ABOUT LIAN DOLAN
& HELEN OF PASADENA

Lian is known for her humorous take on day-to-day issues facing women everywhere.

— OPRAH.COM

Helen of Pasadena is down but not out when her life is turned upside down and she is forced to start over. Readers will cheer the modern-day Helen in this smart and charming tale of second chances.

— LINDA FRANCIS LEE, *NEW YORK TIMES* BESTSELLING AUTHOR OF *THE DEVIL IN THE JUNIOR LEAGUE*

We always knew our sister Lian was warm and funny and sexy and trying to figure out a use for that degree she earned in Classics. But we did not know she was secretly whipping all of that into a warm, funny, sexy novel about contemporary women faced with classical dilemmas.
Hello, Helen of Pasadena! Welcome to the family.

— JULIE, LIZ, SHEILA & MONICA DOLAN: THE OTHER SATELLITE SISTERS

With its likable heroine and colorful supporting cast, Helen of Pasadena *is a warm and entertaining read. Lian Dolan offers a modern tale of rediscovery and shines a humorous light on universal issues of self-esteem, commitment and identity—issues to which every woman can relate.*

— JODI WING, AUTHOR OF *THE ART OF SOCIAL WAR*

Every reader will see something of herself in Lian Dolan's likable heroine, Helen of Pasadena. Offering up every woman's worst fear, Dolan pulls the rug out from under Helen, and we get to watch as she recovers and reinvents herself with wit, charm and smarts. Dolan's Helen Fairchild is reminiscent of Nora Ephron's Rachel Samstat: strong, determined and fearless.

— SALLY BJORNSEN, AUTHOR OF *A SINGLE GIRL'S GUIDE TO MARRYING A MAN, HIS KIDS AND HIS EX-WIFE*

Lian is "sassy, the smart one.'"

— *NEW YORK TIMES*, ON THE SATELLITE SISTERS

She's down-to-earth, witty and doesn't take herself too seriously.

— DAILY CANDY

A send-up of a 40something mom who finds herself suddenly widowed, broke and forced to reinvent herself... [Lian Dolan is] opinionated, energetic and funny.

— NPR'S MANDALIT DEL BARCO, *ARROYO MONTHLY*

I loved this book.... I wonder how long I have to wait for her second book?

— BOOKWORMWITHAVIEW.COM

I loved Helen... a lovely, flawed, insecure, endearing protagonist. Great storytelling... top-notch writing.

— LARRY WILSON, *PASADENA STAR-NEWS*

HELEN *of*
a novel PASADENA

BY **LIAN DOLAN**
OF THE SATELLITE SISTERS

PROSPECT PARK BOOKS

Published by Prospect Park Books, a division of Prospect Park Media
prospectparkmedia.com

Distributed to the trade by SCB Distributors
scbdistributors.com

Special Sales
Bulk purchase (20+ copies) of *Helen of Pasadena* is available to companies,
organizations, mail-order catalogs and nonprofits at special discounts, and
large orders can be customized to suit individual needs. For more information,
contact Prospect Park Media.

Library of Congress Control Number: 2010931359
Dolan, Lian, 1965—
Helen of Pasadena / Lian Dolan—1st ed.
         p.   cm.
1. Fiction.   2. Pasadena (CA)—Fiction.   3. Archaeology—Fiction.
4. Private Schools—Fiction.   5. Humor—Fiction.   I. Title.
ISBN: 978-0-9844102-2-4

First edition, third printing
⊕ Printed in the United States of America on recycled paper.
Cover design by Joseph Shuldiner
Map art by Alexis Chong
Interior & production design by Color Show

TO
BERICK

la cañada

Rose Bowl

Orange Grove

The Gamble House

Helen's Pasadena

Sacred Sisters

Candy's House

Cloverfield

The Norton Simon

City Hall

charming Shoppes

Pasadena Town Club

The Hearth

Petite Petals Patisserie

Mitsy's Condo

Raleigh School

Orange Grove

California

Korean Day Spa
& Downtown Los
Angeles

Ignatius

Helen's Forever House

Redwood School

San Gabriel Mountains

Bungalow Heaven Adjacent

Washington

Best Tacos in Town

Hill

Vroman's Bookstore

In Vino Veritas

Bistro 47

Colorodo Blvd.

★ The Panda Incident

Stephen Stephens Salon

Porto Viaggio

Lake

San Marino / Viviennes

Caltech

The Langham Pasadena

The Huntington Library & Botanical Gardens

CHAPTER 1

Now I knew: I'd get a full church at my funeral. What a relief. It was the kind of thing I lost sleep over at night, being a planner and all. How many times had I sat at funerals, counting the hundreds (or, more depressingly, dozens) of mourners in the pews and thought, *Who would show for me? Do people like me more or less than Jane's mother? Do I know a hundred people who would care? Two hundred? Who should cater?* Now I had my answer: full church. Because if this many people could show up for my husband, my *late* husband, then I'd get almost this many, right?

One thing I'd never planned on was my husband dropping a bombshell on me and then dropping dead.

That would have been good to know.

At least Merritt would have been pleased at the standing-room-only situation in the church. Merritt was a big deal in his world, and to prove that, there were the partners from the firm and the fraternity brothers, town officials, boards of schools and organizations, a Pasadena who's who. Merritt's people, many of whom he had known his whole, short life.

But there were lots of my people, too: the thin, young mothers from Millington School turned out in their best black suits, Prada purses and Tory Burch flats despite the economic downturn; the formerly thin team moms from a decade on the sidelines of every sport from basketball to soccer; the lovely sustaining members of the Symphony Guild, whispering together in the back rows about losing such a big donor in such a tough time; the handsome dads from water polo contemplating if they'll be next. Half of them longing for a drink, the other half wondering who did the flowers.

Their presence meant the world to me.

I was shocked by Merritt's death, maybe even in shock. But I was not devastated. I was relieved.

Very, very relieved.

"It's a tragedy when a husband is taken from his wife, when a father is taken from his son, when a son is taken from his mother, when a citizen is taken from his community, as Merritt Fairchild was taken from his lovely wife, Helen, his brave son, Aiden, his adoring mother, Mitsy, and his beloved hometown of Pasadena," sang out Monsignor Flaherty, working his Irish brogue and his gift of oration from the altar of St. Perpetua's, the most socially progressive and socially acceptable Catholic church in town.

Merritt had donated the altar. That's the kind of big, public gesture he liked to make. It was a simple, hand-carved mahogany altar influenced by the Mission at San Luis Obispo. Merritt had asked me to do the research and make the recommendation to the Church Restoration Committee. It was all a little contrived for me, but I'd risen to the occasion, loving history and architecture as I do. I still preferred to slip an anonymous $25 in the envelope at collection. Merritt never understood that. "Why give a little every week when we could just write one big check at the annual auction?" he'd say.

The Monsignor was a cult figure, inspiring the kind of following that most Catholic priests could only dream of these days. Maybe it's because he understood the power of myth, because he was certainly spinning one now.

"Merritt Fairchild will be missed," continued the Monsignor. "His sense of generosity, his sense of humor, his sense of dignity. This is a man who will be missed."

Thank you, Monsignor, on behalf of my son, who will miss him, even though he never knew him that well. Or maybe precisely *because* he did not know him well. I squeezed Aiden's hand. How did he get so big? Not 20th percentile anymore, so I guess all that worrying paid off. Thirteen years old and now he has no father. After two days of alternating between sobbing and silence, Aiden looked surprisingly strong, sitting there in the itchy Nordstrom suit that I barely remember buying, even though it was only two days ago. My God, what a two days it had been! I thought you were supposed to get five stages of grief; I got about 36 hours.

Hold it together and get through this performance.

"He was a man who honored his commitments deeply."

Until he didn't. I used to be in love with my husband—really, really in love. When I first moved to Pasadena to become Mrs. Merritt Fairchild, I thought I was the luckiest girl in town. Marriage to Merritt meant stability and social status, something I never had growing up. Central Oregon wasn't too big on cotillions and country clubs. Who needed to socialize in formalized groups when there was plenty of pot and bootleg Grateful Dead tapes to share? My parents meant no harm, but, really, a life selling macramé and scented oils out of a VW camper van was not for me. I read everything I could get my hands on, from Walker Percy to *The Preppy Handbook*, made good grades and got out of Jerry Garciaville as soon as I could.

Enter Merritt Fairchild, a straight-arrow Berkeley law student in a blue blazer and khakis. I was an archaeology grad student working at the food co-op when Merritt strolled down my aisle, solid, graceful and slightly sweaty after a game of Ultimate Frisbee. Merritt feigned interest in the eternal question: quinoa vs. bulgur. After he asked me out, I actually looked over my shoulder to see if there was a sorority girl behind me. I loved it when he introduced me to his law school buddies as his "yurt-raised hippie chick" or his "genius Greek-speaking goddess." Like he appreciated my past but believed in a future free of weekend craft fairs. When he asked me to marry him six months later, despite his mother's objections to my unorthodox upbringing and my parents' objection to his conventional upbringing, Merritt was my hero.

I sailed through the early years, thinking how very clever I was to have found Merritt and given him a healthy, strapping baby boy. Merritt was a solid citizen in the solid, suburban town of Pasadena, home of the Rose Parade, the Norton Simon Museum, Caltech, Greene and Greene homes and old money. Old, old money. The kind of credentials that could only be sexy if you grew up in a town like Sisters, Oregon, which had more bead stores than banks and featured "art" galleries full of tree trunks shaped into beavers by chain saws.

Merritt was busy building up a law firm and then making the switch into capital investments; I was busy building friendships and navigating the social waters with complete naiveté. I happily traded in my grad-student status for membership in the young mothers' club of Pasadena. I think it was the car. Not admirable, but I loved that Volvo. It was new and shiny and not at all like the rusty relics I'd seen at the Oregon textile symposiums of my youth. That car was the most beautiful shade of blue. Hello, keyless remote entry. Goodbye, archetypes of the feminine in classical mythology.

I'll just take a few years off, I thought once I was pregnant. I'm only 26, I'll finish that thesis someday. But for now I had money to raise for the new children's museum. Merritt used to laugh, amazed that I was asked to be on the board at Kidseum with my natural-fiber past and subscription to *Biblical Archaeology* magazine. He'd tease me in front of his clients, but all in good fun, I'd thought. But in the last few years, the teasing had stopped being funny. It had started to feel real.

Still, that was no reason to feel relief at his death.

"Merritt Fairchild was the kind of man who inspired others to be their best, raise their game, achieve more. He brought out the best in those around him."

Or their insecurities. Should I have paid more attention to social obligations? Or my grooming? Or any of the other minutiae that mattered to Merritt? I'll never know now.

"It is fitting that a man who gave so much to his community should die in service to the organization that he loved so much." Monsignor let it go at that, but I thought I heard snickers. A manicured hand squeezed my shoulder warmly, then my friend Candy McKenna, scented by Michael Kors and coiffed by Stephen of Stephen Stephens Salon, whispered in my ear, "Jackie Kennedy, Jackie Kennedy, Jackie Kennedy." My Candy-recommended mantra for the next few days. Be the stoic widow, Candy directed. I conceded to her in matters like this.

Candy had a profound sense of the appropriate, being a former Rose Queen, the pinnacle of teenage social success in Pasadena. Out of thousands, literally thousands, of fresh-faced candidates, Candy was chosen to reign. Rising to the top of the Rose Court through excessive grooming, academic achievement and community service is usually a prelude to a charmed life in TV news or charitable works. Candy had been a spectacular Rose Queen, squeezing every ounce of extra camera time and connections out of her moment in the sun.

Then came the fall.

She called it "an unfortunate case of misjudgment," her Vanessa Williams incident in the late '80s. Candy had taken her 1987 reign as Rose Queen right to the Ivy League, only to discover that no one at Brown cared that she'd worn a diamond crown and waved to millions on New Year's morning. Being Pasadena's Rose Queen meant nothing to the jaded East Coast undergrads of Providence, Rhode Island, especially to her roommate, a women's studies major with a minor in comparative feminist lit. By her sophomore year, long after her official reign ended, Candy was desperate to reclaim her status. So she posed for *Playboy*'s Women of the Ivy Leagues issue. Back then, a naked photo was shocking, not like today, where every beauty queen has some X-rated video posted on the Internet. Once the Tournament of Roses caught wind of her, umm, exposure, she was shunned. Not officially tossed out of the Tournament family, but not welcomed back for reunions either. Candy reeled, transferred back to UCLA to plead her case and wound up the black sheep of the Rose Queens.

Now, twice divorced with two kids, the same killer body she had in high school and a midcentury modern house on Linda Vista, she made her living as a digital media maven, running the hugely popular gossip and entertainment site candysdish.com. She covered events and news stories from all over Los Angeles, including Hollywood. But she paid the rent with her local stories. Candy spilled about everything that mattered to Pasadenans, from proper black tie events to preschool blackballing. She was respected, fawned over and feared. Almost an insider, but not quite.

Candy, true to her Rose Court training, had rushed to my side when she heard the news about Merritt. God, everyone in town had heard the news before the Rose Parade was even over. How could you not read the headlines? Rose Parade Volunteer Killed by Float. And underneath, the details unfolded: Police Investigate Collision of Scooter and Giant Panda Float Sponsored by the Chinese Tourism Board.

In the 112-year history of the parade, no Tournament of Roses volunteer, or White Suiter, as they are known to locals because of the white suits and red ties they wear on New Year's Day, had ever been killed during the actual parade. The White Suiters were CEOs and lawyers and bankers with deep social connections and a sense of civic duty, hand-chosen to oversee the parade, the football game and the myriad events associated with the Tournament of Roses. They knew how to handle rain, cold, flower shortages, war protesters, crowds of millions—but a Death by Float? New territory for these pillars of society.

"Making Lasting Memories" was this year's Rose Parade theme, and Merritt certainly did, as he plowed his official Honda scooter into the oncoming panda. He was texting at the time, but only I knew that.

And only I knew to whom.

My feet were starting to swell. They were jammed into the Ferragamo boots with heels that Tina Chau-Swenson said would elongate my calves. Tina, Candy and I met in a mothers' group when our kids were infants; now we were the best of friends. Once we figured out that all the third-generation Pasadena mothers with their six-week-old infants already on the waitlist at St. Simon's Preschool were not going to talk to us because, well, because Candy was disgraced, Tina was back in her skinny jeans and I was not from there, we bonded.

If Candy represented Pasadena's past, Tina Chau-Swenson embodied its future. New everything: money, style, citizenship. Tina was first generation, the daughter of wealthy Hong Kong merchants who saw the writing on the wall and high-tailed it to California with their newborn daughter and pillowcases full of cash before the Chinese came to get their island back from the British. Tina did what she was told: She was the first Chinese-American valedictorian at the exclusive Martindale School for Girls; she earned entrance to Yale and Yale Law School; she received an offer to practice will and trust litigation at Ye Olde Prestigious Law Firm in Los Angeles. She was right on track for a life- and fortune-affirming wedding to an old family friend with ties to Hong Kong when she met Anders Swenson at the law firm's summer associates' picnic. Tall, blond and Minnesotan, he was the next frontier for Tina's assimilation. It was love at first sight.

Mr. and Mrs. Chau were less than pleased, but they only talked about Anders behind his back in Cantonese. At least he made partner. That appeased the Chaus a bit.

Tina and Anders had three lovely daughters, Lilly, Rosie and Heather, to prove just how right they were for each other. "And multiracial is so trendy now," Tina cooed the other day. "It's hip to have halfsies!" That was Tina in a nutshell: all style, some substance, no bull.

Tina Chau-Swenson was in charge of my funeral outfit, and she'd made me promise not to wear Naturalizers, my preferred footwear. "So unflattering, don't do it," Tina had warned. "People will notice. You know those Cloverfield moms."

Yes, the Cloverfield moms. Rival school, rival committees. I'd never be a woman who cared about shoes, no matter how many years I spent in Pasadena, but Tina was right. Those Cloverfield mothers would notice every buckle. *Why give them material for the next mothers' coffee?* So I'd zipped my short calves into the boots, wrapped my soft midsection in several layers of binding underwear and wedged my encased body into the Escada suit Tina bought at a downtown discount boutique. (*You are a 10 if you believe you are a 10!*) Then I fastened the triple strand of pearls my mother-in-law had given me on my wedding day and accepted the big Chanel sunglasses as loaners from Candy. On my very best day I looked like Kate Winslet on her very worst.

Now, two hours after the service, here in the green and chintz foyer of the venerable Pasadena Town Club, I just wanted to stop shaking hands and nodding my head, accepting condolences and "thoughts and prayers." No more thoughts and prayers, I wanted to scream. Just get me out of these boots!

It was the suddenness of Merritt's death that got most of them. I could sense what everyone was thinking: One day you could be president-in-waiting to run the Tournament of Roses, and the next, panda fodder. That was too much for people who had been living in the same town since birth.

Aiden had already asked to step out of the receiving line to go "hang with my friends." Dozens of Millington classmates had come with their parents and were treating the funeral reception like a school dance, laughing, flirting, exchanging cell phone numbers. Adolescent narcissism can be a gift at a time like this. *Go,* I said, *I'll handle this.* And I could.

My own family—my out-of-place parents and my handsome

little brother, Des—stood in the corner, munching on chicken salad tea sandwiches (*do they know there's meat in there?*) and making small talk with one another. Classic Castor family behavior when they come to visit. My parents, now in their late 60s, had repositioned themselves as fiber artists and gallery owners in the growing vacation-home market of central Oregon, which had completely transformed from my youth. High-end restaurants, bookstores and antiques shops had replaced the empty storefronts. The area was now rich with Nike, Microsoft and California millionaires looking to decorate their large log homes with the giant pieces of tufted wool art that my father churned out. But my parents had not abandoned all their hippie ways. Hence the formal Birkenstocks and the clear violation of the club's shirt-and-tie requirement for men; it was their way of sticking it to The Man. Even on the happiest of occasions, a trip to Pasadena was like a foreign exchange program for them.

My mother, Nell, had been lovely over the last 24 hours. All those soul-searching workshops in the '70s made her particularly good at tragedy in later life. And the twelve-step program for marijuana addiction had given her clear eyes and a sense of purpose. She took a quiet and pragmatic approach to adversity: soup, tea, Joni Mitchell.

My father, Peter, was overwhelmed with emotion, not that he and Merritt ever had any deep bond. The two had almost nothing in common, except me, Aiden and a love of backgammon. But my father, too, had a giant well of empathy bubbling inside, and he felt the sadness of the situation deeply. Unfortunately, unlike my mother, he could not control that well. He'd cried nonstop since landing, sobbing dramatically at the church, much to the discomfort of the entire Fairchild clan and the board of Fairchild Capital. Even Aiden started to laugh at the waterworks. Raw emotion was not a Fairchild family trait.

Letting it all hang out was a Castor family trait. Which is why I usually took Aiden to visit my parents in Oregon only when

Merritt was away on business.

My brother Des, a ski patroller at Mt. Bachelor in the winter and a rafting guide on the Deschutes in the summer (yes, he *was* named after the river), was trying to rehydrate my father with white wine, a suspect choice. At least he'd stopped crying.

Merritt's mother, the imposing Millicent "Mitsy" Forester Fairchild, stood near me but not next to me, which pretty much sums up my relationship with her for the past fifteen years. She had her own receiving line going, which normally would have annoyed me, but today I let it go. Merritt's older sisters, Mimi and Mikki, flanked their mother in matching black suits. I was glad I didn't have to stand with them. Their sorrow was genuine.

The receiving line went on for hours. I welcomed the mayor of Pasadena, the president of USC and various movers and shakers of various vaunted institutions. The headmistress of Millington, Adele Arnett, and her husband, Michael, gave me deep hugs. Over Aiden's nine years at the school, I'd come to know them quite well. Would I replace Merritt on the board of trustees? Or would they just name some other father who managed a fund of some sort? God knows there were plenty of them at Millington. Another worry.

Then came the squads of women who had stood next to me at games or school plays or holiday look-in tours. The women who had worked alongside me at charity events or religious-ed pizza-dough sales. So many of them were crying or choked up. Were they really that fond of Merritt? Or was it just that when they looked at me they thought of their own lives? I wasn't sure, but it was touching. Their pain made me feel, well, good—which in turn made me feel odd.

Then, of course, came an army of slightly peeved White Suiters, whose thoughts and prayers, I'm guessing, included the hope that there would be no legal action on my part. Believe me, there wouldn't be. I needed to move on.

Tina stood behind me, plying me with Arnold Palmers, the

half lemonade, half iced tea concoction that fueled most of the lunches in town. There was no rum in the punch, but I was thinking I could use a little right about now. Candy stood to my right, employing her amazing facial identification skills, honed over years at the best parties, whispering names and relationships as the crowd moved through the line. Dexter Olmstead, Historical Preservation commissioner of Pasadena. Nancy Tully, president of Near and Far Bank. Jeff Smithson, managing partner, the Capital Fund. I'd met all these people at all the fundraisers and galas and award dinners over the years, but I was never good with name recall, except when it came to history, and today, my brain was a sieve. Mercifully, the line was coming to an end when I heard Candy harrumph.

"What is she doing here? It's just tacky to bring a news van to a funeral. I can't believe the club even let her in the parking lot," Candy fumed.

I looked up and my legs buckled inside my calf-elongating boots. Freaking Roshelle Simms, Fox 11 news anchor and the woman my husband was texting when he hit the float.

"I need a big fucking drink."

CHAPTER 2

"That news ho slept with Merritt?! I'm going to freakin' kill her!"

"Thank you, Tina, because I'm not sure the cater waiters heard you the first time. Now that the staff of the Pasadena Town Club knows my husband was about to leave me for Roshelle Simms, I can stop the grieving widow charade," I hissed, between sobs and deep breaths, head in my hands as we sat on the tasteful striped couch in the ladies' lounge.

Candy regrouped, as she always did. "Start at the beginning. What are you talking about?"

I glanced at Anna, the lovely Guatemalan attendant who has managed the ladies' lounge at the club for two decades. Always ready with a tissue, a kind word for a botched Botox or a cup of coffee for a drunken bridesmaid, Anna was discretion personified. Her giant haul of holiday tips was proof that she knew more about moneyed Pasadena than the CIA. I knew she could be trusted, and she knew I'd make good next Christmas.

"Merritt was leaving me for Roshelle Simms. He told me New Year's Eve, right before he had to report for duty at the parade. He said he was madly in love with her, she was his "soul mate," only she understood his needs, and it was over between us. Fifteen years and he was leaving me for a woman who wears teal suits and can't pronounce *cinco de Mayo*."

"Jesus, did he actually use the words soul mate?"

"Tina, please!" Candy commanded. "You know her real last name is Slusky. I think that says it all. And she was only a Rose Princess, you know. Not the queen. And the '90s were not a good decade for the Rose Court."

"Really? More relevant than the soul mate bit?" Tina snapped.

Candy refocused. "Let's support Helen. Merritt told you New Year's Eve? Did you know about the affair, about any of this?"

"No, no idea. I felt like such an idiot. Totally duped. You know that I barely saw Merritt. His work was endless. He had a million meetings. Or, at least he told me he had a million meetings. He had his life; I had mine. We had Aiden, the house, the club—it was all very quiet and easy. Not exhilarating, but not awful. But I never thought he'd do this to me. To Aiden."

"Oh my God! Did he meet her at the benefit last year?" Candy gasped, eyes wide with recognition. Yes, he did. The benefit that Candy, Tina and I had chaired to Save the Deodar Pines in the Arroyo Seco. "Give Green, Go Green" had been our adorable theme, and Roshelle Simms had been our adorable Mistress of Ceremonies. How great to get a minor celebrity, we'd all thought. A news anchor! Even if she did work for Fox.

All the major celebs lived on the other side of Los Angeles, the westside, home to the Above the Line types: movie stars, big-time producers, directors, studio heads. The Below the Line folks lived in the Valley: crew, caterers, accountants. In Pasadena, we had the Between the Lines crowd: studio executives, studio lawyers and regular lawyers, bankers and real estate investors. Plus character actors and lots and lots of news people, from the anchors to the weather guys to the producers. Roshelle lived in a condo in the hip Old Pasadena area. So convenient for her to get to the studio when news broke, and to entertain the many married suburban dads who lived nearby.

Like Merritt.

At the gala, all Roshelle had to do was thank the sponsors and introduce a short film, "The History of the Deodars in Pasadena." She was wearing a pale blue low-cut evening dress that she'd gotten off the rack at Loehmann's, even though the invitation said "Green Attire Encouraged." She'd gushed about how wonderful it was to "give back to the community" but failed to mention that she'd been giving back to my husband in her dressing room.

"Yes, it started that night, and Merritt seemed compelled to tell me all the details, like ... like I could understand that it was 'bigger than him.' That's what he kept saying, 'I couldn't stop it. It was bigger than me.' Nothing's ever been bigger than him. He's not a guy who gets carried away. His life has been completely predictable since the minute he was born: Millington, Ignatius, USC, summers at Camp Longbow, vacations in Hawaii, living two miles from his childhood home. This is a guy who doesn't like to shop at Brooks Brothers because the suits are 'too modern.' But one night with Roshelle and it's bigger than him."

Anna produced a perfectly limed Tanqueray and tonic from her broom closet of cures and I carried on.

"And get this, Merritt wanted to stay in the house like we were the happy couple. Oh, he was still going to sleep with Roshelle, but he wanted to get my blessing to stay until April. Good father that he was, Merritt didn't want to hurt Aiden's chances of getting into Ignatius."

Tina and Candy shook their heads in disgust. Next to parade season and the mixed-doubles tournament at the club, the most important day of the year in Pasadena was the Friday in April when the private school acceptance letters went in the mail. From preschool up through college, school acceptance was the one topic of conversation in which every Pasadena parent could engage. Endless discussions about which school was better, more exclusive, had the most homework, did the most with arts education, offered the finest language program, had the highest rate of Ivy League acceptances. At Hospital Guild meetings, Y basketball games, in parks and at nail salons, mothers engaged in behind-the-back conversations about which 4-year-old was "Millington material," which hedge fund director's son got into Cloverfield because his dad promised a new theater, which school had "too many legacies" or "too many siblings" in the application pool, which girl would never get into Martindale because of a Facebook page scandal involving the P.E. teacher. Private school admissions wasn't a sport, it was a full-time occupation.

And it didn't stop at acceptance.

Parents spent years justifying their school choice, long after the letters had been mailed. Even Merritt, with his blue-blood pedigree, appreciated that.

Merritt was not going to jeopardize his son's acceptance into the prestigious Ignatius Prep for Boys with a scandalous affair and a messy divorce. That would be admissions suicide, particularly at a Catholic school. He'd wait until after the acceptance letters went out to announce our separation. That's what he'd told me on New Year's Eve, anyway, shortly before putting on his official white suit and heading out the door to do his civic duty at the parade.

The Pasadena police had recovered his Blackberry at the scene of the accident. I checked the texts. The deed is done, read the message sent to soulm8 seconds before the collision. Yes, the deed was in fact done.

"I'm sorry he died, but I'm not sorry he's dead," Candy said.

"Me either," Tina echoed.

"What's going on in here, Helen? The mayor is waiting to say goodbye to you before he can go. He's talking about renaming one of the streets off the parade route in honor of Merritt. Isn't that kind?" Mitsy Fairchild, in a vintage black-and-white St. John Knit suit, burst through the ladies' lounge door. Tall, athletic and looking like she'd be ready for a set of doubles on a minute's notice, she still terrified me after fifteen years in the Fairchild family.

In the study of classics, scholars spend a lot of intellectual time on "myths of origin" of the gods and goddesses, trying to determine their beginnings in a religious, artistic and archaeological sense. My theory on Mitsy's creation, formulated while I was hiding out in the kitchen during holiday events to escape the Fairchild family's hyper-competitive games of Trivial Pursuit, was that Mitsy had been born to be a matriarch, like the ancient Minoan Snake Goddess, one part civilized, one part untamed. Depictions of the Bronze Age Snake Goddess show her holding an angry, writhing snake in each hand, illustrating her threatening power and her connection to the natural world. If someone immortalized Snake Goddess Mitsy, she'd be holding a vodka martini with two olives in one hand and a checkbook in the other.

Mitsy had been widowed at 50, when Mitchell Fairchild dropped dead on the 17th green, but she hadn't missed a beat. She used her Amazonian stature, solid breeding, sharp intellect and patronage of the arts to build her reputation. She gave her presence more than her money to good causes, going to every theater, opera, symphony and gallery opening. ("My God, if I have to write one more description of your mother-in-law's elegant evening gown and dramatic bejeweled wrist cuffs, I will cauterize my eyes," Candy had complained once.) Mitsy could speak knowledgeably about the importance of the arts in underfunded public schools in the Rotunda of the Athenaeum at Caltech, then walk outside and cut the valet parking attendant down to his knees if the radio of her Mercedes had been turned up too loud. Like the Snake Goddess, she could be benevolent or she could be destructive, but she could not be denied.

Funny though, with all her reading and study of the human experience through the arts, one thing she could never understand was Merritt's attraction to someone from Oregon. Connecticut, of course. Even some counties in Ohio, maybe. But *Oregon*?

Now, here in the PTC's ladies' lounge on the day of her only son's funeral, I saw the familiar Were You Raised in a Barn expression on Mitsy's superbly tightened signature Dr. Weismann face. "Pull yourself together, Helen. You can break down tomorrow. No one will be looking then."

The words were on the tip of my tongue. I could feel the slights of fifteen years rising up in my gut, the comments about my lack of style, my housekeeping, my choice of gardeners and their tendency to plant marigolds, the tackiest of all the bedding flowers. *Hey old lady with the two-carat diamond! Your son died because he was texting a 27-year-old news anchor that he was sleeping with at the family beach house! That's right, your beach house! Yes, perfect Merritt was about to leave your beautiful grandson in the middle of a holy mess. And speaking of holy, you can just forget about getting the best table at the St. Perpetua's annual auction, because Monsignor frowns on adultery! How do you like that awkward social situation, you freakishly tall Minoan Snake Lady?*

Oh, I would have enjoyed that moment of truth after an exhausting day of cover-up. But that's when I remembered the promise I'd made to myself, right after getting the call from the Pasadena Police. Merritt's dirty little secret would stay my dirty little secret. If I'd learned anything in my years in Pasadena, it was the truth of the old dictum: Discretion is the better part of valor.

In other words, keep your mouth shut and you've won half the battle.

I knew I could trust Candy and Tina. They had their own skeletons and wouldn't reveal mine. But with Mitsy, it was more than just withholding information, it was self-preservation of my reputation and Aiden's. And truthfully, I really didn't know how she would react to her son's behavior.

We'd never shared a single personal conversation. We'd discussed logistics of birthday parties, news events not related to politics, the latest Masterpiece Theater production ("The only television worth watching," Mitsy said more than a hundred times, even though I knew she watched *Regis and Kelly* on the sly.) The two of us were more comfortable dissecting the decline in pickup-and-delivery dry cleaners than the state of our souls. Revealing Merritt's bad behavior would be new territory for us, and the prospect terrified me.

I knew I would miss Merritt, just not today. He had given me Aiden and an entrée into his life that I wouldn't trade for the world. Someday, maybe soon, I would forgive the affair and grieve his death, but right now, I had to keep acting. Telling Mitsy about Roshelle Simms would be indulgence of the highest order. I'd rather she resent me than Merritt. That's all the love I could muster right now.

Mitsy cocked her head. My short silence must have been unsettling to her, as I usually stammer along until I can muster up a cogent thought to blurt out. But not this time. *Jackie Kennedy, Jackie Kennedy, Jackie Kennedy.* Tina and Candy watched me expectantly. Candy was actually licking her chops.

"You're right, Mitsy. Give me two minutes. Thank you."

"Oh, and I told that awful newsperson Roshelle to leave. What kind of a name is that? Roshelle? She actually wanted a statement from the family. Can you imagine? Really, I knew her grandmother Cecilia. She once served cheese from a can! At a luncheon! Do something with your face, Helen."

And with that, Mitsy was gone, and the air returned to the ladies' lounge.

"Ohhh, that was good. You were magnificent!" Candy lauded, diving into her pocketbook in search of her touch-up bag. "She owes you and she knows it."

"Owes me? What do you mean?" I said through pursed lips, as Candy wielded her Bobbi Brown lip liner on my melted face.

"Mitsy Fairchild would not have personally taken care of the 'awful newsperson' unless she had some suspicions. I've observed your mother-in-law for years at all those parties, and that is not her normal behavior. She never speaks to the press, not even to me. The Mitsy I know would have commanded Carmen at coat check to take care of the news van and the reporter. But Mitsy went and spoke to the news ho in person. And knew her name. That speaks volumes."

As usual, in matters of manners and mannerisms, Candy was on to something.

"She won't say a word. And she's on your side," Tina agreed. "That's where you want her."

I had no idea how right they were.

I was exhausted beyond words, drained literally and figuratively. Every tear, every smile, every sliver of polite conversation was sucked from my body. I was so grateful the day was over. Recently I'd read about a new business that planned funerals that were more of a party and less of a solemn occasion. Balloon drops, margarita machines, DJs spinning tunes. "Putting the Fun Back in Funeral" was their motto. At the time, it seemed like a great idea, like really buying into the eulogy cliché, "So-and-so would want us to all go out and have a beer instead of being here mourning!" But now I knew that kind of funeral would fall short, not allowing for the anger and the missing that follow any death.

Even a death like Merritt's so filled with contradictions.

There was no way I could have toasted Merritt with a margarita today. And yet, here in the bed I'd shared with Merritt for so many years, I was unspeakably sad. The man I'd lived with for fifteen years, who had slept with me when my body was twenty pounds thinner and stretch-mark-free, was gone. Goddamn it, Merritt.

Couldn't you have died *before* you told me you were leaving?

My parents and brother had come back to the house after the reception and put out a simple dinner. Aiden and I were too wrung out to eat much of my mother's famous vegan carrot bisque. I let Aiden watch an inappropriate movie with Des while I collapsed on the couch, not saying much of anything. My mother, humming Joni Mitchell's "Down to You," quietly cleaned up, started some laundry, hustled my drunken father to bed and reassured me about the next day. "Sleep in, poor thing. Don't get up for us.

Do you need anything before we go to the airport? I can't believe we have to get back for that felting symposium."

I said I'd be fine. If being fine meant living with murderous thoughts about TV newswomen. I kept that sentiment to myself.

But now, lying in the dark, I couldn't get that worked up about Roshelle. I hadn't been married to her. I had been married to Merritt.

"Mom?" Aiden's voice interrupted my thoughts.

"Aiden, are you okay?"

"Yeah, I just had a bad dream or something. Can I stay in your room? I have my sleeping bag." At 13, he was too old to snuggle up in bed with me like he would have done two or three years ago. He knew it and I knew it, though I wished it wasn't so.

"Of course. Do you need a pillow?"

"Sure."

I got up, tucked a pillow under his head and gave him a kiss on his shaggy bangs. Maybe I should have made him cut his hair before the funeral. "I'm right here. I'm right here."

"I know. 'Night."

CHAPTER 3

The law offices of Owens and Hapstead were in a charming 1920s Craftsman bungalow just south of City Hall, restored to National Register of Historic Places standards while winning a Gold Arrow Award from Pasadena Heritage for the "reclamation of priceless period light fixtures." Those kinds of honors led to a celebratory cocktail party and many photos in Candy's column. Merritt and I had attended, of course, because Billy Owens, Esquire, an award-winning architectural reclaimer, was not just our lawyer, he was also like a brother to Merritt. Billy had been Merritt's best friend since kindergarten at Millington right through graduation at USC. Without any of the drama that a lifelong female friendship endures, the two men had gone from sandbox to frat house to country club smoothly. They routinely played golf, drank martinis and tailgated at football games while calling each other by their frat nicknames, Billbo and Merles. Billy was the first person I called after the accident. I ended up comforting him.

I liked Billy. Funny, smart, not too smug for a Trojan. Though his insistence at getting completely drunk at USC football games had begun to bother me more and more the closer my own son got to college age. *Isn't he getting too old for that*, I'd ask Merritt, who would roll his eyes. What was I missing? I've never understood midday drinking. Where's the appeal to being tired and cranky at 4 in the afternoon? And in a football stadium, no less.

Billy's wife, Lacey, was a California blonde from San Diego, full of energy and good intentions, fueled by Diet Coke and an addiction to spin class. My God, she must spin two hours a day! Where does she find the time with those three kids? Lacey also worked in fundraising at Crown City Hospital, putting her genuine spirit to good use. We'd been out a million times with the Owenses, but the call I got from Billy the day after the funeral gave me an uneasy feeling.

Please meet me at the office. Bruno will be there, Billy had said in a somber tone. Bruno is our, well, now *my* accountant. I knew I'd have to face the money issues soon enough, but I didn't think it would be so soon.

"Helen, come in. You're here. Good, good. How are you? Are you okay? Patrice, get Helen a latte. You look like you need a latte. Patrice will get you a latte," Billy said in a rush.

How unusual. Billy was like a well-educated maitre d'-at-large, cool and casual in any social or business situation, always appearing to be in charge of hospitality even if the get-together was not his to supervise. But not today. Was he nervous? "Obviously, you know Bruno Purcelli," he said.

Bruno nodded. So solid, that Bruno. Merritt had said you should always have an Italian accountant because they understand blood money. An Italian accountant would never cheat you because he knew that someday, you'd get him back. Bruno had been doing our books for years, but I only saw him every April, when we met to get the tax rundown. I'd done a lot of nodding in those meetings, understanding about 30 percent of the information. I had Merritt. Why get all worked up over the particulars? Now I was regretting not paying closer attention. But I had confidence in Bruno. He would help me get through the next few years. I knew there would have to be changes, but Merritt had always assured me that he "was covered," whatever that meant.

"Helen, I don't know how to say this," Billy stammered. Now I knew he really was nervous.

Shit, this was not good.

"You are not in good shape—I mean financially, not physically. As you know, this is a tough time and the economy is a mess. Merritt made some bad investments, and when the credit meltdown happened, he got caught short. Really, really short. You are in a pretty deep hole."

Bruno nodded confirmation.

Breathe, breathe. Speak.

"I don't understand. How could this have happened? Merritt didn't say a word. Nothing. Not 'stop spending.' Nothing. Obviously we talked about the stock market plunging and the recession and his business, but he just kept saying that he would be fine. How bad is it, Bruno?"

Bruno painted a picture that included a wiped-out stock portfolio, an overleveraged home-equity line, high credit-card debt and unpaid insurance premiums. Personally, our finances were in shambles. And thanks to the stock market decline and clients fleeing like rats, Merritt's stake in Fairchild Capital was virtually worthless. Even if Merritt were alive, we'd be in trouble.

Fuck, fuck, fuck. Fucking Merritt. "The house?" I asked.

"You'll have to sell. Hopefully, you can get the price you need to cover your debt and have money left over for a down payment on, you know, something, somewhere."

"Aiden's school?'

"They have financial aid. Or maybe Mitsy can help."

This is what it feels like to get punched in the gut.

Fantastic, I am now a 40-year-old widow with half a master's degree in an arcane subject who has to rely on her mother-in-law to pay the bills. It's like a freaking Jane Austen novel. Maybe I can get a parson to marry me. I was going to lose it.

"How did this happen?" I repeated over and over again. I was met with silence. In my mind, I replayed conversations with Merritt over the past few years, and none reflected anything more than slight concern over our finances. Sure, it had been a bad eighteen months, but Merritt was not concerned. We're good, Merritt had said when I'd asked him weekly about the economy crashing down around us.

We're good? We were screwed, and we'd been screwed for

some time.

"Billy, I just don't understand. Even if Merritt were here, alive, how was he going to get out of this?" Billy looked down for a moment, like a frat boy caught in a hazing ritual by campus security, and I knew. Oh, I knew. He knew about Roshelle. It was written all over his face, his truly shame-filled face.

Now I understood. "Did she have money?" I leveled at Billy. "Was that how Merritt was going to get out of this? Dump me, marry her, blame his financial mess on our divorce and live off her money?"

Bruno pretended not to hear and looked out the window, suddenly fascinated by the drought-tolerant California native sage garden recognized by *Sunset* magazine as "One of the 10 Best in 2006."

Then I remembered what Candy had sniped at the funeral. Her real name was Slusky. Of course! She was Shelly Slusky of Slusky's Wash & Wipe, 64 stores strong, the awful ads always clamored. I'd learned from my years in the Golden State that if you were the first at *anything* in California—from car washes to orange juice bottlers to real estate development—you were loaded. That was it! Merritt was trading in our debt for her fortune. In turn, she would become the proper Roshelle Fairchild, rather than the unfortunately named Shelly Slusky.

Billy was not so calm and cool now. He was now the reluctant apologist for his dead best friend, a lying, cheating and financially reckless father. "Helen, I tried to tell him. I tried to get him to slow down with everything. To think. Just stop and think. The investments, the, umm, changes in his life. He just made one bad decision after another. Lots of guys did, Helen, guys in the capital business went nuts. Everybody went crazy. Merritt was just one of them."

"*Changes?* Is that what you boys call leaving a wife and child broke and humiliated for a weathergirl? And nuts? He borrowed against his life insurance policy. That's not nuts, that's mean.

That's crazy. My God, poor Aiden. How can we afford high school, never mind college?"

He shook his head, afraid to meet my eyes. All the anger I'd felt toward Merritt about his betrayal, I now wanted to dump on Billy for things that were absolutely not his fault, yet somehow he had allowed.

"Billy, all the tailgating, the dinners, the laughs … I thought you were *my* friend too, not just his. How could you let this happen and not even tell me? And you," I whirled around to Bruno. "Didn't I have a right to know that everything was gone? Wasn't my name on those papers, too?"

"No."

"What?"

Bruno looked me straight in the eyes, like the good Italian accountant he was. "You signed away everything years ago. All those papers you signed, turning everything over to Merritt, I never understood why you did it."

Because Merritt told me he would take care of everything, and I believed him.

By the time I was 12, I was the financially responsible one in our family. I paid the bills, balanced the checkbook and made sure my brother had lunch money. I kept the books for the craft business as soon as I figured out Nell and Peter were on the verge of doing time for tax evasion. (My parents weren't criminals, just woefully disorganized.) When I became Mrs. Fairchild, I gratefully gave up the business of life. Let somebody else worry about money; I've got a million other things on my worry list.

That was the unsaid deal Merritt and I had struck. Like lots of husbands and wives. I kept up my end, leaving my studies, raising a family, creating a home. I thought Merritt was keeping up his end.

I trusted my husband. *That's why, Bruno, but you would never understand.*

"I wish you had asked more questions, Helen."

"So do I, Bruno, so do I."

Patrice knocked and entered, bearing a latte in a tall mug on a William Morris reproduction tray. "Here's your coffee, Mrs. Fairchild. Can I get you anything else?"

"Yes," I said standing up and downing the beverage like a shot of courage. "Make copies of every document in that stack and send them to my house. Better send them today. I may not have a house tomorrow, Patrice."

Poor Patrice, in her Talbots tweed skirt and cardigan. She looked like someone had just asked to borrow her toothbrush. I was not usually this forceful in this office.

Billy stood up. "Helen, I'm sorry. If there's anything I can do...."

I cut him off. "No. No, thank you. Remember, I grew up in a yurt, not Pasadena. I'm used to having nothing."

I sat in the driveway of the Monterey Colonial that Merritt and I had bought twelve years ago, when the market was down and we were flush. "It's a fixer, but what a neighborhood!" said our agent, Nancy Taunton, a striking, early 50s divorcée in a size-6 Dana Buchman suit. Nancy enjoyed stating the obvious, as the house was a wreck inside but on a picture-perfect street. The Oak Knoll neighborhood of Pasadena was filled with traditional landscaping and long, curving driveways leading to architecturally significant homes of the 1920s and '30s. To say it was a dream neighborhood for someone like me was an understatement. It's not *like* a movie set, it *was* a movie set. *Father of the Bride, Mr. and Mrs. Smith, Brothers & Sisters*—all shot on this street. As a kid, I hadn't known anyone who lived like this, and now, somehow, it was me. When I started to cry, Merritt and Nancy pretended not to notice.

"It's our forever house," I said, repeating a phrase I'd heard Cissy Montague use at Mommy and Me aerobics. Cissy and her husband, Bart, childhood sweethearts and one-time Cloverfield classmates, had just purchased an enormous house in the same neighborhood on fashionable Jordan Road. A house on Jordan was the big time, another realm of real estate, within reach to only a select few. And that select few included Cissy McMurphy Montague and her prematurely balding but decent husband.

Thankfully, Cissy had full-time help, so she could spend many hours a week chasing down highboys and hand-printed toile wallpaper with her decorator, Pierce DeVine, while the nanny Maria watched McMurphy Montague, first-born son. The renovations had been rumored to be in the millions, which was a lot of money in the mid-'90s, and included moving the pool. Move a pool? I didn't even know that was possible, but Cissy wanted that pool to get more sun, so she moved it.

"She's only 30. How can they afford a place like that?" I'd asked Candy at the time. Hey, Merritt and I had some money, but not move-a-pool money.

"Oh, aren't you cute, little wood nymph from Oregon! Cissy's family founded Standard Oil. She's loaded, and she wants to move the pool. So she's moving it."

I would later learn that when I asked about the origin of someone's wealth in town, the response always seemed to be "they were a founding family of Standard Oil." If only my family had known that crude oil was more profitable than patchouli oil. At the time, this bit of intel about Standard Oil seemed like incredible good fortune for someone like Cissy, who was not exactly a rocket scientist.

"Bart and I decided that this is our forever house," Cissy announced to all of us in aerobics one day, using little McMurphy for a bicep curl. My heart had opened up to Cissy. So she moved a pool, and she had a full-time nanny *and* a cleaning woman. That's okay. She wanted to make a home for her family. I could forgive her the endless supply of Cole Haan loafers. Such confidence in the future, such security in her husband's love. In that moment, I wanted to be Cissy more than anything.

Now my forever house would go on the market and be sold at a huge loss, financially and emotionally. So would the iceberg rose hedge, the portico with the Brown Jordan furniture where I loved to read, Aiden's giant tree swing and my white-tiled Pierce DeVine kitchen with the Viking stove, the Miele dishwasher and the hand-blown Italian light fixtures. Goodbye to the red dining room that Tina insisted was the "must paint" color of 1999 and the ridiculous upscale urinal Merritt put in the poolhouse loo. Maybe this was why my parents eschewed traditional housing situations. It was hard to get emotionally attached to a seasonal rental.

I mourned my real estate more than my late husband. I'd truly become a Californian.

How was I going to tell Aiden? *What* was I going to tell Aiden? *Well, son, you're a teenager now, and I know you thought your dad driving into a panda was as bad as it could get, but I have worse news. Your father lost all his money and most of yours, he took up with a woman who got a boob job for her 21st birthday, and you may not be able to go to college. So get over the grieving, cause we've gotta pack!*

Cynicism in a time of anger can be like prayer.

Where was my road map? I needed some sort of agreed-upon timeline for my situation: Recently Betrayed and Bereaved and Bereft. I was not a big fan of forging new paths. Me, I'll take the road more traveled and be satisfied with the result.

Growing up, I knew my situation with my tie-dyed parents and my haphazard home schooling with the occasional semester in public school was not like the other kids. My best friend was Jessica Holstrom, who had a television (we didn't), a mother who wore pantsuits (my mother wore Indian-print wraparound skirts long after their day) and a Brady Bunch lunchbox (I took my pita bread sandwiches to school in a string bag). I wanted that Brady Bunch existence. What a lovely home, Mrs. Brady.

But the Castor household lacked anything resembling structure. Other families seemed to be executing a time-honored plan. They wore new clothes in September, not hand-me-downs, attended church on Sunday instead of selling crafts under a tent, and wrote to Santa Claus instead of celebrating the winter solstice. I watched Jessica's older brothers taking the SATs and getting into the University of Oregon. Slow, steady, completely expected steps that lead to an adult life circumscribed by order, not the Grateful Dead's tour schedule.

Even though my parents seemed uninterested in the calendar that the rest of society was following, I wanted to play along. I begged them to go to a regulation public high school in Sisters, Oregon, rather than "experience education through life," which was their ill-conceived plan. (A teenager can only read *The Electric Kool-Aid Acid Test* and *On the Road* so many times before she asks, "Why don't these people get jobs? What is wrong with them?") I loved high school: the textbooks, the lockers and the ringing bells announcing class changes. My classmates were the sons and daughters of lumber mill workers, Forest Service and Department of Transportation employees, parents with uniforms and time clocks and permanent addresses. My teachers had full curricula; we were busy every day.

I gravitated to history and literature, soaking up the names, dates and patterns, taking honors classes and independent studies. I happened into Latin with a well-meaning teacher, Mr. Berman, who guessed I might like the precision of translation, and he was right. It was Mr. Berman who helped me get into Willamette University in Salem, Oregon, on an academic scholarship.

At Willamette, a beautiful liberal arts college founded by the Methodists, I thrived. I discovered dorm food, plentiful and mediocre. I ate meat with abandon, after years of eating macrobiotic food before macrobiotic food was edible. I gained twenty pounds the first year, but not because of beer and pizza, the usual culprits. (My parents had been offering me home-brewed beer since the eighth grade.) I put on twenty pounds of bacon and chipped beef. I liked being surrounded by normal kids with normal traditions. Carol singing around the Christmas tree on the quad! Sign me up!

I focused on classics immediately, never even considering another major. Classical Greek, history of religion, mythology, literature, philosophy. (My worst subject. Too theoretical for me. More facts, less rhetoric, please.) I reveled in my complete immersion in an ancient world filled with mystery, sex and romance. But also filled with discipline—the strict rules of classical architecture, the complicated but elegant language of the Greeks. It all got me. Like every other kid in America at the time, I wanted to be Indiana Jones, without the spiders, the giant rolling boulders or the theft of sacred ancient artifacts, which I was firmly against, of course.

And I was on my way there in grad school at Berkeley when I met Merritt. He wasn't exactly a Bronze Age hero, more like a favored king. But what he offered appealed to me: a life on schedule, on course, with a purpose.

Now where is that beaten path that I loved so much? Now what the hell am I supposed to do?

I've watched what divorced women do in Pasadena: They sell the big house, move to the lovely two-bedroom condo off South Lake Avenue and lose twenty pounds through a new regime of stress and yoga. Somehow, in that first year post-divorce, they find the will to blow dry their hair and attend the school holiday program solo, smiling a lot and laughing wildly at wildly unfunny comments. Eventually they get their real estate license or land a job at a local charity, hopeful that someday, once their kids are out of high school and through the eating-disorder/painkiller-addiction/low-GPA phase, they'll meet a nice man, remarry and travel to Europe as a couple. Until then, they'll tell you that they're happy reconnecting with their women friends and going to the movies when the kids are at the ex's ("Finally, after so many years of animated movies! One with real people in period

dress! I love that James McAvoy. What else has he been in?")
Just like Nancy Taunton, the former real estate agent who was
now Nancy Nelson, retired and living in a condo in Solana Beach
with husband number #2. Good for Nancy; it only took her a
decade to get there.

My mother always says, "First things first," which was a pretty
funny personal credo for someone to whom the "first thing" used
to be a cup of chamomile tea and a bong hit. But she was onto
something. What I have here is Operation First Things First. I
can do this, with enough coffee and denial.

I took out my iPhone and texted Candy: need real estate agent
pls advise

There, first things first.

CHAPTER 4

"Don't worry. I know the market is down, but not for a property like this. This is someone's dream. We'll get offers on the first day," Rita Beghosian, my new Armenian real estate agent, told me. "Priced right. And such class."

Candy had recommended Rita. "She's a killer. She's the only one making money in the downturn. Armenians are tough and Rita is the toughest. You know, they are the best salespeople. They've taken over the sales floors at Macy's and Nordstrom. They are good. They started at TJ Maxx and Mervyn's and worked their way up right into DKNY. Rita started in apartment leasing, and now she's selling $5 million homes. She won't let you down."

Candy was right about the Armenians and about Rita. The Pasadena area now had the largest population of Armenians outside of their homeland. They brought their delicious chicken and their great bakeries, and they started taking over small businesses from limo driving to Pack N' Posts. The women staked out retail sales for their territory, and now they dominated every department store and discount store in the area. Rita was a trailblazer in real estate, selling her way right into a top neighborhood, Anne Klein suits and a Cadillac STS. Who knew they made cars that color purple?

Tina was doing the walk-through with me. "You are not signing another legal document without me, do you understand?" She'd put that dusty Yale Law degree to work and reviewed the stack of papers I'd gotten from Bill Owens' office and shuddered. "You did some really stupid things. Merritt was setting you up for his next life and you fell for it. There's nothing I can do now, but I won't let it happen again. It just floors me how smart women like you can be duped. I say that with love."

And I took it with love.

Tina wanted to check out that Rita was on the up-and-up, and I needed the moral support to walk through my house pointing out the special features as if I were a disinterested third party. In a steady voice I called out, "Here's the temperature-controlled wine closet," and "Make sure you include in the brochure that the tiles around the fireplace are Batchelders, original to the house and considered some of the finest in Pasadena."

This is not my beautiful house.

When I told Aiden that we were going to have to make some immediate changes in our life, like selling the house, he didn't understand.

"Can I still have a graduation party here?"

Merritt had promised that he would have a "kick-ass" eighth-grade graduation party, with a DJ, lights and deluxe taco cart. Now I'm wondering how he thought we would pay for all that, but I kept my mouth shut. Keep the myth alive.

"Aiden, if we sell the house, we won't be here when you graduate. We'll get together with your friends, just not here."

"Can't we just stay here until I finish at Millington? Why do we have to move now?"

"Because we can't. The house is a lot to keep up, and we just can't manage it without Dad."

"Can't you get a job?" His tone was increasingly angry, almost furious.

I was tempted to fire back, *Yes, women who have spent many years raising their children and volunteering at pumpkin festivals are highly valued in the marketplace.* But I didn't. The school psychologist told me that a little dose of reality was fine, but giant waves of real emotion on my part could put a lot of pressure on Aiden. "Aiden is not your partner, he is your son. Don't start treating him like he is a stand-in for Merritt."

So I continued carefully. "I will. But first things first. The house is a big financial drain, and we need to move into someplace more manageable," I said in what I hope was a firm but gentle tone.

"Here's the list."

Rita handed me a to-do list (*Yeah!* I love a list!) of minor home repairs to complete before the open house. Did I really have to paint my red dining room?

"Yes, red is very last millennium. Try blue, it's soothing. It's a new day. People want spa, not power. I'll send my men over. Juan is in charge. He can do this all in about a week or two. We'll have this on the market by the end of the month." Rita squeezed my arm. "You'll get through this, and we'll find a place for you that you love, well, almost as much." And off went the lilac Cadillac into the lilac sunset.

Tina looked at me. "Are you okay?"

I nodded. "Okay" had become a relative term. I was okay in this minute, but maybe not five minutes from now.

"Is it déclassé to tell you that you look thinner? I think you've lost weight," Tina said, climbing into her new Prius. "I've gotta go get the girls at school then we're off to ballet. Do you need me to get Aiden?"

I shook my head no. "He's covered. Jan Gamble is bringing him home. She's been a saint. I just hope she doesn't show up with another casserole."

Every day for the last week, Jan had arrived at my house bearing a covered dish and bag of salad from some well-meaning Millington mother. Word had gotten around that Jan was taking Aiden to school, and she'd become the de facto Courier of Casseroles. I'd come to think of the dinners as the currency of the uncomfortable. Apparently, people who wanted to say, "I'm sorry for your loss" found that lasagna did the job much better than a sympathy card or a phone call. My housekeeper, Emilia Sanchez, now spent an hour a day organizing and redistributing the casserole overload to her large family with my blessing.

"Well, obviously you haven't been eating all those carbs because you are slimming down. Silver lining!" Tina was a big believer in the silver lining. When she was blackballed by the Junior League by a former high school foe? Silver lining, more time for kickboxing! And when she totaled her husband's new black Jaguar on its maiden voyage? Silver lining, she could now get the blue one she really wanted! So the fact that she viewed my husband's death and my subsequent financial ruin as a weight-loss opportunity only made me laugh. Everybody needs an optimist on the payroll.

Just as Tina was heading out, a black Range Rover was heading in. Melanie Martin, former exec now turned benefit chair, crunched her way down the gravel driveway, tooting the horn slightly to signal her arrival. Candy referred to women like Melanie as a Neutron Mom: once-powerful business executives, now at-home mothers whose loss in status results in instability and possible implosion at any minute.

Melanie Martin was a poster girl for the Neutron Mom Syndrome.

Despite what that doctor on the radio says, some mothers should not leave the workplace. The transition from business to parenting is too much for their ego. Meet Melanie. She was the senior VP of marketing for the Langham Luxury Hotel Group until the birth of her twins, Dustin and Denzel. As the VP of marketing, she'd enjoyed high-level strategic thinking, exciting travel and lavish budgets for events that only the very best attended. As the at-home mother of twins, she enjoyed almost none of those things. At her big job in her big office, she had a big support staff: underlings getting her coffee, scheduling her day, filing her expense reports and making things happen when Melanie uttered her favorite phrase, "Make it happen." At home, she had only the nanny to boss around, and as a result, she'd spent years watching lovely women from Central America quit after a month because, as they would tell my Emilia, "Mrs. Melanie is crazy."

Melanie used the Scorch and Burn Method to reach the top of the Pasadena charity chain. Melanie was so controlling, so unpleasant to work with, that fellow volunteers just got out of her way. Mind you, these moms had Stanford MBAs or law degrees, too, but they had made the adjustment to civilian life better than Melanie. If Melanie wanted to do everything herself, from choosing the typeface for the invitations to designing centerpieces, then so be it—such was the prevailing attitude of others. Why dig your heels in with someone that power-hungry? Now Melanie had risen to the chair of the Five Schools Benefit, and her minions included everyone else on the committee, like me.

The Five Schools Benefit was held every May in Pasadena. It was the event of the season. In short, the parents from five predominant private schools held an auction to raise money for the city's public schools. The tradition was more than 75 years old, which tells you a lot about how long the public school system has been underfunded and how long the parents from the private schools have waged rivalries. Hundreds of thousands of dollars come pouring in, the fruit of tremendous labor, delicate inter-school diplomacy and generous alcohol distribution. Millington, Cloverfield, Redwood, Martindale and Raleigh rotated the co-chairmanship, each school getting it once every five years. The result was a nomination coveted by many because it came around so rarely. Typically, only once or twice in your child's educational career at say, Redwood—the school with no grades and no uniforms but an enormous tuition for all that freedom—would your name even be eligible to be considered to run the benefit. A secret nominating committee comprised of the schools' development people and former co-chairs tightly guarded the selection process, like Skull and Bones for the socially upward suburban set.

Melanie Martin's kids went to Raleigh, the pre-K through 12 school famed for an Ivy League acceptance rate so high it warranted mention *on the front page* of the *Wall Street Journal*. (The article created an e-mail frenzy in Pasadena, and hundreds of hours of discussion continue to this day.) Melanie neutroned her way to the top of the Raleigh mothers by leading a shining capital campaign for the new student center. (Yes, every school does need a sushi bar in the cafeteria.) Now she was expending all that pent-up executive energy on Save the Date cards to announce this year's theme for the Five Schools Benefit: The Best and the Brightest.

A small cadre of mothers from each school was chosen to fill out the all-important committees: everything from Decorations to Invitations to Menu. Tina, Candy and I had been selected to represent Cloverfield on the executive committee, the result of our wildly successful, and now fateful, Save the Deodar Pines Fundraiser. Tina was in charge of Invitations, Candy was honcho-ing Public Relations, and I was chairing Corporate Sponsorship. Honestly, in the past ten days, I hadn't given Melanie or the benefit a single thought.

So what *was* Melanie doing here?

We were friends because I'd quickly concluded that being her enemy could be life-threatening, but we're not close. A couple of soccer teams together when the kids were little and many encounters at the gym and hair salon. She liked me because I humored her, asking her opinion about everything from finding the best math tutors to buying organic turkey. Like many Type A men, Neutron Moms were happiest when they were highlighting their own accomplishments. Finding the best math tutor was an accomplishment in Melanie's world. But I would never drop by her house to say hello.

Frankly, she scared me.

As a freshly coiffed Melanie hopped out of the SUV, the answer became clear. She had a casserole dish. "Helen, I just can't believe it. I *cannot* stop thinking about you and Aiden. My heart breaks. How are you doing? Did you see me at the funeral? I

had to leave before the reception. Can I give this to your girl?"
she said, not pausing for an answer to the question about my
well-being. She headed into the house, waving around the frozen
spinach lasagna from Vivienne's Gourmet Shoppe and calling for
Emilia.

Yes, Melanie, I did see you at the funeral, and my first and
only thought about you was, *What are you doing in the third row?*

The lasagna stored in the Hall of Casseroles and a fresh cup
of coffee in our hands, Melanie and I settled into the chairs in the
eat-in kitchen. I noticed Melanie turned over the pillow as she
sat down, looking for some sort of label that my pillow was lack-
ing. She took a big sip of coffee, put the cup down dramatically
and turned to me with her best "I'm-the-boss-and-I-know-what's-
best" look of empathy.

"Helen, the executive committee of the benefit had an emergency meeting today to discuss your situation, that's how concerned we are about you."

What meeting? As far as I knew, Tina and Candy hadn't been
contacted about any emergency meeting.

"You do not have to worry about a thing. Jennifer Braham is
stepping right in to fill your shoes for Corporate Sponsorship. Do
you know her? She's a Martindale mom, lives near the Arroyo,
husband is at Nestle in marketing. She'll be great! She did Corporate Sponsorship for the Colorado Street Bridge Summerfest.
She's on top of it and I'm sure you'll send her your notes and
contacts so we won't miss a beat. This is going to be a tough year
to bring back those sponsors and we don't want you to stress one
bit with everything else going on in your life." Melanie paused
briefly for air intake. "I know what you're thinking, and yes,
your name will still be on the invitation as 'Honorary Committee
Chair.' We like that language, don't you? Are you *so* relieved?"

Actually, I was *so* stunned.

The chair of the Corporate Sponsorship Committee usually went to a woman who could do the math and write the proposals and who enjoyed taking mid-level corporate executives to lunch because the Big Boss said it was good for the company image. But the key factor in getting such a prestigious post was your husband. Yes, even in this day and age, your husband's connections created your value. A powerful and successful husband could make the phone calls to the Big Bosses and get the corporate commitment. The lunches with the company PR person or the community marketing person? Simple follow-up and paperwork that any on-the-ball corporate wife could handle. When IndyMac Bank melted down in 2008, Chrissie Sears resigned her post on Corporate Sponsorship because her husband had lost his job at the bank. And their big, beautiful house. Tongues wagged, but everyone understood that Chrissie had done the right thing for the good of the benefit. Chrissie retained some personal dignity and slinked away to Orange County to live with her parents "to care for them in their old age." Sure.

Melanie's announcement made it clear that Merritt's death had reduced my standing exponentially. I could no longer pull in the big donors on my own. Melanie was giving me a graceful way out. And I had no option but to accept her exit strategy. My name in the program was my personal-dignity bailout package.

I bet she plotted this at the funeral. Wasn't Jennifer Braham sitting next to her? The Best and the Brightest.

I had to take the deal. I didn't have the strength to hold out until consulting with Candy and Tina. I know they would urge me to fight on, but now didn't seem like the best time for a power struggle with Neutron Mel.

In the same voice I used with my mother-in-law when I knew I was defeated but wanted to project otherwise, I responded, "Oh, Melanie, what a relief. How gracious of Jennifer to step in for me. She's the best. Please let her know how much I appreciate her efforts. And your quick action, Melanie. Takes a huge worry off my plate."

Melanie clapped her hands in agreement (or victory) and leaned back, enjoying her second slug of coffee even more than her first. "It must be overwhelming. Having to figure out everything by yourself. Like money." Melanie tilted her head, allowing an even better view of her ginormous diamond earrings. My God, as big as Oprah's! And like Oprah, Melanie knew her way around a balance sheet after managing a multimillion-dollar advertising budget. She came in for the kill.

"Was that Rita the Armenian I saw going down the street? So, when does the house go on the market?"

This time Melanie did pause for an answer, smiling while she waited.

The sound of Aiden's backpack slamming to the ground shook me from my seething rage after Melanie left.

"Hey, Mom, I'm home. Mrs. Gamble has another casserole for you. She's waiting out front."

Before I could make eye contact with my son, he was up the stairs to hide out in his room, where he'd spent a good portion of his time since Merritt's death. I could hear Jan at the front door.

"Hey, Helen. Today's offering is beef bourguignon! Nice upgrade! Sophie Wright made it and she can cook. She used to work at the Hearth before having kids."

The Hearth was the standard-bearer for all caterers in town. No event was complete without its signature Mashed Potato Bar or Pâté with Pomegranate Seeds. Thank you, Sophie, for a noodle-free dinner. The last time I made beef bourguignon was Christmas 2004, and Mitsy had declared it "not bad for a first attempt." I'd made it at least a dozen times at that point. Now I had Hearth-worthy beef stew to soften the blow from Melanie. Silver lining!

Jan lingered in the front hall. "Helen, Aiden said in the car that you have to sell your house. Is that true?"

Unlike Neutron Mel, the concern in Jan's eyes was genuine. And her motives were pure. She was one of the most respected mothers at Millington, known for her generosity, discretion and complete lack of flash. Jan didn't need a $1,200 pocketbook to prove her worth.

Jan had four kids and two black Labs and drove a big Suburban. Her son Will had been in Aiden's class since preschool. She could always be counted on for carpooling or room parenting. Or just writing the check to fund an entire hospital wing. Though she'd married into the Gamble family, she had no attitude. Yes, *that* Gamble family, as in Proctor and Gamble. Not like Jan and Ted were actively involved in the diaper business anymore, but they had inherited a good deal of blue-chip stock. Ted also imported wine and Italian oil paintings, which made for many tax-deductible trips to Italy and France.

The original Gambles came to Pasadena from Ohio in the late 1800s, along with a host of sun-seeking Eastern and Midwestern industrialists: the Wrigleys (gum), the Gillettes (razors), the Scripps (newspapers). These families were looking for sunshine and citrus and the area had plenty of both. They built their glorious houses on what became known as Millionaires Row. The Millionaires brought their household help, many of whom were African-American, thus helping to establish Pasadena as home to one of the oldest and most successful black communities west of the Mississippi. Then, thanks to Hollywood, Caltech, great natural light and lots of land, the movie people, the scientists, the architects, the artists and the real estate developers settled in Pasadena. Now the town was home to 150,000 people of every race, creed and class.

And yet some days, Pasadena felt more like a big high school than a small city.

Though many of the mansions of Millionaires Row were now luxury condo complexes, the offspring of the Gambles and other founding families have remained in the area. Jan, full of good sense and excellent breeding, married Ted Gamble straight out of Harvard. They lived in a huge Mediterranean villa near Caltech.

There was nothing Jan Gamble would not do for a friend, and I was lucky enough to be one. I knew the spin clock was ticking, now that Neutron Mel had sighted Rita the Armenian. Every woman on the Five Schools committee would know by sundown about my housing situation, as Neutron Mel loved the "Here's an Update" group e-mail. If anybody could counteract the Melanie-generated rumor mill, it was solid, steady Jan Gamble. So I spun my story.

"We are putting the house on the market. I want to be very conservative with the estate. I just want to make sure Aiden has everything he needs for his future, and I don't want to take any chances in this economy. You know, Jan, these houses can be a lot to keep up. I think a place with less upkeep and less stress would be best for Aiden and me right now."

There, the half-truth was out and I felt about 50 percent better! The house was too big, too expensive and too much for me, but there was no need to add the part about bad investments, massive debt and an estate worth virtually nothing. I knew that part would leak out later, as I'm sure some of the parents at the school were also clients of Fairchild Capital. But at least among the parents of Aiden's friends, I could maintain my façade.

"I totally understand. That is so sensible. If I didn't have Ted, I'd be overwhelmed. You're doing the right thing."

"Thanks, Jan."

I almost lost it. Having Jan's approval meant a lot to me. I have no doubt she'd been the senior class president at Atherton High School, her alma mater in Northern California. She still had that aura of accomplishment and moral authority.

'We miss you at school. Not that I mind taking Aiden," Jan was quick to add. "But we just miss you."

"I am the glue that holds that place together." We both

laughed. It was a joke Jan and I had shared since the day when our boys were in third grade and their classmate little Elliot Merriman had asked me during Colonial Day candle-dipping, "Mrs. Fairchild, do you own the school?"

"No, Elliot. I am just the glue." I'd replied, amused but not surprised by Elliot's observation. I did spend more time there than the other mothers in the class, simply because I had more time. While Jan, Candy, Tina and the others were off having second (old-school yuppie), third ("Three is the new two!") or fourth ("We have so much money we can pay four tuitions!") children, I just had Aiden.

I'd plowed all my energy into volunteering as a distraction from the secondary infertility. I could be there at a minute's notice to fill in for the field-trip driver who didn't show or the library reader who had a sick child. I was always available for meetings mid-morning. I had plenty of time to do all the extra legwork on any project, from stuffing envelopes to braving trips to Michaels craft store, otherwise known as Hell on Earth. What I lacked in social connections, I made up for in sheer man-hours. I came to be regarded as essential to the school, the glue that held the place together, even to Elliot Merriman.

Now I didn't even want to get in the carpool line.

Ten days since Merritt's death, and I hadn't been to school, the grocery store, anywhere. It wasn't the grief; it was the fear. Honestly, I'd been hiding out from the public because I was terrified I would just break down and spill the whole awful truth to anyone who gave me a willing ear. I needed to steady myself before I could face those women again.

Those women? Most were my friends, but now my entire existence was up for reinterpretation. My encounter with Melanie confirmed that instinct.

"I'm almost there. Maybe next week, I'll show up for my shift at the book fair at school!" I said to Jan, hoping for a light touch.

"No pressure," Jan responded quickly. "Just wanted you to

know that you are missed. Oh, and I saw Melanie at the nail salon this afternoon. She told me that you had resigned from the Five Schools Benefit. Totally understand. Though, I thought you were doing a great job. Maybe another year."

Unbelievable. Of course Jan would know my status, as a former co-chair and a selection committee member. Could she read the shock in my face over Melanie's bald-faced lie? Once again, I had to play along.

"Well, it's all part of making life for Aiden and me very manageable at this point. Priorities!"

Sometimes I find a single word can convey an entire thought without really saying anything all. *Priorities!* Yes, Melanie's, not mine, but priorities just the same.

"Enjoy the beef bourguignon! I hope you have a decent cabernet. That's what you need: vino! Forget the bag of salad! I'll see Aiden tomorrow at 7:45. History test tomorrow for the boys." Jan, with her trusting, discreet nature, climbed into her Suburban and headed home.

I called Candy and Tina for our own emergency meeting.

"My God, this meal is spectacular! I mean, I know you had an awful day, but let's just take a minute to toast Sophie Wright," Candy said, raising a glass of Cabernet that I'd busted out of Merritt's collection. "I don't think I've ever heard that poor thing say one word in my entire life. She always looks so downtrodden in all those black clothes. We all know she's from New York, enough with the black turtlenecks in May. She sure can cook, though."

"Candy, does it ever occur to you that you never stop talking? Maybe that's why no one can get a word in around you?" Tina enjoyed alerting Candy to her foibles. Candy liked having that kind of reputation.

"Back to business. Helen, do you want us to resign in protest?

You know we will. That would freak Melanie out. I love seeing her lose her grip."

I had just re-created the entire conversation with Neutron Mel, complete with coffee-slugging, and the follow-up with Jan. As I'd guessed, Tina and Candy had not been part of the fictitious "emergency executive meeting," and their outrage over my ouster was over the top. So were the names they called our girl Melanie. Now, as we sat around in my kitchen, contemplating retaliatory measures, I felt my own frustration drain. The truth is, I really didn't have the time to raise money so other people's children could get a good education. I needed to raise money so my own child could.

"Stay on the committee. Melanie is the type who wouldn't even understand that the protest was about her. I don't think she does a lot of self-reflection. And really, she's right. Without Merritt, I don't have an entrée into that world. I couldn't raise the money, not in this economy, not on my own."

"That's not true," Tina said, always the cheerleader, even if her team was losing.

Candy poured herself another glass of wine. "It kinda is true. Sorry, Helen. But when Chris and I divorced, I lost a whole Rolodex of contacts. Pretty much the entire commercial real estate industry would no longer take my calls. I mean, really, he's the one who was gay and it's my fault that we divorced?"

Candy's first husband, Chris Lincoln, was a commercial real estate broker and closeted gay man. She was 24, a news producer at the NBC affiliate, using most of her paycheck to maintain her newly tinted red hair. She met Chris at a Brentwood salon (red flag!), and they eloped to Vegas six weeks later, after seeing George Michael in concert (red flag!). Candy loved that Chris seemed to really enjoy shopping and having white-wine spritzers at lunch (red flag!). Chris needed Candy as cover to avert suspicion at his testosterone-filled downtown firm, though he didn't exactly articulate that in the wedding vows. The marriage lasted three years, most of them spent living apart after Candy discovered Chris in bed with her hairdresser, Arthur, two weeks after the wedding. By the time the divorce was final, Candy was an entertainment reporter with blond hair, and Chris was a major player in the redevelopment of Melrose Avenue into a shopping Mecca. Candy got a nice settlement and a lifetime of free highlights from Arthur, now Chris's husband, at least in Massachusetts. She actually had the highlights written into the divorce settlement.

"I mean, really, I did nothing but nice things for Chris and still the real estate brethren shunned me. Oh, sure, fourteen years later they talk to me at events and they want good press for their charitable underwriting, but in the early '90s? Forget it," Candy moaned.

"So there's nothing you want us to do to Neutron Mel?" I shook my head at Tina's question. I was too tired to seek revenge. Tina gave me the buck-up smile. "We want to be here for you, Helen."

"You know what I need, Tina? I need a job, an actual paying job. Not a committee head position where I donate all my time and skills for free. I need somebody to pay me for my work. And I don't even know how to start."

"I know just the girl for you. Elizabeth Maxwell, headhunter. She used to call me all the time about law firm jobs; you know, being an Asian female I was in high demand. But now we're everywhere. Still, she owes me a favor. I helped get her kids into kindergarten. I'll call her," said Tina, typing a note to herself into her Blackberry. "You should get a new suit. You're going to need it for all your interviews."

Mitsy Fairchild had done the proper thing for a Pasadena woman of a certain age and status. She'd sold her big house in the San Rafael area and downsized into a condo on famed Orange Grove Boulevard. The street was lined with luxury buildings featuring pristine landscaping, million-dollar units and many "For Sale" signs, due to the high turnover in that age group. Mitsy lived in a dark gray French-style complex, humbly called Le Trianon. Apparently, calling the building Versailles was a little over the top for the inhabitants. Mitsy's penthouse corner unit was more than 3,000 square feet of antiques and art treasures collected from her decades of annual trips abroad. Of course, she'd worked with a decorator, but her own personal taste was impeccable. Her home was a showstopper.

And she rarely invited me there.

Mitsy preferred to entertain at the club, more conspicuous and less personal. So when I got a phone message that she'd love to see me for lunch at her place, I braced for impact.

Although, at this point, what could she possibly say to me that could make my situation any worse? Bring it on, Snake Goddess.

I gave the big brass lion head a good knock. Mitsy opened the door, wearing slim tan trousers, a cashmere V-neck in warm yellow and the classic Tiffany yard of diamonds, her midweek uniform.

"Helen, I'm glad you're on time." My one saving grace over the last fifteen years with my mother-in-law. I am habitually early, always on time, and never late. "Come in and have an iced tea."

Lunch was predictable and already set out on the table: quiche, a side salad with oil and red wine vinegar dressing and a basket of French bread. The iced teas were poured, each with a gleaming slice of lemon. No sugar or butter or salt and pepper on the table. This lunch was strictly business. We sat down and simultaneously put the linen napkins in our laps.

"I spoke with Billy. I am aware of the financial situation."

Well, so much for attorney-client privilege. Apparently Billy crumbled under the pressure of Mitsy Fairchild, too, and for some reason, that buoyed my spirits. Actually, having Billy let Mitsy know that her only son was on the verge of financial ruin was a relief. Better him than me. I nodded and took a bite of the stone-cold quiche.

"And I understand you are putting the house on the market. Is that correct?"

Neutron Melanie must have filled in the older ladies at the club's popular mid-morning water aerobics, and the word had cycled back to Mitsy. This method of communication appealed to my non-confrontational side. I nodded again, sensing Mitsy was not really looking for a conversation but only a confirmation.

"Well, it sounds like you've had to make some quick decisions, and I can understand that. When Merritt's father died so suddenly, I, too, had to educate myself rather quickly. It's a good thing you're so much younger than I was. Being 40 today seems decades younger than being nearly 50 when I had to restart my life."

I waited for Mitsy to continue. She seemed on the verge of sharing something personal, but the moment passed and she carried on.

"What are your plans?" she asked.

This time it appeared I had to answer. I chose my words carefully. I had no idea how she expected me to react. And I was always conscious of falling below her expectations.

"I am still absorbing the information about the finances, but I am trying to move forward."

"What does that mean?' Mitsy snapped, hating any kind of language that could be construed as "new-agey." I guess "moving forward" qualified as too vague for her. Now I was annoyed.

"Here's what moving forward means, Mitsy. It means that I am trying not to lose it and obsess about what my husband did with all our money. So instead, I'm selling what possessions we need to sell, like cars and art. I'm looking for a job and hoping that after the house sells, we'll have enough money for a down payment on a small place and money for Aiden's high school. If not, we'll have to consider relocation to a more affordable part of the country. That's what moving forward means."

Wow! I surprised myself with my clear thinking! My tone and conviction seemed to impress Mitsy. She relaxed her arched right eyebrow and studied me. Then, she conceded, "I wish I could help. Unfortunately, the economic downturn has required me to make my own financial adjustments."

Did Merritt have something to do with that? Mitsy would never tell me something like that. "I would have gladly contributed to Aiden's education, but now that is not possible."

Back to nodding for me. I wasn't so sure she was being honest, at least about the "gladly contributing" part. She'd never made any grand gestures before, no college funds or trust funds set up in Aiden's name. Mitsy espoused a belief in self-reliance, but I think she was just stingy, especially when it came to people.

"Helen, I'd appreciate it if you didn't advertise your situation all over town. Not that you have! It's just, for Aiden's sake, it would be better if you didn't discuss the particulars with your friends and such."

I've noticed over the past fifteen years that wealthy people routinely engage in denial and illusion. Mitsy, an old-money maven, pretended that it would violate the rules of good taste to mention money, or lack thereof, to friends and distant family. The truth was, she just didn't want anybody to know that her son's widow and her grandson were now in a much lower tax bracket.

Now I knew why she'd invited me.

"It's not my intent to 'advertise' my situation, but I will do what it takes to take care of my son. And if that means putting the house on the market, getting a job and applying for financial aid, that is what I will do. I grew up taking care of myself and my family. I'm not afraid to do that again."

Now Mitsy was trying to choke down the cardboard quiche. She looked up at me, her eyes wet, and she struggled to get a hold of her emotions. It was then I remembered that she was a mother who had just lost a son, imperfect as he was.

"I know you will, Helen. I just thank you in advance for upholding the Fairchild name."

If Mitsy hadn't been so clearly upset, I would have howled at the idea of upholding the Fairchild name, the irony thick, as it was Merritt who'd put the name in peril in the first place. But I realized that, for better or worse, in sickness or in death, I was a Fairchild, too.

"Of course. For Aiden." And we both nodded.

I did not miss Merritt during the day. Between the painting and the packing and the selling off of my antiques, I was too busy during the day to think about him. And really, he'd never been part of my life during daylight anyway. We weren't the kind of couple that talked a dozen times on, say, a normal Tuesday. Occasionally a question might come up mid-afternoon about picking up Aiden at practice or buying tickets to something, and I'd ring Merritt at the office. But usually, we practiced a communication blackout during the day.

Which is why his homecoming at night was a big deal. And why the silence at 7 o'clock was now deafening. Aiden and I started watching *The Simpsons* to fill the void. No doubt, someday, Aiden's college girlfriend, a pretty psychology major from Scottsdale or Houston, would have a field day with the significance of Aiden replacing his dead father with Homer Simpson. She'd blame me for allowing Aiden to process his grief so inappropriately. But seeing Aiden laugh in the moment was much more important to me than protecting myself from future blame.

The only problem with Aiden's devotion to *The Simpsons* was that it was on the Fox Network, as was Roshelle Simms. So every night, while Aiden and I ate the casserole of the day, we watched TV and I waited for the inevitable: My late husband's mistress was sure to pop up sometime during the half hour to do a promo. *Is this lingerie too sexy for TV? You be the judge at 10.* Or, *Is this pill the secret to a bikini body? The revealing before and after photos at 10.* If the editorial content of Fox News seemed questionable before the Panda Incident, now I took its overtly sexual nature personally. Where is the FCC when you need it? It took every ounce of discipline not to throw my fork at the television. I'd come to think of her as Shelly Sleazy.

"That woman has a weird face," Aiden commented one evening (*Can more action in the bedroom make stretch marks disappear? Take an undercover look at 10!*) while helping himself to a large portion of Enchiladas Especial from the Gutierrez family. "What's wrong with it?"

High Def and collagen are a lethal combination.

I clicked the mute button and changed the subject. It was one thing to be stoic in the face of infidelity; it was another to be blasé.

"You know, you have your Ignatius admissions test coming up in a few weeks. I scheduled some test-prep classes today." Because that's what parents in Pasadena did, shelled out hundreds of dollars on all sorts of academic extras, because that's what everyone else did.

"Please don't make me go to that guy with the freaky hair."

Guilty as charged. Aiden had endured some Spanish tutoring from a Donald Trump look-alike named Señor Tom. Neutron Mel had said Señor Tom was "the best in town." Unfortunately, the hair had proved to be such a gigantic distraction for Aiden that his grades went down, despite Señor Tom's $75-an-hour fee. Some days, Aiden would get into the car after class and his gag reflex would kick in just thinking about the comb-over. "No más Señor Tom!" Aiden had begged.

So I started throwing a few extra bucks Emilia's way if she'd go over his homework, a much better solution. But the damage was done. Señor Tom remained a dark memory for Aiden, and his resistance to tutoring was steadfast.

"No Señor Tom. You and Lilly Chau-Swenson are going to go together to a totally normal college kid who's going to give you some tips, just pointers. It will be fun."

Why did I say that? Of course it wouldn't be fun. "Rock Band" is fun. Grammar is never fun if you are Aiden. At least Aiden liked Lilly, and she was smart as a whip. A top test-taker.

"Okay. If I have to."

Aiden was a C-plus student. After years of being threatened and tutored and attending an "academically rigorous" school, he was still an average student. In a world of seemingly extraordinary 13-year-olds who play perfect violin, make the traveling team for volleyball and compete at Mock Trial, all while thriving under the intense academic pressure of their parents and teachers, an average student like Aiden was nothing special to a high school admissions director. Hence the test prep.

I had come to terms with Aiden's totally average performance in the classroom. I would have loved to have gone to a school like Millington with rigor, rules and hours of homework. But Aiden shrugged off the work, turning out a maddeningly uneven academic performance. When it came to school, I was Sisyphus and he was the rock. Why couldn't he just care a little more about his GPA and a little less about Legos, I'd whine after another average report card.

Merritt had mocked my worry. "The kid will be fine. The Asians may get all the As, but Aiden will get the girls in high school."

Even Tina Chau-Swenson had concluded the same.

"Of course our kids get better grades. What do you expect? Your people want your kids to be popular. We don't care if our kids go to birthday parties. We want them to go to Yale."

Tina had a point. Aiden was born into a certain life, and his future seemed to include a free pass into a decent high school, a pretty good college and a respectable career, if he could just hold it together and not do drugs, get into a car accident or get some girl pregnant. Aiden didn't need the Ivy League; he was a Fairchild. Up until New Year's Day, his life had been a series of expected steps on a clear path, just like I'd wanted at his age. In December, I hadn't been worried about Aiden getting into Ignatius. That's why he'd applied to only one high school. But now? He was just some average kid with a dead father and no economic influence, as Neutron Melanie had so clearly illustrated to me. He needed to get into Ignatius now more than he did a month ago.

But first he had to nail the standardized test.

"Yes, you do have to do the tutoring. You want to go to Ignatius, right?"

Aiden shrugged. Didn't he want to go to Ignatius? Of course he did. Merritt had been taking him to Ignatius football games since he was little. He loved his Ignatius T-shirt. It was his dream to play water polo for Ignatius, wasn't it?

"Aiden, I know right now it may not seem that important, but next September, you'll be glad you made the effort." I could see by the look on his face that "next September" might as well be a million years away. He clicked the unmute button. The conversation was over.

The Shelly Show was back. *Is your teen sexting while at school? Tune in at 10 and see what's really happening on your child's cell phone.*

Hey, Shelly, F-U! Try this promo: *Is your husband sexting me while driving? Watch out for that panda at 10 o'clock!*

Oh my God, did I just say that out loud?

"Mom, are you okay? You were talking to yourself."

"Lots on my mind. More enchiladas?"

CHAPTER 5

"I have to be honest. I have nothing for you, because you're not really qualified for anything at the executive level, even junior executive," said Elizabeth Maxwell, a tall, striking African-American woman in her early 30s. I was mesmerized by the most beautiful family photo I have ever seen, displayed prominently on her sparkling desk in her sparkling office at Maxwell and Mathers Executive Search, Inc. Elizabeth's cool voice forced me to focus. "I have out-of-work MBAs who can't even get interviews for entry-level jobs. There's nothing on your resume that screams, 'Hire me.'"

The only reason she didn't hoot and howl at my situation was because I was a friend of Tina's and a fellow Millington mom. The new widow bit was a plus, too. Her use of the word "resume" was the tip-off. My "resume" consisted of a list of charity activities compiled by me and jacked up by Tina to make my years as a mother, wife and community volunteer sound like actual work experience. My time on the decorating committee became "design and branding expertise." Tina transformed my years as room mother into a position requiring "team-building skills" and "negotiating contracts." (*With whom? The charter bus company for field trips?*) And the many charity dollars I brought in for various organizations were re-purposed as "raising capital" and "budgeting P&L." My abandoned graduate studies at Berkeley had been redefined as "master's track coursework." The woman on the paper was someone with a career.

I had never had a career.

I had nothing to "go back to" but a half-finished thesis. I had no law firm like Tina or marketing department like Neutron Melanie to return to on a part-time basis. Instead of building a career in my twenties, I was building a family: getting married at 25, having Aiden at 27, happily staying home and being a mother. Now I was trying to pretend that all those experiences amounted to a job.

All those experiences amounted to a life, but not a job.

Even my new Banana Republic suit (*on sale in size 8*!) felt a little ginned-up for the occasion; I never wore tailored shirts or stockings during the day. And the bright pink silk scarf around my neck? Tina said it would make me look younger.

"If you refuse to use fillers like the rest of the women in town, then you'll have to do something to cover up that neck!"

I'd rejected the traditional 40th birthday gifts of Botox, Restalyne or tummy-tuck surgery in favor of a nice dinner with friends. Tina had thought I was crazy. Apparently, my punishment was this scarf. I thought it screamed "Clinique Salesgirl at Bonus Time," but what did I know?

Elizabeth Maxwell was not fooled by the resume or the outfit, but she was kind. "I've seen a lot of women like you in the past few years, going back to work after the kids get older. Maybe they need money for college or the husband has lost a job or taken a pay cut. Honestly, your prospects are really grim. You're capable of doing a job in marketing or communications. And I think your real-life experience is worth as much as any MBA. But corporate America doesn't see it that way. You'll end up making less than your housekeeper."

Not for long, because I have to let Emilia go, but I knew she was right.

As I studied the young, successful Elizabeth Maxwell, I wished for the hundredth time since Merritt's death that I could have a do-over of the last fifteen years. Obviously, I would never trade Aiden, but why wasn't I more ambitious for myself? *Don't cry. Do not cry.*

"Do you have any advice?" I squeaked out, hoping I didn't sound too pathetic.

"You've done a lot of volunteer work at the Huntington. Maybe there's something there in the development office or public relations. They know you, so your dedication to the institution will make up for your lack of job experience. You're bright, articulate, connected in the community. You just have no street cred in the real world. Start with the Huntington. You need to get your foot in the door and get some real experience."

Among the moms at school and on the sidelines at games, I'd built up a reputation as a Scholar Lite, thanks to my academic past and my hours volunteering at the Huntington. The Huntington Library, Art Collections and Botanical Gardens—the official name, though no one in town ever called it anything but the Huntington—housed one of the finest rare book and document collections in the world, in addition to spectacular gardens and a first-class art and furniture collection. The Huntington was established on the former estate of Henry Huntington, railroad baron and book collector, and his lovely wife, Arabella, philanthropist and visionary garden designer. It stood on a marvelous piece of property on the border of Pasadena and San Marino, a quieter, even higher tax bracket to the south.

In addition to being a tremendous public space, the Huntington was a world-class research facility, thanks to the rare books and papers in its collection. Only select scholars were granted access to the collections for research. They repaid the Huntington by giving lectures on their esoteric areas of study. I served them tea and cookies.

Over the past ten years, I'd worked my way up the volunteer food chain, from Preschool Docent to Scholar Hospitality, by virtue of the fact that I was a quasi-academic and about 25 years younger than most of the other volunteers. The lovely retiree volunteers tended to talk the ears off the visiting scholars and curators, so my attentiveness minus the need to tell everyone about my grandchildren made me a favorite to staff the public lecture series. Tea and cookies were always served to those who could attend the midday talks. Sometimes, I was even allowed to introduce the speakers, giving out their long lists of credentials as if I was their equal. I loved it.

For the mothers at school, I did my own lecture series. I could take an hour-long lecture by a Distinguished Fellow of Historical Minutiae at Impressive East Coast University and boil it down to a couple of salient facts for busy women who didn't have time to go to talks on a Wednesday afternoon. Sociability in the British Enlightenment (*Who knew the entire study of science started with well-connected British guys who could entertain the ladies with amusing stories of the natural world!*); the Reign of Charles I (*Disastrous king! The George Bush of England. Pious, but bloody. Executed as a result of civil war!*); Money Talks: Commerce, Classics and Taste in Late Imperial China (*Wow, those women of the Ming dynasty were every bit as label-conscious and conspicuously consumptive as the Hollywood wives. Think Late Imperial* In Style *magazine meets* Architectural Digest). Those lectures, and my retelling, kept me intellectually stimulated, staving off the boredom of motherhood. And earned me the nickname "Professor Fairchild" from the Millington mothers.

In all the years that I'd volunteered at the Huntington, it had never occurred to me to work at the Huntington. Thank you, Elizabeth Maxwell.

"I'm going to steal that phrase for my interview. 'No experience but much dedication to the institution,' that's me!" I chirped a bit too brightly.

"Please do."

"Can I ask you something?"

"Sure."

"Did you ever consider giving up your job when you had your kids?" I nodded toward the photo of the whole family in the shallow surf in Hawaii. Two adorable girls in hibiscus print suits and

Elizabeth in a big floppy hat and pareo. Cute husband, too.

"My mom was a single mom. I believe in work."

"Simply put. Thanks, Elizabeth. I appreciate your advice."

"No problem. Will I see you at the book fair?"

"Maybe. I could be running the development office at the Huntington by then." I laughed. So did she.

"Yes, you could."

"Mom, what are you doing here?" Aiden said, climbing into my Audi wagon in the carpool line. "And why are you dressed like that?"

I had to hand it to him. He could be very observant when he wanted to be, just not when looking for his backpack or water polo gear.

"I am here to pick you up. It's time for me to get back into the world," I declared, slowly pulling away from the curb, grateful that I didn't bash into the SUV in front of me that suddenly stopped. "And I have just come from my first career counseling session."

"What career?"

"Yes, exactly, what career? I believe you are more qualified to get a job than I am. At least you have your lifeguarding certification." I looked over at Aiden, who was smiling for the first time in three weeks. I went with it. "Would you mind dropping out of school and lifeguarding to support us?'

"No problem. As long as I get to drive Dad's BMW to the pool." And we both laughed, really laughed, together for the first time since Merritt's death.

Then, Aiden asked me the question that I'd been preparing to answer every night when I lay in bed and prayed for guidance.

"Mom, are we going to be okay?"

I stared straight ahead, watching the road and my words. "Aiden, we will be okay, but there will have to be a lot of changes. You know about the house, but besides that, we just won't have as much money as we're used to. We'll sell the house, I'll get a job, and we'll be okay. But life will be different."

He nodded, his brown hair falling into his eyes. "We're kinda broke, right?"

Surprised, I snapped, "What do you mean?'

"I heard you talking to Candy and Tina, um, Ms. McKenna and Mrs. Chau-Swenson," Aiden corrected himself. Pasadena was a "last names for grown-ups" kind of town. "It sounded kinda bad."

I bit the bullet, trying to remember that he was my son, not my partner. "It is kinda bad now, but it will get better."

"I don't have go to Ignatius. There are public schools. And I can get a job. I can help."

"Don't worry. We can handle tuition, and your priority should be school, okay?"

"Yeah. I love you, Mom." Aiden was never embarrassed to say that to me. He rarely said it to Merritt, who wasn't a big fan of expressing emotions, not even in the 'I love ya, buddy' way that men use as a default. Merritt used to pat him on the head and say, "Good boy." Like he was a Lab.

"I love you, too, Aiden," I returned, squeezing his hand, then to ease the emotion, "Do you like my scarf? Do I look younger?"

"You look like a dorky French girl."

"*Merci.*"

I figured it out. It was that vacation to Mexico about five years ago that was the beginning of the end for Merritt and me. Lying in the dark night after night, unable to sleep, I became obsessed with pinpointing the Incident That Changed It All. Figure that out, I convinced myself, and the rest of this mess would begin to make sense.

I settled on the Mexico trip.

"You make the plans," Merritt had tossed out at me one morning in January before he headed into downtown L.A. to build his empire. "Wherever you want to go! Surprise me!" I think he'd even kissed me on the way out the door.

So I had, because I am a planner. Good at details, long-range calendarizing, airline reservations, packing lists, transportation supervision, weather charts, day trips, travel documents and shot records. "Good planning makes for good fun" was a needlepoint pillow credo that I lived by. I'd plunged into my new task. I was an early adapter to Internet vacation planning; it made me feel like I was back in school doing research. I thought Spring Break 2003 would be a high point in Fairchild family vacation lore. And in our sex life.

We'd spent the previous six years trying to have a second child, to no avail, despite the specialists and the fertility drugs and the planned-to-the-minute, medically inspired intercourse. Really, it's a stretch to call that kind of coupling *sex*. Secondary infertility, the doctors called it. I was pretending not to be heartbroken, but Merritt hadn't bothered to pretend anything. He blamed me, though Dr. Weston hadn't come to that conclusion.

This vacation was going to be our big breakthrough. One last shot to relax and conceive before I threw in the towel. Not that Merritt and I discussed the matter much anymore at that point. But I thought if we could find an exotic new spot, we could cut loose and be our old selves.

Merritt hadn't appreciated my creativity.

"Mexico? That's not Hawaii. That's not the Mauna Kea."

"We always go to the Mauna Kea. You said, 'Surprise me,' so I thought we might try somewhere new, something different. Like an eco-resort in Puerto Vallarta! We might see some celebs."

"Helen, Mexico is not America. Mexico is *Mexico*. Do you know what that means? I won't be able to drink the water or check e-mail. What about security? What about terrorists? And I don't want to see celebrities. What were you thinking? What's next? A cruise?"

"You've been working so hard. We never see you. I thought it might be fun to have an adventure. As a family." I did not mention the word "baby."

"I want a vacation, not an adventure."

We had neither, really. Oh, Aiden and I loved the place, with its slightly run-down, not-quite-America ambience. The "wild-life" promised on the website consisted of one old decrepit sea turtle that slept on the deck of the restaurant. The waiters and waitresses had "performed" the evening entertainment of bad skits that featured an unusually high number of cross-dressing sight gags. Merritt had pouted and pounded watery margaritas while 8-year-old Aiden and I did the limbo to Ricky Martin songs. Nobody got sick or attacked by terrorists, and I certainly did not get pregnant.

But we never quite recovered.

We got home to Pasadena and Merritt's message was clear: I want a marriage, not an adventure. My unusual background was no longer an asset, it was a liability. I think those were his exact words. Asset, liability, risk, loss. That's how he thought about our marriage.

The next year, we went back to the safety of the Mauna Kea with half the members of the Pasadena Town Club in beach lounges beside us, sucking down mai tais and talking about golf. Merritt regaled his people with tales of our "third-world camping trip in freaking Mexico!" Everyone laughed at his over-the-top descriptions of the vacation, confident in their own excellent hotel choices. Everyone but me.

He never mentioned Mexico again, not even on New Year's Eve when he told me about Roshelle. But I know, *I know*, that was the Incident That Changed It All.

Good. Moving on.

CHAPTER 6

The long, tree-lined drive into the Huntington always filled me with pleasure. From the first time I saw the site of the *beaux-arts* mansion with the unending lush landscape, from the authentic Japanese garden to the proper English rose garden, I knew this was a special place. The fountains and sculptures tucked into sun-dappled corners all over the property always surprised me. The tasteful Galleries, once the Huntington family's private residence, had just been restored with glorious chandeliers and gleaming parquet floors. Mary Cassat's *Breakfast in Bed* and Gainsborough's *The Blue Boy* hung on the silver-blue walls, lovely reminders of motherhood. But most of all, I relished the cool, dark Library building filled with treasures, from the first-edition Gutenberg Bible to Albert Einstein's letters to an original "Shakespeare's Folio." I loved pretending to be a part of this world.

But on that Friday in late January, I was filled with dread. I had to ask someone for something. I had to ask for a big favor. I was used to being the one asked, not the asker.

Get used to it.

I met Sarah White at the outdoor coffee cart, just inside the Entrance Pavilion. Sarah White was about 50, one of those women who went gray early and still looked sexy, her hair the perfect shade of silver and her skin vibrant. She'd come from the admissions office of Wesleyan a decade earlier, venturing west to start a new life after a divorce. She rose to power as an assistant in the development office by raising millions of dollars for the new Chinese garden, thanks to the area-wide influx of people and money from China. Now she had her finger in every pot at the Huntington. As the newly named public relations director, she was the ultimate source of information.

Sarah brought that veneer of East Coast snobbery that Californians loved, her accent awash in New York's Upper East Side and Miss Porter's. She could drop phrases like "our summer place in Cos Cob" and "My mother had a Saturday night series at the Met" and the donors would nod their heads in solidarity, pretending to know what she was referring to. But I'd seen Sarah with her hair down on several occasions, after a little too much wine at the volunteer dinner. She didn't scare me at all.

At least, not until this moment.

"Helen," Sarah hugged me, giving my shoulder an extra squeeze, like she meant it. "I've been thinking of you."

"I've missed it here. It's good to be back."

"I was surprised to get your call so soon. You don't have to worry about your shifts. You know that you cannot be replaced, but Arlene in Volunteers can find the subs. Mrs. Smithson is thrilled to step in and do the lecture series." We both laughed. Mrs. Smithson could take twenty minutes to ask you what time it was. "Coffee?"

"Great," I said, accepting the latte from adorable little Annie, who ran the espresso bar during the week. Annie studied photography at Art Center. She'd come to the funeral, along with so many others from the Huntington. "Thanks, Annie!"

"Look at you, Helen! Good to see you." Annie smiled hard, her good cheer rubbing off on me. "We need you back here." And then she winked because she's a winker.

I winked back uncomfortably.

"Let's walk. I have to drop off something over at the Scott Gallery," Sarah commanded, taking long strides toward the step and pathway.

Once again, in my Banana Republic get-up, I felt like a pretender. The combination of the straight skirt and the mid-heel pumps made it difficult for me to catch the sprinting Sarah White. And goddamn, I didn't want to spill the steaming hot latte all over my tailored shirt. Tina would kill me.

Slow the fuck down.

I panicked, attempting to keep up with Sarah Longlegs, forgetting my job pitch that I'd actually written down and rehearsed several times in front of the bathroom mirror. *(I think my dedication to this institution has been proven in deed and commitment. I'd love a chance to become more than just a volunteer. I want to be part of the team.)* In an effort to slow my companion down and get it over with, I blurted out, "I need a job. I'm not really *qualified* for anything but I would *do* anything. Anything. Do you have anything?"

Sarah turned—her stunned face, gleaming hair and just-right lipstick set off by the giant bamboo forest in the background— then she smiled. "Oh, that's what you needed to see me about. Why didn't you tell me on the phone? I've been there, too!" Sarah said, referring to her change of status after her divorce, a comparison that I was starting to resent a touch, but I let it go.

"We'd love to have you here as an employee. But it's not the best time to be looking. Let me think. Nothing in my office right now. We're holding on for dear life, trying to ride out this economy without losing too many people."

"Anything in other departments? I'd dust the Magna Carta if that's what it takes." The Huntington did have a copy of the Magna Carta, which I do not believe they would let me dust, but I was just trying to make a point.

"There is something I just heard about. Karen in Library mentioned it to me this morning. We have a DS visiting for this semester. He needs a research assistant."

DS was a Distinguished Scholar, and by "semester," Sarah meant he would be staying until May or June. Perfect. My foot in the door.

"That would be perfect!" I was breathless, maybe because my

binding underwear was starting to cut off the oxygen supply to my lungs, and Sarah had resumed her nine-minute-mile pace toward the other side of the gardens. This was a poor outfit choice.

Sarah laughed. "Don't you even want to know who he is or what he is researching? Or the pay?"

All excellent questions, I acknowledged.

Sarah filled me in. The hourly pay was slightly better than Emilia's but less than a lifeguard's at a children's birthday party. And all she knew about the researcher was that he was an archaeologist who specialized in Troy. He was here to catalogue some new papers that had been discovered in a Caltech professor's attic and had to do with famed archaeologist Heinrich Schliemann and the original excavation at Troy.

"Sorry, I don't know his name. Let me drop this off and we'll go talk to Karen right now. Maybe he's still here and you can meet with him."

Meet with him? Now? Oh my God, no. I can't work for a classical archaeologist! Anthropologist? Sure. Botanist? Great. Early American history scholar specializing in wildlife prints by that Audubon guy? Fine. I love birds. But an actual classical archaeologist? No way. He'll bust me. I'm not smart enough. He'll know right away that I'm a grad school dropout, that my Greek was weak twenty years ago and certainly has not improved in the last decade. The face of every professor I disappointed in grad school flashed before me. "Oh, well…"

"Wasn't that your field? Archaeology? It's kismet!"

That's the sort of phrase you don't hear every day. Now I wanted to kill Sarah, because I was sweating right through my tailored blouse and I could feel a run in my stockings creeping up the back of my right leg. "Yes. Well, it's been a few years. Maybe I should call Karen and come back later…"

"Helen, once this job gets posted online, you're toast. Most of the research assistants we place are Ph.D. candidates themselves. Young, qualified Ph.D. candidates. If you want this job, you have to make a case for it now. Catch my drift?"

Catch my drift? That's some tough talk from a Miss Porter's girl. But Sarah had a point, the same point Elizabeth Maxwell made. At 40 and jobless for fifteen years, I was neither young nor qualified. And I was getting less so every day I hesitated. I thought of Aiden. I thought of getting that foot in the door.

"Okay. Let's go meet this archaeologist."

I was still breathing heavily as I pulled up in front of the Scott Gallery and waited for Sarah to drop off her envelope and locate Karen from Library. My God, when had I gotten so out of shape? How long had it been since I'd done that Shreadmill workout my trainer had designed? Before or after Meredith Viera left *The View*? I'd really let myself go, just like Merritt had said. Put that on my list for my new life: more cardio.

Stop! This was exactly the kind of pathetic mind-babble that I should be stomping out. Focus, focus. Try to remember anything you ever learned about Troy. *Made famous by Homer in the Iliad. Scene of ten-year siege in, like, 1200 BC Bronze Age, just say Bronze Age, that works. Helen of Troy, wife of what's-his-name, most beautiful woman on earth, abducted by Orlando Bloom. Spartans try to get Helen back. Achilles, blah, blah, blah, greatest warrior. Big horse, Troy falls, Spartans win, Helen goes back to what's-his-name. Menelaus, that's his name! Much debate among scholars: Did Trojan War really happen or was it just Homer's fiction? In 1800s, German businessman slash amateur archaeologist Heinrich Schliemann uses his wealth to prove Troy really exists. Finds site in northern Turkey. Calls it Troy Something. Troy 1. Troy 2. Okay, pretty good. It's all coming back to me.*

A voice interrupted my History of Troy for the Academically Inept. "Excuse me. Can you tell me…"

Automatically, I reverted to docent mode, even before I turned to face my inquisitor. I was standing in front of the famous bronze statue *Diana the Huntress* by Houdon, a stop on the Huntington audio tour, but not one of my personal favorites. Diana, or Artemis to the Greeks, had been my area of study in grad school; this stuff I knew cold. I felt like I had to defend her legacy.

"This Diana was sculpted by Jean-Antoine Houdon in 1790. It is admired for its fine musculature and the beautiful depiction of the face of the powerful Goddess of the Hunt. But really, this poor goddess couldn't kill a rabbit with that tiny bow, not to mention a charging boar! Furthermore, she's buck-naked, which is not helpful when riding through the forest at top speed. Talk about chafing. And let's face it, it's hard to fight off an unwanted paramour when you're nude! Obviously sculpted by a man."

Oops, that's not in the official script.

"Actually, I just wanted to find a water fountain."

I turned to face the bluest eyes I had ever seen on a man. Along with the eyes, there was a deeply tanned face, a great head of dark hair and a very amused smile. Must be mid-40s, good height, nice, nice nubby chocolate-brown sweater. He wore a messenger bag slung over his shoulder and had a guide to the grounds curled up in his right hand. No ring. He looked like a very thirsty Gerard Butler, and there I stood, sweating and blushing and speechless. If I could have strangled myself with my kicky scarf, I would have. Seriously, I would have squeezed my own head off.

"Oh, I'm sorry. So many visitors ask about the Diana statue, so I just assumed that was your area of interest and I expounded without thinking," I babbled on, sounding like a Japanese tour guide on speed. "But really, you just wanted a water fountain. I can do that, too! The water fountain is near the Garden of Flowing Fragrance. Just follow the path along to the left, beyond the camellias. May I help you with anything else?"

Please say no and just back away while I try to regain my dignity.

"No, though I have to agree. She is seriously disadvantaged

with that weapon. And I hope she's wearing a lot of sunscreen. You're right to be up in arms."

"Thank you. I'll take it up with a curator."

"Oh, you're not one? You seemed to really know what you were talking about."

Was this guy flirting me with? Or just trying to smooth over my obvious embarrassment? Really, it had been so long since I'd had a conversation with a man that did not involve business, golf or Merritt, I had no idea what was happening. On the other hand, I recognized my feelings of inadequacy from high school and college, so maybe he was flirting with me. But then again, why would Gerard Butler in a nubby sweater be flirting with *me*?

"No, I'm a ... well, I'm hoping to work here, but right now, no. I'm a ... just a freelance, volunteer docenting person." *What? What does that mean?*

Just then Sarah and Karen from Library came bursting through the double doors. Karen was a Master Librarian, a term I thought existed only in children's books, but no, Karen was the Queen of the Dewey Decimal System. She knew every volume, every document, every drawing in the Huntington's collection—a walking card catalogue. She wore the same red blazer every day of the year, even when the temperature hit the triple digits in August. She claimed it was the "insane air conditioning"; I thought *she* was the insane one. But I liked her intensity.

"How great. You've met!" Karen shouted, nodding at me and Nubby Sweater. I was confused and so was Nubby Sweater. Karen from Library was oblivious to most human emotion, preferring pages to people, but Sarah was not. Sensing our confusion and noting Nubby Sweater's tall, athletic build, she stepped up to correct the situation, using her best public relations voice.

"Dr. O'Neill, so nice to meet you. Heard just great things about your work. Welcome to the Huntington. I'm Sarah White, in charge of public relations, for all you see before you." Dramatic hand gesture combined with humble head bow. "I'd be happy to help you with *anything* you need."

Judging by the open lust on Sarah's face, I knew she was not kidding about the anything. And now I knew exactly who Nubby Sweater was. Damn.

"Helen, this is the visiting scholar I was telling you about," Sarah continued, turning her velvet voice to me.

Please don't let me emit a whimper.

"Dr. O'Neill, I understand from Karen you're looking for help in organizing your work. Helen would be a perfect research assistant. She's very qualified. She's been with us a long time."

Could it be any worse? I think not.

Dr. O'Neill, Dr. Nubby Sweater O'Neill, extended his hand first to me, then to Sarah. "Patrick O'Neill. Nice to meet you. I hadn't gotten Helen's name but I was already impressed by her passion and her position here as a 'freelance volunteer docenting person.' Delighted to hear that you are interested in the research assistant job."

And then he smiled for real at the whole group and I thought Sarah was going to resign her current position and apply to research whatever the hell it was that Dr. O'Neill wanted researched. Even Karen had to unbutton her blazer. Hot flash?

"Yes, very interested in the job." Short phrases seemed like the safest conversational gambit right now. "Love archaeology. Super organized. Prompt." *Prompt?*

Dr. Patrick O'Neill looked straight at me. With his arms crossed against his chest and his right hip cocked to one side, he took in my whole package, as if he were examining yet another statue. His face was neutral, not giving away any emotion that might assuage or increase my anxiety. I was pretty sure that I was everything his prior research assistants had not been: a mother, a widow and a woman who just turned 40. The khaki suit, the headband and the stockings didn't exactly scream, "Ready to get down in the dirt and dig!" Plus, he had much better hair than me.

"I just have one question."

Oh, no, please don't talk to me in ancient Greek and expect me to answer back with a pithy comment. Please, God, no.

"One of my students told me to be sure not to miss La Estrella. Apparently they have the best tacos in town. Do you know where it is? "

I was thrown for a second, then I answered triumphantly, "Yes!'

He waited. He wanted the full answer. This was my test. And I was gonna pass! When I was pregnant with Aiden, I ate nothing but tacos and popsicles for the first four months. I'd secretly frequented taco stands ever since, despite Merritt's warning of food poisoning.

"There are several La Estrellas in Pasadena, but the original is over on Fair Oaks and Washington. It has the best carne asada tacos in town. And they carry the Coke from Mexico with the real sugar, not the American Coke with corn syrup."

"Are you a freelance volunteer docenting taco person, too?"

"Sometimes."

Karen was mystified and Sarah looked a tiny bit jealous.

"Then, we're all set. Can you start next week? Or at least bring lunch to my office?"

"Both."

I was a tad giddy when I returned home to share my triumph. Even the sight of Shelly Sleazy on TV reporting on the effects of caffeine on the male libido couldn't dim my spirits. Though the pay was small and the commitment was only a few months, it felt like a really important step in my life. Tina and Candy, my daily dose of good spirits, dropped by to confirm what I was feeling: I would make it out of the darkness.

Aiden's first reaction to my new job as Dr. Patrick O'Neill's assistant was, "Cool, you're going to work for Indiana Jones!" Maybe this would help bring Aiden back into the world a little, too. I hadn't even considered that as a by-product. Score one for Mom.

Candy wanted to know if he was single. I told her he wore no ring and she told me that meant nothing.

"He digs all day in the dirt," she pointed out. "Surgeons don't wear rings either."

It seemed futile to try to explain to Candy that he wasn't going to be doing any actual digging at the Huntington. She enjoyed using wild exaggerations to make her point. And seeing as how I did not really want to elaborate on my personal life with my new boss, I was hardly going to quiz him on his personal life.

"Candy, my plan is to work for the guy, not marry him," I reminded her.

"But I might want to marry him!" she reminded me. "Get the scoop."

Tina wanted to know if he was honorable. "You're going to be alone with him all day. What do you know about him?"

So like a good research assistant, I did my research. What did suspicious minds do before Google? Dr. Patrick O'Neill had more than twenty pages of mentions on Google, so many I stopped clicking through. A Google search on me turned up two pages, most of the entries reading, "Merritt Fairchild and his wife, Helen." I hoped Nubby Sweater didn't Google me.

There were articles by, books by, filmed lectures by Dr. Patrick O'Neill, Ph.D. He even had a Wikipedia page, which really impressed me. That meant he had some pretty devoted students to create the entry or that he paid somebody to write the entry, a common practice here in the land of Hollywood. Candy and Tina stood over my shoulder and we read:

Current Position: Dr. Patrick O'Neill holds the Walter F. Beady Chair in Classical Archaeology at the American School of Classical Studies in Athens, Greece. He is also the Executive Vice Chairman of the Ancient City of Troy Foundation and Director of Excavations of the Troy site in Hissarlik, Turkey. Currently, he is on sabbatical in Pasadena, California, as the Mortimer Levitt Distinguished Scholar at the Huntington Library.

Current Research: Dr. O'Neill is one of more than 350 scholars, scientists and technicians from nearly two dozen countries collaborating on the excavations at the site in northwestern Turkey. The Troy site began as an early Bronze Age citadel in the third millennium BC and ended as a Byzantine settlement before being abandoned in AD 1350. Dr. O'Neill's research focuses on excavating, mapping and time-lining the entire site. His research has lent credibility to the Homeric texts as historical sources. Dr. O'Neill is also recognized for his work as a biographer of Heinrich Schliemann, the German archaeologist who originally excavated Troy and is considered the father of modern archaeology.

Background: Dr. Patrick O'Neill is an American, but he grew up all over the world. His father, Thomas O'Neill, was an expatriate executive with Questum Pharmaceuticals, and the family lived in Sao Paolo, Brazil; Athens, Greece; and Geneva, Switzerland. Dr. O'Neill graduated from the International School of Geneva and Amherst College with a B.A. in Ancient History. He received his Ph.D. in Classical Archaeology from Princeton University. His interest in Troy and the Homeric Interpretation was kindled as a child at the International School in Athens and the family's frequent trips to Mycenae and other Bronze Age sites. His work at Troy has helped to rekindle the enthusiasm for the site among scholars, foundations and interested amateurs.

Works:

The Big Three: Homer, Schliemann and Troy (2005)

History without the Histrionics: Fact, Myth and Interpretation (2001)

Why Homer Matters (BBC documentary)

Articles:

see links at www.ancienttroy.org

"Where's the personal stuff?" Candy asked.

"Where's the photo?" Tina added.

"Where's the wine?" I wanted to know. This guy was the real deal, everything I wanted to be and then some.

I was not just intimidated, I was terrified.

CHAPTER 7

I have found that four in the morning is the best time to worry. It's that perfect hour wedged right in between getting a good night's sleep and being fully awake. Four in the morning was not so early that I stressed about getting back to sleep, but it was way too early to actually rise and make coffee. So instead, if I woke up at four, I'd lie in bed and let my mind work through my Worry List.

I'd run through all the worries I had lined up for the day. I'd pick my top three and either figure out a solution or decide to continue to stress until I was convinced by a friend that I had nothing to worry about. As in, "Oh, Helen, you know that someone will step up and sponsor the t-shirts for the school fair. They always do!" Then poof, that worry would disappear because, yes, someone did step up to do the underwriting.

Before Merritt's death, a typical early February Worry List consisted of items like the booking of a hair appointment, the probability of a terrorist attack at LAX, the likelihood of sex on the weekend with Merritt, and the location of that little card from the dentist about my next cleaning.

After I'd formulated the Worry List, then I could attack it with some action plan, right after that third cup of coffee and drop-off. Nothing I could do about the terrorist attack or that long-lost card from the dentist, so those items dropped to the bottom of my action plan. But there were worries I could jump on. I'd make that hair appointment! I'd book a bikini wax because Candy had made me see the errors of my razor ways, or at least shamed me into more maintenance in that area. I was on top of things!—or so I thought.

Back then, I really had *nothing* to worry about.

I'd always suspected that my life was pretty stress-free, but now I knew for sure that I had a good thing going. I used to actually worry about whether I was happy, whether I was making Merritt happy, whether Aiden was completely fulfilled. What a luxury to worry about happiness.

In recent days, my Worry List was filled with real worries about selling my house and getting enough money out of it to cover my debts and buy a crappy condo. I worried about getting myself more life insurance because, God forbid, what if something happened to me? I worried about the trees on the property being overgrown and crashing into the garage after a giant rainstorm, even though we'd just had them trimmed a year ago. I worried Aiden would start sniffing glue as a way to mask his anger, because I'd seen some terrifying statistic on teenage boys and glue-sniffing on *Good Morning America*. I worried that I would never have sex again with another real human being. I worried I would die alone.

At least these were honest-to-goodness worries.

Now I had a whole new frontier of worries to add to the Worry List: the workplace. My eight-hour orientation (Paid! Bringing home the bacon!!) prior to my first official day on the job consisted of a few hours at Human Resources, and then a grueling training session with Karen from Library. At HR, I had to fill out all sorts of paperwork, most of which seemed unnecessary for a temporary, 30-hour-a-week job. But Min Cho, the HR person, just kept repeating, "good to get in the system," and I agreed. It had been so long since I'd been in a system of any kind, just draping my Huntington employee ID around my neck gave me a sense of accomplishment.

Then I entered the vortex of Karen from Library, bedecked in her red blazer. Karen took her work very seriously. I supposed if part of my job was to insure the health and safety of an original draft of the Gettysburg Address for future generations, I'd be a hard-ass, too. As a lowly volunteer, I'd never seen this side of Karen; now as a research assistant, I was under the scrutiny of a Master Librarian. My new greatest worry was about keeping my hands clean at all times so as not to "soil or stain the pages" with my, gasp, "personal body oils."

I would be working with notebooks that were roughly 140 years old. Karen debriefed me as if I were about to embark on a secret mission and she could only reveal a few details at a time or else my very existence would be compromised.

"Here's what I can tell you at this time. There are fifteen notebooks, numbered Roman numeral-style, that have been gifted to our collection. The notebooks belonged to the nephew of noted archaeologist Heinrich Schliemann. The nephew was Rudolph Schliemann. The notebooks were discovered over a year ago in the attic of one of the houses owned by the California Institute of Technology. At one point, the two elder Schliemann brothers came to California from Germany to make their money during the Gold Rush. Heinrich's brother died, and his widow relocated to Pasadena with their son, Rudolph. Dr. Rudy Schliemann became one of the first professors of engineering at Caltech, but the diaries predate his work at the University. He was on the original excavation crew at Troy. The notebooks detail the original site prior to and during the excavation. That is all I can say."

I half-expected Karen from Library in her red blazer to self-destruct after the debriefing. But instead, she smiled her crazy smile and handed me a pair of soft white gloves. "Never, ever touch these notebooks without these gloves. Any violation may result in termination."

Termination, as in death? Or as in being fired? This new Karen was capable of both.

Karen then took me through the "document scanning protocol," or "DSP," as Karen referred to the process by which I would photograph the individual pages of the notebooks, scan them into the computer and create a working file for Dr. O'Neill, as Karen kept referring to my future boss. She explained in great detail the daily check-in and check-out process. Then came an excruciating examination of the inner workings of the camera, the bookstand and the computer. She even broke down the fiber content of the gloves vs. the fiber content of the paper in the notebooks. It felt like slow motion watching Karen. Didn't she realize that I'd constructed my own document scanning protocol when helping Aiden with his history projects? I can scan in my sleep, I wanted to scream. Finally, she allowed me to practice the technique on comic books, then on one of the real notebooks, hovering over me.

After several hours of tedium, Karen suggested we break because of the "intense pace of the training." A brisk walk and one of Annie's espressos shook me from my stupor.

At the end of the day, Karen declared that I was approved for Level One DSP, the lowest level of scanning.

"I don't want to see you touching the Gutenberg Bible," Karen actually joked.

I almost self-destructed.

Now at four in the morning, unable to sleep or relax, I amassed my Worry List for Day One of my employment:

Don't forget white gloves or risk termination.

What do I call Patrick O'Neill? Dr. O'Neill? Professor O'Neill? Patrick? Pat? Dr. Dig? Hey there?

Should I tell him about my failed master's? Or just pretend that I am an archaeology enthusiast with no formal training so I won't have to reveal my shameful academic past?

Do I mention that my husband just died? Should I tell him about Aiden? Of course I should tell him about Aiden, but should I mention my age?

Should I ask him about his family? Is that legal? Aren't there laws in the workplace now about questions like that?

What do people in offices do for lunch? Always together? Always alone?

Can I possibly work for a man as attractive as Patrick O'Neill?

I constructed my action items. I would call him Dr. O'Neill, as that seemed to be the standard at a formal place like the Huntington. No reason Dr. O'Neill had to know about my master's or any other part of my life, like that fact that I used to have money and now I did not. I would mention Merritt's death and Aiden if asked, but I didn't need to offer up details as small talk. I'd bring my own lunch, ask only about his work, and hope that I didn't fall for this guy.

Because he probably had a gorgeous Greek girlfriend waiting for him in Athens.

There, I had a plan. I just needed to stick to it.

Top-notch Distinguished Scholars earned top-notch office space at the Huntington. I knew that Dr. Patrick O'Neill ranked high in the super-competitive academic world when I saw that he'd scored Scholars' Cottage #7, one of a dozen small, tile-roofed bungalows scattered about the grounds at the Huntington. Middle-of-the-pack academics worked in carrels in the Library itself. Dr. O'Neill rated private quarters, outfitted with a temperature-controlled office suitable for valuable papers, all the Level One scanning equipment I would need, the best computers and high-speed Internet access and some lovely antique furniture, a gift from one of the Huntington's benefactors. There were vintage photos on the walls, a fleece throw on the couch and fresh flowers on the coffee table. Cottage #7 even had a patio where, presumably, Dr. O'Neill and I would take tea and confer like colleagues.

It was an oddly unprofessional place to work. More like a really nice hotel suite at the Ojai Valley Inn and Spa (where Merritt and I had spent our tenth anniversary) than an office. I was tempted to call room service. The couch made me uncomfortable.

On day one, I was early, of course, arriving just after 8 for my official 9-to-3 work day. Karen had ordered, "Wait for instructions from Dr. O'Neill before initiating the DSP." Those were her exact words. She didn't even have to use the phrase "risk termination." I took the opportunity to scan the premises for any of my boss's personal effects: family photos, knickknacks that could have been made by a child, random faxes left on the fax machine that held valuable private information. But there was nothing, not even a Post-It. Dang.

So I did what I knew how to do: made coffee, cleaned the fridge, re-arranged the flowers, swept the porch, tidied up a bit and waited for Nubby Sweater to arrive.

Stop being the wife, I had to remind myself. *You are a research assistant now. You have important work to do. You will be scanning and organizing information that could redefine one of the most important ancient sites in history. Secrets revealed! Insight gleaned! You could ignite the archaeology world and get back some of the dignity you lost when you dropped out of Berkeley. You are a scholar, not a wife. Get on that computer!*

I was online checking the schedule for Aiden's weekend water polo tournament in Mission Viejo when Dr. O'Neill strolled into our cottage around 10. He was wearing another fantastic sweater and a deep blue cashmere scarf that I really shouldn't have noticed. The messenger bag was over his shoulder, and a laptop was under his arm. His hands were rough and tan from years in the sun and dirt. Despite his shiny appearance, I could picture him at Troy, walking slowly behind a bulldozer, covered in dust and sweat, dying to get at the newly unearthed layer of information. Like the archaeologists I'd worked with in the past, he did not seem entirely at home in these posh surroundings. He cocked his head at me as he tossed his bag on the couch.

"Hard at work already, I see."

Aiden had taught me his trick of switching web pages quickly when busted by a teacher during study hall, so I brought up the Huntington home page to hide my real activities. I don't think I fooled the great archaeologist.

"Just getting oriented," I offered up, hoping to sound as if I had previous experience in this position and knew the ropes. "Do you want some coffee? And I brought some scones from a terrific local bakery down the street. Cranberry Orange. May I get you one?"

Oh, for God's sake, I sounded like a hostess in the first-class passenger lounge. Where was my snappy hat? Shut the hell up, Helen!

"Wow, usually my research assistants are too hungover from a late night of dancing and drinking to bring baked goods."

"Well, you know, I'm a single mother. My drinking and dancing days are over. I am up early, now that everything is my responsibility. The bills, selling my house, raising my son. I just think that nothing beats fresh coffee and a good breakfast. That's what I tell my 13-year-old. I mean, minus the coffee. Though sometimes, I do make him a little café au lait in the morning, especially since his father just died. I'm trying to create that moment of connection for the two of us, so he doesn't sniff glue and drop out of school."

That really could not have gone worse. I think the only thing I declined to mention about my life was my failed attempt at grad school. That would probably come out by lunch.

"So, scone, Dr. O'Neill?"

"If you feel that strongly about scones, sure, I'll have one. And you can call me Patrick when it's just the two of us. No need to be formal here."

"I apologize. I'm nervous. I haven't done this in a while." I replied, handing him a cup of coffee and plate with scone, jam, butter and a cloth napkin. "Worked, I mean. Not... served scones."

"Understood." Dr. Patrick O'Neill did appear to understand, judging by the sympathetic smile on his face. "Let me get settled in and then we can go over your responsibilities. And what I'm looking for."

"Roger. Check. Okay."

So much for my action plan.

"Oh, and I'm sorry about your husband. Sarah told me about your situation. My condolences." Patrick gave me a nod, indicating that he did not expect a response other than 'thank you.'

Of course Sarah White, in her dulcet tones, had said something. So that's what I was: a situation.

"Thank you."

By noon, Patrick had explained the expectations he held for this new research: absolutely none. As far as he was concerned, the next several months in California amounted to little more than a paid vacation and a chance to raise the money that his foundation desperately needed to continue his research at Troy by tapping into a new pool of donors. The Schliemann notebooks, touted by Karen as "a highly valuable source of new information on what might have been destroyed in the original excavation," were, in his words, "a boatload of uniformed musings by a guy who didn't know jack about archaeology."

"Rudy was young and inexperienced, and he never really took to archaeology. He became an engineer. He knew even less about preserving the site than his uncle. Hack and dig was their method. They dug a trench across the entire site at Troy with men and pick-axes. Even if he had seen something important, Rudy Schliemann would not have recognized it as such. Heinrich Schliemann plowed under thousands of years of archaeological evidence to get to what he thought was Troy. That evidence is gone forever. I don't expect there will be anything in those notebooks I can really use, except a few colorful anecdotes about ol' Uncle Heinrich, which are always helpful at fundraising cocktail parties. But the idea that there could be some truly important revelations about the site is pretty far-fetched," Patrick said. "Still, the Huntington gave me the money and wanted me to come and check out the notebooks, so here I am."

And there went my chance for archaeological redemption. At least now I didn't have to stress so much about my personal body oils jeopardizing an entire academic discipline. Just then, his iPhone came alive with the ring tone "Dig" by Incubus, which I thought was pretty clever, and I thought I was pretty clever to know, thanks to my 13-year-old.

"You better dig it," I said, in what I vowed would be my last archaeological pun. And I excused myself to clear the scone plates, resuming my comfortable role as helpmate now that my brilliant career appeared to be over before it had begun.

I heard Nubby Sweater's voice change. It was definitely a woman.

"Yup, I'm ready. See you then." Patrick hung up and continued on with me, no explanation offered. I hated that. Not that I had any business knowing Patrick's business. It used to drive me crazy when Merritt would take a long call without any explanation, and now this guy. As it turns out, maybe I should have asked a few more questions about Merritt's calls.

"So, Helen, here's the deal. Let's scan the notebooks, see what's in there, transcribe the stuff, but don't kill yourself. Glad to have your assistance for the grunt work." Patrick sat casually back on the couch, stretching out his legs and conversing with complete confidence in his theory about the notebooks. He was treating me like a colleague. No wonder his students adored him enough to keep up his Wikipedia page.

Oh, maybe there was a Patrick O'Neill Facebook fan page! I should check at lunch.

I continued clearing the coffee mugs, trying to hide my curiosity about him and his phone call. "It's just that Karen made the discovery of these notebooks seem so critical to your work."

Patrick laughed and, my God, he had some great looking creases around his eyes, the result of two decades on site in the glaring Turkish sun searching for history. "Karen is a librarian! She thinks every old piece of papyrus holds an ancient secret.

That's why she spends her days in temperature-controlled cata-combs. Some old stuff is only valuable because it's old, not be-cause it's important."

"Well maybe there's *something* in there that's useful." I of-fered in my most hopeful, Tina-like optimism.

"Maybe. Knock yourself out."

Just then a familiar voice rang out. "Hello, it's me. Patrick?"

Sarah White swept into the cottage, looking stunning as usual, in a terrific navy blue suit, white scoop-neck sweater and the sort of large, chunky cut-glass necklace that I would have neither the guts nor the height to pull off. So … Sarah White, available di-vorcée, was the mystery woman. Maybe she was just welcoming him on his first day of research, an official obligation, not social at all. After all, her work in PR was tied to high-profile projects, like what were now being called the Schliemann Journals.

Why did I care?

"Helen, congratulations on your first day. This project is so perfect for you and so fascinating. Patrick told me all about his work on Saturday night. We went to the Steak House. Big fil-lets, great booths. I love it there. Anyway, he filled me in on the intriguing notebooks while we shared the fillet for two. Are you settling in?"

Okay, not official at all. Definitely social, which may have accounted for Sarah's dramatic jewelry on a Monday, the day the Library was closed to the public and most employees dressed down. Sarah was bedazzled by Dr. O'Neill. Well, apparently he hadn't told her what he'd told me about the notebooks. Patrick let her believe what the Huntington wanted to believe. He knew how to play the game. And so did I, thanks to so many years with Merritt. Score one for the research assistant.

"I feel lucky to be here. Really looking forward to the next couple of months. Thanks for everything, Sarah."

And then, after a big smile to me, Sarah gave Patrick an awk-ward kiss on the cheek. Patrick responded stiffly, then gathered up his phone, his computer and his cashmere scarf.

"Are you ready, Patrick?" Sarah asked, turning her back to me and making it very clear that I was not invited. "We're off to that La Estrella place. I love the food there, too!'

Liar, liar pants on fire. Sarah White had never voluntarily eaten a taco in her whole privileged life, unless it was prepared by Wolfgang Puck and served on catering china. She was after this guy big-time if she was willing to risk an outdoor taco stand for him. Well, fine. I had work to do, anyway.

"Do you want to come with us, Helen? You must know exactly what to order." Patrick asked, completely unaware of the look of shock on Sarah's newly unlined face. Recent trip to the derm?

"I'm going to get right at those notebooks. Plus, I brought my lunch!" I said, waving about my bright pink lunch bag, a table gift from a breast cancer fundraising fashion show last fall. Nothing says "downsizing" like a brown-bag lunch. Or in my case, a pink bag lunch.

"You're so thrifty, Helen. Good for you! Let's go, Patrick."

Sarah White! Who knew she could play hardball like that?

"Helen, I may not be back this afternoon. I'll see you tomorrow. Thanks for the scones." And with that, my new boss left me alone in my office/honeymoon suite.

I had three more hours to kill, I mean work, before I could go pick up Aiden. Maybe there was something in those notebooks.

The sound of my cell phone snapped me out of my scanning stupor. I was so enjoying the slow, rhythmic monotony of the DSP that I'd completely lost all sense of time. It was Candy.

"Hi. I'm at work!" I announced.

She whooped an inappropriately high-energy whoop, like I'd just announced winning the lottery, followed by, "So ..."

"So?"

"So is he married? What's the scoop?"

"Oh, I thought you cared about my professional fulfillment, but you just want the dirt. So to speak."

"That's my job."

"No photos of gorgeous wives or girlfriends, no phone calls from Athens, no incriminating faxes. But he did appear to go out on a date with Sarah White. And now they are out to lunch together," I reported to my gossip columnist friend—then immediately regretted my choice of words. Oh my God, what if Candy put that in her column this week? "Candy, please don't print that."

"I wouldn't. Nobody knows who he is, and Sarah White has been mentioned a lot lately, and she's starting to annoy me with her perfect hair. You're lucky I'm tired of her. But that's the only one of those you'll get. Don't tell me stuff you don't want me to use." I knew she was joking. I think. "Anyway, I thought Sarah White and Tiny Tim Winston were an item."

"Tiny" Tim Winston was a short but world-renowned thoracic surgeon who was business partners with Candy's second ex-husband, a short but world-renowned cardiologist, Sam Kennedy. Candy and Sam's six-year marriage had produced two beautiful children, Mariah and Ian, and many hours of ranting and raving. Candy was not cut out to be a doctor's wife; she couldn't take the long, lonely nights and the weekends on call. And Sam Kennedy was not cut out to be anybody's husband; he liked the ladies. They were the happiest divorced couple I'd ever seen. You'd never know that they were not together unless you'd seen the moving van come and take Candy's white furniture to her new place on the other side of the Rose Bowl. At the kids' birthday parties, basketball games and holiday programs, Sam and Candy came together and behaved better than most married couples.

I'm sure Candy and Sam still slept together, too, but she had too much pride to let that slip.

I think her interest in my archaeologist was really for my benefit, to get me back in the swing of things. "I don't know about

Sarah and Tiny Tim, but I can tell you, off the record, that Sarah claimed to love tacos, just to get him to go to lunch with her."

"*Quelle horreur!*" Candy said, using the only French phrase she knew besides *mon Dieu*. "Why didn't you just ask him if he's married?"

I didn't know why. If Merritt had been alive, if I'd been a wife instead of a widow, I would have had no qualms about sussing out his marital status. But now it seemed safer to be ignorant than informed. "It seems so personal."

"Right, and we wouldn't want to get personal! You've been a Fairchild too long!"

I looked at my computer screen. It was time to get Aiden. "Maybe. I have to finish up here. Talk to you later, Candy."

"Bye, sweetie. Hang in there." Click.

Day one of work had come to a close. I hadn't thought of Merritt and Shelley Sleazy in six hours.

Victory.

CHAPTER 8

Millington School was built on the grounds of an old tuber-culosis sanatorium in the foothills of the San Gabriel Valley. The restored complex, built in the latter part of the 19th century, once housed respiratory patients who had relocated to Pasadena seek-ing relief with clean air and never-ending sunshine. The sanato-rium fell into disrepair in the '20s and stood empty for a decade, until Eustice Millington snapped up the property to create a K through 8 private school, just like the fine academies on the East Coast. Now that the air quality in Pasadena qualified as some of the worst in the country, it was the perfect spot for young children to learn, to thrive and to stay indoors at recess during fire sea-son. Millington was more than 75 years old, ancient by California standards, and every time I entered the gates and drove around the circular drive, the perfect beauty of the place struck me.

Schools like Millington did not exist in central Oregon: ornate stucco buildings with a touch of Mediterranean flair, open-air courtyards and wisteria-covered walkways between classrooms, acres of manicured playing fields and jungle gyms, all surround-ed by groves of olive and orange trees. Like so many places in Pasadena, Millington was camera-ready all the time.

Every year in February, the Millington moms put on the week-long Word-Write Fest, a high-minded fundraiser that included theater performances, a public-speaking competition among the students, big-time author signings, a lecture series and, of course, the sale of books worth thousands and thousands of dol-lars. The event was so well respected that even the other schools in the area attended the lectures. Signs outside the gates announced this year's theme: Mysteries Revealed!

I was going to swing by a committee meeting for a few minutes before picking up Aiden. I'd been in charge of Word-Write when Aiden was in lower school, and now I held a sort of emeritus position, using my acquired know-how to help with any crises that arose. Chairing Word-Write had been my entrée into the upper echelons of Millington moms. When I got the call from the head of the Millington Parents Association (MPA), asking me if I was interested in running Word-Write, I was thrilled. Even Merritt was impressed.

"Helen, we have full confidence in you. You seem to read a lot of books," Nan Mitchellson, the MPA president, had told me over the phone, without a trace of irony. "You could really add something to this event."

I threw myself into organizing a dynamic week of authors and speakers like I was mounting a presidential campaign. Our theme that year was "The Final Frontier," and I scored a huge coup by securing the local glamorous geek squad at the Jet Propulsion Lab, the team that had just landed the Rover on Mars a few weeks before the event. The project manager went live to Mars onstage with some of the first pictures of the Red Planet, a Word-Write coup that garnered national press attention. Needless to say, the presentation was a huge hit and secured my place in the pantheon of Word-Write chairs. Along with the Rover, I booked astronauts and science-fiction writers with abandon. Astronaut Sally Ride did a special panel for middle-school girls on pursuing their science dreams. Ray Bradbury thrilled or upset the parents, depending upon their party affiliation, by comparing the Bush Administration to the Firemen of *Fahrenheit 451*. And of course, we made thousands of dollars selling books, a new event record.

Nowadays, the Word-Write Fest happens in the Fairchild Performing Arts Center, a gift from Merritt and myself during a capital campaign and after a particularly good year in 2006.

We made the donation in honor of Merritt's parents, and Mitsy had stolen the show on the day of the dedication. She attended the ceremony dressed like a modern-day Queen Elizabeth and declared that the next 100 years at Millington would outshine the Elizabethan Age. Frankly, I thought that was quite a bit of pressure to put on a bunch of fourth graders and their underpaid English teachers, but I said nothing. She was in her element, on stage in the spotlight.

More than once since Merritt's death, I wished I had that donation back. But money doesn't work like that.

As I strolled through the Millington campus, I could feel myself start to relax. I was at home here. I knew the secret code to the office copier. I had a key to the supply closet on my key ring. I even knew where the Diet Coke stash for the staff (and me) was hidden. I welcomed the waves and nods of the mothers lingering in the courtyard, waiting for their little guys. There was Hattie Thompson and Cheryl Knowles, both super-skinny runners who were constantly in training for something. I mouthed hello to Donna and Shihfeng, chatting away in Mandarin, the chess club moms who used trays of orange chicken and pork dumplings to lure kids to practice after school. Camille Dryer was violating the "no cell phone in the courtyard" policy, speaking loudly enough for all of us to hear about her kitchen remodel. Even the headmistress Adele Arnett wandered through the courtyard at that moment.

Adele gave me a swift hug, her good tweed jacket smelling like Chanel No. 5 and Play-Doh. "I've just been in with the kindergarten. They get cuter every year. Do you have a second? I was going to call you today."

"Sure, I'm on my way to a Word-Write meeting, and then I'll swing by your office. Will you still be here?"

"Board of trustees meeting tonight. I'll be here late."

Adele hustled off in her capable way, a good educator and a gifted administrator. She was tough, but firm. And how she managed to stand up to that collection of egos on the board of trustees was a tribute to her fortitude. Merritt was just one of the Masters of the Universe who had contributed large enough amounts to attain a seat on the board. I supposed that was what she wanted to talk to me about, assuming Merritt's seat on the board.

The more I thought about it, the more I wanted that seat. I felt like I'd earned it with everything I'd done for the school. I may not be the typical board member with the MBA and the blank check, but the work I'd done at the school meant something to the kids, to the life of the school. I was beginning to believe I was as qualified as any, maybe even more. Even if Aiden was moving on, there was no reason I couldn't still have a voice at Millington. It was my theater, after all!

I saw the Word-Write committee gathered in Eustice Courtyard, a collection of about a dozen mothers, all clinging to Starbucks venti lattes and frantically typing information into their Blackberrys. If all the women had been in suits, this would have looked like any business meeting in any company in Los Angeles, with a mix of races and faces. But the yoga wear on half the participants was a dead give-away that this was a gathering of Pasadena mothers. At any given moment, in any given hair salon, grocery store or tart yogurt emporium, 50 percent of the mothers in town would be decked out in lululemon yoga pants, even if the last class they had been to was in 2004 before Pilates ate suburbia. I myself had fallen prey to this trend, leading Tina to beg me one day, "Buy some pants with an actual zipper or no one will take you seriously."

As I surveyed the table with half suits and half yoga pants, I wondered where I would fit in now, with my job. Would I make Team Yoga Pants feel inferior now that I had to wear clothing with zippers and tailored shirts?

No, these were all my people. Nothing to worry about here.

There was Dependable Jeanie from publicity and art director Sandy from decorations sitting next to Kate and Sally, the speaker series girls. Cris and Kathy, the hardest-working women on the food committee, were squeezed in next to the go-getter book donations team of Sun, Jinny and Jeku. This was an all-star cast lead by Dr. Natasha Natarova, an orthodontist from Pasadena by way of Russia who wore four-inch heels every day, everywhere, because being 5' 11" apparently wasn't imposing enough.

Natasha's husband, Yuri, had many mysterious meetings in Moscow, despite the fact that he allegedly owned a chain of gas stations here. Was he bringing the gas back from Moscow himself? Natasha had immigrated to the U.S. at age 6 but still had an accent strong enough to inspire many "Boris and Natasha" imitations, but only behind her back. She straightened the teeth of most of the middle-school students at Millington with an iron fist. She was a mover and a shaker who had jumped at the chance to "take Word-Write global!" At least that's what she'd told me over coffee at an informal meeting last June. Now her plans for world domination had hit a snag.

She'd called my cell phone in a panic about an hour ago, screaming the words "disaster" and "cancellation." She begged me to come to the meeting for my sage wisdom.

"Helen!" Natasha shrieked. "Crisis averted! But thank you for rushing over to help. You are too much."

Natasha explained that the keynote speaker, so spectacular, so big-time that the school was actually worried about security if the speaker's name was advertised ahead of time, had backed out at the last minute. Just this morning, she got a call from the agent explaining that the Mystery Speaker had eaten too much sushi and was under medical observation for mercury poisoning. Hence he would be unable to be the main mystery of Mysteries Revealed!

"Who was it?' I asked, naturally.

"I promised to keep it quiet, but I can't. Stan Black. Stan "I-wrote-the-*Michelangelo-Coda*-and-ate-too-much-sushi' Black," Natasha spit out in her angriest accented English. "I hate his books. So unbelievable and stupid. The same book over and over again. But he is very popular, when he is not eating sushi. All over the world, people love Stan Black. It would have been a huge story to get him for Millington. But oh no, too much sushi! Don't think I'm not going to leak this story to your friend Candy."

I was about to point out that it wouldn't be the best possible PR for the school or Word-Write to humiliate a top-selling author, but I held my tongue. Let Dependable Jeanie deal with that. Or the Russian mafia.

"I called you for brainstorming because you read so much. And then I had a brilliant idea. I just called Sarah White at the Huntington to see if they had anyone in town that could be mysterious. A great speaker. And guess what?"

I knew what.

"Indiana Jones is in town! Some famous archaeologist who digs up treasures somewhere! Troy, I think. And Sarah said he is a dynamic speaker. Mesmerizing, she said. So he's all set. I forget his name."

"Dr. Patrick O'Neill," I provided. "I work for him."

A collective gasp escaped from the committee. Knowing looks accompanied the gasp. Since the Meltdown, lots of these women had quietly taken part-time jobs to bolster their husbands' shrinking paychecks. Hourly wages at boutiques, bookstores, clothing resale shops. Now even Helen Fairchild, of the Fairchild Theater, was in the workforce.

"I started today as his research assistant," I announced, acting as though I'd been chosen for a plum assignment, not just working a J-O-B.

And then the shock turned to admiration. I was Professor Fairchild again.

"That is marvelous, Helen," Natasha purred. "And is he dynamic, your archaeologist?"

"Oh, yes. He is brilliant."

"Tell him to bring his bullwhip."

As I made my way back to Adele Arnett's office, I spied Aiden hanging out with his friends in the middle school courtyard. I'd texted him that I would be a few minutes late and to meet me at the office. Now I gave him a brief wave; I didn't want to interrupt his social life. When he was little, he used to love to see me at school, serving up hot lunch or selling popsicles at the school store. Now, in middle school, we both pretended not to notice each other. I respected his space. And, knock wood, he respected me for that.

Aiden's friends weren't the cool kids (the lacrosse boys and the drama girls) or the smart kids (the students in the top math class called themselves the Asian Einsteins), but they were solidly in the second tier of popularity. His crowd occupied the social strata just below the Bad Attitudes, the sophisticated kids with older siblings, solvent trust funds and wayward parents, but way above the Puberty Busters, those who either had hit puberty really early and were gigantic and blemish-ridden, or those who had yet to experience the magic of getting taller, getting hairier, or getting breasts. Aiden and his friends, a mix of about eight girls and boys, had settled into their above-average spot comfortably, free of major angst or rebellion.

Even a worrier like me didn't worry too much about sex, drinking or drugs with his group. Well, in truth, I worried about the sex, because that was free and easy to procure. And the girls in his class seemed about a decade more knowledgeable than the boys in matters of the flesh. When I drove the carpool to games, the boys dished away like I wasn't even in the car. I loved getting the fly-on-the-wall viewpoint of these man-boys and their daily concerns. Those concerns did not include Tiff, Karly or Morgan.

Listening to Aiden and his classmates talk made me realize that the hours I'd spent agonizing over Keith Von Brockitsch in eighth grade were a complete waste of time. Thirteen-year-old boys are not thinking about the finer qualities of thirteen-year-old girls. They are debating the finer points of video games and paintball guns.

I'd start worrying in earnest next year, when Aiden went to high school and his new friends might be sufficiently savvy enough to steal pharmaceuticals or beer, but for now his friends seemed more interested in iChatting and going to the movies together than breaking into their parents' liquor cabinets.

I couldn't really say the same for that jaded lacrosse crowd. I kept my eye on them.

Before I turned into the headmistress's office, I took one more look at Aiden. He looked absolutely nothing like Merritt and everything like my brother Des. Merritt had been tall and thick, his features broad and open. He had been handsome in a prep school kind of way: neat, clean, blue-eyed, blue-blazered. Merritt told me once he thought he looked like Ed Harris with more hair. With more hair and less intensity, I concurred.

Marriage is a series of little half-truths and hasty agreements that add up to a life. I certainly wasn't going to spoil my husband's vision of himself.

But Aiden seemed to have come entirely from my gene pool in terms of looks. Someday he'd be tall and lean like my brother, with great dark eyebrows and a cute face. Now he was just growing and eating and trying to keep up with all the changes. When Aiden was little, I loved that he looked like my side of the family. I was surrounded by Fairchilds, but Aiden was so clearly a Castor. With Merritt gone, maybe it was too bad he didn't inherit something other than bad debt from his dad.

"Come on in, Helen!" Adele's voice broke my reverie. Right, time to talk to the headmistress and accept that board seat.

Adele Arnett's office was warm and cozy, with dark stained beams, Oriental rugs and a seating area with two brown leather chairs and an olive green chenille couch. Adele was sitting at her large, neat, antique oak desk when I strolled in. Even as involved as I was at Millington, I hadn't spent much time in Adele's office. Aiden wasn't in trouble much, and Merritt and I weren't the type of parents who complained over every little grade or indignity suffered on the playground.

"Suck it up," Merritt would tell Aiden when he came home with another horror story about the unfairness of the touch football game at recess. "It's a dog-eat-dog world. You've gotta learn to deal with assholes. You know why you suck it up now? Because someday you'll be managing those assholes. Then they'll have to suck it up."

Classic Merritt.

"So, tell me how the testing went at Ignatius. What did Aiden say?" Adele jumped right into the conversation. I appreciated her efficiency.

"He said it went fine. But he says that about everything, and then we get the C-minus." I laughed. It was true! "Fine" was the kiss of death for Aiden.

"When's your interview?"

"On Friday afternoon. I'm nervous," I admitted. The admission director at Ignatius had put off our interview until the last possible date because of the "circumstances." Now, after my meltdown with Patrick O'Neill, I was afraid I was going to come across as a complete nut job. Merritt was a master in this type of situation, so I'd usually deferred to him. Now I was on my own.

"Don't worry," said Adele. "They're good people at Ignatius. They understand. And really, the interview is about Aiden, not you and your life."

That was a lie and both Adele and I knew it. At all of the local private schools, the "interview" was more about checking out the family than the kid. When Aiden had "interviewed" at Millington, he was 5 and really had no opinion about the kinds of questions that we'd been asked, like mounting a successful capital campaign or measuring our commitment to the Millington community. Aiden sat in the corner and played with a dump truck.

The admissions director at Ignatius had already met Aiden on several occasions. Millington was a feeder school that set up private tours for their kids to ensure a high yield of acceptances. It was me Ignatius wanted to see.

Me without Merritt.

"And don't worry, Helen, we are not going to alert Ignatius about Aiden's grades. Obviously, he's just checked out since his dad's death. Who can blame him? We'll give him some incompletes for this quarter if it comes to that, and he can make up all the work in the last quarter." Adele poured herself another cup of coffee from a sleek Cuisinart machine on the antique side table. She splashed in some milk and waited for my response.

I was dumbfounded.

"I'm sorry, Adele. What do you mean, 'checked out'?"

"Well, you've seen the progress reports. He hasn't turned anything in, hasn't passed a test. It's understandable. And we know you have your hands full with everything you're dealing with. You couldn't be that much help to him."

What was she talking about? I hadn't seen any progress reports, had I? I would have noticed them in my inbox; the teachers e-mailed them every week if there was a problem. And did she really need to add "you have your hands full"? And "not much help"?

Headmistress Arnett's patented warm voice was starting to sound a little sharp to my ears.

"Adele, I haven't seen any progress reports, and my hands are not so full that I would ignore Aiden. He is my first priority."

"Of course. I didn't mean to imply that. It's just that we've been updating you on Aiden's lack of effort," she said, moving over to her desk and pulling up the progress reports on her computer. "Here we go. Three sent in the past three weeks to your *merritthelen* address."

Of course! I hadn't checked that address in weeks. One of the first things I did after Merritt's death was get a new e-mail address. It was a tiny, tiny expression of anger. I didn't want that old address anymore, the one that Merritt and I had coined when we got our first e-mail account and Merritt never used himself. Only I answered to *merritthelen*. Once I found out about Shelley Sleazy, I wanted a fresh cyber-start.

Obviously, I'd forgotten to inform the school, and the reports were going to the old address. But why hadn't the school noticed my auto-reply with the new address?

"I have a new e-mail address. This is the first I've heard of Aiden's issues." I felt myself on the verge of apology, but something cool in Adele Arnett's expression stopped me from segueing into a sob story. I concluded concisely, "I'll get on Aiden. We'll turn it around."

"Good. We have the greatest sympathy for him, but we can't let him graduate if he doesn't pass his classes, *all his classes*. You understand, Helen. We have the school's reputation to think about. The expectations for our students are very high, because the high schools they will attend will demand it. Aiden cannot be an exception."

Every generous thing I'd ever thought about Adele Arnett dissipated in that moment. She was talking about a 13-year-old boy who had just lost his father, not his mind. So he had missed some homework and failed some tests? For God's sake, he'd been at the school for nine years and now he needed some understanding, not tough love. Aiden was grieving, not selling drugs, threatening teachers or cheating on exams. If he wasn't an exception, he should be. We were talking about the eighth grade, not medical school.

Sometimes, the years of living with Merritt paid off in unexpected ways. Like right now. I wanted more than anything to pummel her with the big Waterford crystal apple that must have been a gift from one of her exceptional students. But if I killed Adele Arnett, then Aiden surely would not graduate.

I sucked it up.

"Understood. You have the school to think about."

"Speaking of thinking about the school, Helen, we have a board of trustees meeting tonight. It's when we nominate new board members for next year," Adele transitioned so smoothly, I barely had time to grasp the conversation's new direction.

Was she kidding? Did she really think that after threatening to fail my son, to ruin his entire scholastic career to preserve the reputation of Millington as a top-notch academic school, *a school my money had help to build, by the way*, that I was going to spend one more minute of my valuable time steering the future of her heartless institution? Adele Arnett could go to…

"And we've decided to ask Yuri Natarov to fill Merritt's seat. We hope you understand. We have the future of Millington to ensure."

I could no longer suck it up.

"No, Adele, I don't understand. Please explain."

Then Adele Arnett displayed the mettle that enabled her to stand up to the corporate CEOs on the board. She got nasty.

"We need the seat for someone who can afford to support the school financially in a substantial manner. We need that now more than ever. I don't believe that is within your capabilities anymore. It's time for somebody else to have the opportunity."

I stood up and was grateful that I was wearing the fashionable wide-legged trousers that Tina had picked out at J.Jill, so that Adele Arnett, Headmistress of the Damned, couldn't see my knees shaking.

But my voice was strong.

"Aiden is going to graduate from this school, regardless of whether he passes *all* his classes or not. And if Ignatius calls, you are going to support his admission. Or else I let it be known to the people who still consider my opinion important, like Candy McKenna, gossip columnist, my good friend Natasha Natarova and my mother-in-law Mitsy Fairchild, who still has a healthy checkbook, what you just said to me. And your reputation, Headmistress Arnett, will suffer. Not mine. I hope *you* understand."

Headmistress of the Damned raised an eyebrow, then nodded slightly.

Merritt was right about one thing: Someday I would have to manage the assholes.

"Hey, Mom."

"You ready to go?" I said in a tight voice that I hoped sounded normal. "Hi, guys! Did you learn anything today?" I turned in the direction of Aiden's buddies, Dex and Connal Ramsey, fraternal twins, IVF-style.

"Not a thing, Mrs. Fairchild," red-haired Dex answered without missing a beat. Connal, the adorable one with the brown hair and the high IQ, guffawed. Someday, Dex would host his own late-night talk show, I had no doubt. He was sharp, funny and media literate well beyond his years. Both his parents were TV writers of some fame. Until his turn behind the desk, though, Dex would have to weather the curses of adolescence, bad skin and a giant nose, with a series of Best Sense of Humor honors. "We have a sullied reputation to uphold here at Millington, and we're doing our part."

I laughed. "Good for you."

"What were you talking to Mrs. Arnett about?" Aiden tossed out, trying to act nonchalant. He asked the questions in front of his friends for protection. I'd never laid into him in public, and he knew I wouldn't do it there in the middle school courtyard.

Under normal circumstances, like a month ago when he had a father and I had money, I would have jumped all over him for a progress report filled with Ds and Fs the minute we got in the car. I would have harangued him the whole way home for his irresponsibility. Today, I wasn't even going to lay into him in private.

"Not much. I'll tell you later. Dex and Connal, what are you guys doing now? Do you want to go for some paninis at Porta

Viaggio, and then I'll drop you at home?"

Aiden looked pleased, like I was back to my old self, because that is something my old self had done all the time, load up a car full of boys for food and entertainment.

"Sure, Mrs. Fairchild. Let me call my mom. We were just gonna stay after school. We have a Spanish test, but, you know, we can study later. Right, Connal?"

Connal made a sort of thumbs-up, shoulder-groove, head-shake gesture that signaled his approval of the plan. He enjoyed talking about the *Lord of the Rings* and *Battlestar Galactica*, and that was about it.

"Great," I agreed with Dex. "Paninis now, Spanish later."

"I think I'll use that as my yearbook quote, Mrs. Fairchild. Very Judd Apatow."

"Thanks, Dex."

When we pulled into the driveway, it did not surprise us to see the light purple Caddie of Rita the Armenian and the familiar white truck of Juan Sanchez. Juan's team of painters, gardeners and cleaners had been at the house almost daily for several weeks getting everything in tip-top shape. Anything that screamed pre-millennial was transformed into something fresh and "eco-green," according to Juan. Of course, Juan also boasted that his secret brand of cut-rate paint went on just like Benjamin Moore.

"Super-sellable," Rita repeated over and over again, as if just saying the word made it so, despite the dismal market and unattainable credit. The new spa-blue living room with dark gray trim? Super-sellable! The outdoor fireplace and retreat area replanted with lavender and rosemary? Super-sellable! The family game area refreshed with 'blackboard" paint and new curtains from Target? Super-sellable! Rita assured me that the lifestyle my house offered some lucky family was recession-proof. I would make money and I would rise again; that's what Rita the Armenian promised.

I wanted to believe her.

But I didn't really feel like talking to her right now.

I had to deal with Aiden and his homework issues at some point. And then there was that large glass of meritage I'd been thinking about since my meeting with Adele Arnett. But both would have to wait as Rita flagged me down with her wild gesturing, flashing a giant aquamarine ring and multiple gold bangles. Wow, that was some cheetah print blouse.

The open house would be this weekend and, thankfully, Aiden and I would be in Orange County at a water polo tournament. Youth sports can suck the lifeblood out of your family, but for this weekend's excuse to leave town, I was grateful. I didn't think I could be there to watch the hordes of curious neighbors and tire kickers traipsing through my house, speculating on what would become of me. Off to the Courtyard Marriott in Mission Viejo we'd go, pretending that water polo was the only thing that mattered.

Aiden and I hopped out of the car. "Okay, do what you need to do, and then get ready for practice," I instructed. Five nights a week from 8 to 10, Aiden was in the pool. Two mornings a week from 6 to 7, he was in the weight room. Usually, two weekends a month, his team played in a two-day tournament somewhere that required an overnight stay or long drives. I liked the water polo scene, but I didn't love that our entire life seemed to revolve around it.

Club water polo had been Merritt's idea. He'd been a swimmer all his life, disciplined and fit. Merritt dreamed of water polo glory for Aiden at Ignatius; we both knew he'd never be big enough or good enough to play in college. Of all the tasks that Merritt had left me to face alone, shuttling Aiden back and forth to the pool was the most tedious.

"Do I have to go to practice?" Aiden asked, for the third

straight night. Merritt never allowed him to skip practice unless the sky was falling or he had floor seats at the Lakers game. Tonight, all I wanted to do was drink the wine and read the pages of the notebooks I'd scanned. The last thing I wanted to do was make the water polo run.

Aiden formed the prayer sign with his hands, "Please, can't I just skip it this once?"

Of course he could. We both could.

"Sure, but make sure that homework gets done. I will be checking." Aiden gave me the double thumbs up and headed into the house.

Juan tooted his horn as he pulled out of the driveway. I noticed Emilia popped her head out of the back door and gave Juan a special send-off. Was something happening between the two of them? I walked across the gravel to meet Rita. She gave me her usual two-cheek kiss and started right in on her plan.

"We are in great shape. Everything is set for this Sunday. Juan has done an amazing job. It looks wonderful. Super-sellable. So..." Rita hesitated dramatically, "There is just one thing I need to ask you. Please understand that I think this is for the best."

"Okay," I answered cautiously.

"I think you should remove Merritt's things from the closet and the bathroom. I think your late husband was very well known, and I don't want people to come here to disrespect your privacy," Rita said in a heavier-than-usual accent. "I want potential buyers to see this house as a new start, not something ... cursed or haunted. Please understand this is hard for me to ask."

Oh my God, of course she was right! It hadn't even occurred to me that people might come to look at the house because of Merritt's notorious death, out of sheer morbid curiosity. For weeks, I'd only been thinking of the house as mine. But it was Merritt's, too. And that was its own macabre draw.

And then, there was Roshelle Simms. The thought of her

walking through my house, my life....

"Umm...."

That's when the sobbing started. The honest-to-goodness heaving and sobbing that had eluded me since New Year's Day. Until that moment, I'd kidded myself that I was just dandy, fueled by anger, fear and huge amounts of caffeine. But the thought of removing Merritt's possessions so that real estate looky-loos didn't paw through our closets looking for evidence of how I was coping sent me over the edge. The affair, the house, the money, the new job, Aiden's grades, the scene at the school, Mitsy—it all came rushing at me in a giant White Diamonds wave as Rita squashed me toward her cheetah-printed chest.

"You poor thing. I am so sorry. I should not have asked."

"No, no, you're right," I said between sobs, and then gasps, as Rita's ample bosom closed in around my nose and mouth. I managed to pull away and free an airway before suffocation, but the crying continued. "I hadn't even thought of it. There are so many things I've had to do, so many hard things. I haven't actually taken the time to miss him."

More sobbing.

Rita the Cheetah pounced again, wrapping me in silk and sympathy. "You are strong, like an Armenian woman. Tough, so tough. Usually, you American girls can't take care of yourselves. But you can. You can do this."

"Umm...." The sobbing was subsiding now, but not quickly enough for a coherent answer.

"But ... if you want, Juan can clear out the closets." That Juan can do everything! God bless Juan.

I pulled away again. The crying had ended and the frantic wiping away of mascara had begun. That's what I get for wearing makeup to work. I breathed deeply. "That's okay. I can get it done by the open house."

Rita looked pleased and relieved as she patted her sopping shirt with a tissue. "It's a good decision. Good for you and for your son. And for the house." Rita checked her watch and opened the door of her car. Time to go! More homes to sell. "We'll talk before Sunday. And don't worry. It's super-sellable."

Aiden was lying on the couch, laptop open, earplugs in, *The Simpsons* on the TV in the background. The contents of his backpack, which included gym shorts and a Nerf gun, had spilled out all over the couch. I doubted that a lot of homework was getting done; more likely he was IMing his classmates with important messages like "S'up?"

Or maybe something more suspicious, because he quickly got out of the screen he was studying when I tapped on his shoulder.

"Aiden," I called out, making the international hand signal for Remove Your Earplugs While You Talk to Your Mother. He did. "Do you want anything else to eat? I have some phone calls to make."

Aiden's recent growth spurt required what seemed like an extra million calories a day in any form, healthy or otherwise. Entire frozen lasagnas as a snack before dinner, four packets of instant oatmeal for breakfast, gallons of Gatorade after practice. *Just keep the calories coming* had become my nutritional strategy.

"Hold up, Lydia," he said to the microphone on his laptop, before looking up hopefully from the screen. "Chocolate ice cream?" I could hear a girl's voice coming out of his earplugs. Was she reciting poetry? How cute.

"Who's Lydia?"

"My friend from camp? You know, the girl who's a really good dancer? We did that skit together on parents' night?"

Oh, right. The skit Merritt said was like an unfunny version of an already unfunny SNL bit. "She was very talented. Say hi."

I took this moment of attention to go over my plans. I tended to speak loudly and slowly when he was engaged in multiple digital activities at once, like he was hard of hearing and a non-native speaker. "I'm going upstairs to call your aunts. I need their help with something."

I got my third thumbs up of the hour.

He can never know.

Merritt's sisters had never been anything but nice to me. We'd never be giggling girlfriends or spinning buddies, well, because I didn't giggle or spin and they did, but we had a fine relationship. They were younger, thinner and blonder than me, but they never made an issue out of that. Their lifelong ties to Pasadena had provided them deep friendships and vast community connections, as well as two very good marriages and a bunch of fairhaired Fairchild grandchildren.

Mary Claire Fairchild Bellweather, a.k.a. Mimi, and Madeleine Grace Fairchild Purcell, a.k.a. Mikki, were very close. They were best friends, charity co-chairs, on the phone with each other a half dozen times a day. I'd never seen sisters like Mimi and Mikki, without any issues or rivalry. Their husbands, Lawyer Bart and Broker Ben, had become best friends, golf buddies and soccer coaches. It was a tight, tight circle, and sometimes I felt like I was standing on the outside, looking in at the prom kings and queens of Pasadena Privileged Class of '95.

But, as Candy had once advised, "That is *your* issue, not *their* behavior. They're nice girls."

The Candy Seal of Approval.

They adored their big brother Merritt. Merritt was six years older than Mimi and eight years older than Mikki. He stepped up when his own father had died so young and was the father figure the Fairchild sisters, then teens, had needed to get through high school, college and their careers before marriage. Merritt had walked both sisters down the aisle of St. Perpetua's on their respective wedding days. They missed him tremendously, which was obvious from their frequent phone calls and visits to me since his death.

To them, Merritt was a hero, not a philandering husband or a failed money manager, which is why I asked them to meet me. Over the course of the last month, the sisters had offered dozens of time to do anything, anything I needed.

I needed them to clear out Merritt's closets and drawers.

I didn't want to ask over the phone, that seemed so tacky, so unFairchild. Instead, I asked them to meet me for coffee before work because I needed a favor. Of course, both sisters had agreed without hesitation. There was no mention of having to clear schedules or arrange sitters. Just a simple yes from both Mimi and Mikki.

When I walked into Petit Petals Patisserie, Mimi and Mikki were already there, drinking coffee from large white ceramic cups and wearing almost identical workout clothes and one-carat diamond earrings. They had inherited the long, lean physique of their mother and the ability to keep full-time help from their husbands. Mimi had three girls under the age of eight (Maddie, Mayson and Merri) and Mikki had a kindergarten boy (J.B.) and a pre-K girl (Callie), but you'd never know they had procreated by their bodies.

Mikki's blond head looked up as I walked in, and she waved. Mimi turned and waved, too. I teared up a little. How could I ask them to do something I couldn't possibly do myself? *Pull yourself together. This has to get done.*

"Look at you! In your work clothes! You're amazing, Helen," Mimi gushed as she popped up and gave me a hug. Tina had put together seven days' worth of work outfits, using my existing wardrobe and some fresh accessories. Like Garanimals for adults. I was in Work Outfit #3: J. Jill chinos with a fashion-forward boot cut, black turtleneck and black boots with low heel. "Classic but contemporary," Tina had said as she threw some long gold necklaces, courtesy of the sale rack at Forever 21, around my neck. ("From a distance, these look like Chanel!" she'd lied.)

Mimi voiced her approval, too, making the same lunging hug and kiss motion. "Helen, you look great. We ordered you a latte. Nonfat, right?"

That was very thoughtful. Now I felt really horrible.

"Yes," I sunk into one of the groovy mismatched chairs covered in Marimekko fabric and took a deep breath. My patience for chitchat was limited these days.

"I am just going to ask what I need to ask and you can say "no" without any hard feelings. My real estate agent thinks I should clean out Merritt's belongings from the bedroom and such. She doesn't want any gossips coming through the house for sport. And I think she's right. It's just that…I can't do it. Not by Sunday, maybe not for a long time. I thought maybe you could…."

I didn't even get to finish. Mimi and Mikki, with watery eyes and understanding nods, jumped in to save me. "Of course. We'd be honored." The sisters spoke in solidarity. It was clear that they appreciated being asked. They wanted to help.

"Thank you. I'll pull out a few things for Aiden—like Merritt's USC jacket and some other items. And I'm sure there are some things you may want. I think Merritt even had some of your father's ties and that great navy blue overcoat. Please keep those. If you want anything, it's yours. If I miss something that you think Aiden would like, leave it. Emilia can pack up the basics and have them delivered to the resale shop for the hospital. I can't tell you…."

"No need to say anything. We all can't believe how well you are handling this. All of us," Mikki said, and Mimi squeezed my hand in agreement. The implication was clear: Even Mitsy approved.

"I'm at work all week. You can come anytime on Thursday or Friday. Just let me know so I can have Emilia available," I said, getting up from the table. Thank God I had a job and an excuse. I should have gotten a job years ago. I loved having somewhere to go and something to think about that was completely unrelated to my life. "Thank you, both."

The blond Fairchild sisters bobbed their heads. So did I. For once, we were all in the same circle.

One giant To Do list item down, one to go. I texted Tina: Open house this weekend. Worried Roshelle might show. Can U watch for her? Make sure she doesn't steal anything.

Merritt's sisters could take any keepsake they wanted. Merritt's mistress could not.

Tina texted me right back: U r so rt ... slut would take something ... I'm on it.

CHAPTER 9

To my surprise, Patrick was already at his desk when I arrived at 8:55. He was staring so intensely at his computer screen, he did not even acknowledge my arrival. He sat with remarkable stillness, his right hand on the desk, hovering over the mouse. His blue linen shirt sleeves were casually rolled up, and I noticed the size and strength of his forearm. His tanned skin, with just the perfect amount of dark hair, set off his stainless steel watch. Was that a tattoo on his left arm?

Snap out of it, Helen!

"Morning," I offered in a quiet voice. Again, another office protocol issue. Do I disturb him if he's working? Or do I leave him alone and slip quietly into scanning mode? His greeting told me I was within professional bounds.

"Hey, you're here!" Patrick said brightly, looking up at me with the same intensity he'd had when studying the screen. "I made the coffee today."

"Thanks." Now he was making me a little nervous with his gaze. I had no witty repartee planned after "Morning!" Tomorrow, I'd work on a few one-liners to fill in the gap between "Morning!' and "Lunchtime." Why was this so hard? I talked to Merritt's buddies all the time. I fell back on my surefire conversational trick when trying to engage the men in Merritt's circle: ask about their work.

"What are you working on?" I tried for a casual tone, as I dropped my large Land's End canvas bag and headed over to pour myself a fourth cup of coffee. I didn't want to be rude, even though I was already swimming in caffeine. I took a sip and gagged. Really gagged. "Wow, this is sludge!"

Patrick laughed like he was expecting the reaction. "It's Turk-ish. You get used to it. After spending so much time there, I've learned to like the chewy quality."

Of course. His dig site was in Hissarlik, Turkey, home of sludge-y coffee and beautiful linen, like the shirt he was wear-ing. I took a smaller sip this time, like I'd seen in the movies.

"It's a meal all right. My coffee yesterday must have tasted like dishwater."

"No, it was refined. Like you." Patrick countered, turning back to his screen.

Refined? Really? Compared to Sarah White and, oh, almost everybody else in Pasadena?

He brought up a slide of what appeared to be a huge excava-tion site as I moved around behind him. I assumed it was Troy. My research so far did not include memorizing the aerial views of ancient sites, as my college archaeology class required. "Take a look at this."

I made my way over to his side of the desk. I stood off to the side of his right shoulder and immediately worried about my breath.

Yoga breathing, yoga breathing, through the nose.

"Here is what I'm calling Troy 10, the last known city, or lev-el, to be occupied. Most folks think there are only nine cities on the site, Troy 1, Troy 2, Troy 3 and so on, dating from 3,000 BC to 600 AD. Built and destroyed, built and destroyed. But I think this right here is Troy 10. I think it was occupied starting about 850 AD." The computer screen held a high-quality aerial photo of the entire site. Unlike so many ancient sites, there were no ruins at Troy, no outward signs that there had been civilization of any kind. The archaeological evidence was buried under layers of dirt, covered by grass. Patrick pointed to a slight mound of grassy dirt on a vast plain at the edge of the excavated levels. "I think it's the key to determining whether or not Troy was a major trading city of the medieval world."

Frankly, I couldn't see anything in the photo. Was there a city under that mound? Was there really even a mound? Looked like a soccer field to me, not the key to anything. "And your academic rivals would prefer the 'or not,' right?"

Patrick's face registered surprise.

"I read your Facebook page. Well, technically, it's the Bringing Sexy Back to Archaeology page, but you're featured prominently." Oops, that sounded like I was stalking him.

"It came up when I googled Troy. And there you were." I rushed through my explanation, hoping he wouldn't register exactly what I was implying. "There's quite a lively discussion taking place on the boards about the validity of your assertion that Troy was a powerful trading city well into the Middle Ages. You have some detractors, Dr. O'Neill."

"I didn't set up that page." Was he blushing a little bit?

"I figured. You don't seem like the kind of guy who would describe himself as 'one part Indy/one part Apollo'."

"Are you kidding me?"

"Yes, I am." I wasn't, but he seemed so genuinely embarrassed I thought changing the subject was a good idea. "I'll be honest. I don't see anything in that photo but a great place to play soccer. What are we looking at?"

"Come closer," Patrick instructed.

Oh, no, he smelled fantastic, like he'd showered with Dr. Bronner's soap and then rolled around in lemon verbena.

He took his index finger and ran it lightly over the illuminated screen, circling a random area of the green field. "This is satellite imagery. Right here is where I think the marketplace, the agora, stood. Can you see the elevation change?"

"Oh, sure," I lied, just wanting him to back away so I could get a grip.

"I don't believe you. My undergrads try to pull that. Sit here," Patrick ordered, gracefully switching places with me and taking ahold of my shoulders to line me up in the proper position. He ran his finger softly alongside my face, directing my eyes to the top right area of the image. *Is that a tattoo on his fine forearm?* He barely whispered into my ear. "Follow my finger with your eyes. Relax your focus, scan the slide slowly, let your eyes see the differences in the topography. Notice the slight elevation change. Can you see it?"

Who knew "topography" could sound like a come on? I was having a bit of trouble relaxing *anything*, much less my focus. My mind was zeroed in on the sensation of his solid shoulders pressing into mine and the gentleness of his voice.

"Relax," he told me again. Obviously, my uptight but refined, body language was talking loud and clear.

Yoga breathing again.

It was working. As I let my eyes soften and focus in on the screen, I could see the slight circular outline of the marketplace, the line where Patrick had traced his finger before. It was there where it hadn't been before. "I see it!"

I sounded like a preschooler who found Waldo.

Patrick laughed, stepping away from the back of my chair, sadly for me. "This time, I believe you." He walked around to the front of the computer. How had he found a shirt that matched the color of his eyes? "Sometimes, it's not about the finding—it's about the looking."

Now I knew why this man has such an ardent following. I scooted out of his seat, wondering what to say next. He beat me to it. "Bring your chair over. Let me show you some other stuff."

Close physical contact was not part of the Document Scanning Protocol, but I was in no position to argue. I was just the assistant.

"Two glasses of that sounds great. Do you usually drink at lunch?" Patrick asked me as he settled onto his barstool and reached for an olive from the tasteful hand-painted ceramic bowl in the signature yellow-and-blue colors of the In Vino Veritas Wine Bar.

No, I thought to myself, but clearly he did. Nobody ever looked more at home drinking wine, eating olives and striking up a conversation than Patrick O'Neill.

I usually eat cottage cheese and Wheat Thins standing over the sink, in between aerobics, committee meetings and mani/pedis. But that sort of answer seems slightly provincial given the morning I'd shared with a world-famous archaeologist, so instead I opted to save face.

"Not if I'm driving carpool." Which is true, even if some mothers I know don't follow the same set of standards.

In Vino Veritas was owned by Ted Gamble, Jan's husband, diaper heir and wine aficionado. Back in the day, Ted was a mergers and acquisitions lawyer, even though the interest on his trust fund would have sufficed for a very nice life. He became so good at lawyering that he made oodles more money. Then, after September 11th and the death of his best friend on the United plane bound for San Francisco, Ted retired early and opened up a small wine shop with an informal, satisfying sandwich and tapas bar. The service was slow, but the ham was Parma. And Ted was a delightful proprietor, the perfect companion for a solo diner. I used to stop by every couple of weeks to buy a case of wine, Ted's picks, and a sandwich.

My wine budget now was more Trader Joe's than In Vino Veritas, so it had been a while since my last visit. When Patrick suggested lunch together, I said I knew the perfect place. I got the distinct impression he wanted some out-of-the-way spot where Sarah White would not materialize. He mumbled something about finding a place "not known to the rest of the Huntington staff." Veritas was up the street, but out of the way.

Ted's eyebrows raised slightly when I walked in with Patrick. I'd never even come in here with Merritt, who had no patience for a place like this. But I could see the question on his face about my lunch date. I hadn't seen Ted since the funeral, and my guess is that he and Jan had other things to talk about at the end of the day than me. I quickly introduced the two men and they both seemed pleased. Ted was well read and a world traveler with high-profile political and business connections. And Patrick was comfortable dealing with guys like Ted.

As Patrick and Ted exchanged the social niceties of who, what, when and how long will you be in Pasadena, I sipped my Pinot Grigio (*delicious... maybe I should drink more at lunch*) and thought about the last three hours.

Patrick had walked me through the bulk of his research, slide by slide. Like a semester of Trojan Archaeology in one morning. I remembered what made me fall in love with archaeology twenty years ago. Unraveling a mystery, shard by shard, using the physical, the literary, the linguistic and the historical data to re-create a civilization gone for a thousand years. Patrick was trying to put together a complete, complex picture of Troy, a legendary city that had disappeared. His work was like a game of Clue, but on a grander scale.

He was patient with my questions and enthusiastic with his responses, like the best teachers. And it was obvious that he not only knew his stuff, he knew everybody's stuff: about Greece, Homer, Troy, history starting in the Bronze Age and moving forward to today. Patrick spouted off on Constantine, Byzantium and the *Aeneid*. He cited ancient trade routes and their modern-day counterparts. He threw in some Greek, Turkish and Latin, along with philosophy and geology and recommendations for the best local food. And he wrapped it all up in a Trojan horse of humor and enthusiasm.

Now I understood why what was in those notebooks meant nothing. Patrick's work was so much bigger, so much broader than a few observations by an engineer 140 years ago. Patrick was out to change the accepted map of the ancient and medieval world, to upset the accepted academic standards. What Rudolph Schliemann might reveal in those journals was a tiny piece of a magnificent puzzle. Just like Patrick had said, "a few colorful anecdotes," but nothing on the scale of mapping the entire 4,000 years of a city called Troy.

Ted's voice snapped me out of my reverie. "So, are you married, Patrick? Is your wife here with you?"

Brilliant, Ted, brilliant! Once a lawyer, always a lawyer. Fire away, counselor. Let's get the whole scoop. I feigned interest in the menu while I waited for the official response.

"I was married once, a long time ago. For about an hour and half. It didn't work out. She didn't care for all the dirt I tracked into the house." Big laughter from the boys. "She went back to London. She likes creature comforts. I don't really care about that stuff. That's where my daughter lives, too."

What?! An ex-wife in London? A daughter?

"How old is your daughter?" Good work, Ted.

"Cassandra is 20. She's studying fashion design. She wants to be the next Stella McCartney. Her mother is a designer, so she gets that from her, not me."

"My oldest wants to be a park ranger. I never even took her camping!" More laughter from Ted and Patrick.

My mind was racing. Inexplicably, an image of Jane Seymour popped into my head, even though I'm sure Dr. Patrick O'Neill had never been married to Dr. Quinn, Medicine Woman. Who is Artsy Wife? How long is "a long time ago?" And when exactly did Artsy Wife "go back to London"? Does he see his daughter? How often? Why did he name her Cassandra when the mythological Cassandra was killed by her own mother? And when he sees his daughter, does he have tea and crumpets with Artsy Wife? And if he has a 20-year-old daughter, surely he's older than me, but how much older?

Keep talking, Ted. Keep talking.

But Ted did what all men do when the conversation turns good and intimate: He changed the subject. "Let me ask you this. Why don't the Greeks make better wine? They've been drinking it for thousands of years. Why isn't it better?"

And off they went on a thousand topics, all of which were entertaining, but none of which were related to anything personal. They talked about the best restaurants in Paris, the English Premiere League, American politics versus Russian politics, the ruins at Ephesus, seeing Bruce Springsteen for the first time. Everything under the sun but people and relationships. Almost two hours later, after a few cups of coffee for me and a few more glasses of wine for Patrick, all on the house, of course, we headed back to the office.

"Great place. Great guy," Patrick said, slipping into the front seat of my car.

A budding bromance? How nice for both of them.

"By the way, you're on your own until Monday. I'm going out of town for a few days."

We were back in the honeymoon suite. I was packing up to leave for the day, already late to pick up Aiden. Patrick's statement caught me off guard. I hoped my face didn't register too much disappointment.

"Oh, okay. What would you like me to get done by Monday?"

"Let's try to get the first half-dozen notebooks scanned and input. If you have a chance to transcribe the material, great. Your notes would be really helpful, and typed pages would be easier for me to go through than the handwriting. After five or six journals, we should have some idea if the notebooks contain anything interesting about the original excavation. Then, I'll spend a couple of days formulating some kind of hypothesis, or people might get suspicious about what we're doing all day," Patrick said, a little too warmly. Maybe he wasn't used to drinking at lunch. "I need to be ready in case Sarah starts grilling me again over tacos."

Apparently, he wasn't going away with Sarah White. That knowledge improved my mood. But Sarah got me this job, so I wasn't ready to sell her out either.

Patrick logged onto his computer, clearly getting ready for a few more hours of work as I raced off. "And I was wondering if you could help me with something. I have to do a presentation for a bunch of middle school kids next week. That's not really my usual audience. Isn't your son about that age?"

"Yes. In fact, he goes to Millington. Your presentation is for his school."

"Small world."

He had no idea.

"Can you take a look at my Power Point and see if it's something that kids his age would like? I could use a gut check. I'm worried it's too academic."

"Sure." I was astonished. A couple of glasses of wine and now I was the Gut Check Monitor for Dr. Patrick O'Neill. "Let me give you my e-mail. Just send it to me. What's the basic premise of the presentation?"

"Oh, you know, basic Trojan War history, a bit of the Heinrich Schliemann story, and then I wrap up with my work there. The subtext is that archaeology is like solving a mystery, with high-tech tools like image intensifiers and computer models, and old-fashioned grunt work."

"As in digging in the dirt?"

"Yeah."

"Wow, teenagers do love image intensifiers! And digging in ditches."

"I thought they liked computers." Patrick got defensive.

"Where's the excitement? The action? How about throwing in the fact that the father of modern archaeology, Heinrich Schliemann, was a bootlegger and con man? He made his millions trading arms. The guy was barely educated, was a pariah among the academics of the time. But he had the audacity to discover Troy. And he married a mail-order bride, Sophia, who had to take a test on Homer before he would agree to wed. How about throwing some of that in for the kids? That's exciting. Computer imaging, not."

"I'm a professor, not a screenwriter."

"And I'm just a mother, not a Ph.D. But I think you should liven it up a bit. Or you may scare off an entire generation of potential archaeologists. Didn't you get into the field because of stories like that?"

Patrick paused, thinking about my question. "No. I liked the structure of academics. The rigor. Not the romance."

It was my turn to pause. "Good to know, Dr. O'Neill. Send the PowerPoint. Aiden and I will take a look. Here's my cell number in case you need anything while you're gone." I jotted the contact information down, then lingered at his desk. What was I waiting for?

"Thanks," Patrick said, looking at me directly and for a touch too long. "How many hours does it take to get to Santa Barbara from here?"

Santa Barbara, paradise on Earth. Who or what was in Santa Barbara? "About two, depending upon the traffic. Don't leave at rush hour. It could be days. Do you have family there?" Fishing for facts. I hoped I wasn't too obvious.

"No, my family's on the East Coast now. I'm staying with a former student, now colleague. Teaches at the university, doing interesting work relating trade routes to changing religious beliefs from Bronze Age to present-day Near East civilizations. I'm going to visit for a few days. Exchange notes, that sort of thing."

"I hope it's sunny. Have fun with him."

"It's a her. And I'm sure I will."

CHAPTER 10

"Just how many women does he have? First Sarah, then Artsy Wife in London, then Santa Barbara? How many more are there?" I demanded of Candy, as we pounded our way around the three-mile loop of the Rose Bowl. Every morning, hundreds of Pasadenans made their way around the famed football stadium as part of their daily exercise routine: the young, the old, the dog-walkers and the mom squads. Candy and I were just two of dozens of mothers, clad in black tights and baseball caps, to walk the walk that morning. We'd already seen posses from Millington (the South American moms, speaking Spanish, walking slowly and wearing full makeup), Martindale (Cole Haan "sneakers" and no body fat) and Redwood (*Who walks in clogs?*).

Candy called out to each group, addressing each woman with her signature, "Cheers, doll!" She made no social distinctions. Everyone was a friend to Candy. She literally knew everybody in town. You never know when you're going to need somebody, she always said.

I looked over at her in her quilted silver down vest, capri tights and top-of-the-line Nikes. Was she panting?

"Helen, let's back off the pace a little. You're a maniac this morning."

"I'm sorry. I'm just in a hurry. I have to get to work and everything."

We rounded the final corner, Candy's big Lexus in view. She slowed considerably and put her hand on my arm to get my attention. "Don't take this the wrong way, but I think you need some therapy."

I did take it the wrong way. Totally the wrong way. "I spent my whole childhood watching my mother try consciousness-raising and primal screaming. So no thanks. I'm fine. Or I'll be fine. I just need some time."

We were in the parking lot now. Candy spoke to me with a genuine concern, "Helen, usually this walk is when I gossip and you nod and laugh. I was all set with a great Neutron Melanie story from the last Five Schools meeting, but I couldn't get a word in. You just spent the last three miles going off on Adele at Millington, high school admission counselors, real estate prices, your accountant, the water polo coach and some woman in Santa Barbara that you don't even know."

"I needed to *vent* my feelings. Not get in touch with them."

She reached into her vest pocket and pulled out a fully-loaded Louis Vuitton key chain. "I'm not a big fan of self-reflection, either. That's what vodka is for. But honey, you are angry. I love anger. It serves a purpose. But not forever. I think you need to talk to somebody. This is not about a high school interview or the board of trustees. This is about Merritt. You're pissed off he died and left you to deal … with everything."

For someone with multiple ex-husbands and personal scandals attached to her name, Candy was surprisingly free of issues. If she thought I needed help, maybe I did need help.

Damn.

I had been so focused on Aiden, I never thought to consider myself. I'd even tried to talk Aiden into a summer camp for grieving teens but he smirked, "Yeah. Sounds fun, hanging out with a bunch of kids with dead parents."

Maybe I was the one who needed a summer camp? I didn't even know where to start. I leaned up against my car and pretended to stretch out my calves.

"Merritt's sisters are cleaning out his closet today. I can't even face his blue blazers. How can I face all …" I hung my head. "… all the rest of it?"

"I'll call around and get some names. Somebody good and experienced in grief counseling."

It surprised me that she would use that term. Candy had been so harsh about Merritt and the affair. It was almost like she was admitting that she had judged the situation too quickly. Had I, too?

"Just talk to somebody a couple of times. It couldn't hurt. Okay?'

"Okay."

Candy climbed into her SUV and started the engine. Beyonce came blasting through the speakers. "You wanna be my date at the Symphony Gala this weekend? The PR person gave me an extra ticket. I bet Mitsy will be there. And maybe some nice older single gentlemen. And I do mean *older!*" Candy back to being Candy.

"Darn. I'll be at a water polo tournament. Have some sherry for me." Me back to being me.

"Will do. Cheers, doll." And off roared my good friend.

The office was quiet except for the low hum of the scanner and the sound of the radio in background. With Patrick out of town, I used the opportunity to wear jeans, listen to NPR and think about what Candy had said. Normally I was the type of person to over-think every decision, researching and mulling over a situation ad nauseum before acting.

But since Merritt's death, I'd done the complete opposite, re-acting quickly, even rashly. I thought that was what I needed to do. Get the finances in order now, grieve later. Was I wrong?

Maybe I *should* talk to someone. Just because my mother made a full-time job of therapy didn't mean that I had to spend the next two decades finding myself. I bet a few quick sessions would do the trick. Or, I could start by opening up a few of the books about grief that Monsignor had sent over. I was a freshman in college the last time I read Kübler-Ross. I was lost in thought, completely ignoring Document Scanning Protocol Rule Number One: Focus on the work.

That's when I heard a terrible tearing sound.

Oh, shit. I'd turned Page 122 of Notebook VI too quickly and torn it slightly. Okay, maybe more than slightly. Maybe three-fourths of the way down the page. Damn, damn, damn.

What if Karen from Library checked the pages every day when I returned the notebooks? Please, please, please don't let Karen from Library check the pages. I don't want to lose this job.

I don't want to lose my *life*!

Once, when I was 13 and was cat-sitting for our next-door neighbors, I locked one of the cats in the basement for a week by mistake. I made the illicit trip to the basement to check out the rumor that the Mills family grew shrooms down there. I expected to find boxes of dirt and fungi under Gro-lights. Instead I found the traditional crap stashed in basements: broken ornaments, old luggage, rusting barbecue grills. The Mills family did not appear to be shroom farmers, just pack rats.

After my sleuthing, Snowball went missing. Six cats accounted for, one cat MIA. I just kept putting food in the Snowball bowl and pretending that he was eating, because I was too terrified to tell anybody that I'd lost Snowball. When the neighbors returned, they heard him mewing wildly from the basement and found an emaciated Snowball curled up with the Christmas decorations. I played dumb, as if Snowball had been bouncing around all week and must have just gotten trapped in the basement on his own.

It was such a mystery, Mrs. Mills kept repeating. How did he get in the locked basement? Despite the clear trauma to Snow-ball, they bought my story. Stupid hippies. Maybe they *were* growing shrooms. I have felt guilty ever since.

My plan with the ripped notebook page would be the same as the Snowball Incident. Play dumb. Deny all allegations. The notebook was already ripped when I scanned it, that was going to be my line. Wait? Can they do carbon-testing to determine the age of the tear? I was so screwed.

Just then somebody knocked on the door and I was 13 again. The irrational thought of Karen hearing the rip clear across the Huntington grounds zoomed through my stressed-out brain.

"Umm, just a second," I yelled in a shaky voice. I knocked over a tasteful leather pencil holder and a box of extra-large paper clips in a rush to hide Notebook Number Five. I shoved the notebook under the couch pillows, readjusting the fleece throw to hide the bump. My heart was pounding.

Relax, relax. Was that breathing at the door?

Another knock, this time louder. "Helen, are you in there?'

Thank God, it was Sarah White, not Karen. I could feel my heart rate slow. I flopped down on the couch, hoping Sarah would buy my casual repose. "Oh, sure, Sarah, come on in!"

She entered cautiously, looking around the cottage for signs of Patrick. When it was clear the true objective of her visit was absent, she focused on me, lounging on the couch in the middle of a workday, no work nearby. Her face registered disgust. "What are you *doing*?"

I popped up, praying that the notebook did not fall to the floor. "Just taking a break. Want some coffee?"

"No, thanks." That was a relief because I didn't have any made and my hands were shaking so much, I wouldn't have been able to measure out the beans. "I'm looking for Patrick. Is he around?"

So, Patrick hadn't told Sarah about his trip to Santa Barbara? Perfect. Now I was on the hot seat. "No, he isn't. I don't expect him in for the rest of the week."

Yes! That was good assistant language. Very neutral, but indicating that I am not at liberty to discuss.

"Why?"

"What?"

"Why? Where is he?" Now Sarah White wasn't playing fair.

Conundrum. If I told her where he was and she tried to track him down, he might get annoyed. But if I pretended I didn't know and Sarah found out that I *did* know when he returned, she would get annoyed. So, I opted for the halfway solution.

"He's working in Santa Barbara. He'll be back on Monday. That's why I have to get back to work." I loosely pointed toward my desk, hoping Sarah wouldn't notice that there was no actual work on the desk because I'd stuffed my one allowed notebook under the couch to hide its disfigurement.

"What is he working on in Santa Barbara?"

I shrugged my shoulders in a dramatic fashion, "Bronze Age trade routes. He has my cell phone for an emergency, but I don't have his." There, I think I shut down that line of inquiry.

Not so fast. Sarah did not seem entirely satisfied. She moved in closer. "I noticed you two were gone all afternoon yesterday. Field trip?"

Was Sarah White stalking my boss? "Lunch, a long lunch. Patrick has been filling me in on all his research so I'm up to speed. Helps me to put this project in context," I explained, quite satisfied with my tone. "It's taken a few days, but now I'm fully on board."

Lots of good mumbo jumbo in there. I sounded like a pro.

Sarah was now circling Patrick's desk, pretending she wasn't reading the few papers left there. "You know, we've been out a few times. Has he mentioned me?'

Now it was Sarah's turn to act 13.

"We've just been talking about Troy. I don't ask a lot of personal questions. That's not the relationship I have with Patrick."

"Of course not," Sarah bristled, brushing imaginary lint off her tailored cream-colored suit. "I thought I just might come up, you know, in the course of conversation."

If this is going steady in midlife, it doesn't seem much different than going steady in middle school. That depressed me. "He doesn't say much about his private life."

"You know his ex-wife is Susanna Ashford, the fabric designer? Marimekko and Laura Ashley rolled into one? Apparently, they fell madly in love for about six months and had a child, but then she fled back to London when she realized that Patrick cared more about his work than her work."

Of course he'd been married to Susanna Ashford! Why wouldn't he have a fabulous first wife? That explains the dirt and the creature comforts comment to Ted at the bar. Still, I was shocked that Patrick would reveal something so ... so *self-aware* to Sarah over tacos. "He told you that?"

"Oh, not all of it. Just that he had a daughter. So I googled Cassandra O'Neill, the daughter, which led me to Susanna Ashford, which led me to an interview with her in *The Guardian*. She didn't mention Patrick by name, but when she said 'my first husband, the archaeologist,' I knew it was him. Apparently he inspired her new line of bedding. The ancient design, I mean, not the concept of sheets."

That was a relief. I didn't really want Patrick opening up to Sarah, but I didn't know why. I felt a little disloyal, so I added, "He's an interesting man. I'm sure you have a lot in common."

That was nice of me.

Apparently, Sarah didn't think so.

"I'll let you get back to your *work*," Sarah said. My loyalty dissipated. "If he calls, can you tell him I stopped by?"

And once Sarah White made her exit, I got back to my "work," trying to minimize the damage I'd done to the notebook. I remembered what Patrick had said: objects are not inherently valuable because they are old. Or something like that.

Maybe these notebooks would really turn out to be useless. That would be great.

I was propped up in bed, trying to transcribe the scanned documents. It was slow going trying to slop through Rudy's century-old handwriting. I was about halfway through the first notebook, a fairly tedious description of the logistics of the trip to Troy. Train, boat, caravan. Even a detailed packing list, which I'm sure some scholar would find fascinating, but not me. It didn't look that much different than Aiden's list for summer camp.

Except the dried venison jerky that Rudy Schliemann was taking by the barrelful.

Though the transcription was painful, I was finally putting to use that typing course my guidance counselor had made me take in high school. "Just in case that Latin thing doesn't work out," Miss Tetherow had winked, bedecked in a burnt-orange pantsuit, trying her Mary Tyler Moore best even in central Oregon.

I felt a little nauseated when I realized that maybe Miss Tetherow was right.

I closed the computer and shut off the bedside lamp. A glow came from the closet, now half empty. I'd taken to sleeping with the light on. I pretended that it was for Aiden, in case he wanted to come in at night and sleep on the floor. But it was for me, too.

Being scared of the dark was a new feeling for me.

I turned on the light, opened my laptop and started typing up more of the transcribed journal. What the … ? All of a sudden, Rudy's description of packing lists turned to his fantasies about the young Sophia Schliemann and what she might be wearing when he arrived on site. Or not wearing, that is, as he described her "naked, slender ankles, absent of boot or stocking."

Rudy, Rudy, Rudy, you bad boy, you.

CHAPTER 11

Aiden and I had debated the merits of a shirt and tie most of the morning. I thought he should wear one for the Ignatius interview. He disagreed. "Mom, it looks like I'm trying too hard," he argued.

"A shirt and tie simply says you care. You'll have to wear one every day for four years when you get in. What's the big deal about wearing one to the interview?" I hissed in that special mother hiss. Honestly, his moods were all over the place these days—understandable, given what he'd been through. But why, why, why pick a fight over a shirt and tie? I pulled the car into the school parking lot, observing the high ratio of Mini Coopers and old Volvos in the student spaces.

Compared to the lush, green surroundings of Millington, Ignatius was as urban as Pasadena could manage. The old stone buildings, originally a Jesuit seminary and retirement home constructed in the 1920s, were covered in ivy and jammed up against a freeway onramp. A small chapel, with a stained-glass window featuring the names of Jesuit colleges, stood off to the right. The pool and sports fields rolled out beyond the chapel, an endless rectangular strip of green and concrete alongside the freeway. A brand-new football stadium, complete with a million-dollar turf field, press box and deluxe locker rooms, was at the far south end of the campus. (One very loyal, very successful former third-string quarterback had donated the entire stadium. Benchwarmer's revenge, Merritt had laughed at the dedication ceremony.)

The campus was not beautiful, but it reeked of tradition: the broad stone steps in front where students gathered in the morning; the worn wooden crucifix touched for luck by a thousand boys a day as they entered the gates; the drafty dining hall where the seniors lead grace before meals. Ignatius, despite its Catholic heritage, was the closest Southern California came to the elitist prep schools in Massachusetts and Connecticut. The big difference was that it wasn't actually elitist.

The children of the rich, the poor, the immigrants and the powerful of all colors and creeds came to Ignatius from all over Los Angeles County. Long before prep schools grew endowments to cover financial aid for needy students, Ignatius had prided itself on a "write the check" admissions policy. If the son of a gardener or cop or mechanic was deemed qualified to attend, some alum would simply write the tuition check on behalf of that student for four years. It started 60 years ago with Father Michael at the helm and continued today with Father Raphael. The beloved Jesuit would scan the alumni directory and pick up the phone. The lawyer or real estate mogul or judge would never meet the kid he sponsored. And the student hoped to someday repay the debt in the same way. It was quiet and discreet, and it built the most loyal alumni in the area. Most Ignatius Crusaders considered their high school allegiance to be even deeper than their college or fraternity connection.

I wanted Aiden to have that connection. I felt like I could still give him that, even if so much else in his life had changed.

As I redid my lipstick in the rearview mirror, I took one last stab at Aiden. What was wrong with him? "It would be a sign of respect to school tradition to wear a tie."

"Fine. Just… whatever, fine." And he put on the tie and a dramatic scowl.

Super, I noted to myself. Terrific day to come down with Attitude.

And it got worse from there.

Hank Pfister, the director of admissions, ushered us into his cramped office. Humility in all things, the needlepoint pillow on the couch advised. So I've learned lately, I thought.

"So Aiden, what are you reading in English this quarter?" Mr. Pfister offered up as his first question. I knew that he knew exactly what an eighth grade student at Millington would be reading this quarter: *Romeo & Juliet* and *To Kill a Mockingbird.* Twenty-five boys from Millington had applied to Ignatius; Aiden was the last to be interviewed. Only about a half-dozen would get in. Aiden was a legacy and a decent kid who had just lost his dad, but his grades were not good. He needed this interview. I got the sense that Hank Pfister knew that, too.

I appreciated the softball question.

"Umm, umm ..." Aiden started, not looking up from the floor for a second of eye contact. Then the fidgeting began, leading to the chair twisting. "Umm, Romeo and, umm, Juliet. That's pretty good. And then that one about the lawyer dude defending the African American guy. The Mockingbird one."

The lawyer dude? Shakespeare is "pretty good"? Who is this kid?

"Oh, Aiden," I fake-laughed, hoping to diffuse the growing discomfort in the room. "I'm glad you think William Shakespeare is *pretty good.*"

"Tough audience," Hank Pfister responded, playfully jerking his head toward my son. God bless you, Mr. Pfister.

Then playtime ended.

"If you can't understand a single word the guy writes, how great can he be?" Aiden snapped, his voice full of defiant energy now. "I could read that crap all day long and still it wouldn't make any sense. What's the point?"

There is no sound in the world quite as deafening as the sound of all hope leaving a room. *Please, Aiden, please pull it together.* But I could see that he was just getting started with his Angry Young Man phase.

We struggled through another ten minutes of questions and

answers. Even the routine questions about water polo failed to elicit a civil response from my son. Eventually, it was Mr. Pfister and me talking about Aiden while Aiden checked his imaginary watch. We carried on the charade, including handshakes and wishes of good luck, until the end of the interview, but we all knew one thing for sure: This Aiden was not Ignatius material.

My mother was very good at silence. It was her greatest parenting asset. Of course, it made me crazy as a kid when she would call out in front of my friends for "a moment of silence and meditation" if we got into an argument over the rusty trampoline in our backyard. "Let's all close our eyes and take a deep breath. Exhale the dark energy," my long-haired mother in the flowing skirt would instruct my bewildered church-going friends. "Breathe in the light."

She would remain very still for about a minute while my friends tried not to laugh and I tried not to die of embarrassment. Then, she'd return to the moment with a big smile and a solution. I think the solution was that the horror of the mediation made everyone involved in the "dark energy" completely forget what the fight was about. Nevertheless, we were all calmer and the trampoline play continued without incident or need for further meditation.

But I was never more grateful for the lesson of silence than on the way home from Ignatius. The fifteen-minute drive felt like fifteen hours. Aiden and I did not exchange a single word. I did my best to breathe out the dark energy; he stared out the window, barely breathing at all.

Both Tina and Candy had texted me with the same "How'd it go?" message. I wasn't ready to answer that question yet. I turned the phone off. I could hear my mother's soothing voice, "Let it go. Breathe out and let it go."

She had a point.

When we arrived back at our house, the "For Sale" sign was being hammered into the front yard in advance of the weekend open house by a couple of guys on Rita's team. "Tasteful typeface and classy colors!" Rita had promised. I'm sure the neighbors would appreciate the art direction. I turned off the ignition and sat for a second. So did Aiden.

"Aren't you going to say anything?" Aiden challenged me when we finally got out of the Audi.

I can't remember a time when I'd ever had less to say, except maybe when Merritt told me about Roshelle Simms. Or when the accountant had told me about the money. I couldn't possibly comprehend what had just happened, so I certainly had nothing constructive to say about it. I simply stated the obvious.

"I guess you really don't want to go to Ignatius. I thought you did. We'll figure something out."

Aiden's face registered surprise, as if he'd expected me to rip into him upon our arrival home. And certainly, if he'd behaved like that in front of Merritt, there would have been serious consequences: yelling, accusations of letting down the family name, no computer or cell phone for a week. But in the last few months, I'd lost all sense of how to measure the importance of events. Was blowing the Ignatius interview less important or more to Aiden's life than having to sell his house? Who knew? I wouldn't know for decades the impact of Merritt's death on our lives, so I certainly wasn't going to jump to conclusions now. "Let's just order pizza so we don't mess up Emilia's clean kitchen."

"Mom, I'm sorry. I messed up. Are you mad at me?" That was the most emotionally complex thought Aiden had uttered all afternoon. I got an acknowledgement, apology and acceptance of responsibility.

"No," I said truthfully. Saddened, disappointed, scared, but not mad. "No, I'm not mad. We'll figure it all out."

"Okay." The One-Word Wonder was back.

I knew we'd have to return to this conversation someday, like in a month when we got the rejection letter from Ignatius and the reality of the awful interview would sink in for Aiden.

In the meantime, I changed the subject. "Hey, can you take a look at a PowerPoint for me? It's Dr. O'Neill's, and he wants to make sure it's cool enough for your class. Ten minutes while we wait for the pizza. Would you mind?"

A smile from the kid!

"Sure."

Three hours and one mushroom and sausage pizza later, Aiden and I had transformed Patrick's studious PowerPoint presentation about the Trojan War into a multimedia spectacular. The original was, as Aiden said, "lame." Our version, with music, animation and moving graphic sequences was, as he said, "cool."

We added in the action, mystery, romance and intrigue that Patrick had left out. And a few action photos of Patrick on site that I'd found on Facebook, to please the female teachers and mothers who attended.

"E-mail it to your boss, Mom. Now." Aiden was convinced I would get a huge promotion based on our soundtrack choices alone, from Green Day to The Weepies. I'd had just enough wine to think that he might be right.

I hit "Send."

"Time for bed. Big weekend."

"Yup."

I meant selling the house. Aiden meant the water polo tournament.

As I watched Aiden drag his sleepy body up to bed, I made a decision. I would talk to Billy Owens, Esquire. He was an Ignatius alum, and he would make it right. Plus, after knowing about the money and the affair and saying nothing, he owed me one, and he knew it.

There is no better place to avoid your life than at a youth water polo tournament. In between the constant whistles, the over-enthusiastic crowds and the roar of the reverberating aquatics center, I literally could not hear myself think. (Which was perfect, considering what I was trying to avoid thinking about.) *So what* that hundreds of looky-loos were traipsing though my dream house, commenting on how sad it was that I had to sell? *So what* that my kid had blown his only chance at happiness and would undoubtedly begin experimenting with marijuana soon? *So what* that I had to cancel my gym membership, move to a cheaper hair salon and sell the R. Kenton Nelson oil painting of the Colorado Street Bridge that Merritt had given me for our tenth anniversary—just to pay the second half of the Millington tuition?

I had plenty of sunscreen, a $12 floppy hat from Target and a Diet Coke. Life was good.

I was seated on a hot, reflective aluminum bench at the Mecca of Water Sports: the Mission Viejo Natatorium. The Orange County town of Mission Viejo turned out more Olympic swimmers and more Olympic water polo players than any hamlet in the country. It was a chlorine-fueled factory, where the local kids were genetically gifted and simply bigger, stronger and faster than other mere landlubbers. There was no way Pasadena was going to win, despite the fact that we were tied 1-1 in the first quarter. Soon, MV would open up the score and crush us like they always did.

I pretended to watch the game, our second of the day, sitting alone to avoid conversation with my fellow parents. I had no desire to keep up with the chatter: playing-time issues; the effectiveness of fitness training; the must-win situation at the 4 o'clock game to advance when we lost this one. Usually I feigned interest in these topics to play my part, but today I had no patience.

These were nice people—the Gambles, the Barneses, the Keegans, the Villanuevas. Parents who had paid their money and wanted to see the highly qualified coach, a former UCLA and US National team player, shape their children into polo-playing machines. I could see that they only wanted the best for their kids, but some of them had out-of-whack expectations.

Aiden had some talent, some drive, but probably not the size to be the "impact player" that the other parents talked about endlessly. I'd never harbored the delusion that he'd be attending USC on a Division 1 water polo scholarship, unlike many of the parents who crowded the stands that day in Water Polo Mecca.

After that interview at Ignatius, I did not harbor any delusions at all.

Then my Blackberry signaled a text. It was 1 o'clock—the open house had started. Tina, acting as my eyes, ears and security guard, was checking in with a first report. Packed. Line to get in when doors opened. Did you see pic in LA Times today?

Yes, I'd seen the full-page ad in the real estate section, touting the house, my house, as "the perfect home in which to raise a family and create memories. "A rare opportunity to own a piece of Pasadena history at an attractive price."

And a big piece of my history at an attractive price.

I turned back to the game just as Aiden pump-faked with the ball, then let a bounce shot rip from about seven meters out. Goal! Goal! Goal!

I went wild. I may not understand the constant whistles that signals fouls, or the "five meter" call, no matter how many games I watched, but I loved seeing Aiden's face when he scored. Pasadena up 2 to 1 at the end of the second quarter. Unbelievable.

Another ping. Emilia is in kitchen serving coffee and cookies. Nice touch. Does she come with house?

Aiden came out of the game to rest. I gave him a thumbs up for the goal. He ignored me. I should have known better. When he was playing soccer at age 6, he'd come off the field seeking my approval. Now he just listened to the coach, the guy who went to the Olympics, not his mother, who didn't know the first thing about water polo.

Ping. Many gay couples. Did you promise martinis?

Ping. Made walk-through. Everything OK. No media if you know what I mean. Juan the painter is here with Emilia. Is something going on?

Ping. Spotted: Neutron Mel and Hubby. She is Very Overdressed in Calvin Klein suit. He is in golf wear. Hasn't she seen your house a million times?

Yes, yes she has. Could she actually be there to look at it, as in buy, my dream house? Melanie and her husband lived in a perfectly lovely place in the lower Arroyo, a classic California ranch with a view of the bridge and a grove of eucalyptus trees. Please don't let me have to sell my house to Melanie. That would be too humiliating.

Ahhh! A giant air horn signaled the end of the quarter and I nearly fell off the bench. I frantically typed to Tina: Tell me how long she is in there.

"Great shot by Aiden! They are going to love him at Ignatius next year!" Chip Barnes bellowed from several rows below. I gave another stupid thumbs up to avoid crying. At six feet already, Chip's son Randy was an "impact player," and rumor had it he was being "highly recruited" by schools all over the area, including Ignatius. At least that's what Marika Villanueva claimed at practice the other night, adding in a dismissive tone, "It's a good thing he can play, because he can't add."

"Thanks, Chip. I think we've got a chance today!" I returned, as much to be social as to keep my mind off Neutron Mel going through my medicine cabinets. At least I'd hidden all the sleeping pills, as Candy had suggested.

"He's going to do great things next year," Chip shouted for all to hear. Since Merritt's death, I'd noticed that the fathers on the team had rallied around Aiden, giving him extra attention after the game, taking the time to tell him how well he played even if he hadn't. It was very sweet.

Ping. Mel still in there. Gay couple out front examining plantings. Heard them say they love the roses and the kitchen. These guys look like the real thing. Driving Range Rover. Gays are so good for property values.

Ahhh! The air horn signaled the start of the next quarter, and the Pasadena crowd stood and chanted, in an effort to whip our team into a frenzy. I applied more sunscreen and hoped that Melanie hated the wallpaper in the guest bathroom and the Gays loved the rosemary hedge and the French lavender beds. *Maybe I should have planted the tulip bulbs; they were just so expensive.* Aiden was back in the game and swimming hard. It was nice to see him work.

Ping: Mel not out yet. Maybe she is trying to hire Emilia away from you. Heard she fired another nanny. Gay couple calling friends to come over and see the place. Rita circling for the kill.

Yes. Let's go, Pasadena! Let's go, Gays!

Ping. OMG. News Slut is HERE. You were right. She is still wearing skinny jeans. So sad. I'm going in.

My head started to swim. The game seemed to move in slow motion. I threw myself into the action, cheering wildly for every pass, block and stop as the third quarter ended and the final six minutes of the game began. The other parents turned to look at me, surprised at my newfound enthusiasm. At one point, I even yelled at the ref, which was a huge stress reliever and an absolute no-no in the Parents' Code of Conduct. When Randy Barnes rifled a shot past the Mission Viejo goalie to put the team up 3 to 1, I leapt to my feet and cheered like we'd just landed a man on the moon.

I decided: If Pasadena wins this game, the Gays will buy my house.

Cheers erupted again from our crowd. Randy Barnes scored again with the clock ticking down the final seconds. We'd slayed the dragons. Pasadena beat Mission Viejo in their home pool!

What an upset! I climbed down to hug Chip Barnes, and there were tears in my eyes.

Ping. News Slut broke down in the living room and never even made it upstairs.

As the celebration continued around me, I read the text in disbelief. Was it grief? Or did she finally understand that Merritt's "other life" with a wife and a son and a home was very real?

And exactly the life she had pictured for herself.

Just then I heard a familiar voice call, "Mom!" I looked down at my son, in his Speedo and cap, surrounded by his joyous teammates. Aiden gave me a thumbs up, then pointed to the sky. Our eyes met; mine filled with tears.

My phone rang at 8:30 Saturday night. I muted the volume on the TV in my suite at the Courtyard Marriott. Back in the day (like two months ago), I would have booked myself in the nearby Ritz-Carlton, but nowadays, the free breakfast buffet was a big selling point.

The hardest-working real estate agent in Pasadena, Rita the Armenian, was on the line for the fifth time in three hours. She was at a raging wedding at the Glendale Westin, but that didn't stop my girl from making her deals. She had the other agents fax the offers to main desk at the hotel to review in between the ceremony and the reception. Then she faxed them to me at the Courtyard Marriott. I'm sure the 19-year-old at the desk thought I was quite a wheeler-dealer.

"It's fantastic. We have two really great offers. See, I told you. The right price makes all the difference!"

"Take the Gays," I replied.

"But the other offer from Melanie is a little stronger. It's $69,995 more and a quicker close."

It's rare in life that you really get to answer the question, *How much is my dignity worth?* Here was my opportunity. Not having

to see Melanie, or any other Pasadena family that bore any re-
semblance to mine, in my house was worth $69,995. Easy.

"I'll take the other offer," I replied. Over the last few hours
of phone calls and faxes, I'd become very fond of Greg and Tony,
who said in a personal letter to me that the house "sang" to them.
How could I not appreciate that sentiment? And maybe they
could become my new friends when I ended up in a tiny one-
bedroom condo, home-schooling my son. "You can counter, but
I don't really care. I want Greg and Tony to have the house. I'll
make up your commission on the difference."

"If that is your decision, that is your decision. And you know
what, I didn't like the way that Melanie tried to hire Emilia at the
open house. Very tacky. Okay, I'll let you know in the morning. I
have to go dance."

Yeah, me too. I knew the reality of moving would hit me soon
enough. But at that moment, I felt nothing but elation. So I did a
little dance right there in room 447, by the light of the soundless
TV.

CHAPTER 12

The Fairchild Performing Arts Center was packed, a stand-ing-room audience hanging on Dr. Patrick O'Neill's every word. He came to life in front of an audience, his intensity turning theatrical, as he entertained the students, teachers and carpool moms with the drama of the Trojan War, the archaeological au-dacity of Schliemann and his own humble passion that led him to a lifetime of discovery.

Sure, the amped-up PowerPoint and the blue jeans and linen blazer ensemble helped the overall quality of the presentation. But when Patrick spoke about the great battle between Achil-les and Patrokolas and their ambiguity at being "heroic," it was like he'd witnessed the scene in person. When he described Schliemann's determination to find Troy, despite his rogue back-ground and lack of formal training, he made everyone in the room want to take up bootlegging or archaeology late in life. And when he waxed on about his own personal epic journey, with Homer as his constant companion as he moved from city to city as a boy, well, every woman in the room wanted to comfort him. Judging from the reaction of the students, teachers and mothers, Patrick could have been holding up a cardboard diorama and wearing a hospital gown and I'm pretty sure the effect would have been the same.

I scanned the back row, finding the familiar faces of friends and frenemies who had chaperoned their middle school students to hear Patrick's Word-Write lecture. Tina and Candy were riv-eted, as if Nubby Sweater was lecturing about the *Real House-wives of Ancient Troy*. Cissy Montague looked lovely and slightly confused by all the big words. Jan Gamble was actually taking notes. Even Neutron Melanie had put aside her Blackberry to give full attention to the speaker, a first. I noticed that she and her henchman Jennifer Braham were starting to dress alike, which was good news for the shoulder-pad manufacturers of America.

As Patrick was answering questions from the animated audience of sixth, seventh and eighth graders, Word-Write Chair and Dentist of the Doomed, Dr. Natasha, caught my eye. She bowed her head, making the international "palms together, head bow" gesture to show she was forever in my debt. In her eyes, he was a rock star and I was his Penny Lane.

I'll take that rep, I thought.

Just then, Patrick began his wrap-up from the stage, "Thank you, students, for your attention. It's a great pleasure for me to stand in front of you and share my work. Someday, I hope you find something that you love doing as much as I love archaeology. I spend my days with my hands in the dirt, uncovering, literally and figuratively, our past. And in doing so, I glimpse into our future by working with some of the most talented students from all over the world. It's humbling. Maybe in the future, one of those students will be you."

Did I just hear a collective sigh from the seventh-grade room moms?

Patrick continued, "And I would be remiss if I didn't mention one Millington student who really helped me with my presentation. Aiden Fairchild, are you here? Can you stand up, please?"

Aiden, seated about eight rows from the front, awkwardly rose, looking like his head might explode with embarrassment and pride. The other kids applauded.

My heart melted.

"Fantastic job, Aiden. You should be a film director. And thanks to Helen Fairchild, my very talented research assistant," Patrick sought me out in the back of the room and made eye contact. The eyes of every mother in the room turned to me as well.

"Thanks, Helen."

Now my head was about to explode with embarrassment and pride.

"If you have any other questions, I'll be here for a few minutes. Otherwise, study hard, challenge yourselves and find something you love to do."

After the lecture, while Patrick was mobbed by slouching, shy teens wondering how they, too, could spend a life digging up clues, I stood off in the corner, receiving my share of kudos. Team Yoga Pants from the Word-Write committee rushed to my side with praise and admiration. The Chess Club moms nodded their heads and patted my arm. Even the teachers made the effort to come over and tell me how impressed they were by Patrick *and* by Aiden.

Then, Headmistress Adele Arnett made her way to my growing circle, clearly determined to reach some kind of détente after our face-off.

"Helen, what a thrill it must be to work with such a scholar. I'm sure his research keeps you very busy and stimulated. How satisfying it must be to have the time to devote to such important work. And to be able to include Aiden is a wonderful benefit for his academic future."

"Yes, it is. But Aiden has always been interested in history, so it's no surprise to me. You heard what the man said! Aiden could be *a film director!*" I said formally, with what I hoped was a touch of insouciance. "And Adele, I've always been able to multitask. I care deeply about the work I do, be it volunteer or paid. Assisting Dr. O'Neill doesn't preclude me from doing other things I'm passionate about."

Yummy, that felt good. I turned my back on her to face Candy and Tina, who had finally recovered from the post-lecture coma.

"Okay, let's review. You work in a small, confined space with that man?" Candy jumped in.

Tina laughed. "We need to work on your whole undergarment

situation, just in case there is some 'emergency excavation' going on in the office."

"You are bad. Shut up, here he comes. Remember, this is my boss, not some guy I met on Craigslist, like the men in your life, Candy. Please try to be appropriate." I turned to face Patrick, who appeared a tad flushed himself from all the attention. I couldn't help but smile. "That was really great."

To my surprise, Patrick leaned over and gave me a kiss on the cheek. "Thanks to you and Aiden. You really made the visuals 'rock,' as the kids say."

Was it me, or was he still holding onto my arm?

Candy mouthed, "Oh my God!" Then she rebounded with her Rose Queen-turned-gossip-columnist charm. "Dr. O'Neill, you were fabulous. Where has Helen been hiding you? You can't spend all your time in the library, digging up things."

I rolled my eyes, "Patrick, these are my dear friends Candy McKenna and Tina Chau-Swenson. Dr. Patrick O'Neill."

Sadly, he released my arm to shake their manicured hands. "It's good to meet you. Helen's been keeping me very busy, staying on task. She seems to think I should be spending my sabbatical working, not socializing. She keeps giving me notes, reworking my presentations, making epic discoveries. Is she always such a slave-driver?"

Just then Neutron Mel busted into our happy circle, sucking the oxygen out of the atmosphere. I'd been trying to avoid eye contact with her all morning, terrified she was going to shake me down for details on the house deal. Surely, she thought she'd been outbid. If she knew that I simply didn't want her to have the house, she could make life very ugly for me.

Please, Melanie, no real estate talk.

I was hugely relieved, and slightly breathless, when she embraced me as if I had just found her the nanny of her dreams. "Helen, I am so carried away with inspiration by your Dr. O'Neill. You *must* introduce us."

Why was she talking like a Masterpiece Theater production? And why was Jennifer hovering two steps behind with a clipboard and a pen at the ready?

"Of course. Patrick O'Neill, this is Melanie Martin. Patrick, Melanie is ..."

All eyes turned to me. Melanie is what? A force of nature? A blood-sucking vampiress? A frustrated marketing exec who should just go back to work and leave the child-rearing to a lovely woman from Guatemala?

I was in a generous mood. "Melanie is a mover and shaker here in Pasadena. Nothing happens without Melanie's knowledge. Patrick, I'm sure she'd be fascinated to hear about your foundation."

I didn't even bother to introduce Jennifer. It was my own passive-aggressive payback for the fact that she took my spot on the Five Schools committee.

Melanie stepped right into the middle of the action, commanding the moment with the confidence of a women who had run a giant marketing team. "Dr. O'Neill, I would love to hear about your foundation. Really. In fact, I have a proposal."

Patrick didn't miss a beat. "I was married once and I think that's my limit. But best of luck to you."

Candy almost fell off her inappropriately high platform shoes. And I laughed a little too loudly.

Melanie was unperturbed. "Please, Dr. O'Neill. Once is my limit, too. And I just happen to have him around still, making the situation that much more complicated. I'm talking about a business proposal of sorts."

"Let me guess. Helen of Troy mud masks made with actual dirt from Troy?" Candy piped up. There's nothing like a love/hate relationship for generating cattiness on a grand scale.

"Oh, Candy. You are too funny. And I'm sure you've tried every product on the market to look younger, so you know where the gaps are in the beauty category. But no, not that," Melanie struck back. "I am talking about the Five Schools Benefit. Wouldn't Dr. O'Neill be the perfect honoree? Think of it! 'The Best and the Brightest' is our theme. Who is better or brighter than Dr. Patrick O'Neill?"

Tina and Candy looked stunned, as if Melanie had just announced that she was changing the event to benefit graffiti "artists" and their contribution to the community. The benefit honoree had already been chosen, a beloved public high school chemistry teacher and track coach who was retiring after 45 years of service. Melanie wouldn't dare drop Mr. Thurmond, would she?

On top of that, you can't change the theme of a huge event eight weeks from the date. Thanks to Tina, the invitations were on the way to the printers. Candy had already issued the press releases. A sub-committee of ten had chosen the menu. And poor Leonora Dillard on the decorating committee! Her idea of "Best and Brightest" was lots of white lights and some big metallic stars. She was going to have a fit over re-creating an ancient city in two months.

Most important, committee members had already bought their dresses! How were they supposed to interpret "The Glory of Troy" in an evening gown with only two months lead time?

Patrick turned to me for support, "I'm not sure I follow."

I tried to fill in. "We have a big benefit here in town to raise money for the public schools. Every year, an educator or artist or philanthropist is honored for his or her work. Melanie thinks you would be, um, great. It's just … Melanie, I know I'm not on the committee anymore, but what about Coach Thurmond? Isn't he scheduled to be the honoree?"

Melanie flashed her Blackberry at me, as if it held the answers to all the questions in the universe. "You didn't hear? Just got a text this morning. Coach Thurmond is not going to be available. Something about steroid use in his sprinters. Seems the chemistry teacher knew his way around the lab. Very messy. But it explains all the record-breaking performances. Anyway, we're moving on. And you, Dr. O'Neill, would be a heroic honoree. Get it? Heroic?"

Here comes The Branding. I could tell from previous experience with Melanie *(Don't think of this as a playgroup. This is The Pathway to a Shining Future!)* that she'd re-thought the entire benefit while Patrick was lecturing. That's why she wasn't checking her Blackberry; she was brainstorming with herself!

"We could use Troy as a leitmotif for invitations, decorating, food. We could create a Greek temple at the Huntington. Huge swaths of white fabric billowing in the wind. Golden accents, glorious food from the Mediterranean. And Dr. O'Neill accepting the honors on behalf of schoolchildren everywhere, for his inspirational work. And here's the business part—it's a chance for Dr. O'Neill to meet eager donors for his foundation. It would be spectacular."

I had to give it to Melanie—other than the fact that the Trojans weren't actually Greek, it would be spectacular. One look at Candy and Tina told me that they were blown away by the speed at which Melanie operated. This morning? Local hero Rex Thurmond. By lunchtime, Melanie was riding in on a Trojan Horse.

And she was right. I had to back her up on this one. Patrick needed the exposure. And I needed a cause.

"Melanie, that is a wonderful idea." I turned to a skeptical Patrick. "The event draws everybody. And generates a ton of press, national press even—*Town & Country* and the *New York Times*. Great visibility for your work and your foundation. You might want to do it. I mean, you might want to *accept the honor*."

Patrick looked around at the circle of eager committee members awaiting his response. "I have two questions. When is it?"

"The end of May. Plenty of time to get your tux. Will you still be in town?" Melanie cooed.

Patrick nodded.

"What's the second question?"

"Helen, will you be my date?"

I've never liked convertibles with the wind, the noise and the constant need to replenish sunscreen on my Oregonian skin. But I enjoyed the ride to Laguna Beach with Patrick in his rented Pontiac Solstice. It was the most spontaneous thing I'd done since the latter days of the Clinton administration. And it involved bikini waxing, which I discovered was quite painful.

After the shocker at school, Patrick declared that we had to get "back to work immediately." Candy was suspicious, I could tell by her stink eye. And by the text she sent immediately after I left the scene. Short and elegant: WTF?

WTF was right. WTF was I doing in a convertible, speeding along Pacific Coast Highway with Nubby Sweater? I was somebody's mother, a recent widow. A member of Save the Deodars. This wasn't me.

Patrick had pulled the bait-and-switch in the parking lot, after commenting that my friends were "a little intense" and "we needed a breather" after the success of the presentation. He tossed me a black baseball cap with a big orange "P," the only reference he had ever made to his prestigious academic background, and declared, "Put this on. We're going to the beach."

I took the hat and hopped in the car. He was my ride and my boss. I had no choice, right?

"Why Laguna?" I shouted above the music, Elvis Costello circa 1985. Laguna Beach was a wealthy, artsy town tucked away on the coast of Orange County. Its charm was genuine, protected by an isolated location and incredibly high real estate costs. Sometimes the high cliffs collapsed under mudslides and fires, sending zillion-dollar homes into the ocean, but when the weather was good, it was hard to beat. Like today.

"It reminds me of home," Patrick shouted back. He even looked good in a worn Arsenal cap.

"What home?" He did live in several places: Athens in the winter and Troy in the summer.

"All of them."

"A bottle of the pinot grigio and the sand dabs to start, please. Then we'll have the steamed mussels and shrimp skewers. And a caprese salad to share. Can you make that a little bigger than usual? Oh, and some water?" Patrick ordered without hesitation, then as an afterthought, added, "Do you like fish?"

I nodded, because blurting out "Fish is good" would have sounded as juvenile as I felt, like a freshman girl at the senior prom. What was happening here? Boundary-infringement!

We were seated on the patio of Casa de Sol, a spectacular cliffside restaurant high above the main beach in Laguna. The water below was wine-dark; in the distance, dolphins bobbed in the waves. Once again, I was grateful for Tina's help in putting together Work Outfit #2: navy blue wide-legged pants and a white boat-neck sweater, perfect for the setting and for my emerging collarbones.

Patrick put down the menu and looked out at the ocean. "I love this place. As a kid, I spent one summer here while my dad did some work in Irvine, and I've never forgotten it."

That detail didn't make his Wikipedia page. "I'm surprised. You've got some pretty great beaches in your part of the world."

"Well, it was the place and the time. I was about your son's age. And I discovered girls. And they don't make 'em any cuter than they do in California."

"I thought Homer was your only companion?" I teased, referring to the portrait of the lonely, studious boy he'd painted in the presentation.

"Busted. I had Homer, California girls and the Clash."

The wine arrived, and while the tan, blond waiter made a show of opening the bottle, I studied Patrick, who chatted with the waiter as if they'd known each other for years. He had a quality I admired: being at home wherever he went. You can't fake that. At least I couldn't, not for the last fifteen years and not now when my insides were churning like the Pacific.

"Yamas!" Patrick said, lifting his glass in my direction. To our health. *Please don't let mine include hyperventilation due to my extreme uncoolness.*

He settled into his chair and his wine, then spoke. "How did you know what I was going to say in that presentation? The PowerPoint. I gave you some slides and a rough outline. It was like you read my mind." He set his glass down and leaned forward, as if he wanted to gauge my reaction. "You seem to do that a lot. How?"

Cyberstalking. But that seemed like a bad answer.

"It was nothing. I did a little research. Used a little imagination."

"But you nailed me. My story. You had just the right visuals, the right music, without knowing exactly what I was going to say."

Cyberstalking again. And the fact that your story is my story: finding a place in another time. I had your dream, only I didn't have your guts, so I bailed. Well, I bailed for love, but mainly I just bailed. But I couldn't tell him all that. The disclosure would be too much and the sun and the wine were already making my face flush. "Hey, I saw *Raiders of the Lost Ark*, too. Every kid wanted to be Indy. You just actually did it. That's an easy story to tell."

"Could you read your husband's mind, too? Did you have that connection with him?"

Whoa, not what I expected. "No, not really. Merritt wasn't easy to read. His story wasn't that familiar to me. Even after many years of marriage."

Now I didn't just *feel* uncomfortable, I *was* uncomfortable. Don't talk about him! I wanted to scream. I don't want to think about him now.

Obviously, Patrick perceived my discomfort. "I'm sorry. I shouldn't have asked. You just seem very different than those women I met today. And I was wondering how you got to Pasadena, to where you are."

"I'm not that different than those women. Well, other than the fact that I hatched from a giant egg."

Patrick laughed sharply, "Ah, like Helen of Troy. Or at least, that's how one of her origin mythologies goes. Nice reference. I had no idea you shared her unusual birth."

"Yes, well, that type of thing still happens in central Oregon. My parents were very understanding. They seemed to have been conceived on another planet, so they didn't mind the egg."

Patrick laughed again. "Hence the name?"

"Actually, I was named after Mount St. Helens."

"The volcano? You were not."

"I was too. Only, it was just a mount when I was born. Top was still on."

"Do you have a sister named Vesuvius?"

"No, but my brother is named after a river. The Deschutes. Not Styx."

Phew, subject changed. And mercifully, the waiter arrived with the sand dabs, lightly breaded and sautéed, to put the subject of Merritt away entirely. He refilled my wine glass despite my slight objections.

"I think I'm picking up on something in the journals," I started to explain, but was cut off.

"You are a slave driver! You know, archaeologists like to talk about things other than archaeology."

"I know. I'm not quizzing you on your trowel preferences. But I think this is kind of juicy." Now I leaned forward to gauge Patrick's reaction. "I think our boy Rudy is developing a thing for his uncle's young wife."

"Really? Are you sure?"

"Think about it; it makes sense. Our Rudy is only 23, much closer in age to Sophia, who's barely out of her teens, than his uncle. And he's swept up in the whole adventure of the excavation. He appears to be dazzled by her, even before they officially meet. He fantasizes about what she'll be wearing, how she smells. Then he describes the first meeting in great detail. He notes everything about her clothes, her skin. He describes her eyes as 'liquid amber, burning into my soul.' He is clearly taken with her."

"Didn't he give a loving description of the venison jerky, too?" Patrick said, giving me the business, reaching for a piece of rosemary foccacia that had just arrived along with the rest of the meal. "I mean, from your notes, the kid seems to go on and on about everything."

I conceded, "Yes, he did enjoy the jerky. But he refers to her as "lovely Sophia" or sometimes just S."

"Take it from me, men do a lot of really stupid things when they are 23."

Obviously, a reference to his marriage to Artsy Wife, but I let it go. "Well, it's very romantic, if you ask me."

"There you go again with the romance. The qualifier 'romantic' goes over very well in academic journals. That's persuasive research. I think if I was able to prove that Rudy and Sophia were having a fling, then the whole rest of my theory about Troy being a major trading center well into the Middle Ages would just fall into place." Patrick was clearly having fun with this topic. "Have you been reading a lot of romance novels? Is that your inspiration for this?"

"Yes, that's what lonely research assistants do in the middle of the night. Read romance novels and reinterpret history based on bodice-ripping fantasies." Now I was having fun. Whoops, too much wine. "It *could* be important."

"How? Why? The personal life of the archaeologist shouldn't actually affect the archaeology."

"What about that bogus Priam's Treasure find? The stash of

artifacts, the ones that included the gold necklace and earrings that Schliemann claimed to find at Troy and draped around Sophia's neck. It was a classic PR move back before there was PR! It could explain why Schliemann might trump up something so spectacular. Maybe he had to win his wife back from hot, ripped Rudy. He planted the necklace, dug it up, plopped it on his young wife's neck, took the photo that made Sophia famous all over the world and won his wife back. You never know."

"It's never been proven that the necklace was definitively bogus."

"But I bet you'll lay awake tonight thinking that it might be," I said triumphantly, reaching for another mussel.

"Helen, my work is not the slightest bit romantic. It's based upon ground-penetrating radar surveys, 3-D laser scanning and electromagnetic soil analysis."

"So, Dr. Soil Analysis, how do you explain the tattoo of Achilles's shield?" I pointed to his forearm, a celestial body peeking out from underneath his rolled sleeve. I launched into some Homer. *"The earth, the heavens, the sea, the untiring sun, the moon at the full.* That's some heroic ink you have there."

Patrick raised his eyebrows in surprise. "Too much ouzo."

I carried on. "History is full of love affairs that altered the course of world events. You might not want to dismiss my theory out of hand. Let's face it, you'd be out of a job if Paris hadn't fallen so hard for Helen and kidnapped her and brought her to Troy." I was feeling pretty smug about that comment. "There'd be no Troy at Troy. What would you be doing?"

Just then the waiter appeared, to clear our plates and pour the last of the wine into our glasses. "Can I get you anything else? More wine?"

Please God, no. It was 2:30 in the afternoon. And I was already over my limit.

Patrick piped up, "I think we'll have the chocolate soufflé for two and some strong coffee."

"Just to let you know, the soufflé will take about a half hour," the waiter said, in a tone that suggested he was scheduled to get off his shift and would prefer if we canceled our order so he could surf.

"Perfect. That gives me just about enough time to convince my assistant here that her feminist interpretation of *poor* Helen as a victim, kidnapped and dragged to Troy, is tired and tedious. She just got sick of her cranky, power-hungry husband and left with the young stud. So yes to coffee and yes to the soufflé."

And yes to spending the rest of the afternoon on this patio, debating esoteric subjects with Dr. Patrick O'Neill.

It was well after 9 p.m. when we arrived at the Huntington after our five-hour lunch and the long drive back. We'd kept the top down on the dark drive home and didn't say much. We were talked out in the best way. Patrick pulled in next to my car, alone in the vast parking lot.

We both got out of the car, slightly stiff from the drive and the walk down the beach after lunch to work off the wine. I felt sandy and salty with a touch of sunburn, the same satisfied feeling as when I was a kid after a day on the Oregon coast. Beach-washed, my mom used to call it.

Patrick looked and smelled the same. Beach-washed.

I handed him his baseball cap, "Thank you. That was ... just what I needed."

He took the cap and held my eyes for a second. Everything about that moment seemed slow and filled with possibilities. But I was paralyzed with the strangeness of the situation. It had been so long since I'd felt this kind of anticipation, this ache in my chest from wanting someone. But it seemed so soon, too soon. I couldn't have made a good decision to save my life.

What happened next was all up to him.

He leaned in, the salt air clinging to his shirt and skin, and he brushed my cheeks with his lips. "You were right. I will be up all night," he said softly, his mouth just inches from my ear. "Thinking about ... those journals. And other things."

Then he moved his mouth toward mine and kissed me full. It was soft and strong at the same time. His rough hands moved from my face to my neck, down my shoulders to the small of my back. And stayed there while I returned the kiss.

A first kiss. I'd forgotten that feeling.

Patrick pushed me back gently against the car door, leaning his full weight into my body. I struggled to stay in the moment, enjoying the pressure of his lean legs against my own. His hands around my waist now. His lips, mine.

But my mind was racing. *Don't think about everything else in your life. Stay here. With this man.*

But I faltered. I withdrew slightly and he noticed.

He stepped back to gauge my reaction. My God, he was something. *What was my problem?*

He was unflustered. That made one of us. He reached out and smoothed my hair. "Thank you for today, Helen."

No, really, thank you, I wanted to shout. *You brought me back from the dead.* But instead, I whispered, "You're welcome." Which made him laugh.

The laugh got me. Okay, paralysis lifted. All systems go! Now I had the wherewithal to run my hands all over his chest and take him down in the parking lot. But he was already backing away, backing off for now.

I let him go. I opened my car door and found my voice. "See you in the morning. I'll be in a little late."

Patrick nodded. "Take your time, Helen. No rush."

Why didn't I rush? Damn, I wanted that moment back.

I hadn't thought about having sex since Merritt's death. I'd thought plenty about *not* having sex. As in, who would ever have sex with me, a 40-year-old mother with pragmatic panties and unreliable personal grooming habits, when there are so many younger women with Pilates abs and regular waxing appointments to have sex with?

Or, please don't make me start online dating. I don't want to sit through all those horrible coffee dates, like Candy does, just to meet someone who might someday touch me with something that does not have a battery.

Those were the kind of sexy thoughts I'd been having for months. But actually wanting to have sex with someone? It hadn't crossed my mind until tonight.

And now, because I am me, I went right from a blissful, "I can't believe he kissed me!" feeling to complete panic. Lying in bed, I became consumed with the logistics of me having sex with my boss. Where? How? Was that wise? Ethical? What if it was awful and we had to go back to working in the honeymoon suite after terrible sex?

Oh my God, what if *I* was terrible at sex? Maybe that's why Merritt…?

Nope, not going there. Not. Going. There. I'd already spent weeks lying awake at night replaying the Merritt/Helen sex tapes in my mind. And truthfully, I thought I'd kept up my end of the bargain over the course of our marriage. Our attraction was immediate and exciting. I had no hangups in that department, and Merritt had a few, so I was an ideal partner. Sex was the glue in the early days of our relationship.

But were we crazy like newlyweds after Aiden and the infertility treatments and my few extra pounds? No. My guess is that nobody I knew had that kind of married sex life. But I put out on a regular basis. Merritt never lodged any formal complaints about frequency. Even on days when we had nothing to say to each other, we usually had something we'd want to do to each other.

So I surmised in my own late-night self-analysis that the affair with Shelly Sleazy was more about midlife than sex. He wanted younger, shinier and thinner, but not sexier. That's what I'd been telling myself for months, and that's what I was sticking with.

If someone like Patrick found me attractive, obviously I was not unsexy in the empirical sense. Men like free-spiritedness, right? I still had that left over from my Oregon days, sort of. And every once in a while, I'd catch one of the dads at school looking down my shirt at my real, unadulterated breasts. That counted for something, right? So, damn, why did I hesitate with Patrick? Maybe I'm just not a hookup kinda girl.

Sleep was a joke. I turned on the light and flipped open my laptop. I brought up the newly scanned pages from Volume XIV. Maybe Rudy and Sophia were getting lucky under the Trojan moon. That would take my mind off of Nubby Sweater.

Maybe.

CHAPTER 13

"Yes, they were having sex!" I announced triumphantly as I waltzed through the door of Scholars' Cottage #7 in Work Outfit #6. An early morning consult with Tina resulted in what she called "a fresh new take on the safari look." Tina's photographic memory of other people's wardrobes gave her the ability to style over the phone. (*"You know that khaki jacket with all the pockets you used to wear after Aiden was born? Do you still have that?"*) I thought I looked pretty cute in my fitted DKNY khaki jacket circa 1997, A-line dark brown linen skirt and *Out of Africa* boots. My black belt, one Candy left at my house a year ago after too many margaritas, had a touch of zebra print. I even dug up a chunky wooden necklace that said "world traveler." Or so I thought.

I was feeling a sort of *joie de vivre* that I hadn't felt in years, despite getting only five hours sleep. The journals were as juicy as I had predicted, and I couldn't wait to share the news with Patrick, so for emphasis I added, "Totally doing it!"

"Who is totally doing it?" responded a female voice, oozing with culture and an accent belonging to some remote, long-forgotten corner of the British Empire.

I dropped my scones.

"Oh, I'm sorry. I thought, I mean, that was for Patrick. Dr. O'Neill. Dr. Patrick O'Neill," I bumbled, thrown by every aspect of this woman. Her wild, dark hair pulled back in a printed scarf, her armful of silver bangles, her tanned, slim shoulders and big hoop earrings. Damn, if she wasn't in a khaki jacket and a linen skirt, too. Her "fresh new take on the safari look" was much more authentic than mine. She was a knockout.

And vaguely familiar, I realized, just as Patrick opened the door carrying a tray of coffees and more baked goods.

"Helen, you're here," Patrick said, flashing an award-winning smile. "Great, there's someone I want you to meet."

"Helen Castor? I knew that was you under that flak jacket. Helen, It's me. Annabeth!"

Simultaneous light bulb and dagger through my heart!

Dear God, this would be the perfect time for that big earthquake the folks at Caltech have been predicting to swallow up the Huntington and me. Especially me. Right now, so I don't have to face questions from my college nemesis Annabeth Sturges. *Of course*, the silver bangles, the hair, that great skin. She hadn't changed one damn bit, except to become even more beautiful and exotic.

But what was with the accent? She didn't have that in college. She was from Cottage Grove, Oregon, not Rhodesia!

"Annabeth? I knew you looked familiar! Wow, Annabeth! Gosh...."

Annabeth Sturges was the one woman at Willamette who could make me feel stupid and inadequate in every way. She was two years behind me in school but light years ahead of me in sophistication, ability and life experience. Her parents had been missionaries and they'd traveled all over the world, spreading the Word and building schools. While her parents tended to their flock, Annabeth immersed herself in local languages, cultures, art history, mythology. She was a freaking sponge for information, the perfect archaeology student. I studied archaeology; she absorbed it. Her parents sent her to Willamette because of the religion tradition; Annabeth stayed because she had half the male population eating out of her hands. And probably other things.

I was wildly jealous of her. She was wildly oblivious to my jealousy. She may have been my nemesis, but I was not hers.

Now we were standing in the same room after nearly two decades. She looked like Catherine Zeta-Jones with a doctorate.

Nothing like insecurity to take me right back to my college days. I met her genuine hug with trepidation.

Patrick, handing out coffees to all, jumped in, "You two know each other. How?"

Annabeth shot out of the gate with the first answer. Teacher's pet. "Helen and I went to college together. She was my hero, a couple of years ahead of me in the Classics department at Willamette. Professors loved Helen. So thorough. She studied so much harder than I did. Of course, after graduation she went on that fellowship at Corinth. Then grad school at Berkeley, right? And we kinda lost touch. And now here you are! In Patrick's office. Stone me!"

Faux Brit vocab to match the faux Brit accent. Brilliant.

My turn. Patrick's mouth was wide open as the hidden details of my academic resume came pouring out of such an unlikely source. I had nowhere to go to make this end well. "It sure has been a long time."

I knew Annabeth was dying for me to ask about her meteoric career. But I couldn't find the good manners. After I got married, I tried to keep up with my former classmates in the very small world of classical archaeology. But, as my motivation for finishing my thesis diminished, so did my curiosity about others. I'd made a point not to google anyone from my former field; I didn't want to know about their successes. It was too depressing. Annabeth was on the top of that Do Not Google list.

So she tried again. "Are you working with Patrick?"

"Helen's my research assistant on this project. She was at the Huntington before I arrived," Patrick answered in a tight voice. His expression was stunned. "You worked at Corinth with Guy Summers? What did you study at Berkeley?"

Annabeth let out a giant guffaw, as if Patrick was quite the kidder. "Well, I don't know, Dr. Oblivious, maybe archaeology! She is your R.A.! If you didn't know that, how did she get the job? The same way I got mine with you at Troy?" Then she winked at

Patrick and let out another randy laugh.

The image of the two of them naked in a trench popped into my head.

The barrage just kept coming. "Did you ever finish your thesis? I thought I heard that you didn't. Didn't you leave Berkeley to get married or something?"

From her tone, I surmised that she truly did not know about my academic decline. I'd done a good job of staying undercover.

"Yes, I got married and no, I never finished my thesis. Life, you know—life happens." I couldn't look at Patrick. I felt like the grad school version of Hester Prynne with a giant "F" on my chest. Time to change the subject. "How do the two of you know each other?"

"Princeton, then Oxford for post-doc, then, of course, working at Troy with Patrick. Now I'm at UCSB teaching during the school year and in Greece during the summer," Annabeth said, as if we all could have such a resume with a little effort. Did she pick up the accent at Oxford? Lame. "Patrick was my professor, then my advisor, then my colleague. We've been in touch ever since. Right, handsome?"

"Yeah. Annabeth is the one I went to visit in Santa Barbara. Her research is groundbreaking, very important."

Yeah, I bet her *research* is amazing, I thought. Although, in fairness, Patrick seemed as uncomfortable as I was. This whole encounter couldn't end soon enough for either of us.

Annabeth appeared to be enjoying the moment immensely. Like she really had been wondering what happened to me. "Helen, next time I'm here, let's catch up for real. We've got so much gossip to trade about everyone from school. Unfortunately, I've got to be off. I have an afternoon class, but I had some exciting news to share with Patrick in person, so I forced myself on him today. We had a lovely morning, didn't we?"

They must have had sex on the couch right here in the cottage. I thought I was going to be sick. "Let's! Catching up sounds great."

"Patrick has my contact information. Thank you for everything, as usual, darling," Annabeth said theatrically, wrapping
her arms around Patrick's elbow. "Walk me to my car. Then you
must rush right back, because Helen has some exciting news
about people having sex! Right, Helen?"

When he returned, Patrick did not appear to be in the mood
to discuss sex, either the possibility of us having sex or the cer-
titude of Rudy and Sophia getting busy. Very, very busy, as I'd
learned last night.

His face was stern, like I was a naughty child who had disappointed him greatly.

"So, small world, huh?" My attempt at humor did not please
him.

"Why didn't you tell me you'd been at Berkeley? You worked
at Corinth with one of my best friends, Guy Summers. You know
Annabeth. You let me think for a month that you were, you
were...." He struggled for the right words. The right words were
clearly *a bored Pasadena housewife,* but he couldn't say that. So
he said, "You were ... *new* to all this. But you're not. You have
better credentials than most of my research assistants in Athens.
No wonder you've accomplished twice as much in half the time.
Why didn't you tell me?"

His confusion seemed so genuine that a smart answer like
"You never asked" seemed the wrong tack to take. So I did what
I do best: I rambled. "I didn't think it was that important. Please
understand— Berkeley, Corinth, Annabeth—that is like another
lifetime to me, Patrick. I left grad school for Merritt and Pasadena. Do you think I'm proud of that? I dropped out of a prestigious program to get married and have kids and be a docent, for
God's sake, when I wanted to be a professor. I wanted to be like
you. To be like Annabeth. That's not something you tell your new

boss when he has this huge impressive resume and a Facebook fan site."

I saw his face soften with a glimmer of understanding, so I rambled on. "Patrick, I was a grad student fifteen years ago. Now I'm just a single mother who likes history. That's who I am and that's the person you thought you were hiring. And we both know that."

Recognition flashed on Patrick's face. Then I saw it all clearly: I was his project as much as the Schliemann Journals. He wanted to free me from my domestic shackles by teaching me about Troy, by saturating my intellect. I wasn't some easy mark, like the lovestruck shovel bums who populated his dig site every summer or the junior-year-abroad students at the American School in Athens. I was a whole new breed: the lonely widow! How epic! How Homeric! How positively Penelope! He was going to save me from my tragic self.

Just like Merritt had saved me from my poor academic self by bringing me to Pasadena.

Patrick crossed the room purposefully, gesticulating with his latte for emphasis. "Now I know how you identified my Achilles's shield in Laguna. Quoting the *Iliad* to me. I thought that was pretty sharp. You let me go on and on about my work and my research. The lunches, the dinner, the endless conversations about Homer, the Greeks, Helen of Troy. All the background information that you must have already known. I feel like an idiot."

I was getting angry. Who did this guy think he was? "Because you wasted your time?"

"No," he said, looking straight into my eyes. "Because I wasted your time."

Now I felt like the idiot. I barely knew what to say.

"Patrick, the last month wasn't wasted. Truly. It was the fifteen years before that I wasted. But not the last month."

Silence. A big, fat, I-can't-believe-I-said-that silence.

Then, the familiar call of Sarah White, Press Officer with

Extraordinarily Bad Timing. "Yoo-hoo! C'est moi."

I instinctively smoothed out Work Outfit #6 and fluffed my hair. Patrick recovered without any grooming necessary. "Come on in!"

Sarah glided into the cottage. "I hope I'm not interrupting any important research. Or maybe I do, because that's what I came to ask you about." She laughed at her own joke, mostly from nerves.

Patrick rebounded quickly, ease seeping back into his manner, almost as if he was relieved at Sarah's appearance. "What can we help you with, Sarah?"

"I just got a call from someone at that TV channel, the history one. I had to rush right over. From a producer on a new show called *The Dirty Archaeologist*! Isn't that a great title? So racy!"

"And they'd like me to co-host?" Patrick deadpanned. I laughed, despite the fact that I wanted to be mad at Patrick. Not that he deserved my anger. But it was a conditioned response, from years of post-tiff silent treatment with Merritt. But I couldn't pull it off. It felt all wrong with Patrick.

"No, apparently they were wondering about your research. Isn't that odd? This producer knew about the Schliemann Journals project. He said he'd heard through the grapevine that there may be some astonishing news. And they'd love to break the story on the premier episode of *The Dirty Archaeologist*!"

I was dumbfounded. As far as I knew, the only conversations about the Schliemann Journals had occurred between Patrick and myself. And he didn't even seem that interested. Who else could have known about the affair? Maybe Patrick had talked about the research to others, but it seemed unlikely. He was so focused on raising money for the foundation. Quite a mystery.

Sarah stared at Patrick, waiting for a response. I thought her Chanel headband might pop off her head with anticipation. "Well? What's in those journals that has *The Dirty Archaeologist* so, so … excited?"

"I'm going to let Helen tell you." Patrick leaned back in his chair for emphasis. Was this payback? Oh, yes. He wanted to put me on the spot, like I'd put him on the spot with Annabeth. "Helen. Didn't you come bursting in here this morning to tell me something about the journals?"

I tried not to make a mess of it. "It's clear from the diaries that Rudolph Schliemann and his very young step-aunt, Sophia, were having a torrid affair. And once they started sleeping together, you can forget any actual information about the excavation or the archaeological methodology." I was trying to put it delicately, for my sake more than Sarah's. Rudy's journals were just downright dirty. Which, of course, made me think of Annabeth and Patrick in a Trojan trench. Any kind of confidence I felt as I walked in the door that morning was gone. Kaput. Replaced by a keen awareness of my own lack of sexual prowess, despite my animal-print belt. So I stalled and then offered, "Let me just say that in the journals, there's a lot of heaving breasts, but not too much heaving of dirt."

Patrick shook his head. "Wow! That's some serious scholarship."

"Really!" Shock registered on Sarah's face. Was it the shock that her high-prestige research project had devolved into ancient adult entertainment? Not exactly the sort of thing that makes great press for the Huntington. But then, Sarah Longlegs surprised me. "This is fantastic! Talk about a dirty archaeologist! I love it. We were just saying at the board meeting last week that it would be great if we had some projects here that weren't so super stuffy. Even the director said that we need something sexy. Sounds like we've got one!"

I think I blushed a tad.

"Your hunch was right, Helen," Patrick conceded. "But let's be clear, it's not exactly going to change the entire course of Trojan history. That being said, it's worth delving into a little bit deeper. There may be something that emerges, other than heaving breasts."

Definitely blushed at that. Okay, so it wasn't exactly the academic breakthrough I'd envisioned for myself, but it was *something*. And it had gotten Patrick's attention.

"Can I tell them the interview is a go? Is there enough in the journals to make for a scintillating story?" Sarah asked, staring directly at Patrick. Clearly, I was not going to be part of the PR plan. He was the telegenic Ph.D.; I was just the research assistant in khaki. "Will you be ready to shoot with them in six weeks? Can you pull something semi-academic together by then? That's the date they need to do the interview."

"Will we be ready, Helen?" Patrick challenged me.

"I'll need to finish scanning the journals and transcribing them, but I think I can get you up to speed on everything you need, Dr. O'Neill."

I added the "Doctor" for effect. It had none.

"If Helen can finish scanning the journals and pulling some things together for me, I can make this work. We may need some extra help doing the grunt work so I can put Helen on some additional research."

Sarah looked very pleased. "Whatever you need. This *and* the benefit honor. You've certainly created quite a buzz for yourself, Patrick. I'll call the producer. Get ready to get dirty. Oh, and we've scheduled your Distinguished Scholar lecture here at the Huntington for the middle of May, right before you go back to Athens. I'll send you an e-mail with the date. I'll copy Helen, too. So exciting!" With that she practically skipped out the door.

Patrick's delightful demeanor vanished as soon as Sarah was gone. Obviously, my secret resume was still on his mind. "We have a lot of work to do. It's a juicy story, yes. But I'll need to work hard to make the fact that Heinrich Schliemann was nothing but a cuckolded husband relevant to my research. I'm sure you can see that. We can't really afford any distractions over the next few weeks."

By "distractions," Patrick clearly meant long lunches with wine, drives by the ocean and make-out sessions in the parking lot. Hopefully, it meant early morning "meetings" with Anna-beth, too.

"Got it. Of course. I understand," I said with what I hoped was a care-free, I'm cool-with-that attitude. The exact opposite of what I was feeling. "I wonder who the Dirty Archaeologist is? And how did they find out about what was in the journals?"

Patrick crossed his arms over his chest, looking smug. "You didn't guess?"

I shook my head.

"It's Annabeth. And you told her."

CHAPTER 14

"You are shrinking before our very eyes. It's like you're a college girl in love." Tina huffed, as we pounded around the Rose Bowl in our matching black tights, white hoodies and baseball caps.

I colored self-consciously. I hadn't breathed a word about my kiss with Patrick to Candy and Tina. Patrick, I maintained to all, was my boss and nothing more. Frankly, I wasn't entirely comfortable with the whole Merry Widow scenario myself. Any hint of indiscretion could get completely blown out of proportion in a town like Pasadena. Even though Candy and Tina knew about Merritt's affair, the rest of my social circle, including my in-laws, did not. And hardliners on the subject would still want an acceptable year of mourning before any other dalliances, especially for a woman. Plus, there was Aiden, always Aiden. So what made Tina say that? *Did she know somehow?*

Candy barked in agreement, "Yes. I'm sorry for your loss and all that, but look at you! Fabulous."

Phew, a comment about my body-fat percentage, not my guilty conscience.

Candy continued, "Oh! I just thought of a great slide show for candydish! Dramatic Death and Divorce Weight Loss pictures! People would love that. Have you seen Suzy Ivers? She is a stick since Bill left with his law partner. Same with Jamilla Hopkins after Beau split. Down like four sizes. I saw her in the petite section at Nordy's the other day. *Look at me*, she screamed in the dressing room. *I'm shopping with all the Asian women! I look like Jada Pinkett Smith!* You look just as good, Helen. I have my camera in the car. Would you mind?"

"You're kidding, right?" I was flattered, but not enough to be lumped in with Suzy Ivers. Yes, I had seen Jamilla at Whole Foods (*I was just buying the store brands!*) and she did look fantastic. I suspected an eye lift along with the weight loss, but I kept that to myself. Candy would put that on candysdish.com as a blind item in the "Surgeries We Suspect" column. Furthermore, Suzy had lap-band surgery post-divorce and that didn't seem in the spirit of the Misery Weight Loss method. "This is not exactly my best look!"

Tina agreed. "Get some shots at the benefit. You'll be dolled up. Have you gotten your dress yet, Helen?"

I love my friends, I thought. I truly do. But they had absolutely no idea what the last three weeks of my life had been like. It had been a rollercoaster of preparing serious academic work and navigating unusual emotional territory. Trying to analyze the Schliemann Journals and preparing all the backup material for the producers of *The Dirty Archaeologist* while feigning disinterest in Patrick every time he showed up in another nubby sweater *(how many could one archaeologist own?)* was exhausting. Throw in the everyday stress of packing, moving, working through Rita the Armenian's punch list, fielding daily phone calls from Mitsy about Ignatius and dealing with a teenager facing an uncertain academic future, and the result was complete stress.

Another dress size down.

I was a machine with no time for contemplation, except for the 45 minutes where I excused myself to "take a power walk" around the gardens at work so I wouldn't have to face the awkward lunch hour with Patrick. I was determined to adhere to the "no distractions" policy. Lunch equals distraction. So I let him go to Veritas alone while I tried to walk away my impending sense of doom:

What if the sexy theory damages Patrick's reputation?
What if Annabeth uncovers flaws in my research?

What if Patrick finds me doodling "HF hearts PO" on my notebook?

The fact that I could squeeze in the time for today's three-mile trip around the Rose Bowl was a testament to friendship, not work/life balance. *So, no Tina, I haven't summoned the energy to contemplate evening wear.*

But clearly, Tina had.

"Hello? Helen, have you gotten your dress yet?" Tina demanded, knocking me out of my reverie. "All the good ones may be gone. You *are* going with the guest of honor. You will be photographed. Guaranteed. And not just by Candy. By actual press."

"Hey, I'm actual press!" Candy fired back. "As much as *Us* magazine, anyway."

"Maybe the black one with the rhinestone buttons will work?" I suggested. A dress I'd worn nine million times over the past decade. It had the timelessness of a St. John's Knits, or so I thought. And the miracle fabric seemed to grow and shrink along with my waistline.

Candy's response? The eye roll/groan combo with uplifted hands.

Tina stopped dead in her tracks, risking a knee injury for the cause of fashion. "No. No, no, no. You are not hauling that thing out of your closet. Not when you look so great and you have such a hot date. In fact, when you move, you are leaving that for the Gays. I'm sure their lovely 65-year-old mother will enjoy wearing it to movie premieres. I will take charge of this. I need something to take my mind off the fact that the admissions letters will be arriving on Saturday. This is perfect. I'll be your personal shopper. Leave it to me."

Ah, yes, Saturday was D-Day in Pasadena. Decision Day. Private-school admissions letters—from preschool to high school—would be arriving in mailboxes on Saturday. Every school in the area mailed the letters on Friday, a result of collusion, or as the admissions directors preferred to call it, "a long-standing agreement." Thanks to the most efficient postal service in America, on Saturday, the word would be out about the chosen few and the not-so-chosen many.

I'll never forget the day Aiden got his acceptance letter to Millington nine years earlier. Merritt had only allowed me to apply to one school, Millington, his alma mater. I thought it was risky, considering that Aiden was a wiggly boy and everybody *knows* that schools like placid, dull boys. By mid-afternoon, still no letter. I was so distraught that I tracked down the mailman two streets over, demanding my mail. The Millington envelope was large and thick. I felt a gigantic sense of relief, then a tiny bit of smugness once the good news set in. I'd been so worried that Aiden might be rejected because of his average "fine motor skills" and reckless "hopping on one foot" during the kindergarten testing.

Merritt comforted me with mocking. "Really, Helen. This is Pasadena. It's not a meritocracy. He's a Fairchild. They don't give a fuck if he can hop. They give a fuck if we can donate a lot of money."

But as I've learned over the last few months, being a Fairchild isn't a guarantee for a charmed life. And despite the fact that I'd pulled out all the stops after Aiden's disastrous interview with pleading calls to Ignatius alum and trustee Billy Owens *and* the all-powerful Monsignor at St. Perpetua's, I was still on edge. And Mitsy's daily phone calls reminding me of the great Fairchild tradition didn't help. But what was Tina worried about? "Tina, Lilly will get into Martindale. You know she will. She's a lock."

"She should, but you never know. There are only 47 spots...."

Oh, here we go: Admissions Math. Parents all over town played this game, a statistical analysis of available spots based on hearsay, innuendo and flat-out misinformation. Admissions Math factored in a complex set of variables including, but not limited to: grades; gender; race; test scores; teacher recommendations; parents' job titles; mother's willingness to head up school auction; whether older sibling got into Brown; minutes played on club soccer team; years of violin lessons; current and previous zip codes; degree of separation from any Hollywood figure; and/or large pool in backyard for school swim parties. Tina had a doctorate in Admissions Math. She'd been handicapping school placements for years with remarkable accuracy. But the stakes were high now that she was computing Lilly's chances.

"… and I heard this year they had 22 siblings applying. Believe it or not, some of the siblings are actually smart, except the mayor's triplets, but they have to get in. So that leaves 25 open spots, and at least six of those will go to scholarship kids. Then I heard half the cast of *Desperate Housewives* is applying their girls, so we're down to, like, fifteen spots. And everybody I know with a half-Asian girl has suddenly decided they want to go to Martindale because of the new Chinese immersion program, so Lilly Chau-Swenson is just one of many halfsies," Tina panted. "For the rest of the spots, I heard Martindale was only looking for lacrosse players, Hispanics and daughters of lesbians."

"Is that a box you can check now on the application? Daughter of Lesbos? I wish I'd known, I would have gone lesbian to get Mariah into Raleigh," Candy cracked. Or, maybe it wasn't a joke, because Candy is the type to go to that extreme for the right high school placement. Candy wanted back in the good graces of the Rose Court. Mariah's admission to Raleigh was the first step in her master plot to have her daughter follow in her footsteps. Candy would never admit it, but she wanted to ride down Colorado Boulevard one more time on New Year's Day. Mariah ascending to the throne was the next best thing.

I laughed at Candy while I reassured Tina. "She'll be fine. Lilly is a smart girl with great test scores, award-winning piano skills and an alumni mother. And she's raising money to build schools in Malawi for all the kids that Madonna couldn't adopt. What more could Martindale want?" Lilly was a perfect a

Martindale girl, through and through. No doubt she would publish a novel by 19, change the world by 22 and get married and trade it all in for a big house in Pasadena by 35. "I kinda think anyone who can pay full tuition has a good shot at getting in these days."

Tina and Candy shot me a look. Had I broken some code, stating the obvious and not playing into their Worry Fest?

"I'm just saying …"

There was an uncomfortable silence for about 1.8 seconds.

"Well … we'll all know in a few days," Tina covered. "I promise to call you guys if you'll call me when you get the letter."

Tina was referring to the common Code of Silence that enshrouded Pasadena on D-Day. Communications between parents, schools and students, so frantic in the days leading up to D-Day, went underground. The schools shut down for a day or two after the letters were mailed, claiming "in service" days so they didn't have to answer the phones or talk to disgruntled parents of the unaccepted. Parents shared information with only trusted friends, but not until the acceptances and rejections were sorted out and rationalized. Some kids even stayed home from school if the news was bad, waiting out the initial few days of their schoolmates' elation, before they returned to class.

"I'm sure we'll all get good news, right?" Candy added. "Our children are perfect."

We all laughed. Uncomfortable moment forgotten. I knew Tina and Candy would know the outcome of the entire Millington graduating eighth grade before sundown on Saturday.

"You know what else is arriving on Saturday?"

"PMS?" said Candy.

"Zappos?" guessed Tina.

"My mother," I said.

CHAPTER 15

The mail hadn't arrived, but Nell Castor had.

"I'll just come down to keep you and Aiden company. You must be lonely," my mother had said over the phone, when she shocked me by announcing her itinerary and flight numbers. Usually I had to pull her away from central Oregon for a visit to Pasadena. She had the gallery to run and my father to manage. And there was always some Sisters Arts Council symposium or speaker series that she was hosting. And of course, there were her meetings and the fact that she was a sponsor to about half the recovery population in town. In the past, I'd made all the arrangements because she had not fully embraced the paperless-ticket concept. Or air travel in general, preferring buses and Volkswagen Vanagons. But this time she had even booked the flights herself. "What good is global warming if the winters just seem to be getting longer?'

I worried that if my mother was feeling colder that meant she was also getting older. But seeing her in my kitchen in her boy-friend jeans, silver clogs and wearable-art wool-and-feather "ki-mono" warmed my spirits and calmed my worries.

"Well, you're very brave," she sighed, taking in the half-packed kitchen and the bare walls of the family room, stripped of the fairly decent California plein air oils that had gone to the dealers for auction. I missed them, too. "You are so very brave. To do everything you've already done. Very brave. Isn't your mother brave, Aiden?"

Despite his discomfort, Aiden did his best to acknowledge my mother's emoting. "Yeah, Nell. Yup. My mom's great."

It was not a Fairchild tradition to call attention to one's feelings or single out others on their good work, other than the occasional, "Good work." One of the reasons I was attracted to Merritt was his lack of willingness to let it all hang out, a trait my family did not share. But I appreciated that Aiden played along when my parents were in town by trying to tap into his feelings. We'd laugh about Crazy Nell Castor later.

"You're both brave. I've been thinking a lot about the two of you during my meditation. I can see you're coping, but not thriving. How about some Kamboucha mushroom tea?"

"What's that?" I asked skeptically. Every time I saw my mother, she was pushing a new super-food or supplement. She may have given up pot, but she still believed in miracle drugs. Echinacea, ginkgo biloba, açai—if it had dubious origins and no medical science behind it, my mother ingested it. And usually long before it went mainstream and ended up in smoothies at Jamba Juice.

"It's a tea with live active cultures made from organic mushrooms. It's like liquid detox. The cleansing properties are, whew, amazing!" she said, whipping around the stove, flicking on burners and nearly setting her feathers aflame. "I'm telling you. Helen, it will renew you inside and out. Look at my skin. And you won't believe the bowel movements. I had to smuggle it through airport security in a three-ounce shampoo bottle."

"Is it tea or a hallucinogenic?" I asked nervously, mainly wanting to change the subject from bowel movements before Aiden started howling with laughter.

"Tea! But it's *alive*! Not dried, but full of active cultures. You cultivate it from starter, like sourdough."

Aiden and I exchanged Crazy Nell looks. "No thanks! I'll stick to orange juice," Aiden called from the couch, putting in his ear buds and returning to what looked like Baz Lurhmann's *Romeo & Juliet* on his laptop. Great, anything to pass that last English test, even if it meant learning Shakespeare from Leonardo DiCaprio.

My mother waved her illicit tea enticingly, her face so hopeful. Who couldn't use a little detox every now and then? "Sure! Why not? Cultivate me a cup." Maybe it would be good for me to have my mother around. I was lonely in the house, and she always brought a certain amount of life with her.

She handed me a mug of what smelled like steaming sauerkraut juice with a touch of mud. "Breathe it in, then drink it down. Then please tell me what the big deal is about going to a private school. Why are you both so uptight? You went to public school, got a wonderful education, and look, now you're an archaeologist."

Maybe it wouldn't be such a picnic having her around. A week sounded like enough time.

To buy a few seconds to form a response that my mother could understand, I took a big swig of the Tea of Great Bowel Movements. How is it possible that it tasted worse than it smelled?

"Slowly! It's a blessing. Receive it as such," my mother said with a straight face and her signature wild hand gestures. "Now, why is this school thing such a big deal?"

I looked at Aiden to make sure he was embedded in the silent world of electronics. I didn't want to make him self-conscious while I explained the private school ethos. The truth is, if he didn't get into Ignatius, he would be going to a local public school. And as much as I hated to admit it, my mother was right. I'd gone to a standard public high school and turned out just fine, at least academically. How could I ever explain to her the attitude in Pasadena—that a public-school education wasn't a risk that most parents who could scrape the money together were willing to take? Or something that longtime Pasadena families like the Fairchilds had not considered since the dawn of time. It was simply not an option.

So I lied. I repeated the prepared speech I had given to the admissions director, the Monsignor and Billy Owens when begging for mercy after the botched interview. "It would mean a lot to Aiden, and to me and all of Merritt's family, if he could continue in the Ignatius tradition. The values that Merritt lived by were the values instilled at Ignatius. Going to Merritt's alma mater would be almost like having his father here by his side."

My mother, her mind detoxed by the tea, was suspicious of my little speech. "Well, I think he's a great kid. And he'll do fine anywhere. Why does he need all the *la-di-da?*"

That's what really bothered my mother: the la-di-da. That was her phrase for all the money, social jockeying and zip code mobilization. La-di-da. One thing I'd always admired about my mother was her inability to see class, in a good way. Maybe it was all the drug-sharing back in the day. *You holding? You're in.* She didn't buy into the notion that money bought respect. She treated everyone with the same warmth and kindness. It had won her dozens of admirers in Sisters, Oregon. In a world full of hypocrites, my mom was the genuine article.

Ironically, my mother-in-law Mitsy was, too, in the complete opposite way. Mitsy believed deeply in the class system, understood exactly where she sat (right on top) and treated everyone as was appropriate to their station. No apologies, no fake smiles. And she had her own legion of admirers. Go figure.

"It's just the way it is here, Mom. I didn't make the rules," I said, trying to end the conversation with a cop-out. But she wasn't letting go.

"You know, you could move back to Oregon. It would be such fun, having you there. Aiden could go to *your* alma mater. There are values there, too."

Yeah, like skipping exams for fresh powder on the mountain or the beginning of hunting season. And let's not forget the bountiful crystal meth production in the suspicious trailers on the outskirts of town. But I held my tongue. Until Aiden perked up on the couch.

"Really, Nell? You want us to move there? Mom, we could do

that! I love Oregon. I'd move there in a second. It's so much fun there. Much more fun than here."

I hadn't heard that kind of enthusiasm for any high school in Pasadena, never mind Ignatius. I wanted to wring my mother's neck. I'd worked so hard to get Aiden through everything: moving out of his childhood home into a smaller place, applying to high school despite his obvious disdain, going to water polo practice come rain or shine, readjusting to life without a father. How could she suggest a gigantic move, like she was suggesting a weekend camping trip?

It would be fun?

Yeah, fun for about five minutes until he realizes that there is no mall, one movie theater and no water polo team. It's a small town in the middle of a small state. Not Pasadena, a small town in a big cosmopolitan city. He'd end up befriending the girl with dyed black hair and a nose ring and her tall, skinny emo boyfriend. What would happen then?

I gave my mother a hard look with raised eyebrows, which she ignored, while I spoke to Aiden in my best faux-understanding tone, "Aiden, let's see what the mailman brings, okay? That's a huge decision that we'll need to talk about when we know all the facts about your future."

My mother pretended she hadn't heard me at all. One of her least admirable qualities, forging ahead with her agenda despite objections from others. Her aging hippie appearance could mask her tenacity. "We'd love to have you, Aiden! And you could get that dog you've always wanted. Everyone has a dog in Sisters!"

Now she was a dead women. A dog was the Holy Grail to Aiden, forbidden because Merritt had allergies.

Just then the tell-tale metallic clank of the antiquated mail slot sounded. From the sound of the struggle, Tran the Mailman was trying to shove a large, fat envelope into the slot designed in 1926 before business-size envelopes were invented. Tran and I had bonded when I hung a red and gold Happy Lunar New Year banner on the front door several years ago. Aiden had made it in class, and Tran, originally from Vietnam, appreciated our cross-cultural efforts. From that initial conversation, we moved on to good restaurants, $20 foot-massage emporiums and the lack of public transportation for the newly immigrated. Tran had a tendency to talk my head off about USC football, so occasionally I hid in the kitchen when he delivered the mail to avoid a half-hour discussion about the merits of the BCS system. But today, he held Aiden's future in his hands. I bolted for the front hall, tore open the door and lunged at the mailman.

"Stop. Just hand me the mail. Don't fold the envelope! I'll take it," I screamed, scaring the poor man into paralysis. He held out the stack of letters and the one glorious fat, white envelope with the Ignatius seal on the front. He was in. *Thank God, he was in! Thank you, Monsignor. And thank you, nice admissions man.* Schools wouldn't send the official calendar along with a rejection, everybody knew that. I hugged the mailman. "Thank you, Tran. Thank you."

"It's a big day, yes?" he said, the mailbag over his shoulder weighing twice his bodyweight. "Everybody happy to see me today. Oh, some not so happy. I understand."

"Well, it's just that some kids are waiting to hear from schools...." I tried to explain, feeling suddenly uncomfortable for my brutish behavior. Poor Tran. La-di-da.

"No, I understand. My son Bernie got into Raleigh. Lots of money for high school but he got scholarship. I was so worried. I sneak into work, look hard and found the envelope at the post office last night!"

Oh my God. Wait till I tell Candy that the mailman's kid got into Raleigh. Second thought, maybe I shouldn't tell her that.

"That's great, Tran. Congratulations to Bernie. You must be very proud."

"Yes. It's hard to get into Raleigh when you are Asian. Because there are so many smart Asian kids that apply. That school could be all Asian kids. White kids have much better chance to get in. Okay, go open your letter. I see you going for Ignatius. Good school. Good luck, Missus."

I shut the heavy oak front door. La-di-da indeed. Then, I focused on the task at hand, calling out in a singsong. "Aiden, there's something here for you!"

"You can open it," he called back. But I didn't. I wasn't going to take this moment away from him. I skipped back into the kitchen and handed Aiden the envelope. I gave my mother the thumbs up. Aiden took it casually, then got distracted with his movie again.

"Open it now. Or I will kill you," I threatened.

"Okay, Mom. Geez!" He tortured me by opening the seal as slowly as possible, then staring at the words on the letter for a long time. Or at least, it seemed like a long time to me.

"What does it say?" my voice escalating with every second.

"The Brothers of Ignatius would like to welcome me into the class of 2013," Aiden announced with weariness in his voice. I was sure it was just an act. Wasn't it? "I'm in. See, you had nothing to worry about, Mom."

Then, I suddenly teared up. Actually, teared up and then sobbed in full, the weight of his future off my shoulders. I did it. He did it. We did it. I gave Aiden a painfully tight hug, but I couldn't speak in between the sobs. He hugged me back, as much as he could, given that I had squashed his arms and the magic letter with my gratitude and enthusiasm.

My mother surrounded us both with her feathers and wool. She rubbed my back as she reassured Aiden, "They are lucky to have you."

Aiden pulled away from the group hug. He'd reached his touchiness limit. "Thanks, Nell. I'd still rather move to Oregon and get a dog."

"Mariah was fucking waitlisted at Raleigh. Can you believe

it? Waitlisted!" Candy's outrage came through the cell phone. "You know who got in? Those freakin' twins—Layla and Madison St. Clair. *Both* of them got in, the Dimwit Twins. And not Mariah! Waitlisted!"

No, now would definitely not be the time to mention the mailman's son to Candy. Or the fact that the Dimwit Twins were both on the Rose Bowl Aquatic Center's National Junior Diving team and Olympic hopefuls. So while their test scores were not outstanding, their degree of difficulty far outweighed Mariah's. That being said, she did have a point. Mariah was a powerhouse. If a school didn't want her, it's a wonder anyone got in.

I was about to offer my condolences when Candy's ire reared up again. "It's me. It's those goddamn Playboy pictures. If this were a school in North Hollywood, they would take Mariah *because* of the pictures. Oh, but not here in Pasadena. Twenty years later and I'm still apologizing. Now she has to pay for my mistake—THAT I MADE AT 19! I hate these people."

By "these people," I think Candy meant the admissions staff, the current parents, the new parents, anyone associated with the Tournament of Roses, pretty much anyone who had ever heard of the nationally renowned Raleigh Prep, including her friends, family and readers. I couldn't say that I blamed her. Plus, I felt awful for Mariah.

"But she's in somewhere, right? Sacred Sisters is a wonderful school where she will get a good education. I know it doesn't have the same, um, the same academic reputation as Raleigh. But those SacSis girls are very solid. Mariah will thrive anywhere. But vent to me, not to Mariah. She needs a positive spin on this," I cautioned.

"You're right. I can't believe it. All that money spent on Millington and for what? To get waitlisted at Raleigh? And SacSis is fine, it's just not, not ... it's not Raleigh. It's a chain school."

"Candy, it's not a chain," I corrected, somewhat annoyed. "The Order of the Sacred Sisters has been around a thousand years. I know you are not Catholic, but please, it's hardly the DeVry Institute. It's a very fine school. And apparently, the nuns have no problem with your past transgressions. That says a lot about their interpretation of forgiveness. You're not getting that at Raleigh."

"It's just ... it used to be a sure thing, getting into Raleigh with good grades from Millington. Now you never know who they'll take." She drew in a big breath and exhaled. I thought of Tran's son, the new ideal Raleigh candidate, whether Candy liked it or not. "Lilly got into Martindale, of course.'"

"I heard. Tina texted me."

"And I assume Aiden got into Ignatius?"

Candy's assumption threw me. I thought everyone perceived my position as precariously as I did. "He did."

"And is he *so thrilled* to be an Ignatius Crusader?"

"He is!" I lied. But I wasn't sure why.

Apparently, Candy bought my false enthusiasm, because she was off. I could barely keep up as she spit out the names of kids and the lists of accepted and rejected schools. Meryl *(Mean like her mother!)* into Martindale. Donovan *(loaded!)* into Ignatius. Aiyala *(Looks like Vanessa Williams and sounds like Michelle Obama! Rose Queen potential!)* into Raleigh. Brandon *(Dumb Jock. How'd he get in?)* into Andover. Carter *(super smart but zero personality)* into Hotchkiss. Kennedi *(I'd go to boarding school, too, with that messy divorce)* into Cate. Cade *(good kid)* into Raleigh, Morgan into Harvard-Westlake *(Ashton Kutcher coaches JV football there)*. Natalie into Crossroads *(How pretentious. Why drive over to the westside every day when we have perfectly fine schools here? You might as well send her to boarding school, stuck in traffic all afternoon!)* And the commentary went on and on. Her sources were everywhere, texting, Facebooking, calling. I tuned it all out.

When had I stopped caring about other people's children?

Then I had an urgent thought. "You're not going to write

about this on candysdish, are you? That would be suicide for the Raleigh waitlist."

"I don't know. It will kill me not to do my annual rundown of kids and school admissions. It's always a big traffic day. Sponsors love it. Last year, when I did that blind item about Katie Entwhistle, of the Perfect Entwhistles, not getting into any kindergarten, the site crashed." Candy was clearly grappling with the duel demons of good for business/bad for family.

I spoke up, "It's not over at Raleigh for Mariah. Don't say something now you might regret. You know the Raleigh people will hear about it. I'm sure they monitor candysdish."

"If they were so worried about my commentary, they should have accepted Mariah. Plus, I hate to disappoint my readers." Candy was heading into "cut off your nose to spite your face" territory.

"More than Mariah? You gotta work that wait list with all you got. Remember how you got yourself into that *Vanity Fair* Oscar party? You know everybody. You'll get her in. Just don't piss off the school now."

"You're right. Okay, gotta go. Call on the other line. Go Crusaders!" And with that, she was gone.

I knocked on Aiden's door. Again, the quick page switch when I entered the room. When Merritt was alive, I had a strict "no computers in the bedroom" rule, thanks to the many features on *Good Morning America* about the danger of predators on the Internet. *One day they're watching YouTube funny animal videos, the next they are stripping for strangers and broadcasting it via webcam!* As a single parent, I didn't have the energy to fight the battle every night when Aiden asked to take his laptop upstairs. Now, rather than sitting around with me, he could retreat to his room. I knew he was getting the scoop on where everyone had gotten into school.

"Yeah, Mom." Aiden was on his bed, in sweats and a Dodgers T-shirt, computer propped in his lap as predicted. "Will Gamble got into Raleigh. Dex and Connal are going to Ignatius. Connal got into Raleigh, too, but he wants to go to Ignatius. Mariah's going to Sacred Sisters. That's so weird."

"Why is that weird?" I said, setting down the hot chocolate I'd brought up as a bribe in case Aiden didn't feel like opening the door. But here he was, talkative as anything. Maybe that business downstairs was just for show.

"Because last week, she was all, 'Raleigh this and Raleigh that.' Now she says SacSis is so much cooler. Whatever."

Clearly, Mariah had found her coping mechanism. Would Candy? I kept my lips sealed about the wait listing. That was all part of the game. "That's great about Dex and Connal! You'll all be at Ignatius."

"Why can't we go live in Oregon?"

Aiden's directness shocked me. "Aiden, we have friends here, your teams, my job. Dad's family. I know you love Oregon, but we live here."

"Why can't we live there?"

Why? Because this was my home, with its old money and new money and great tacos. I loved the bookstores and culture and architecture. I loved watching all the la-di-da, even if we couldn't really be a part of it anymore. But Aiden wanted change. And a dog. Maybe because he thought that would make everything okay again.

"Let's go slowly. See what happens. I can't make that decision right now with everything going on at work and trying to move out of this house. We just got some great news, let's not make it more complicated," I said, then held out a recycled Nordstrom bag that held the real reason I'd knocked on the door. "Here. This is for you."

"Is it a sweater vest like the other kids wear at Ignatius?" Aiden joked, reaching for the bag.

"No, and they do not wear sweater vests," I laughed. Then, the lightness left the room as Aiden pulled out Merritt's 25-year-old Ignatius letterman's jacket. It was blue leather with white wool sleeves. Merritt's name was embroidered on the left side, just under the school's crest. His year and a swimming patch were on the right sleeve. It was lovingly worn in all the right places, as if Merritt had cherished the jacket and treated it well. I'd never seen it before, except in old photos. When Mimi and Mikki had cleaned out Merritt's closet before the open house, they'd found it hanging deep in the back in a dry cleaning bag. They left a note on the hanger, "For Aiden, the next Fairchild Crusader."

I choked up then, just as I was choking up now. "It was Dad's. He would be very proud of you right now." Whatever Merritt's faults, he would have loved this moment. Aiden nodded, unable to speak without endangering his teenage sense of manhood.

"Thanks," Aiden finally managed, smoothing the leather with his hands, fingering the swimming patch and the embroidery.

"Put it on. See if it fits."

Aiden looked at me. He shifted his feet, uncomfortably, as if he wanted to avoid my scrutiny. "I think I'll do that later. Is that okay?"

I nodded. "Sure. It's yours now. Take care of it."

CHAPTER 16

"I've been thinking about what you said that day at lunch, and I think that's going to be my angle for the interview," Patrick dropped casually while we were working side-by-side in the honeymoon suite. He had been scribbling notes on a yellow pad all morning, while drinking his ever-present coffee and running his hands through his hair. Not that I had noticed.

Patrick and I had settled into a comfortable work routine, with a morning meeting about what we needed to do for the day, very little talking until lunch, when he went out and I went for my walk, back to our computers in the afternoon, then a quick re-cap at the end of the day. Occasionally, I'd tell him an anecdote about Aiden and he'd talk about Cassandra or his students in Athens. We talked about the news or movies we'd seen. Patrick might throw in a fleeting reference to his ex-wife and I might mention Merritt. But we never talked about *that night*.

Even though I thought about it all the time.

But I had no idea what he was talking about now. I was so lost in researching supporting visuals from the digital archives of various museums and universities that it took me a second to re-focus my brain on the conversation. When I did look up from my screen, I met Patrick's gaze. It was the first time our eyes had locked in three weeks. *Keep it professional.*

"At lunch?"

"In Laguna."

Oh, that lunch! Geez, there was a lot of wine involved that day. I hope I didn't say something like, "You're very attractive. If you let your hair grow out a touch longer even Gerard Butler would be jealous of you." Because I know that's what I was thinking that day.

Had I spoken those words aloud on that patio overlooking the sea?

"Drawing a blank. What did I say?" I asked, hoping the answer wasn't too awful.

"You said that history had been shaped by great love triangles. And if there hadn't been a Helen, Paris and Menelaus relationship, I'd be out of a job. There would be no historical significance to Troy without the myth of their great love story and the subsequent war. I'm going to use that concept when talking about Schliemann, Rudy and Sophia. I think you're onto something."

I must have had more wine than I suspected if I suggested that Patrick O'Neill would be unemployable without Helen of Troy. That was a little cheeky of me. "You know, Patrick, I think someone with your talents would have found work in another area of archaeology or another field of study. I didn't mean you'd be unemployed for life."

He burst out laughing. Oh no, what had I said? He leaned back in the leather chair, stretching out his legs and arching his back. The bottom of his black t-shirt separated slightly from the top of his cargo pants, revealing a sliver of tanned, well-toned abs. I didn't notice that either. Then, he relaxed forward, over the front of the chair, hands on his knees, smiling at me. "Not the part about me not having a job! Though I appreciate the vote of confidence. I'll put you down as a reference. I meant the part about the love triangle shaping history."

Oh, right. I'd said that, too!

"There are some nice similarities between the Helen/Paris/Menelaus story and the Sophia/Schliemann/Rudy story. I can draw some parallels, make connections. You know, older, powerful man loses young, hot wife to younger, not-so-powerful rival. Then wife returns to old man when she realizes what she is giving up: money, prestige and outrageous gold jewelry. I really think you were onto something when you suggested that find of Priam's Treasure may have been an old man's way of winning back his wife. I've done some work. The timeline fits as far as I can tell from Rudy's notes. It was during the time of Rudy's affair, spring of 1873, that Schliemann miraculously found the treasure. We've never had an exact date on that find, because Schliemann didn't release the information or photos until after he smuggled the treasure out of Turkey. But thanks to Rudy's journals, I know the date of the find was May 13th, 1873. That's something new and relevant."

"And you didn't think there would be anything useful in these journals," I teased.

Patrick stood up, walked over to my desk and slapped the transcribed pages down. He pointed to the relevant passage. "Our boy Rudy doesn't say anything about the moment they discovered the gold pieces, because when Schliemann dug the necklace and earrings out of the earth, only his uncle and Sophia were at the site by design. Rudy and the rest of the crew were instructed by Heinrich Schliemann to take a break. It was always a pretty convenient find, happening right when Schliemann appeared to need public support and out of the view of objective onlookers. But now, with the revelation that his wife was having a torrid affair with nephew, I agree with you. Pretty suspicious correlation. Did you read that part of the journal yet?"

"No, not yet." Since booking the TV interview and scheduling the public lecture, Sarah had convinced the Huntington to step up the support to get the journal scanned and transcribed. Karen from Library and her crew of grad students had rolled into action. I'd been freed up to organize the supporting research that would be needed for the interview and the subsequent public lecture at the Huntington. And *Archaeology* magazine had asked Patrick to write an article about the Schliemann Journals for its September issue. I spent half my day on the phone with *The Dirty Archaeologist* producers, all of whom seemed to be about 12 and knew nothing about history. For the rest of the day, I dug through research to put the lecture and the magazine article together. I loved it. It was exciting and fulfilling, but I missed reading Rudy's hot journals and reporting back to Patrick.

Now he was one step ahead of me, instead of me being one step ahead of him.

"Well, his primary commentary about the Priam's Treasure find was that Sophia failed to come to his tent that night for their usual frolicking. He has very little description of that actual find, but a lot of moaning about his sex life. And he thinks he may be losing Sophia to her husband. He asks the same question you did: Could Schliemann have planted Priam's Treasure to win his wife back? Your theory is looking very plausible, Dr. Fairchild," Patrick acknowledged.

I was over the moon, but tried to play it cool. I re-stacked some papers on my desk, a permission slip for Aiden's trip to Disneyland and a hot lunch form, with the care and intensity befitting the Magna Carta.

Patrick continued, "Do you think Annabeth and Sarah will find this sexy enough for their needs?"

Dang, why did he have to go and ruin my moment by mentioning those two? I played along. "This could be the most scandalous thing to hit Pasadena in decades: sex, secrets, ancient artifacts. Sounds like my mother-in-law's life. Even if you are never able to prove that Priam's Treasure is a fake, the love affair angle will certainly thrill the women in their Chanel suits who come to hear your final lecture at the Huntington. Show a little skin, Doctor, and those rich old ladies will be throwing money at your foundation for your important research."

"Here I was just thinking about TV. I hadn't even considered the rich old ladies. Maybe you could find some naughty slides for the visuals and that would really shake the money loose."

I hadn't felt this relaxed around Patrick in weeks. I didn't want the conversation to end. "You know, I just threw that out, the idea that Schliemann had trumped up the necklace and headdress for Sophia, before I even knew that Rudy and Sophia were having an affair."

"You must have good instincts about how men and women relate."

I snorted involuntarily, thinking back on the fact that I'd watched Shelly Sleazy on the news every night until the day Merritt died, not knowing she'd been sleeping with my husband for almost a year. "Yeah, not really."

"Then you have good instincts for history. It is, after all, created by ordinary, imperfect human beings. Who do selfish, foolish things and then make others pay for their indiscretions. And usually, that's how the best research comes about: a wild hair of an idea that becomes a reality." Patrick's knees rubbed up against mine inadvertently.

Suddenly, the lunch in Laguna was coming back to me. So was the warm, gooey feeling in the pit of my stomach. "I thought you said romanticism had no place in your research. You were all soil analysis."

Now he sat down on my desk, facing me. "Let's be clear how I feel: there's nothing romantic about one spouse cheating on another. In these two cases, Helen and Sophia, it's the younger women cheating on the older men. And then the older men won the women back, but at what price? War, lives lost, cities destroyed, families torn apart, evidence falsified, governments disrupted. History changed for a few rolls in the hay." Patrick's voice grew somber, serious. We locked eyes again, as if we shared a secret. "Betrayal changes everything, Helen."

Was he talking about me and my resume? Or did Patrick somehow know about Merritt and Shelly Sleazy? Better yet, had Artsy Wife betrayed him and he was still bitter? I was slightly stunned by his last statement, not at all sure what he wanted from me. "When you say it like that, Patrick, it's not a sexy theory at all. It's tragic, epic, very Greek. And a little depressing." I gauged his response to see if he wanted me to go on. He held my gaze intensely. Then, trying to lighten the mood because it all felt too much, I said, "But very dramatic the way you laid that all out."

Patrick broke out in a huge smile, and he actually slapped his knee. 'You bought it! Ooh, I'm good."

"What do you mean, 'I bought it'? Bought what?" I was confused.

"My fake serious academic BS. I was rehearsing for my TV interview. I mean, I think the theory has some merit, but do I give a shit if Sophia was sleeping with Schliemann's skinny nephew? Naaah. That just makes a good story. Something people can relate to because they have no interest in the carbon dating of the gold necklace and earrings. Knowing that Priam's Treasure was fake would be significant. Knowing why? Nobody cares." Patrick jumped up victoriously. "Coffee?"

I felt deflated. Here I was thinking something significant had passed between us, and he *was acting*! "Just tell me the next time you want me to play Uta Hagen to your Marlon Brando."

"Who is Uta Hagen?"

"A very famous acting teacher," I barked, adding silently *Dr. Give-a-shit*. I turned back to my computer with a huge desire to end the conversation before I lashed out at Patrick. But I blurted out, "Betrayal *does* change everything."

Why was I so worked up? Stupid, Helen!

"Helen, I'm sorry," Patrick responded, leaving a mountain unsaid. I was grateful he didn't ask any more questions about my comment.

"The next time you want to test out your TV persona, just let me know. I'm happy to walk you through a mock interview. I've done that with Aiden a million times, getting him ready for oral reports and stuff."

"Helen ..." he struggled, not sure what to make of my anger.

"I'm done with being in the dark."

I shouldn't have lost it with Patrick, but there was something so familiar about the scene. It was Merritt and me all over again, the lousy parts. The parts where Merritt mocked my upbringing in front of his preppy friends. The parts where Merritt waited until the last minute to tell me about a work obligation or social event without regard to my schedule. And especially the part where Merritt informed me that his soulmate was a weekend anchor and not the mother of his child and wife of fifteen years. But obviously, Patrick had no knowledge of my history with Merritt. It was just Patrick working up his shtick for TV.

So why did I react like that?

Fortunately, I had a perfectly legit reason to leave the office shortly after my outburst. At 11:30, I was grateful to throw on my Banana Republic blue blazer, grab my bag and head out the door. I pulled myself together enough to say, "I won't be back 'til 2. I have a ... a thing."

Patrick mumbled in response, "Take your time."

The 'thing' was Millington's annual Eighth Grade Mothers Luncheon, ostensibly to salute the mothers who had served the school for nine years, since entering in kindergarten. But really, it was an opportunity to do some post-acceptance letter rehashing and gossiping. Traditionally, the mothers whose children were accepted at top schools arrived first. The mothers whose children had been rejected by the same schools arrived late to avoid the pre-lunch chitchat and left early to avoid the parking lot conversation. And the mothers whose kids had been waitlisted wore brown and didn't say much. We were all expected to drink iced tea and behave as if everything was dandy.

Frankly, the luncheon was an out-of-body experience for me. Because of my work schedule and my downfall in the eyes of the board of trustees, I hadn't been on campus in months. A place that had once felt like home now felt like a Residence Inn. Had

I not promised Candy I would support her in her state of admissions limbo, I might have blown off the lunch for a giant Dutch chocolate frozen yogurt with Heath bars. And Tina had texted me that she had exciting dress news that she wanted to deliver in person, so I had that guilt motivating me. My spirits lifted when I saw the blue-and-white balloon arch, the "Welcome, 8th Grade Mothers" sign and the friendly faces at the sign-in and name-tag table.

"Helen! We've missed you, now that you have that big job and all. We're glad you could make it!" Room rep and avid scrapbooker DeeDee Nicholas hugged me and name tagged me in one motion. "So great about Aiden. Lauren will be at SacSisters. They'll have dances together. How fun! Look everyone, Helen is here!"

Everyone did look. Light applause and elevated chatter followed. Mothers in their power suits and wrap dresses. The young mothers with great figures and the tired mothers on their last tour of duty at Millington. These people, my people, were really happy to see me. Not just Candy and Tina, who rushed to my side, but the dozens of mothers who had made it through nine years of too much homework, mediocre test scores, after-school flag football games, school fundraising slights, rotten teachers, middle school social drama and impossible final exams. It was great to see them!

My fellow moms showered me with love. *You are something else, everything you've done! You look wonderful, and the news about Aiden is so great. You deserve something positive. I hear good things about you and Aiden. You've done an amazing job getting through this.* So many kind sentiments, I started to think I'd made a mistake removing my name from my Millington commitments. Maybe my gut feeling that I was being 'left off the list' was wrong.

I belonged.

Even the sight of headmistress Adele Arnett, wearing an

indestructible bouclé suit and sensible shoes, didn't bring me down.

"Here comes Cruella de Millington," Candy warned, in between bites of two-bite quiche. "I got your back."

Adele sidled up to me and squeezed my arm, saying, "We are so proud of Aiden. He pulled through, didn't he? It was touch and go. He'll do beautifully at Ignatius, and they were lovely to give him a chance."

Three months ago, I would have responded by screaming, *"Touch and go? Give him a chance? His father died! It wasn't touch and go. It was tragic and awful, you boucle'd bitch!"* But I held my tongue and took a long sip of my mango-infused iced tea. Then it hit me—I really didn't care what Adele Arnett thought of me or my son. We were done here in a few weeks. With that knowledge, I simply nodded and said, "We did it, Adele. We did it."

And by we, I meant Aiden and me.

On the way back to our cars, Tina delivered the dress news. "It's amazing. Vintage. Fabulous. But it's a loaner. I did some bartering with a friend of mine in the clothing business. I'm doing some contract law; she's giving you the dress for the night. But you've had your last meal, got it?"

I chuckled, but Tina did not.

"Seriously, stop eating. It's a real couture size 8." Tina advised. "Oh, and I made appointments for us at the Korean Day Spa on the Friday before. You'll need some major sloughing before going to the benefit."

Tina was a regular at the Korean Day Spa over in L.A.'s Koreatown; it was as authentic as any anything you'd find in Seoul. The place was a subterranean wonderland of small rooms, giant tubs of murky liquids, steamy showers and a very tasty restaurant. The female spa attendants, built like wrestlers and inexplicably dressed in black bras and panties, climbed on top of you and proceeded to rub and scrub *every* part of your body and then some, until it hurt so good. Then they dipped you in a giant vat of green tea, washed your hair like you were a little baby and patted you dry. Finally, the bra-and-panty brigade slathered you in oil and wrapped you in hot towels, leaving you to roast on a heated slate floor. You left the Korean Day Spa with an entirely new epidermis and an appreciation for the Korean commitment to personal grooming, all for under a hundred bucks. It was heaven—and hell—on earth.

"You're right. I have been delinquent about exfoliation since the sudden death of my husband," I deadpanned. Then, we both howled.

When we recovered, I asked, "Aren't you going to tell me what the dress looks like?"

Tina smiled, "It looks like you."

By the time I returned to the office, I was ready to face Patrick: apologetic, energized and free of Merritt flashbacks. *Patrick is not Merritt. Patrick is not Merritt. Patrick is not Merritt.*

But Patrick jumped in first, as soon as I walked through the door. "I was worried you wouldn't come back. Listen, I'm sorry about before. I will be upfront in the future. Starting right now. I can't afford to lose you."

"I overreacted," I countered quickly, but not so quickly that the "can't afford to lose you" line didn't sink in. "There's just a lot going on for me right now—with my life and Aiden and everything. I let it get the best of me."

"No, I was over the line. Susanna, Cassandra's mother, my ex-wife, still accuses me of being so focused on my work that I wouldn't notice if the walls crumbled down around me."

"Is that why she's your ex-wife? The walls were crumbing and you didn't notice?"

A smile broke across Patrick's face. "Exactly. Literally and figuratively. The adventure of being married to a guy who was happy to live in a tent and spend hours in the dirt wore off pretty quickly. She wanted four solid walls and some attention. I didn't get that at the time." For a moment I thought he was going to go deeper, but then he backed off. "But I am working on the noticing part. So, we're good?"

I was slightly disappointed. "We're good."

"Great. I'm going to get back to this," he said, pointing to a screen filled with data. Apparently the conversation was over. I took off my blue blazer and rolled up my sleeves.

The end of the day surprised me. I'd delved into some research on Helen and Sophia, trying to find some cosmic connection between the two women who were separated by thousands of years. I thought it would make an interesting sidebar in the *Archaeology* article. It was another hunch I was following, but I didn't want to give Patrick any details until I knew there was some useful information. I was deep into a doctoral thesis written by a British woman on the worship of Helen as a demi-goddess when Patrick's head popped in over my shoulder, startling me.

He placed his hands on my shoulders. I was disappointed I'd worn a black cashmere turtleneck to work. A V-neck would have been a better choice for that particular moment. "What's this? More revisionist history on Helen from a feminist perspective?" It seemed he wanted to clear the air of any lingering tension from the morning. A shoulder rub and flirting was a mighty fine way to start.

I met him halfway. "Do any of the women in your field respect you?" I asked, not entirely joking and leaning back in my chair just a touch.

"Annabeth!"

Annabeth. Of course. I tensed up.

"Are you busy tonight?" Patrick asked, to my shock and awe,

as he removed his hands from my back. What was going on here?

"I have to take Aiden to water polo," I answered, regretting the truth of the statement. I did have to take Aiden to water polo, a mandatory practice on a Friday night. And I had already imposed on Emilia once too often with all the work and packing. She needed the night off; things were really getting serious between Juan and her.

"Let's trade. I'll go to water polo and you go out to dinner with your crazy friend Melanie Martin," he suggested, not entirely kidding.

I almost died laughing. God bless Neutron Mel. Holding an honoree hostage with dinner invitations to enhance her social standing was brilliant. Maybe it was a good thing that I'd been unceremoniously dropped from the Five Schools committee; I really didn't have time for all that maneuvering now. "Why are you going to dinner with Melanie?"

"She called and told me she had a 'very special live auction item' she wanted to ask me about. You speak her native tongue. What does that even mean?"

His academic background was no match for the specialized language of charity events. A live auction item was meant to bring in thousands of dollars, not a couple of hundred bucks like a silent auction selection. The live auction was the big show at the Five School Benefit, when the partygoers were liquored up just enough to raise their paddles, but not so much that they couldn't sign the check. Tickets to the *American Idol* finals, Golden Retriever puppies, box seats and backstage passes to the Rolling Stones at the Hollywood Bowl—those were the sort of once-in-a-lifetime items that ended up in the live auction. What could Neutron Mel possibly have in store for Patrick? Knowing Melanie, it was probably something pretty outrageous.

I wanted to tell Patrick that he had become Melanie's trophy honoree and he should watch his back, but I held my tongue. He was a big boy. "It means she is going to ask you to donate something for the cause. Something major enough to warrant dinner, so it's big. Your presence alone at the benefit is not enough. There is a quid pro quo, and you'll find out about it tonight."

"I thought I was doing her a favor by being the honoree?"

"That's what she wanted you to think, so you'd agree. Then, she turns it around. She's good. Where are you going for dinner?"

"I think it's called Bistro 47."

Bistro 47 was the Pasadena standard for elegant food, high-priced wine, very good service and top-notch valet parking, which was a must for the Mercedes SUV crowd that had kept the place in business for two decades. Melanie probably had a standing reservation there on Friday nights, as many similar couples did. Merritt and I had been regulars, once upon a time. "That's a great place. Order really expensive wine. Melanie is loaded. And her husband has zero personality, so you'll need it."

Patrick laughed, "Good advice. Sure you don't wanna be my date tonight? Sounds like I could use some backup."

I blushed. "Water polo, remember?"

"But you're still going with me to the benefit, right?" Patrick sounded as if he really was asking, not sure where we stood. "Don't make me face Melanie alone that night!"

Are you kidding, I wanted to scream, *I am not missing an opportunity to see you in a tux!* But I composed myself enough to respond, "Of course. You're the boss."

Patrick gave me an off look, "Great. I'll be in Santa Barbara this weekend if you need me. See you Monday."

I was so not over that kiss.

CHAPTER 17

"Excuse my French, but this is crap!" Rita the Armenian proclaimed as we stood in the kitchen of a ranch house stuck in the '70s but priced in the mid-600s. "Somebody needs to tell these people that it isn't January 2007. This house is not even worth a lowball offer. Let's get out of here before we catch salmonella."

My mother and I had been with Rita all afternoon looking at the next phase of my life: the 2 Bedroom/1 Bath Fixer in a Transitional Neighborhood phase. No wine cellar, no loggia, no Golden Arrow distinction for outstanding landscaping. With the long closing my buyers Greg and Tony had agreed to, I'd put off even looking at real estate until I knew what my financial future held. Apparently, this was it: an outdated ranch house with overgrown bushes in front, wood-paneled everything and several decades of accumulated cat hair in the carpets.

After my latest meeting with family lawyer Billy Owens, accountant Bruno and personal lawyer/shopper Tina, I had an acute understanding of my financial situation: grim, but not deadly. If the house deal went through as planned in a month and none of the shareholders from Fairchild Capital chose to hold me personally liable for their losses, then I could pay off almost everything Merritt owed with the proceeds of the house and the sale of the furnishings, paintings and the high-priced wine Merritt had bought at auction. I would have enough left over for modest shelter—by Pasadena standards—and Aiden's reasonable Ignatius tuition. Provided, of course, that I was able to land a full-time job once my work at the Huntington was done, a provision I hadn't even had the energy to address.

What I wouldn't have money for: my golden Pasadena-blond highlights and lowlights; vacations to any location involving a hotel stay or plane flight; a new car in the next decade; any remodeling beyond painting and some Ikea floor rugs; and a fine college education for Aiden should he make it through high school with a high GPA.

It wasn't the end of the world, but it was the end of my world. In my most self-centered moments, I felt bad about the college fund, but I was really mourning the highlights.

Being naïve, I'd taken for granted that I would be able to find a charming, TV movie-ready home in a decent neighborhood in my price range. I envisioned a cozy cottage built for two, like the Craftsman bungalow I'd seen on the cover of *Sunset* magazine last month. Sage green walls with crisp white trim, chocolate brown couches and splashy orange pillows, patina'd candlesticks on the mantelpiece and soft pink climbing roses peeking through the window. A Downsizer's Dream, the headline had declared. That's exactly what I wanted: a Downsizer's Dream! But where was the "buyer's market" that Roshelle Slusky had struggled to explain last week on the evening news? (She actually used to the word 'escarole' to describe the process of escrow. Soulmate indeed for my financially challenged late husband.) Sure, prices had dropped, but apparently not nearly enough for me.

This house was no Downsizer's Dream. It was just a downer.

Standing in the middle of the avocado-and-puke-colored kitchen, I thought I might cry for the nine millionth time since Merritt's death. I missed my double ovens already.

My mother turned to catch my eye. Her look said it all: You could buy a stunning log home with twenty acres in Oregon for this price. But she held her tongue as I'd asked, reminding her that there were very few jobs in central Oregon, and being employed was a big part of my financial equation. Instead, she just repeated the phrase she'd used in six earlier houses: "I don't get it. I just don't get it."

"These people are crazy!" Rita said, tossing her dramatic mane of black hair and brandishing her wristful of gold bangles like a real estate superhero. "Come on, I have one more on my list. It's not officially on the market yet, but I have a good feeling about it! It's on Sunshine Street! How could it not be happy? And that's what you need: happy, not crappy. Let's go."

I had to postpone the trip to Sunshine Street. We had a mandatory Fairchild event that night and I needed to steel my emotions. First a shower, then a large cup of coffee before I faced the Fairchilds en masse. The last thing I wanted was to throw my own pity party in front of Merritt's family.

We were celebrating Merritt's birthday. It had been Mitsy's idea and I had to admit, it was a good one. According to my three-visit, short course in grief from the therapist Candy had recommended, the 'firsts' were the hardest after the death of a family member: the first Christmas; the first Father's Day; the first graduation; the first birthday. According to my therapist, it was a year of unbearably sad family events before you could move on to the next phase of recovery. Each one was tough in its own way, depending upon your family traditions. For the Fairchilds, birthdays had always been low-key events. They were not inclined to fete individuals, but instead, they chose to make a big deal out of the family holidays. As a result of the non-existent family birthday tradition, my inclination was to spend Merritt's birthday alone with Aiden at the movies. But now that I was standing on the porch of the Pasadena Town Club with a glass of white wine in my hand, I was grateful that Mitsy had taken the initiative.

My mother-in-law had orchestrated a family Mass at St. Perpetua's. Aiden and I arrived early, along with the Odd Couple: Mitsy, in a simple black dress, multiple-strand pearl necklace and Hermès scarf, and my mother, resplendent in what she called her Peacock Wrap and long purple pleated skirt. My sisters-in-law, Mimi and Mikki, wore almost identical charcoal-gray suits, gray silk blouses and two-inch pumps. Their eyes welled up as they approached me and Aiden, already seated in the front row. My brothers-in-law, Lawyer Bart and Broker Ben, dressed in somber dark blue suits with striped ties, both hugged me and squeezed my hand as they slipped into the row behind us. Both men had a handshake and hug for Aiden, which I appreciated, and a polite hug for my mother, who nodded furiously with sympathy for each new arrival. Unlike other parents with young kids, Mimi and Mikki had wisely chosen to leave their collective children, five cousins under 8 years old, at home.

Mitsy included Billy Owens and his wife, Lacey, as part of the family that night. They arrived on time, with their three well-scrubbed, blond teenagers in tow. Seeing Lacey—fitter than ever with her perma-tan and short blond hair—and handsome Billy reminded me of the thousands of hours we'd spent together as a couple with them. I wondered what they did now with their weekends? I certainly wasn't on their list. Though I was glad Aiden would have some friends his own age tonight, I was still on shaky social ground with Billy. He would spend the rest of his life feeling guilty about Roshelle. And I would spend the rest of my life embarrassed knowing that Billy knew my husband had cheated on me. We would probably never recover the ease we once had with each other.

The Mass was sober and quiet, punctuated only by sobs from the sisters whenever Monsignor Flaherty mentioned Merritt's name in the sermon. "Let us remember Merritt Fairchild, on the anniversary day of his birth, as a man who was humble before God. Who lived the Word of God in his actions and in his deeds. And who left behind a legacy of good works."

"Namaste," my mother piped up, much to the horror of my in-laws and the Monsignor. I welcomed the comic relief. I bit my lip in an effort to suppress my laughter and caught Mitsy's eye. Was that a flicker of understanding in her gaze?

Dinner followed at the Pasadena Town Club in the same room where Merritt's memorial reception had been held. The cycle of life and gin and tonics replayed itself over and over again at the PTC: baptisms then graduations then engagement parties then weddings, anniversaries, retirement dinners and, finally, funerals. Guaranteed, like it came with the membership. The green-and-white dining room was always packed on Saturday nights with regulars and relics. For Pasadenans who didn't want to brave the parking or the anonymity of eating at an actual restaurant, the main dining room at PTC was a welcome haven of familiarity and overcooked scalloped potatoes. Friendly faces sat at almost every table, from the Gambles to the Montagues. There is nothing more powerful than belonging, Merritt used to say whenever he pitched a new business idea to me. If you can tap into a person's need to belong, then you've won their loyalty.

The dinner that followed at the club was about as much fun as the Fairchilds allowed themselves to have. Billy Owens stepped into the role of host and MC, not allowing the conversation to turn maudlin. Toasts were made in Merritt's honor, but then quickly, the focus turned to Aiden and his admission to Ignatius. Billy stole the show with lots of stories about Merritt's high school days at Ignatius, from skipping school to pranks to swimming victories. Mimi and Mikki recounted the dozens of girls Merritt dated in high school, from Rose Princesses to softball players. Even Mitsy joined in the journey down memory lane with some rather bawdy tales of her own, about finding a stash of *Playboy*s under Merritt's pillow and a flask of whiskey in the glove box of his Toyota Celica. I doubted the veracity of some of the stories, but didn't question Billy, Mitsy or the sisters.

They had their memories and I had mine; theirs were sweeter and unspoiled. And that's where I wanted to be after a day of looking at real estate wrecks: in Denial Land. I'd heard all the stories before, but seeing Aiden's face as he listened for the first time gave me hope.

"What a bon vivant!" my mother would cry after each new revelation about Merritt's high school and college exploits. I knew she thought the stories sounded rather tame compared to her hippie past, but she was in a fine mood, so I didn't discourage her.

Well-wishers came over to the lively table all night long, to pay homage to Mitsy and raise a glass to Merritt. Watching the Fairchilds, so at ease in this room with all these people, even at an event like this, made me appreciate the certainty of their lives. Yes, tragedy had struck them, with their father's death at an early age, then Merritt's, but the family would carry on. As it always had. It was why I wanted to marry Merritt and why I couldn't conceive of moving Aiden away from all this.

The people in this room were content with their lives. What was wrong with that?

We were wrapping up dinner when Aiden unexpectedly announced, "Thanks for finding my dad's letterman jacket, Aunt Mimi and Aunt Mikki. My mom gave it to me the other night. It's a little big, but I think I'll grow into it."

More tears and choked-up thanks followed. Billy and Lacey hugged and kissed all the Fairchilds, including me. Then it was clear that it was time to go. But not before Mitsy got in one last request, "Helen, can I speak to you a moment on the porch? Here, have the last of the wine."

"Will you be okay?"

The question was vague, but I knew Mitsy was looking for specific information. After the initial news from Billy Owens about Merritt's financial meltdown, I'd spoken to him about not revealing any confidential information to her again. Mitsy Fairchild may be a privileged client who is like a mother to him, but she is not entitled to know my business. Billy apologized and promised to keep his trap shut around Mitsy. Obviously, he had.

Tonight at dinner, he was Billy the Rowdy Best Friend, not Billy the Consigliere.

"I'll be fine," I answered, nodding for emphasis. "Aiden and I will be just fine once the house has closed."

"You'll stay in the area," she stated, not in the form of a question.

"Yes. Our lives are here."

"Tuition?"

"Covered. And we'll make all the adjustments we need to make. Thank you for asking, Mitsy." We managed to cover a lot of ground in the fewest words possible. Clearly, she understood the big picture, but she didn't want to know details. And I didn't want to give them to her. "And thank you for planning today. It was lovely and just the right thing to do."

"Of course," Mitsy concurred, although I'm not sure if she meant, 'Of course it was lovely' or 'Of course, it was the right thing to do.' Or both.

Probably both.

"Helen …" she said, pausing. "Do you need anything?"

I studied my mother-in-law's carefully crafted face. I think she was genuinely asking me if I needed *anything*. Like a hundred grand or a hit man or a prescription for Xanax. In that moment, I believed she could get any of those wish-list items and more. But despite the fact that I would soon have no home and no job, I didn't need anything.

"Not a thing, Mitsy. Not a thing."

"I understand that your little job is ending soon at the Huntington," Mitsy carried on, oblivious to the steam coming from my ears when she referred to my "little job." "But they consider you a hard worker. And the scholar you assist, he's quite something, isn't he?"

Was she fishing for information? Had she heard some gossip or rumors? Well, this fish wasn't biting. "Dr. O'Neill is very accomplished. It's been a great experience working for him."

"What will you do when he leaves?"

Regret that we got no further than a kiss. Eat pints of ice cream, regaining all the weight and then some. Bookmark his Facebook page and click on it a hundred times a day. What do you think, old lady? I'll miss him in a way that I haven't quite missed your son.

"I'm sure Dr. O'Neill will give me a good reference. I'll find something. I have to, so that's what I'll do."

Now it was Mitsy's turn to study my face. "Good work."

Sunday morning at Bob Hope Airport in Burbank was so sleepy that even the fact that we were "very late" by my standards did not stress me out that much. My mother had taken forever to pack her potions, tonics, bangles, leather and feathers. "How did you ever live out of a van with all this stuff?" I asked as Aiden and I heaved her deep blue rollaway bag with tie-dyed ribbons onto the sidewalk in front of the Alaska Airlines terminal.

"It's something I meditate on all the time: Where did I get all this baggage?" My mother laughed at her own double entendre. "Just leave me. Don't come in. I can make it through security on my own. Enjoy the beautiful Sunday with your beautiful boy! Come here, Aiden my dear."

Aiden submitted to a smothering hug with genuine affection. "Bye, Nell. See you this summer!" And with that announcement, he winked theatrically.

My mother winked back, "Break a leg, kid."

"What was that all about?" I asked, feeling like the only one not in on the joke.

"We have a plan we're working on, but we can't talk about. We need some additional intelligence, right, Aiden?"

"Right," Aiden shouted, already climbing back into the front seat of the Audi.

"Mom ..."

"Don't worry. Nothing subversive. We'll let you know when we have it all worked out."

I still didn't like being out of the loop, but I let it go. "Thanks for coming. It was fun. I did need some company."

My mother gave me her "little lost lamb" look before she launched into another Joni Mitchel reference. "You know what you are, dear? Stardust, Helen, stardust."

I knew how Aiden felt when I sang his praises publicly: self-conscious and weird. "I know, Mom. It's just gonna take me a while to get back to that garden."

"I can see that," she hugged me and then briskly turned herself around, pulling her roller bag and swinging her ginormous carry-on. "I left you the live tea culture. Keep brewing! And be grateful. Stardust, Helen! Stardust!"

More like sawdust, I thought, as I joined Aiden in the car. "Wanna go to Ikea and get some meatballs?"

"It's, like, 10 o'clock in the morning," Aiden answered.

"You know my motto: It's never too early for meatballs."

CHAPTER 18

Keeping up with Sarah Longlegs, stride for stride, made me realize how successful my lunchtime fitness program had been. I was not nearly as out of breath as I'd been four months earlier when I gasped out my need for employment to the public relations director. Now, as we pounded around the Huntington's walkways, past the manicured lawns, bouncing fountains and blooming camellias, I could walk and talk at the same time while wearing European comfort shoes and wielding a clipboard. "Okay, here's the rundown for next week, Sarah. On Wednesday morning, we'll submit the article and supporting visuals to *Archaeology* magazine. Wednesday afternoon, we meet with the producers from *The Dirty Archaeologist* for a pre-pro..."

"Oh, listen to you. From room mom to 'pre-pro'—you certainly have made quite a leap in a short time," Sarah quipped a little too sharply, even for her. She slowed to a stop in front of the Japanese teahouse and waited for my reaction.

Listen up, Longlegs, as far as I can tell, chairing the Word-Write book fair involves a lot more creativity, planning and politics than producing a TV show, I wanted to snap back. *TV shows have teams of paid producers and resources to burn. School volunteers have to create something out of nothing all by themselves. This is a picnic compared to that.*

But I held my tongue. I needed to stay on Sarah's good side for any future job references, so I pretended she'd said something delightfully naughty. "You got me. Using the lingo before I have the credentials. Let me re-phrase. Wednesday afternoon, we have a *pre-production* meeting to go over all the details of the shoot the next day. You should probably sit in for that. Then, of course, Thursday is the big shoot. The producers want to set up first in the Scholars' Cottage for the morning, then do some exteriors on the North Vista lawn and along the Camellia Walkway, with the sculpture garden as a backdrop. I know you were copied on that e-mail. They expect to be done in one day. One long day. The crew call time is 7 a.m., so I've made arrangements with security to have the gates opened early. Then on Friday, there's the public lecture in the Founders' Hall. I'll have the PowerPoint ready to go. And on Saturday, the benefit."

Sarah gracefully sat down on a nearby bench, crossing her legs to reveal camel herringboned trouser socks above her JP Tod loafers. How is it possible that her textures blended so well? I could never get that blended-texture thing down. She patted the seat next to her, an invitation to take a load off. I did, with much less grace than she. "Helen, when I first recommended you for this job, I wasn't sure you were up to the task. But I thought you needed a break. And look at you now. I don't know how Patrick got along without you. That man needs a full-time Helen to keep his life in order. He'll be lost without you when he goes back to Athens in a few weeks."

"Thank, you, Sarah." Her words made me wince a little. She made me sound like a dowdy secretary combined with a doting wife. I pictured the ripped biceps and the tanned legs of the many female grad students he must have at his disposal in Athens and Troy. Not to mention the comforting presence of Annabeth, who, according to her producers, was planning a trip to Troy to shoot this summer. I didn't think "lost" was the adjective I would use to describe a certain archaeologist. Patrick would manage just fine.

"You've been a great asset on this project. You've really pulled things together. I'll keep my eye out for an opportunity for you to stay with us here at the Huntington." Sarah eyed me steadily.

Wow, now I was officially blown away. "I would love that. That would be amazing."

"I'm off to meet with the director," Sarah said as she stood up, preparing to charge off in another direction. "By the way, do you know who Olympia Sutton-Majors is?"

Of course, what PBS Masterpiece Theatre viewer in America didn't know Olympia Sutton-Majors? She was a lovely, pale, utterly British actress whose name was synonymous with tastefully produced costume dramas. She'd played every heroine in every made-for-TV series set in 19th-century England for the past decade. Nobody looked better in an Empire-waist muslin dress than Olympia. But recently she created a buzz when she played a brainy, sexy MI6 operative opposite Daniel Craig in the last Bond movie. Her refusal to get breast-enhancement surgery had made her an icon to less-endowed women. Plus, she was constantly in the news with one attractive actor or another. What an odd question from Sarah. "Sure, the actress. BBC, Bond, B-cup activist. Why?"

"Well, Melanie called and said Patrick was bringing her to the Five Schools Benefit. Wanted a comp ticket for her and a seat at the head table. I guess they're an item. Has he mentioned her to you?" Sarah asked, oblivious to my shocked face. She appeared to have no idea that I was supposed to be his date. Oh my God, Sarah must have been waiting for a last-minute invite! And clearly, she didn't even suspect Annabeth as a romantic interest. We'd both been had.

"No, never mentioned her," was all I could squeak out.

"Well, things weren't going to work out with Patrick and me anyway. I'm here; he's leaving in a couple of weeks. It's for the best," Sarah said, holding her head up high and completely misstating the nature of their relationship. There really wasn't anything to "work out" except the occasional lunch and some one-sided delusions. "An actress is perfect for him, all drama. You know how men like Patrick want drama in their lives. Working women like us aren't exciting enough to hold them, of course. Damn, I'm late."

Sarah rushed off as I sat glued to the bench.

Before Merritt's death, I used to think there were two roads you could take in any situation: the high road or the low road. But since then, I'd learned that the only two roads you could take were the slow road and the go road. On the slow road, I could stand by passively, making wild assumptions about the situation, waiting for someone to rescue me. Or I could get on the go road by taking a deep breath, gathering information and making informed decisions. *See, I had learned something in my three sessions of grief recovery!*

I chose the go road.

I started by texting Candy: What do you know about Olympia Sutton-Majors?

Then, I followed up with a text to Tina: Please check seating charts for benefit. Am I at head table?

Finally, I gave myself a little lecture about my unrealistic and slightly immature expectations, hopeful that berating myself would lessen my anxiety and put me in a better position to talk to Patrick minus the hysteria. *He is a world-famous archaeologist. You are a lowly research assistant with stretch marks and a forehead that could use some Botox. He could have anyone; why would he pick you? That thing in the parking lot, the intimate discussions—that's just his style. Seriously—you or Olympia Sutton-Majors? Is there really a contest?*

The worse I felt about myself, the better I felt about the situation, in the sense that I could handle the inevitable: I'd be going alone to the benefit and Patrick would be going back to Greece with a Bond girl. But if that was the case, I was going to find out sooner rather than later.

Once you have nothing to lose, you have nothing to lose.

I popped up off the bench and headed back to the cottage to ask Patrick one question: What the hell was going on?

Believe me, nothing can take your breath away like the sight of a beautiful British actress in a passionate embrace with a beautiful, brilliant archaeologist. Especially when the actress is Olympia Sutton-Majors and the archaeologist is ... *Annabeth?*

Holy shit.

"Oops," I said like a moron, as I stood in the doorway of Scholars' Cottage #7, stunned by the scene in front of me. Had I been in less of a rush to confront Patrick, I might have been able to pull off an unseen retreat once I stumbled upon the secret lovers. But with my usual lack of grace, I made a loud and unattractive entrance. Annabeth and the palest woman I'd ever seen in person separated, very slowly. These two were in love.

Clearly, of the three of us in the office, I was the most embarrassed. By *miles.*

"Helen! You caught us!" Annabeth giggled.

"Annabeth, I'm sorry, I didn't ..." I started to apologize, but she didn't let me finish.

"I didn't mean you 'caught' us. I meant, whoops, you caught us, ha ha! Nothing to hide in here!" Annabeth gushed, pushing the ghost-like Olympia toward me. "Olympia, this is Helen, the one I was telling you about. Helen, this is the love of my life, Olympia Sutton-Majors."

Olympia, in head-to-toe cashmere, embraced me like a long-lost sister and planted a euro-kiss on both cheeks. "Helen!" Olympia sang. "Wonderful!" Oh, she was so soft and smelled like the Cotswalds.

"Welcome to Pasadena!" I was so overwhelmed with relief, random phrases were just flying out of my mouth for no reason. "You're lesbians. That's fantastic!" Olympia was Annabeth's date, not Patrick's! What great news! Patrick wasn't going to the gala with a gorgeous actress; he was going with me. I continued to smile like an idiot. Annabeth and Olympia seemed a little tak-

en aback by my enthusiasm. I tried to explain in my best suburban mother, I'm-an-Ellen-fan manner: "It's just great that you've
found someone to love. To have in your life. Someone so ... special. You two look very happy. And that makes me so ... happy."

"We haven't made it public or anything. It's complicated,"
Annabeth explained while gently patting Olympia's arm. Olympia finished the thought, "We're just waiting for the right time to
tell people. You understand."

"Yes, I understand. Life is complicated. Don't have to tell me.
And you are ..." I could barely carry on a conversation with the
spectacular Ms. Sutton-Majors. Thank God, she was a lesbian. I
didn't stand a chance against her with Patrick. "You are ... my
favorite British ... person." That was awkward. Then, it dawned
on me. *The Dirty Archaeologist* was being produced by Aphrodite
Productions in association with the BBC, according to all the
press releases I'd seen. Duh! Aphrodite must be Olympia! "Wait!
Is Aphrodite your production company?"

"Yes! Well, it's ours together. Annabeth's show is our first pro-
duction. It's so exciting and Annabeth says the whole first epi-
sode would be rubbish without you. You're a wonder, she says."
Now I get it, Annabeth's whole faux-British accent. It wasn't from
Annabeth's post-doc years at Oxford; it was from her years with
Olympia. Lover-ly.

And though I enjoyed the props, I was still trying to wrap my
head around the happy couple. Where did that leave Patrick? On
the inside of this twosome, possible threesome? Or just a willing
beard?

"I've enjoyed it," I said, brushing aside Olympia's compliment
for now, circling back to the really important stuff. I faced Annabeth. "And here I thought that you and Patrick were a thing!"

"Oh, no. A million years ago, but that's all water under
the bridge now," Annabeth confessed, with both she and her
co-star gazing at each other, laughing. "Really under the bridge,
in so many ways. Plus, Patrick is all work these days. For the

last decade, really. The fact that he's still single is one of the great archaeological mysteries of our time. I think he's waiting for someone he can share his work with. He only uses me for my research."

I could live with "a million years ago."

Olympia chimed in, "When he comes to Santa Barbara, he retreats to the guest house with his laptop or the beach with his books and only emerges for cocktail hour." So Olympia had been hiding out in Santa Barbara this whole time and Patrick never said a thing?

And then the movie star and the archaeologist filled me in on their whole romance. Where they met and how (On Crete almost two years ago, with Olympia researching a role as a 19th-century female explorer and Annabeth providing the tutoring), how they settled into their bi-continental relationship ("Santa Barbara sunshine is the perfect antidote to London fog!") and what their plans for the future included (*The Dirty Archaeologist*, a mini-series about Marie Curie and two children by 2014). The two of them prattled on forever, thrilled to be sharing their story with someone.

I barely noticed the time, until Patrick walked through the door in the late afternoon. If he was shocked to see us cozied up on the couch together, drinking tea and swapping stories, he didn't show it. "Well, here's a powerful triumvirate. Did I miss anything?"

Happy hour became a happy three hours. We ditched Patrick at the Huntington and moved our all-female lovefest to Mujares Mexican Cantina, because Olympia claimed there was no such thing as too much guacamole. By the size of her thighs, I'd say her definition of "too much guacamole" was very different than mine. But the change of venue gave me a chance to text Candy from the car.

Star sighting. Meet at Mujares. Keep low profile.

Candy responded: What am I looking for?

I answered: Dirty Archaeologist with Olympia Sutton-Major. Off the record.

In Candyland, keeping a low profile meant snooping from the bar or the table next door when a scoop was unfolding. And Off the Record meant just that: off the record, as in not for posting on candysdish. She needed a pick-me-up after the Raleigh waitlist debacle, and this was just what she needed—hobnobbing with the famous, not gossiping about them.

At first she kept her distance, chatting up Raul at the bar for a good long time over a club soda, while Annabeth and Olympia downed margaritas. When I felt the timing was right, I waved her over to meet Annabeth and Olympia. By the time the enchiladas arrived, the three of them were laughing like old school friends. Candy delighted them with her Rose Queen Gone Bad story, an apologia I'd heard a million times. But she was *on*; it was like watching a one-woman show. The reception from Annabeth and Olympia was so encouraging, she carried on with her whole life story. She concluded by explaining candysdish.com, her way of disclosing that she was a professional celebrity gossip reporter. Annabeth and Olympia squealed with delight, though that may have been due to the margaritas. By the time the coffees were poured, Olympia was calling her agent—Aphrodite Productions wanted to buy the rights to Candy's life story. She was glowing.

"Once this deal hits *Variety*, Mariah will get in off the wait list at Raleigh for sure," Candy whispered to me. "Plus, they're talking HBO series. So don't worry, I won't say a word. I'm going to bide my time on this one. And I like them. I want a weekend invitation to Santa Barbara, don't you?"

Candy agreed to drive the slightly drunk Dirty Archaeologist and her snow maiden back to their hotel. She had a deal to secure, and I had to get home to Aiden. The valet pulled her spotless Jaguar around. "This was so much fun," Annabeth gushed. "I love you guys. Were you always this much fun in college, Helen? I can't wait for the shoot on Thursday. Candy, you must come. We want you to be there, too."

"I wouldn't miss it. Can I bring my photographer? It would be great publicity for your show."

"Oh, that is such a good idea!" said Annabeth the Naïve.

"But a word of advice: Cut out the salt and the chips tomorrow. Just lots of water," Candy warned Annabeth as the trio piled into the car. "Or you'll be bloated and have carb face on camera! Right, Olympia?" Olympia, who had never had carb face a day in her life, agreed heartily.

As I waited for my car, my thoughts drifted off to Patrick. Now that I knew there was nothing between him and Annabeth, I felt more pressure than ever about the benefit.

Was there really something there between us?

CHAPTER 19

"Are you ready?" I asked Patrick two days later, as I watched the stylist smooth the collar of his Turkish linen shirt, in what I'd come to think of as Patrick's Blue. We were standing in a makeshift dressing room at the Huntington in the Friends Hall. Scholars' Cottage #7, which I'd stayed in late last night to clean and accessorize with fresh flowers and important-looking books, was being lit for the interview. All that HGTV proved good for something. Patrick, now powdered and hair-sprayed, was looking impatient. And *fine*.

"Helen, relax. I've done interviews before. And the research is good. This will be great. And then we can all go out and have a beer. It's just TV."

"You look great, Dr. O'Neill. I'll be on set to powder in between takes. Let me know if you need Chapstick," said Mona, the skinny, adorable twentysomething with the carpenter's apron full of makeup, brushes, cotton swabs and safety pins. She turned to me. "Do you need hair and makeup?"

Did I look that bad? Just as I was about to acquiesce, Olympia swooped in. She was dressed in fabulous white jeans and a tawny suede shirt set off by a silver-and-turquoise belt. Mona's mouth dropped open. *There was a Bond girl on her shoot!* "Of course, Helen needs nothing. She's beautiful all on her own. And she's not on camera. But you are, Patrick. So get to the set. Be brilliant." Patrick trotted off while Olympia played producer, pushing Mona out the door, too. "Darling Makeup Girl, go take one last look at Annabeth. Tell her she looks lovely, because she is starting to doubt herself. Go!"

Mona went. Olympia really was a movie star.

"Is Candy here? I want to talk to her about something."

"She'll be here any minute. With a camera crew. She said that you okayed that." I don't know why now I was playing the part of Candy's producer. I just wanted everything to go smoothly for Patrick. And Annabeth. An unexpected camera crew might ruffle some feathers.

"I told her absolutely yes!" Olympia clapped her hands, her beaded bracelets flashing on her wrists. She draped her arm around my shoulders conspiratorially. "Let's go make something dirty, shall we!"

The Huntington's gardens, library, art galleries and koi ponds have been used in literally hundreds of movies and television shows. Leo, J-Lo, DeNiro—you name it, they've filmed on the grounds. You'd think the Huntington staff would be blasé by now about another film crew taking up their parking spaces and messing up their schedules. That was the usual attitude of the citizenry of Pasadena when the klieg lights and Starwagons rolled into town. But there was something electric about the atmosphere surrounding *The Dirty Archaeologist*. Maybe because so many of the staffers had something personal on the line.

Sarah White was vying for professional attention from the director of the Huntington, kudos from the board of trustees and personal attention from Patrick. She was entertaining a cadre of local journalists covering the shoot. Karen from Library, the self-appointed "manuscript wrangler" on set, wouldn't allow anyone but her to turn the pages of the Schliemann Journals during the close ups. Annie the Coffee Cart girl was thrilled to get her first craft-services gig, supplying fresh java. (The big movies used their own people.) The eager grad students who had supplied the extra hands to scan and transcribe the journals toward the end of the project stood around with lattes, whispering about the glamorous Olympia. Even Arlene the Volunteer Coordinator was snapping photos of the action for her slide show presentation for the Ladies' Guild Luncheon in June.

Sure enough, Neutron Mel, not technically an employee but putting in a lot of hours around the place lately because of the benefit, hovered in the corner with her minion Jennifer Braham, who seemed to have aged ten years since she acquired my position. Being Neutron Mel's #2 was not good for the complexion. Melanie was typing furiously on her Blackberry, periodically looking up to survey the scene and check her watch. Jennifer's face was tight as she scanned the horizon, looking for something. Of course—today was the day the massive white tent went up for the benefit on Saturday night. A control maven like Neutron Mel would want to oversee every aspect of the event, even the tent stakes.

Then, of course, there was me. I had everything on the line. That's why I was thrilled when Olympia called me over to the inner circle: the two young, blue-jeaned producers, the prototypical, unshaven director in a baseball cap and Yankees T-shirt, Patrick and Team Aphrodite. The executive producer/movie star spoke in an exasperated tone, "Helen, can you please explain what we went over yesterday? The producers seem to have forgotten the rundown. Exactly what are Annabeth and Patrick going to cover while going to the cottage location, and what are they going to cover while strolling through the sculpture garden? I know you'll remember."

"No problem. I made notes." I flipped through the stack of papers on my clipboard. "Here, I typed this up last night for Patrick." Then I addressed the production team and Annabeth, trying not to step on any toes. "And here's a list of possible questions. I know you have your own, because, um, that's your job. But I gave these to Patrick as examples. I'm sure he didn't look at them." Patrick laughed. "But I made copies for all of you, just in case."

I handed out the rundowns and questions to Olympia, Annabeth, Jonas the director and the crew. Then I handed one to Patrick. "Does this look familiar?"

I swore he winked.

Annabeth was a natural on camera. Any anxiety she had in the dressing room disappeared the moment the cameras started rolling. She was warm, inquisitive and completely comfortable in the role of host and expert.

Patrick, on the other hand, was not a natural. He was scholarly and serious and not having a single bit of fun. What was going on? For a guy who was so dynamic in person, he sounded like a drone! His description of the love triangle, the findings from the journal and the revelation that young Rudy and young Sophia had been sleeping together were about as salacious as a C-Span Senate hearing. Olympia, Jonas and the producers huddled around the video playback whispering about Patrick, citing his "lack of energy" and "geeky academic tone." Jonas kept asking, "Where's the sexy?"

I could tell he was getting self-conscious as the director repeatedly yelled, "Cut!" and "Let's try that again." I felt awful for him.

Olympia called me over. "Seems Patrick has a case of the uptights. What should we do? You know him best."

Hardly. But technically, I'd spent the most time with him in recent months. What could I say that would get him out of academic mode? I remembered the day in the cottage. *That was it!* I offered to Olympia, "Let me talk to him. I think he's just really nervous. Why don't you take five—or whatever you say in the TV biz."

"Work your magic, Helen."

Did this mean I could add "director" to my resume?

"I'm the problem, aren't I?" Patrick said in between sips of coffee (out of a straw so as not to mess up his Chapsticked lips). Mona fluttered around with the powder puff, assessing the shine on Patrick's brow. "I'm terrible."

"No, you're not. You're not terrible, just too serious. It's about the tone. The show is *The Dirty Archaeologist*—they want it to be steamy and intimate. You don't seem to be having fun. You need to bring your personality to the material. You know, the part of your personality that's not so technical and … analytical."

Patrick shooed off Mona. "Okay, okay. You're right. It's just the more that director guy says 'relax,' the more annoyed I get. Tell me what I need to do."

"You need to stop with the dates and the statistics and the soil analysis. Find the heart of the story. The good stuff." Patrick's blank stare meant that I had to go even further. *Okay, here goes.* "Remember that day when we were talking about history and love triangles and you faked me out. Got me all worked up. And I, I … freaked on you."

"Yeah," Patrick responded cautiously, not wanting to go there again. "What about that day?"

"You told me the story with intensity, with passion. Like you were speaking directly to me about something you really felt. And I felt it, too. I thought you knew something about me that I'd kept secret." Patrick was very quiet. I leaned in closer to him and continued. "That's why I freaked out when I found out you were using me to work on your material. I thought it was the real thing." He nodded slowly. "You need to find that intimacy with Annabeth. This is a story about love, passion and betrayal of historical significance. Tell it to Annabeth the way you told it to me. Make Annabeth feel it the way I felt it."

Patrick's face lit up, "You're right. You're right. You're absolutely right. I get it." And he kissed me on the cheek, much to the dismay of Mona, who was monitoring his lip moisture. "Thank you, Helen."

"You're welcome," I said, then dropped my voice. "And if that doesn't work, just picture Annabeth and Olympia naked. That should do it, too."

From the way Patrick smirked, I could tell he already had.

"I don't know what you said, but it worked," Olympia whispered, as Patrick and Annabeth carried on for the camera. Patrick's storytelling and Annabeth's questions were compelling and their interplay downright ... arousing! It was exactly what the director was looking for. I watched the tiny playback monitor and smiled at Olympia's compliment.

"So what's next? Will we ever really know if Priam's Treasure was the real thing? Or simply the desperate gesture of a jilted husband?" Annabeth asked, shaking her brunette mane, practically breathless as she awaited the response.

"Hopefully, I'll know soon enough. I just received permission from the Pushkin Museum in Moscow to examine the treasure next week. It's something I've wanted to do for years, and the invitation was finally issued. If all goes well, I'll have the answer by the end of May."

What? I almost screamed. Next week? He's leaving next week?

"Cut! That was great! Really good." Jonas directed. "Okay, Patrick, we need a pick-up on your last line about going to the Pushkin. This needs to be evergreen. It won't air for a few months. So can you talk about the trip to Moscow without using specific time references or dates? You know, something like, 'I'm going very soon' or 'I'll have answers in a couple of months'—something like that." Annabeth and Patrick huddled for a moment to consider the options.

What followed was a long discussion about how Patrick was

going to frame his impending trip to Moscow for the TV show. But I wanted to know how Patrick was going to frame his intended trip for me. Was he leaving for good? Would he come back to Pasadena after Moscow? Or was this it?

"All right," Annabeth said. "I think we've got it. We'll do the pick-up."

This time Patrick's answer was vague in terms of specific dates but not information. "Next week, I'm flying to Moscow to finally get my hands on Priam's Treasure. Then, I'm headed straight back to the dig site at Troy to compare all the data. I hope to have an answer to your question very soon."

No mention of Pasadena, the Huntington, or me at all.

I was standing next to the craft services table, laden with energy bars, chips and bowls of lollipops, M&Ms and chocolate-covered raisins. Mindful of Tina's warning not to eat anything before the benefit, I was drinking coffee, black. My Stress and Grief Diet had given way to a straightforward Starvation Diet. I felt jittery but thin. I didn't know if the pit of nerves in my stomach was from my excessive coffee consumption or the prospect of Patrick leaving. I'd know soon enough as he swept over to the table, grabbing a handful of almonds. He was very pleased with himself.

"I nailed it, didn't I?" he said, fairly confident of the answer. Could he be any cuter?

"Yes, you did."

"Thanks. You really helped." Now Patrick was less sure of himself. "So that bit about going to the Pushkin, did you hear that?"

Confirmed: The pit was from the prospect of Patrick leaving, not the coffee. "Yeah, that was a surprise. How great! And how timely," I said, ratcheting up the pace and enthusiasm of my response to cover my disappointment. "That all your research should be coming together at once like this is incredible. What luck!" More rambling on the horizon. "And to get to work at the Pushkin? Amazing. You must be super-excited. It's a once-in-a-lifetime opportunity. This could really be a breakthrough. Congratulations." Despite my high levels of caffeine, I felt winded after my speech.

"I was trying to find the time to tell you. We've just been so busy, cranking out everything over the last few weeks. It just slipped my mind." Patrick grabbed a bottle of water and nervously played with the top, twisting it back and forth.

"Totally understand. Hey, I'm here for another month, according to my contract. So I can finish up anything you need: get stuff packed up, ship anything off to wherever—Troy, Athens, Moscow. I'm here." That's me, Full-Time Helen.

"Great. I'm leaving Tuesday." *Tuesday?* That's five days from now. And in between, there's the lecture and the benefit. Freaking Tuesday? "So we can go over everything on Monday, I guess."

"I'll be here," I said again, in case there was any confusion about my future plans.

"What will you do next? When your contract is up?"

"I've already talked to a few people about positions," I lied enthusiastically. "Now that I know things will be wrapping up here, I'll get on the job search. So it's all good." Aggressively Perky Helen making a rare appearance.

"Have you thought about going back to grad school?" Patrick asked, reaching for some M&Ms. I guess the statute of limitations for Misleading Information About Your Academic Credentials had run out. I was forgiven for failing to mention my half-done master's. "I can make some calls to Berkeley, Princeton, anywhere you want. It's not too late to go back to school."

But it was. "Thank you. That's very generous. But I can't afford grad school now. That ship has sailed. I have Aiden and everything. I need more revenue and less debt. So grad school is financially impossible for me."

"There's money out there for someone like you, Helen."

I laughed. "The money would have to be for me *and* Aiden! Does Princeton give double scholarships to middle-aged moms and their underperforming teens?" Patrick looked sympathetic, but not so sympathetic that he corrected the "middle-aged" crack.

Just then, the twentysomething producer in a headset appeared. "Dr. O'Neill. You're wanted on the Camellia Walkway. That's where we're doing the next set-up. We need you in five." Then she darted off, like a nervous rabbit. I gathered up my stuff, intending to head back to the office to mope alone.

Patrick reached for one last handful of nuts. "Aren't you coming to watch?"

"I thought I might go back to the cottage to work on the PowerPoint for tomorrow's lecture."

"Please don't. I like when you're here."

For five more days, anyway. "Sure. Of course."

The champagne was flowing and the volume was rising in the usually sedate Tea Room at the Huntington. Sarah White had arranged a post-shoot celebration for cast, crew and special friends, which was a lovely gesture. The party filled the quaint tea house and spilled onto the Rose Garden terrace, lit by white lights and votive candles. Annabeth and Olympia were nowhere in sight, but the rest of the crew seemed particularly joyful, filled with bubbly and cucumber sandwiches, as if they'd never been invited to anything before in their lives. Was that Karen from Library flirting with the key grip? And Coffee Cart Annie exchanging cell numbers with the producers?

In the middle of it all, Sarah was mingling and laughing loudly. She was clearly a little tipsy. It was a triumphant tipsy, well deserved.

But I, frankly, was too exhausted to partake. And afraid to have more than one glass of champagne on account of my minimal caloric intake. I needed to have my wits about me to drive home, feed Aiden and help him study for a science test. Then I planned on collapsing. I scanned the crowd for Patrick, hoping to at least say goodbye before I went home to Aiden. I spied him in the corner holding court for the Huntington director and several members of the board. The heavy hitters, of course. I was turning to leave when Candy assaulted me.

"Oh. My. God."

"What? What's wrong?" I worried something had happened to somebody somewhere. It was my job to overreact.

"Olympia and Annabeth want to announce their relationship to the world. And they want to give me an exclusive. A sit-down interview, personal pictures, the works. This is huge. This will put candysdish on the map." Candy started to jump up and down like a sorority girl. Then she realized the magnitude of the task—that Olympia might well be putting her career in Candy's hands—and she froze. "Do you think I can handle it?"

The slight twinge of guilt I'd felt over setting up Candy with Team Aphrodite was now gone. I was a natural matchmaker. "Yes, of course. They trust you for a reason. You've been through press scrutiny and come out the other side. You're the perfect person. Wow, Candy, this is fantastic. When?"

"Tomorrow. They want me to come to their hotel room at the Langham with a small crew. I'm going to post it on Friday!" Candy swiped a glass of passing champagne and downed it. "I've been waiting for something like this to get me out of the Pasadena gossip ghetto. This is an international story."

"Are you ready? Do you need anything?" I asked, not really knowing what skills I had to offer in a digital coming-out interview. But maybe she wanted the fresh flowers from our set?

"I am ready. The crew is lined up. My intern picked up my shiny gray Blumarine dress at the dry cleaners; that looks *so* good on camera. And I scheduled an emergency blowout with Mr. Stephen," Candy cooed. "I just put in an S.O.S. call to my webmaster. We need bandwidth! I don't want the site to crash when this goes up! Bye, doll!" A quick kiss on the cheek and she was gone.

"Helen, wait!" Patrick was jogging through the parking lot in an effort to catch up with me. I was just opening my car door. Startled, I dropped a carelessly balanced armload of stuff. Damn. "Sorry, I didn't mean to scare you. I saw you leave the party and I, um, I …"

"Do you need something?" I asked, more snippily than I intended, bending over to recover my clipboard, some research materials, a water bottle and the Starbucks bag full of mini sandwiches, brownies and cheese puffs I'd swiped from the party for Aiden. Patrick knelt to help me. I felt like a bag lady with my contraband food. Embarrassed, I recovered and softened my tone. "Do you need something for the lecture tomorrow?" I avoided his eyes as I shoved the baked goods back in the bag.

"No, no. You've done enough today. Here," He handed me a paper napkin full of chocolate chip cookies as he stood. "I just wanted to say thanks. For everything."

"These are for Aiden," I explained, still fixated on my stolen food. "He eats a lot. And he loves mini food."

Patrick chuckled. "I'll go back in and get that entire tray of chicken-salad triangles if you want. I owe you that."

"No, I'm going to swing by the PETA fundraiser on the way home and swipe some tofurkey." We both laughed. Then the familiarity of the situation quieted us both. There are pregnant pauses and then there are pauses that last the nine months, right through labor and delivery, and continue on to the first birthday. This was one of those pauses: long, intense and slightly painful.

But this time, I knew what I had to do. "I've gotta go. Big day.

See you tomorrow, Patrick." When in doubt, generic platitudes can be enormously helpful. When I'd shut myself in the protective cocoon of my car, I felt safe enough to open my window a touch. "Have a good night."

"You, too," Patrick replied.

CHAPTER 20

On the Saturday morning of the Five Schools Benefit, women all over Pasadena were beginning their pre-party beauty regimes, honed by age, experience and budget. Mothers, matrons and mavens were being pruned, waxed and hot rollered to perfection, or at least as close as they could get to their own Personal Perfection Scale. Tonight, they would be counted among the Best and the Brightest, but right now, they were in their most naked state. And no one looks her best—or all that bright—while bleaching her peri-menopausal mustache. Even the regulars at Stephen Stephens Salon, the closest Pasadena comes to an uptown Beverly Hills salon in price, design and attitude.

Every chair was occupied as I walked in to claim my 10 a.m. appointment. I'd booked my cut, highlight and style almost nine months ago, literally the day the benefit date was confirmed. At the time, I was still on the committee. And I still had a husband. Sitting here now, I couldn't believe I had so little to do in my life that I'd made a hair appointment nearly a year in advance. But I was glad I had. I knew this would be my last appointment with Sammi. At $300 a visit, she was out of my price range now. I would have cancelled if Annabeth and Olympia hadn't given me a generous gift certificate (Candy's suggestion!) as a thank you for all the extra work I'd done for the shoot. I arrived early, determined to enjoy my herbal tea, warm neck towel and lavender-scented smock to the fullest.

Next time, it would be Supercuts.

But today, at Stephen Stephens, a salon appointed more sumptuously than most living rooms, almost every face in every chair looked familiar. The place was crawling with Five Schools Benefit committee members. The Cloverfield Mafia—Leila Kennedy, Mary Claire Meyers and Taffy Hart—were foiled and seated under the dryers. They headed up the all-powerful seating committee, using their skills honed as cotillion co-chairs to assign tables for the night, elevating a few to the lower numbered tables and relegating others to a seat near the exit to the restrooms. Their work was apparently not done, as they were pouring over the chart as the dryers raged.

In Begonia's chair sat Sonia Michelson, a hippie-chic Redwood mother and daughter of one of the dogs of Three Dog Night. Sonia was in charge of securing a decent dance band. (Last year, the band played nothing but reggae, which confused the small but influential over-65 crowd. This year, a No Funny Music edict went out.) Sonia was having her voluminous strawberry-blond hair straightened into submission. No doubt she would be wearing a Kate Hudson-inspired printed maxi dress and dancing in bare feet by 10 o'clock. And everybody would be charmed because everybody loves a token rich hippie.

Nancy and Neicy, a sister team almost as glued to the hip as Mikki and Mimi, were seated side by side in the manicure room. They were in charge of the food, a thankless task, as somebody powerful always hated it, usually my mother-in-law. It was a no-win committee, and they were brave to take it on. Nancy and Neicy were raised in one of Pasadena's first foodie families, if you can call owning a national chain of warehouse grocery stores being "foodie." I did, but others around town were not as generous when the sisters pleaded for the top spot. (*Their stores sell vats of ketchup! Vats! They're hardly gourmet*, one committee member had sniped.)

The salon buzzed with excitement. As Sammi's assistant (*Rinda? Renda? Randa? Why can I never remember her name?*) led me to my chair, I exchanged nods, waves and smiles. *Good to see you, Helen. Looking forward to tonight! Tonight's the night!*

Maybe.

As I walked past Stephen's station, I touched him on the elbow. "Candy wanted me to say thank you. Again. And again. Her hair looked so great on camera!"

"She's my star!" Stephen exclaimed, as he shellacked Blair Becksley's up-do with hair spray. "Did you catch her on ET? She was amazing. I think Mary Hart better watch her back!"

Yes, the Olympia/Annabeth story had broken and, as predicted, it created a global firestorm and unprecedented traffic for candysdish.com. Candy herself was booked on every talk show from *Entertainment Tonight* to *Larry King* to talk about her interview. She'd assumed the role of unofficial spokesperson for the couple, with their blessing. Now that the news was out, Olympia and Annabeth intended to keep a low profile for several months. Once the initial frenzy dissipated, they would speak to Oprah, right before the debut of *The Dirty Archaeologist* in September.

"That's good media planning," Candy had observed, as she called me from the back of a town car on Friday to bail on our Korean Day Spa trip. There was no way she could squeeze it in between Ryan Seacrest and Billy Bush. "I can learn a lot from Olympia. She understands the concept of having your moment."

No doubt about it—Candy would extend her moment for as long as she could.

I arrived at Sammi's station and plopped myself down in the chair. The one reason I loved going to Sammi was that she was not a talker. She was a listener. If I wanted to blab, she would engage. But if I wanted to enjoy back issues of *Cosmopolitan* and *Martha Stewart Living*, she would quietly go about her work, a comfortable silence between us. Today, I wanted silence. I needed focus, not advice.

Plus, I was a little heavy-hearted, knowing I was going to have to break up with her. I didn't think I could tell her today. I was thinking a nice note and a small gift next week would suffice. Easier and cleaner. And I couldn't cry today, because Tina told me not to get my eyes puffy for any reason.

"Sammi!" I greeted her with a hug.

"Helen, I've been thinking about you." Today her hair was deep purple with blond highlights. And yet she was wearing a chic all-black jumpsuit and neutral makeup. She dove into my scalp, examining my root situation. I hadn't been to see her since the day of the funeral. I was long past the days of covering up my need for reinforcement with a headband. Sammi didn't blink an eye. "Same color?"

I nodded. Why not? One last time.

Then Sammi snapped at Rinda/Randa/Renda to mix up a gold 27 with a blond 449 for lowlights, a concoction called Pasadena Blond at most salons. It was a color I shared with dozens of my closest friends. "So ... how are you?"

How am I? That was one of those questions I didn't feel like answering today. So I gave my new standard answer. "I'll tell you a year from now. Right now, I don't know." I thought that had just the right touch of self-awareness mixed with exhaustion and grief. I got it out of a book. To me it signaled: Please don't ask. I don't want to go into all the awful details.

Sammi got it. "Okay. Just relax then. You deserve it. More tea?"

Yes, please. I did deserve it. I leaned my head back, closed my eyes and went over the events of the last few days. It had been an unbelievably exhausting week. As if the shoot and the revelation that Patrick was leaving hadn't been enough, I'd followed it up yesterday with the Scholar's Lecture. Patrick presented his research to an enthusiastic audience packed with familiar faces. I provided visual support and some minimal stage directions. Though the professional stakes weren't as high as they were for his TV interview, the personal stakes were enormous.

Patrick's connection to the benefit, the local press from the TV shoot and the good word-of-mouth reviews from the Word-Write talk at Millington had piqued the curiosity of the afternoon-lecture set. This crowd had changed their watercolor classes and private Pilates sessions to see what all the fuss was about. Patrick had rebounded from his TV nerves to inform and charm the standing-room-only audience, which included most of the women currently at the salon and, of course, my mother-in-law and her cohorts. The presentation had been a huge hit with just enough of the salacious material from *The Dirty Archaeologist* interview to get the ladies twittering.

The biggest surprise of yesterday? Seeing Cissy Montague, she of the "forever house" and the moved pool, on cookie-and-lemonade-detail. My old turf. In her twin set and pearls, she manned the refreshment table with an excited, nervous energy. I gave her arm a squeeze when I greeted her, full of goodwill. "It's so nice to see you, Cissy. Everything looks great. You did a wonderful job!"

"I hope we have enough. This is my first time volunteering. I had no idea these lectures got so packed. I figured it would be a dozen ladies and some tourists. But look, everybody's here!" She was right; the crowd was a who's who.

"Don't worry. These women don't actually eat, at least not in public. Most of the cookies will go back to the staff lounge. And you can water down the lemonade if you start to run out. The kitchen makes it really strong." She nodded gratefully. "You'll enjoy the Huntington. It's inspiring."

She straightened out the cocktail-size napkins for the tenth time. "I hope so. I just felt like, you know, like I needed to get out of the house. Do something different, something for me." Her big diamond flashed in the sunlight, and once again, her good heart shone through.

"Maybe someday you'll end up going back to school, getting your doctorate! You never know!"

"Is that what you're doing?" she asked, clearly astounded at the thought of handling more homework than McMurphy, her seventh grader, brought home.

"Not yet anyway. I'm only a research assistant." Just then Patrick waved me over. Sarah White stood at his side. She certainly wasn't going to let a first-timer like Cissy introduce a Distinguished Scholar like Patrick. Sarah was going to milk this intro for all it was worth. "I'm being called. See you Saturday night, Cissy."

After the lecture, Mitsy insisted on meeting Dr. O'Neill, as she kept calling him, and then acted as if she was granting him an audience. It was quite a performance. I think even Patrick was intimidated. She brought the encounter to an abrupt end, fishing a big buckle of keys out of her Chanel bag, "Best of luck with your work, Dr. O'Neill. Keep us informed."

Keep us informed? Who did she think she was—Queen Elizabeth? The CIA?

Sammi's voice interrupted my reverie. While I'd been reviewing my week, she'd been foiling like a fiend. I was ready for the dryer, then the cut and style. Sammi asked an obvious question, one for which I had no answer. "What are you wearing tonight?"

I snapped back to attention. "I don't know. My friend Tina picked it out. It's vintage and I haven't seen it. She told me to tell you to think, um, 'windswept, flowing and sexy'—those were her words." Obviously, because windswept, flowing and sexy were not words I associated with myself.

"Windswept, flowing and sexy? Got it. I'm going to need more hair. Excuse me." And Sammi went into the back to find more hair, while I closed my eyes.

As I was leaving Stephen Stephens Salon for the last time, I ran smack into Jennifer Barham, Melanie's second-in-command and the woman who'd stepped into my spot on the committee. She made a miraculous catch, as her Blackberry headed toward the ground after impact with my shoulder. What a dive!

"Oh my God! If that broke, I'd be a dead woman." Jennifer

whimpered, the stress of the upcoming event evident in her body language. And her yoga pants looked as if they were going to fall down around her knees. Silver lining! Stress combats Mommy Bleacher Butt! "This thing just doesn't stop beeping!"

I was so glad I was not her. "It will all be over tomorrow. Then you can go back to your regularly scheduled life! I hear you're doing a great job. Even in this economy, you really brought in some big names to buy tables."

"Well, you left me great notes and great contacts. And getting the travel and hotel for the big live auction item—that was huge. Once I got that, I felt like I could breathe again."

Actually, it didn't look like Jennifer had taken a breath since February, but I didn't say that. "What big live auction item?"

"Dr. O'Neill's dig. Didn't he tell you?"

"No." No, he hadn't. Was he auctioning off some relics?

"He donated a fantastic archaeological experience! Two weeks working alongside his team in Troy this summer. Like a real archaeologist. Except with deluxe accommodations arranged, of course. Plus, he agreed to lead private side trips to some of the best sites in Greece on the weekends. Santorini and some other place related to Troy…"

"Mycenae." Of course he would want to take them there. It was Schliemann's other big discovery, home to Agamemnon, who led the Greeks into battle at Troy. "It's the other piece of the historical puzzle of the Trojan war."

"Yeah, that's it. Anyway, it was a major coup. I had to get all the travel and hotel donated, and I never could have done it without your great contacts at Marriott and British Airways. Huge, Helen, huge!" Jennifer's Blackberry buzzed again, but she ignored it. "It's an unbelievable trip for two. Top-of-the-line everything, with a stopover in London to see some statues at the British Museum. Melanie thinks it will go for some crazy amount of money. Like Hollywood money, not Pasadena money. After seeing all those women at the lecture yesterday hanging on Dr.

O'Neill's every word, I think she's right. I wouldn't put it past Melanie to buy it herself!"

"He never mentioned it, but maybe it just slipped his mind." Neutron Mel must have really wined and dined him at Bistro 47 to get him to agree to shepherd around some wealthy Pasadenans in the middle of the dig season. The Blackberry buzzed again. Jennifer looked at the screen. "It's Melanie, I've got to take this. Your hair looks great! It's huge! Huge!"

At least I had that going for me. As I walked out of Stephen Stephens Salon, I thought that it did sound like a dream trip. My dream trip.

"Here you go, Missus. Oh, very nice," said Tran the Mailman as he handed me the mail and pointed to my new 'do. "You look good. Are you going to the big party tonight?"

"Yes, at the Huntington. A fundraiser for the schools." I replied, amused by his interest and flipping through a stack of bills until I got to a large manila envelope.

"I know. We going, too. Outside the party, anyway. My son Bernard is playing the violin in the special orchestra. He has a solo." At the benefit, Pasadena's top orchestra students lined the red carpet and serenaded the guests into the party. It was a lovely tradition. Of course, Tran's son Bernard would be a concert violinist as well as a straight-A student. "That's lovely, Tran. I'll keep my eye out for him. Or at least, an ear out!"

Tran pointed to the envelope. "Good luck with that. My son apply too, for violin. He didn't get in. Good thing he going to Raleigh."

I had no idea what Tran was talking about. Apply where? My face must have registered my confusion, because Tran piped up to clarify, "To the High School for the Arts. The envelope, the big one. What does your son play?"

"Water polo," I responded like an idiot. I looked down at the return address of the large envelope. The Los Angeles County High School of the Performing Arts. Somewhere in downtown Los Angeles. It was marked: To Aiden Fairchild. What the hell was this? I didn't want to open it in front of Tran, and I think my look told him that.

"I don't think they have a water polo team! Ha, ha! Bye, Missus," Tran laughed as he bounded down the driveway. "Maybe see you tonight!"

"Yes. Tonight."

Aiden, still in his pajamas, ripped open the envelope, while I stood there like a stranger in my son's life. "Yes!" he shouted. "Yes! I got in. I made it!" And then the biggest genuine smile of his life passed across his face, accompanied by a fist pump. "Yes! Whooo!"

I was stunned. Seriously, I was stunned. It was like the day the police came to tell me about Merritt and the panda. "How?"

"Thanks for the vote of confidence, Mom," Aiden quipped, doing the end-zone dance on top of the couch.

"I didn't mean that, Aiden. Please stop that!" He did. At least for a second. "I just meant how, how did this happen?"

"I applied and I got in."

I was going to lose it. "Okay, I'm trying to understand this. But you've got to stop being cute with me. You somehow applied to a performing-arts school without my knowledge. And honestly, without my knowledge that you had any actual performing-arts talent—don't take that the wrong way, but you've never even auditioned for a play at Millington. And now you're in and you're thrilled. Aiden, what is going on?"

So he told me what had been going on while I'd been at work, or out looking at houses, or at the accountant's office trying to straighten out our financial mess. In other words, while I'd been absorbed in stabilizing our lives, he'd been thinking about the future. He'd learned about the school from Lydia, the girl from summer camp last year who went to Los Angeles County High School for the Performing Arts *(LACHSPA—that's what everyone calls it, Mom)*. They stayed in touch all year *(ah, yes—the one beaming into our living room on iChat every night)*. She was a dance major, and she thought he could be a really good actor. Or even a director! *(Like Dr. O'Neill said!)* So after he blew the interview at Ignatius *(I'm really sorry I was such a jerk—I just hate those uniforms)*, he got together an application *(a transcript, three essays and a headshot)* and had my mother sign all the legal paperwork *(wait until I get my hands on her!)*. Then he rehearsed an audition piece with Lydia over the computer *(yes, from* Romeo & Juliet, *the same play he claimed not to understand at Ignatius)*, and Emilia drove him to the audition one night when I was working late *(I could kill her, too!)*.

My son, the same one who can barely remember to turn off the water after brushing his teeth, had decided that he wanted to be an actor and managed to get himself into a highly selective performing-arts high school—one that even the mailman's perfect son couldn't get into—all by himself.

If I wasn't holding the letter of acceptance myself, I would have never believed it.

"Mom?"

"I don't even know what to say."

"I really want to go there. And it's free! It's a public school, so we don't have to pay anything!"

Now the real $25,000 question, at least as far as I was concerned. "Why didn't you just tell me you wanted to go to a school like this? Why did you go behind my back?"

"You wanted me to go to Ignatius so bad. It seemed really important to you. I didn't want to disappoint you. And the whole Dad thing. I know Grandmother and everybody wants me to go there. And when you gave me Dad's Ignatius jacket, that made me feel horrible," Aiden said, his eyes welling up. "That's when

I told Nell and she said she would help me. I didn't want you to get mad. And I thought, if I didn't get in, then you'd never know. But, I *did* get in."

Now I was the one blinking back tears, mindful that Tina had warned me that crying equals puffy face. He couldn't tell me because he didn't want to disappoint me. I wanted to strangle him and hug him to death at the same time. But I couldn't ruin my cascading hair with that much close contact.

I looked at the letter. We had a week to give them an answer. I'd only put down a small deposit at Ignatius, and the balance of the tuition wasn't due for months. I had two ways to go here: Fight it or accept it. The look of joy on Aiden's face made the right answer clear. "Okay, here's the deal. I don't know anything about this school, like if they even teach math...."

"They do and all those AP classes that I know you're going to want me to take," Aiden interrupted. I held up my hand, signaling my turn to talk. He wisely shut up.

"I don't know anything about this school. Like how the heck you're going to get to downtown L.A. everyday without injury. But let's go look at the website. I want to see what it has to offer. Then next Wednesday I can take the day off and we'll go visit *together*. I need to see it for myself and figure out if it's going to work for us before I agree. Deal?"

"Deal."

"And one more thing. You've got to show me that scene from *Romeo & Juliet*. I want to see this alleged acting." I reached out for him, for my baby.

"Okay," Aiden said, hugging me and burying his head in my shoulder, much to my hair's dismay. "I love you, Mom."

"I love you, too, Aiden," I said, squeezing tighter, hair be damned. Then I pointed him in the direction of the stairs. "Now go get some actual clothes on, please. Pack your stuff and brush your teeth. Mrs. Gamble is coming to pick you up. You're spending the night there, remember? Because I'm going to the party with Dr. O'Neill."

Aiden sprinted toward the stairs, then turned. "Have fun tonight, Mom."

By the time Tina arrived with my mystery dress, I'd worked myself into such frenzy that nothing but a loaf of bread, a pound of Tillamook cheddar and a chocolate milkshake would calm me down. Really, with hours to go, it was too late to actually lose any more inches, or so I rationalized as I fired up the panini maker. I felt like a felon in my own home when I heard the quick knock, then Tina's voice in the hallway. "I'm here. With your dress!" Tina managed to give the word "dress" about five syllables. I raced to hide the incriminating milkshake remains, but it was too late.

Tina's face registered mock disapproval as she burst into the kitchen holding a long silver-gray dress bag, "I hope the seams don't burst from those carbs!" She unzipped the dress bag dramatically, "Close your eyes!" I heard more rustling, then she ordered, "Open them!"

I gasped—a true, I-can't-believe-my-eyes-gasp. There before me was the most beautiful dress I had ever seen. Better than my wedding dress! Tina held a milky white, one-shouldered, pleated silk dress with a braided gold sash. It was astonishingly beautiful. Classic and modern all at the same time. "Tina ..."

"Isn't it gorgeous! It's a Mary McFadden. From her 1976 collection called something like Grecian Goddesses. How perfect is it? It's almost the same dress that Jackie Kennedy wore to the Met Costume Gala that year. Only the draping down the front is different. Isn't it unreal?"

It was unreal in every way. Oh, God, please let it fit.

"Let's go try this beauty on and make sure you can get into it. I have a backup, but I don't want to go there. This is the dress that dreams are made of!" Tina was going a mile a minute now. "By the way, what have you decided? Are you going to sleep with

Dr. Dig tonight or what?" How did she know that's all I'd been
thinking about all day? Okay, all week. Fine, for the last month.
"Just get that monkey off your back. He's hot and he lives in a
foreign country. Who better for your first time back in action?"

"You sound like Candy!" I countered, hoping to redirect the
conversation, as I followed Tina and the dress up the stairs.

"Oh, no. I sound nothing like Candy. Because she thinks
you've been sleeping with him for months and holding out on us!
I, on the other hand, believe that you've *wanted* to sleep with him
for months, but were too nervous to act on it. Am I right? Or is
Candy?" We reached my bedroom. She held the dress an arm's
length away, implying she wouldn't turn it over until she heard
the truth.

How could I explain that sleeping with Patrick was not "getting a monkey off my back"? It was more than that. It was sex
with someone other than my husband. It was sex for the first time
with a different man in almost two decades! I was the last woman
on earth who thought I'd find myself in this situation so soon
after Merritt's death. Along with all the usual hang-ups about
that, I had the vision of my mother-in-law and Merritt's sisters to
haunt me with their disapproval. They'd be at the benefit tonight,
watching my every move. To top it all off, I was *somebody's mother*! That was a new one for me when it came to sleeping around.
The last time I'd seduced a man, I was a grad student and food
co-op worker, not a water polo mom. The reality was too much to
dump on my friend, who had just arrived with the most beautiful
dress ever. So I economized my words. "You're right. Haven't
done it, but wanted to."

"Yes! Lunch at Vivienne's goes to me!" Tina crowed, then cautioned me, "Helen, don't rush into anything if you don't want to."

But I *did* want to, that's why I felt so conflicted. I just couldn't
admit that to Tina. "Good advice. Thanks."

"All right, let's get you into this dress! Suck it in, Helen!"

CHAPTER 21

Laughter, music and a deep golden light poured out of In Vino Veritas. It was a beautiful May evening, warm enough to go without the lavender silk wrap, a loaner from Tina that I had carefully folded in my evening bag for later. The Gambles had invited about a dozen couples to meet at the wine bar before heading to the Huntington. I'd been so relieved to get the invitation. It was the perfect place to rendezvous with Patrick. The last thing I wanted was for him to pick me up at my house. There was too much of my old life there. With only four days left of his stay in Pasadena, I didn't want him to intersect with Merritt in any way.

I scooted myself out of Tina and Ander's Lexus and collected my thoughts. After our dress fitting/sex pep talk, Tina went home to get ready. Returning a few hours later to act as my chauffeur, she looked stunning in a turquoise Badgley Mischka dress and sky-high golden sandals by somebody important. She stuffed me into my McFadden and zipped me up for the night. "Gotta get those girls in there," Tina grunted as she manipulated my C-cup breasts into the B-cup bodice. "You are now officially a couture size 8, except in the boobs. Lucky you! Turn around."

I stared at myself in the mirror, and my cheeks went red. It had been a long time since I'd been comfortable looking at my reflection. But tonight, something felt very different. Sure, the hair, the dress and a fresh coating of Bobbi Brown "Port" made a huge difference. But it was something more.

It was confidence.

"Thank you, Tina."

"It's all you, Helen."

Even Anders, Tina's serious Swedish husband, gave his approval freely while hoisting me into the back seat. "You look lovely, Helen."

Now, at the door of Veritas, I paused.

"You ready?" Tina asked, fluffing my flowing but slightly de-poofing hair and leading me into the bar to meet Patrick. "Never mind, of course you are. Stand up straight. Relax your shoulders. Let's go."

And in we went.

Patrick was by himself, perched on an oak stool at a table on the other side of the room, in a proper black tuxedo with a proper white pin-tucked shirt and bow tie. He was sipping champagne and watching the door. When our eyes met, a wave of warm excitement rushed down my entire body. *Please don't let the seams split*, I thought. I breathed in as deeply as the dress would allow, catching the scent of night-blooming jasmine from the pergola outside, mixed with the aroma of red wine. *Here we go.*

I had to maneuver through a throng of well wishing and air kissing, attempting to keep Patrick in my sights at all time, like a dancer spotting during a pirouette. I prayed I could cross the room without my knees buckling, especially given the height of my heels. Fortunately, he stood up and met me in the middle of the crowd. He took my hand, brushed his lips against my left temple and said softly, "I have found my Helen. Helen of Pasadena."

Very nice. The words Heinrich Schliemann himself had used in his journals to describe his young bride. With a twist, of course. But I had to bring it back to our common ground.

"Which version? Victim or harlot?"

"Definitely 'the face that launched a thousand ships' Helen."

"Thank you." If the evening had ended right there, I would have been perfectly satisfied. The starvation, the hair extensions, the waxing—everything would have been worth it for that moment. But it got better. "Come with me. I have something for you." He took my hand firmly and led me across the crowded room.

After being swept away, I finally found my voice. "Did you get me a corsage, prom date?"

Patrick laughed. "Sort of. It is a gift. And I believe it will complement your dress, though maybe not as well as the pink carnations with baby's breath I got my actual prom date in 1982." By then, we were at his corner table, and he handed me an elegant silver bag with clouds of tissue paper peeking out the top. "For you, Helen." He poured a second glass of champagne while he watched me unwrap the package.

The bag contained a gold-and-jewel-encrusted wrist cuff; it was spectacular. I was speechless. It was a modern take on an ancient design, dazzling with semi-precious green, blue and purple stones entwined like a snake and set off by delicately hammered polished gold. I knew exactly what it was and what it meant. "Oh, Patrick! It's like the bracelet from Priam's Treasure. It's ... it's lovely. Did you have this made?"

"I did. I wanted to thank you, for everything." Patrick appeared to be struggling with his words. "You've made the last few months very, um, successful for me. In terms of research and, well, in terms of everything. Thank you."

It was the least articulate statement he had ever made in my presence. I slipped the cuff on my wrist and held it up, Wonder Woman-style, for him to see. "Now I feel all-powerful."

"You're more powerful than you think, Helen," Patrick said quietly. The warm rush returned. I reddened, sure I was sending out a strong "take me now" signal. The moment ended too quickly when Ted Gamble bounded up to us with an open bottle of Argyle Sparkling Brut.

"Any one need to be topped off? We should be going to the Huntington soon. Jan's already there, and she said if our whole gang arrives late and drunk, she'll kill me!" Ted said, refilling Patrick's glass and mine. There was a slow shuffle toward the door by the other guests, reluctant to leave the convivial warmth of Veritas for the crush of the benefit. Ted turned to me. "Did Patrick tell you about our alliance?"

"No. Have you formed a softball team? Drinking club?"

"Both good ideas, but no. I'm going to be on the board of his foundation, helping to fund his work and find resources! I know people who know people, Helen." Ted looked like he could not have been more thrilled. "And hopefully, getting in there and doing a little digging myself!"

It was obvious the bromance that they'd started that day at lunch months ago had blossomed into real respect and friendship. "Now I've got to get this crowd going. I'm sure Jan is wondering where all the big spenders are!"

As Ted waltzed away with the last of the bubbly, I dropped my mouth wide open, cocking my head, "That is amazing. On your board and funding your research! How did that happen?"

"I'll tell you in the car," Patrick answered, draining his glass. "But you really should have warned me. I almost blew it."

"Warned you about what?"

"I thought the guy was a bartender, Helen. A well-educated, well-read bartender. Hours of conversation over lunch and he never mentioned that he was that Ted Gamble, gentlemen proprietor with a very healthy trust fund and then some. I almost started laughing when he offered to underwrite the next three years of research."

"That could have been awkward."

"Yeah, thanks for the heads up." He laughed.

"Well, you've learned an important lesson about Pasadena. No one here is what he or she seems at first glance. And it only took you several months to learn that. It took me years."

"I'm a quick study." Patrick offered me his arm. "Shall we?"

The Huntington was dazzling. As beautiful as the magnificent grounds were during the day, by night, especially on this night, it was like being in another world of wealth, privilege and excessive landscape design. The labor of a thousand leaf blowers and temporary workers on ladders had transformed the gardens into Ancient Troy: A full moon, thousands of twinkle lights and a phalanx of potted olive trees leading to a dazzling white tent inspired by a Gehry building. The piece de résistance? An enormous Trojan Horse standing guard at the entrance to the gala, a movie prop generously donated by Warner Brothers, secured by the beaming and exhausted Leonora Dillard, chair of the decoration committee.

"Wow. I'm impressed. I had no idea it was going to be this ... glamorous. Is it always like this?" Patrick asked, fidgeting with his tux for the first time. He led me by the elbow up the walkway into the flashing bulbs and electric energy of the band in the tent. I was glad he didn't take my hand. Someone might have seen us.

"Yes ... and no. Usually there is press and hoopla, but not like this. There's *Entertainment Tonight!*" I lost my cool, then recovered. "But I think they're here for Olympia and Annabeth, um, not you." I tried to soften the blow.

Patrick let out a giant guffaw. "Helen, do you really think my ego is that big?"

"No, no, not at all. As far as TV-star archaeologists go, I think you've got yours in check. I just didn't want you to be *disappointed* if nobody takes our picture. I think the only archaeologist ET appreciates is Harrison Ford."

"Then it's a good thing I brought my bullwhip."

"You did not!"

More laughter. "No, I didn't."

The long walkway up to the tent was lined by earnest young musicians playing the theme from *Ben Hur*. Close enough. I waved to Tran and his wife, standing off in the shadows behind their son Bernard. Tran gave me the thumbs up and Mrs. Tran waved and smiled. I waved back just as Sarah, in Armani and a head set, appeared out of the shadows.

"Finally. We thought you'd never get here," Sarah snapped, giving me the once over, then turning toward the man of the hour, Dr. Patrick O'Neill. "I got him, Melanie. He's here. We'll do the press. then I'll send him in." Sarah barked into her head-set, obviously relishing the telepathic communication she and Neutron Mel were sharing. I was surprised that Sarah would get so involved, but then I realized that in the midst of all the press attention on Olympia and Annabeth, Sarah, ever the public relations maven, did not want the Huntington's message points to be overlooked. She stepped in between Patrick and me, relegating me to third-wheel status. "Okay, Patrick, I am going to walk you through the press gauntlet, let them know who you are, and you do your thing. Be charming and mention the Huntington every chance you get, okay? We've got the *L.A. Times*, the *New York Times*, *Town & Country*, various local news organizations, and then ET, TMZ and that little Candy. Even *Archaeology* magazine sent a photog. Are you ready?"

Patrick looked to me for guidance. "I bet you wish you had that bullwhip now!" Sarah gave me a funny look. I took the hint. "I'll see you inside the tent."

Off he went to have his moment of fame while I strode up the rose-colored carpet alone, hoping my solo entrance didn't have a Sally-Kellerman-at-the-Oscars feel of desperation. Thank God for Candy! There she was, shining in a low-cut black pleated number that looked like an evil Angelina in Alexander the Great. She was waving me over to her prime candysdish.com spot just in front of the tent entrance. I smiled and focused on her, ignoring the press that were ignoring me. Candy made a scene. "Helen Fairchild! Helen Fairchild! Over here, please! Is that vintage McFadden?"

I felt a few camera lenses turn my way, not that I cared.

Finally, I reached Candy. "You look amazing! Where's Dr. Dig? Ah, that she-devil has him. Well never mind, you're getting a prime spot on my page. Below the lesbians, of course, who just called to say they will be here any minute. And let's face it, this town would have a field day if you showed up hand-in-hand with a guy that attractive. Why do you want all those rumors? But, look at you! My God, what is that bracelet?"

I explained the gift from Patrick. Candy said, "That's an impressive gesture. That's good. Have the best night of your life, please, for me? Enjoy yourself and for once, don't overthink everything. Tonight, underthink everything. But don't drink too much. If something happens, I want you to remember every detail. You know, so you can tell me!" Candy's phone buzzed and she checked her text. "Oh, Annabeth and Olympia are here! I've got to focus. Find me later, doll?" And with that, my dear friend of fourteen years practically shoved me into the tent.

I took the opportunity to re-do my lipstick and overthink one last time.

Candy was right. The last thing I wanted was Aiden or anybody else to see "couples photos" of me and Patrick and start to gossip. Frankly, there was nothing to gossip about. I didn't deserve to be grist for the mill for one kiss and several close encounters. That being said, she was also right about the overthinking. I needed to let go of the worrying for one night. Could I do that?

Whoosh, Sarah deposited Patrick at my side. He looked shell-shocked and relieved. Sarah pointed at me and began speaking as if Patrick wasn't even there. He stood behind her, making faces like a 12-year-old. "He needs to give a short thank-you speech at 9:37. Then he'll stay on stage for the auction of Trip to Troy or whatever cutesy name they came up with. That Jennifer gal in the silver tunic outfit will come find him at 9:08 to go backstage. The remarks should be no more than six minutes about education—how important it is and all that. Melanie wants everything wrapped by 10—speech, auction, bidding. Then everyone can dance and revel. I'm sure you have something prepared, yes? Please make sure the Huntington is mentioned. Helen, do you understand?"

"Yes, Sarah. 9:08. Six minutes. Huntington. Got it." That was all I could manage. Patrick was killing me with his immaturity.

"Have a wonderful time, Patrick. Save a dance for me, will you?" He'd regained his composure. Sarah checked her Blackberry. "Ufff. Here comes Annabeth and Olympia—because they just haven't had enough attention lately. Gotta run. Six minutes! That's all!"

As Sarah disappeared into the flashing madness, I said, "Please tell me I'm not that uptight."

"Not nearly. Well, not nearly as often," Patrick replied. Then looking slightly concerned, he asked, "I didn't know I had to prepare any remarks. You didn't by any chance prepare any remarks for me, did you?"

I whipped a folded index card out of my evening bag. "Take back the uptight part and I'll give you the card."

"Is thorough different from uptight?"

"Keep trying," I called over my shoulder, shaking the 3x5 complete with all the important names to thank. I headed into the belly of the beast, straight to Table 1. I heard Patrick call out behind me, "Overprepared? Hyper-efficient? What's the opposite of spontaneous?"

Why did I think this was going to be fun? The next two hours were torture, high-society-style. I felt like I was caught in a slow-motion blender. The people of my former life as Mrs. Merritt Fairchild—Millington moms, benefit committee members, Merritt's former clients, Mitsy and her Pashmina Posse, Billy Owen and the Ignatius crowd, water polo dads, Mikki and Mimi and their Pasadena doppelgangers—collided in a whirring, scary soup with the figures from my new life as Helen Fairchild, Research Assistant—Patrick, Team Aphrodite, the director of the Huntington. I was whip-sawed between the two crowds. I nodded, smiled and accepted good wishes and stale condolences at the same time.

Moving on at the benefit proved to be harder than standing still at the funeral.

The most difficult part of the evening was pretending not to be paranoid about the millions of questions about Patrick from members of the Mrs. Merritt Fairchild circle. *Tell me about your escort*, the Pashmina Posse wanted to know. *Do I see you have a new man in your life?* the benefit committee members asked. *Is that your brother?* Merritt's frat buddies speculated. No, no, I answered. He is my boss, my colleague, a guy I know from work. I talked him into doing this for the good of the schools, I joked. Oh him? He's leaving town Tuesday. The inquisition didn't stop until we sat down at Table 1, surrounded by the New Me crowd: Annabeth, Olympia, Sarah and most of the Huntington board, who didn't know me from Adam.

By the time dinner was served, I felt chopped, grated and pulverized. And the very fitted bodice of my dress wasn't helping much either. I could barely breathe.

That's when Jennifer Barham tapped my shoulder, "It's 9:08. You're supposed to have him backstage. We're about to start the program!" Despite her unpleasant and completely unnecessary tone, I was grateful to have an excuse to hide in a dark corner and get my wits about me. Plus I could bail on the erudite discussion on antiquities acquisition being staged by Annabeth and the head of the Huntington's medieval manuscript collection. I'd added nothing in the last ten minutes except, "Pass the butter." I grabbed my wrap, evening bag and wine glass and tapped Patrick on the shoulder. "We've got to go. I'll go over the remarks backstage."

Patrick, completely engaged in the conversation, rose

reluctantly and excused himself. "Showtime. I've got an honor to accept."

"And then he's being auctioned off to the highest bidder, isn't that right, Dr. O'Neill?" Annabeth added. Olympia hooted, good sport that she was.

"Yes, I'm hoping some rich older woman buys me and keeps me in spades for life," Patrick quipped.

Be careful what you wish for, I thought.

Backstage was not exactly the *sanctum pacem* I'd envisioned. Melanie was in full Neutron mode, sniping at the stage manager and the professional auctioneer. The superintendant of schools cowered nearby, no doubt waiting for his check and a quick exit. In a crowd of men, Melanie's voice stood out like a Siren, but not in a good way. "I am never hiring a weatherman again. Unbelievable. How dare he not show? Don't you think the dead-relative card is a little tired? Thank God we got Roshelle to fill in. Jennifer, how long until she's ready?"

Please tell me no. Please tell me that dapper and dependable weatherman Jackson Snowe—his real name—did not cancel. He does almost every benefit in town with graciousness and warmth. I was looking forward to his weather jokes! Noooo! Please tell me that Shelly Sleazy is not stepping in to fill his shoes.

"She's lip-glossing now. Ready in three."

And then my husband's mistress emerged from the portable dressing room, wearing the same Loehmann's dress as that fateful night of the Save the Deodars event. Maybe she was hoping to catch somebody else's husband. This was now officially the worst night of my life. A small gasp escaped my lips. Patrick heard. "Okay, you're not uptight, efficient or any of those other names I called you. You're the consummate professional. How does that sound? Can I have the card now?"

Tearing my eyes away from the taut, elaborately eye-shadowed Roshelle Simms, I concentrated on Patrick. "Here, every-body you need to thank is on this card. Read the names out loud and let me hear you pronounce them. I'll correct any mispronun-ciations."

Then Neutron Mel was at our side with Shelly. "Patrick, dear, I wanted to introduce you to our Mistress of Ceremonies before we all go onstage. This is Roshelle Simms. She graciously of-fered to step in at the last minute when that damn weatherman cancelled. Roshelle, our honoree Dr. Patrick O'Neill. Oh, and maybe you know Helen?"

Roshelle threw her shoulders back and extended her hand to greet Patrick. "Dr. O'Neill, I've heard so much about you." *Liar. I don't think Patrick's been mentioned in US Magazine, your only news source besides your teleprompter.* "And Helen?" Roshelle then did one of those tilted dog head moves, feigning non-recognition. She looked so ridiculous, I almost felt sorry for her. Almost.

I took some inspiration from an unlikely source: Mitsy. "We've met before, Roshelle. You emceed the tree benefit for me last year. I believe you were wearing the same dress. And then I saw you again with your news van at my late husband Merritt's funeral. Do you remember me now?" My tone was flat, even and deadly. Not one iota of Aggressively Perky Helen.

Melanie and Patrick were struck dumb while Shelly Sleazy whimpered out, "Oh, yes." Victory. A tiny little victory for me.

"Well, that's been established," Melanie interjected. "We've got to get going, Roshelle, let's get you on stage. Can you walk with me, honey? Right, let's get going." With a nudge, Neutron Mel maneuvered a stunned Roshelle to the stage. Shelly Sleazy was going to need some more lip gloss to get through the night.

"You're going to have to explain that to me," Patrick said in an admiring voice.

"Later."

Sometime between Patrick's short speech and Melanie's introduction of the Treasures of Troy and the Glories of Greece auction item, I regained my composure. I could breathe again, at least as much as my ever-shrinking dress would allow. I would survive the sight of Roshelle Simms, just like I'd survived selling my house and consigning my wedding china—with an acceptance of the inevitable.

Could the big lesson in life possibly be "life happens"?

"Do I hear twenty thousand dollars? Twenty thousand dollars?" The professional auctioneer had taken over the microphone, whipping the well-juiced crowd into a frenzy. From my dark backstage corner, I could see a sliver of Patrick, uncomfortable onstage. As quickly as the auctioneer shrieked out dollar values, paddles were raised. Twenty-five, thirty, thirty-five thousand, forty. From my spot in the wings, I couldn't tell who was bidding, but the competition was intense. Melanie looked as though her head was going to blow off with excitement, holding her own paddle by her side, letting others do the bidding. Maybe she was waiting to step in at the very end and be the hero? When the total bidding reached fifty thousand, the pace slowed, the tension built. Just then, Jennifer Barham rushed by me backstage, holding a note. She raced up the stairs and gave the paper to Melanie.

Melanie raised the mic to her mouth and shouted, "Halt the bidding. Halt the bidding!" All she needed was a German accent to complete the effect. The room hushed in anticipation. Or fear for their lives. "I am speechless. Speechless! We have received a bid that is beyond our wildest expectations! The bidder would like to remain anonymous—but I can announce the amount of the bid. Pasadena, are you ready?"

The black-tie crowd did its best to preserve its dignity while sending up an *American Idol*-like round of applause and shouts.

"I am holding a bid for the Treasures of Troy and the Glories of Greece for a quarter of a million dollars. Two hundred and fifty thousand dollars!" Now the crowd cheered for real.

Melanie jumped up and down, waving the note and repeating the number over and over again. Hugging ensued on stage, as if they had all cured cancer and reunited the Beatles simultaneously. Melanie, the auctioneer, the superintendant, Roshelle, Jennifer embracing indiscriminately. Oh please, were those tears in Roshelle's eyes?

Patrick stood to the side and shook his head in disbelief. Who would bid that kind of cash for a trip with him? Melanie was asking the same question, "This is a verified anonymous bid. But would that bidder like to come forward now? Your contribution will make a difference to thousands of Pasadena schoolchildren. Please, let us honor you for your generosity."

Necks strained and nervous applause turned into a driving hand-clapped beat. I peeked through the curtain to see which of Pasadena's old guard or new money would stand up and be recognized. Nobody really wanted to be anonymous, did they? Was it the Gambles? The Montagues? That guy who pitched for the Dodgers? Those people who invented Post-its—the Averys? The clapping got louder, more insistent. Melanie tried one more time, "Please, good soul, let us say thank you?"

And then, from Table Two, the Minoan Snake Goddess rose. Mitsy Fairchild stood up, tall and straight, and made her way to the stage. Wearing an elegant gold lamé dress and a dramatic piece of gold jewelry in her hair, Mitsy owned the night. She took her sweet time, creating a piece of theater like no other. She gestured to Mikki and Mimi to join her on stage, which, of course, they did.

Mitsy did not appear to be looking for me in the crowd.

As I watched her approach the stage from my position backstage, one thing was clear: She'd never had any intention of remaining anonymous. Mitsy removed a tiny slip of paper from her sleeve. Notes for her speech. Unbelievable.

That's when it hit me that this whole thing was scripted. And Melanie was the costar. That's why she hadn't bothered to raise her paddle to bid. She knew Mitsy's bid before the auction had started.

Mitsy greeted Patrick with a false gesture of humility, hands in prayer position, head bowed. She double-kissed Melanie and embraced the flushed superintendant. And, true to form, she completely ignored the open arms of Roshelle Slusky. Absorbing the adulation, she made her way to the microphone. Finally, acknowledging a standing ovation from the faithful at the tables, she began her un-impromptu remarks, "I wish my son Merritt was here tonight...."

Air. I needed air.

"Hey, I've been looking for you." Patrick discovered me leaning against a tent pole out back, staring up at the moon. "Were you hiding?"

"Yes. But I knew you'd find me. You're an archaeologist, right?"

"Did you see that?" Patrick was halfway between amused and bewildered at the drama of the last few minutes.

"You got your wish. A rich old lady won you."

"Yeah. That was weird, wasn't it? Isn't she your...."

"Yeah. She is." There was nothing else to say on that subject. At least, not then.

Patrick reached for me and pulled me into his chest. I buried my head in his shoulder, closed my eyes and pictured that we were anywhere but there. "What do you want to do now?" he asked softly.

I didn't hesitate. "I want to get out of this dress."

CHAPTER 22

"How do you feel?"

"Wonderful. Completely ... satisfied."

Oh, and I did. The deluxe cheeseburger (with sweet potato fries) delivered by room service at the luxury Langham Hotel had lived up to its billing as "the Most Delicious Burger Brought Right to Your Door." Its $36 price tag, plus tax, tip and service charge, was worth every penny. The chocolate shake was overkill, but Patrick had insisted I order it. He drank most of it while I sipped some herbal tea.

The Five Schools Benefit committee had provided the junior suite at the historic Langham Hotel and Spa in appreciation for his auction donation and other services. Patrick had the room for the weekend, he explained as we were fleeing the scene of the benefit. "Are you kidding me? Of course I took it. I do a lot of traveling, but the places I go do not feature five-star hotels. Most of them have goats in the front yard. And the faculty housing I've been in for months is losing its charm, now that the botanist club moved in next door. Botanists can party, I'm telling you."

He carried on amenably, perhaps to distract me from the fact that my mother-in-law, who couldn't be bothered to pay one red cent toward Aiden's education, had just pledged a quarter of a million dollars toward the education of complete strangers. Or that my husband's mistress had shown up wearing the same ensemble as the night she entertained my husband in her dressing room a year ago. He rambled on like I would have, had I been in the driver's seat and he been the stunned passenger. "Plus, the room has a private entrance. No familiar faces, I promise. Just us."

"That sounds perfect. Thank you." I answered.

He was right. We slipped into his suite unseen. The room smelled like clean linens and lavender. The lighting was low, and I could still hear the band from the benefit in the near distance. I didn't feel the slightest bit awkward. Working in such close quarters had given us a natural ease. And the relief I felt to be out of the benefit was palpable.

Priority number one was the removal of my Mary McFadden dress. Patrick's plan was to unhook the top while I took emergency measures to prevent my loosened B-cup bodice from exposing my C-cup breasts. After several unsuccessful attempts, he asked, "Should I call down to the desk for a crowbar?" Which only made me shake with laughter, making the process infinitely more difficult.

"Don't rip it. It's a rental!" I countered, which made Patrick laugh so hard he could barely perform the fine motor skill necessary to finish the task.

Finally, I was free and could take myself into the bathroom for the rest of the dress-removal process. He tossed me some sweats and the original Nubby Sweater, which I gratefully put on. I felt like a college girl in her boyfriend's clothes. There was that smell of lemon verbena again. I took down my hair, tossed the hair extensions and re-applied my lipstick. One quick look in the mirror told me that I'd gone from Helen of Pasadena to Helen again.

At least I had on lipstick.

By the time room service arrived, I'd spilled my life story. Well, at least the short, entertaining version of the last year: my average, unexciting marriage; Merritt's New Year's Eve confession about Roshelle; the death by panda; my dire financial situation that resulted in selling almost everything I owned; Aiden's high school admissions odyssey; and finally, my dread at facing a future with no job, no man, no house. It took me about 25 minutes to go through the whole year. And honestly, by the time I got to the "no job, no man, no house" part, I was feeling downright energetic. "The funny thing is that it hasn't been all bad. Meeting you, working with you, rediscovering something I loved—that's ... that's been great. It's changed me."

And then I polished off the cheeseburger while Patrick finished the shake, taking in my confession. "Everybody has an unexpected story, Helen. Isn't that what we proved this spring? Now I know yours. And, can I add, you're a good actress, so maybe Aiden inherited that from you. I never would have guessed *all that* was going on in your life."

"I wasn't acting at the office. I was escaping. Rudy and Sophia's illicit affair? Or the steamy side of Helen and Paris? Much easier to deal with than my own husband's behavior."

"That's the thing about archaeology. You can get so lost in someone else's life, you forget your own."

"Is that your story?"

"I'll tell you tomorrow." Patrick rolled the room service cart out the door, padding around in bare feet and his tux pants, presumably because I had on his loungewear. *Tell me tomorrow?* "Okay, here's the question: Do you want me to take you and your dress home?" He came closer; I stood up to meet him. "Or will you stay with me tonight?"

There was only one reason to take my dress and go home: I didn't know the plan. I didn't know where one night with him would lead. And in the past, the not-knowing would have stopped me. But not anymore.

"I'd like to stay."

"Are you sure?"

"Completely."

Even the feel of Patrick's warm hands running up and down my bare back couldn't relax me. *Stop thinking, Helen!* I tried to concentrate on the feel of his skin against mine, over my shoulder blades, forearms, hips. Was I shaking? Was it obvious? Patrick bent down to kiss me, but stopped. "You're nervous."

I guess I *was* shaking and it *was* obvious. *Please, don't let me blow this.* I willed myself to press into his body, like physically connecting with him would give me the courage to go on. "It's been a long time since..."

"I know." Patrick smoothed my hair, his lips brushing against my neck, then the top of my ears, then my earlobes. He worked his hands down to my waist and effortlessly slid the oversized sweats off, running his strong fingers over my hips. His sweater reached to my thighs, but I had on nothing underneath, as his hands discovered. A happy discovery, judging by the intake of his breath. And mine.

Patrick kept his mouth moving all over my body, not letting me escape. "Remember that day in the office, when I was first showing you photos of the site and you couldn't see the ancient outline, the change in elevation, because you were trying so hard to see it?"

I nodded as I ran my hands over his chest softly, slightly afraid. "Yes."

His lips found just the right spot on my forehead, my temples, my eyelids. "Then you relaxed. You stopped focusing and you finally saw." Again, his hands scraped down my back and under the limited protection of the sweater. "Do that, Helen." His fingers drifted over my breasts, then back for more. I immediately responded. "Relax." His hips pressed firmly into mine. "Breathe." His legs intertwined with mine. Then, just like the time before, Patrick ran his rough finger lightly against the side of my face and whispered, "Stop focusing."

And so I did.

And when his lips finally met mine fully, I was oblivious to everything but the pleasure, the sensation of being desired. And oh my God, of wanting a man, of wanting Patrick so much. We stood pressed against each other in the middle of the room, the pressure between our two bodies holding the other up. His mouth was gentle, then not. Any doubts vanished. My hands came alive, seeking him. I couldn't touch him enough, like I hadn't really touched another body in forever. I needed to feel his skin next to mine. His dress shirt came off slowly, one stud at a time. Then I unzipped his pants quickly. He let them drop to the floor and elegantly stepped out of the pools by his feet. Dr. Patrick O'Neill wore some very revealing black European briefs. If there were any flaws in this man, I didn't see them. He was wonderfully real. I took him all in: his lovely arms, his deep collarbone that I'd been staring at for months, wanting to trace with my fingers, his perfectly hairy chest. The tattoo of the sun and stars. Oh, he looked good. I lowered my head, too embarrassed by my desire to meet his eyes. I brushed my mouth against his nipples. Patrick moaned, the sound of sweet arousal. "Helen ..."

"I'm not focusing, just like you told me," I teased, rolling my tongue back and forth, first on the right side, then on the left. His whole body hardened.

"How about you not focus in bed?" His knees buckled, as my fingers found the very top of those very tight black briefs. And then inside. I gently pushed him back toward the bed, enjoying his enjoyment. Patrick stretched out on the cool crisp sheets of the generous hotel bed, watching me the whole time as I approached. I kneeled on the edge of the mattress. His mouth curled wickedly, "I think I'd like my sweater back now. I'm a touch chilly."

"Oh, you're never getting this sweater back," I declared as I straddled my archaeologist, squeezing my thighs against his. "It's the Nubby Sweater."

"It's what?" he said, rising up on his elbows, accentuating a very respectable set of abdominal muscles. "The Nubby Sweater?"

"You were wearing it the day we met. By the Diana statue."

"I remember. You were wearing a very cute scarf." Patrick reached his hands out to rub my thighs, then deeper and higher.

His touch was fire; the pressure was perfect. I circled my hips, barely able to hold on. Now it was my turn to moan involuntarily while Patrick took control. "Do you still have the scarf?"

"I do."

"Maybe we can trade."

"Deal." I backed off, not wanting to rush the inevitable.

Patrick relaxed back on the pillow. His eyes looked deep blue, but not playful anymore. "Now please stop talking and take off that sweater."

And so I did.

The clank of the hotel door indicated that it was safe to get up and roam about the room. Patrick had departed, and judging by his outfit, which I spied while pretending to be asleep, he was off for a run. But not before leaving a large coffee, a scone, a shopping bag, assorted sundries and a note on my bedside table.

I turned on the light and grabbed the coffee. The note read: *On a run. Back by 10. Don't leave.*

Don't leave, how romantic.

Stop it. You said you weren't going to be that way, Helen.

I amused myself with the task of opening the bag, rather than dwelling on unrealistic visions of happily-ever-after. It was an adorable sweatsuit from the spa shop. The velour kind with the hoodie and low-slung pants that had been in style, then out of style, then back again, because it was just too comfortable and cute to really ever go away for good. Exactly the kind of loungewear I would never buy for myself, fearing that I could never pull off that sexy casual look with my saddlebags. But Patrick thought I could! In charcoal gray, my color! Again, I had to temper my expectations.

Lecture to self: *He's leaving Tuesday. You are staying. You are both grownups and this was one night. His life will go on. And yours will, too. You got it out of your system. Same with him. It was great, but it is over.*

It was great, but it is over, I repeated out loud to make sure that I understood fully.

And with that, I hopped out of bed and into the shower, slightly reluctant to wash the night away so quickly.

Patrick discovered me sitting out on the balcony of the suite, overlooking the landscaped pool area, unnaturally thrilled about the success of the velour sweatsuit on my body type. I felt happy at a cellular level.

Before he returned, I'd been responding to the texts from Tina from last night, each one getting progressively more frantic, then accepting:

Where r u?

OMG, Shelley Sleazy.

OMG, WTF Mitsy?

R u still here?

Do u need ride home?

OK? Guess not. Good luck.

Call in morning.

Candy had sent just one: Holy Crap. You deserve best night of life. Go get it.

And finally, one text in from Rita the Armenian: Have found your house! 1112 Sunshine St. Perfect. Meet me at 1.

To Tina I responded: Am alive and well. Very.

To Candy, I responded: I did.

To Rita, I responded: See u at 1.

I had just put away my phone when a sweaty Patrick walked through the door, in running shorts and an Arsenal T-shirt. "Hey."

"Hey." Apparently time and life experience have not made this portion of the morning after any easier. I was looking for just the right mix of warmth and cool. "You're quite a provider: food, shelter, toothbrush, velour sweatsuits. Thank you."

"Good thing the spa shop opens so early. I thought that number was slightly better than the fuzzy bathrobe. Though personally, I like anything fuzzy," he said, grabbing a nine dollar bottle of water from the minibar and taking a big swig. "I didn't think you'd want to be waltzing through the lobby in your dress. Half the people arriving for Sunday brunch were at the party last night. They recover fast!"

Of course! The brunch at the Langham was the classic gathering spot for party postmortems! "Well, the Langham has a new executive chef, and he is really superb," I said in my best lock-jawed Mitsy imitation. Then I added in my own voice, "And I think you're fully integrated here if you actually recognize people in the brunch line at the Langham." It was the perfect opportunity to let him off the hook. "It's a good thing you're leaving before Pasadena sucks you in."

"Thanks for the warning. I think I'm getting out just in time," he laughed, and then the easy conversation ended. He seemed to be searching for a way into the inevitable. "Helen, you know, I don't have the kind of life that makes for great relationships. Up until now, my work has been everything. I live in Athens part of the year, then Turkey in the summer. I travel in between. I live on next to nothing…"

My turn to be the hero. I put my hand up. "Patrick, I had a wonderful time last night. But, I understand the reality of your life. Mine isn't any more relationship-friendly. You don't have to explain anything. Please. I know what this is. I get it. It stays here. Nothing more."

Our eyes met and held for an uncomfortable moment.

"Oh, okay," he agreed tentatively, seemingly surprised at my preemptive strike. Did I throw him off? Was he headed in a different direction? "I was just … never mind, you're right. We do have very different lives to get back to, Helen. I guess that's just the way it is. But last night, I, um, enjoyed your company." He breathed deeply, as if that portion of the conversation was over and he was relieved. And then a long pause. "So, what's next? I mean today, what's next today?"

I almost blurted out, "Come see a house with me!" But I managed to contain myself. If this were a normal relationship, if Patrick weren't leaving in two days, never to return, and if I weren't still supposed to be in mourning for my dead husband, there would be nothing sweeter than spending the day with my new man. A personal fantasyland: a long, lazy lunch; house-hunting for an adorable cottage; dinner around the table with Patrick and Aiden getting to know each other better.

But this wasn't fantasyland. And trying to integrate Patrick into my life here in Pasadena would only make Tuesday more terrible.

So I put him off with a complete lie. "I have something really important to do later. You know, with Aiden. It's a Fairchild thing. And ..." the babbling started. "You must have packing and all kinds of craziness going on. Wow, you're leaving in two days. I can't imagine everything you have to do. It's too bad about...."

It's too bad about *what?* That I didn't meet Patrick twenty years ago?

"... the timing."

"Yes, it is too bad about the timing," he gave me a long look. "I do have a few things to do. But any chance you can grab lunch first? Something quick. Tacos?" There was that smile.

"Sure." *Tacos or cardboard, whatever you want.*

"And a shower?"

I cocked my head. "I just took one."

"I think you may need another," said the archaeologist, removing his shirt. "I know I do."

Maybe I could learn to like this no-expectations thing.

The house was never quieter than that night. I'd gotten into the habit of turning on the TV, the radio, the stereo—anything to make noise to cover the silence—since Merritt's death. But that night, I sat alone in the living room embracing the quiet, even ignoring the buzz of my cell phone. A call from Annabeth. Then another. That's odd, I thought. I'd listen to the voicemail tomorrow.

Aiden was up in his bedroom, slogging through history homework without enthusiasm, trying to grind out the last few weeks of Millington. Just pass the classes, I begged. Get out clean and then you're free! He was putting in just enough effort to keep the Ds at bay.

I was nursing a glass of wine and staring at the school calendar, my last vestige of an undigitized life. Everything I needed to do in the next six weeks was scribbled on the appropriate day, old school: Patrick leaves, visit performing-arts school, last day at Huntington, Mother's Day with Mitsy, final artwork auctioned, antiques dealer comes for dining room set, exams for Aiden, meeting with accountant, Aiden's graduation, movers arrive. I added a new scribble on moving day: Close on Sunshine Street house?

As Rita had promised, the Sunshine Street bungalow was perfect, a jewel-box example of Craftsman architecture typical of Pasadena, just like my *Sunset* magazine fantasy. It was small, cozy and in my price range. It had two bedrooms, one bath and a tiny attic where Aiden could escape from my constant gaze. The kitchen was as neat as a pin and about as big as a postage stamp. The living room had a fireplace; the dining nook had a stained-glass window. Outside was a porch wide enough to hold two chairs and a table, so we could sit out front, watching the traffic or the toddlers across the street. The garden was drought-tolerant and guilt-free, and there was a firepit and an outdoor shower in the minuscule backyard. The house was move-in condition in a wash of blues and greens. If my life were a Reese Witherspoon movie, this would be the set.

"If you don't make an offer, I will kill you," Rita had said after our private showing, just before the agent had an open house.

"Do it now, the open house starts in an hour. I want you to have your offer on the table when they throw open the doors to the rest of these people," she said, waving her hands around, vaguely indicating the masses that would soon be my Bungalow Heaven Adjacent neighbors. "You'll be happy here for a few years. You're young, you'll meet a nice man, maybe he's a widow or divorced, and you'll be back in a bigger house in no time. Don't worry. This is not forever. But it's perfect for now."

This is not forever. But it's perfect for now. That should be my new mantra. And, in fact, the house was perfect for now. Move-in condition and a relatively good street, except for the Tanzou Chicken restaurant on the corner. (Silver lining! We'd always have something to eat.) And it was walking distance to the train, the one into downtown that Aiden would need to take to school. He could come and go on his own, an advantage if I was going to be stuck in some office somewhere.

When I told him about Sunshine Street, Aiden simply said, "Good. I can't wait to move. Our house doesn't feel right anymore." He nailed it. It did feel like we were living in somebody else's home: Merritt's home. I couldn't wait to move, either.

I offered full price.

Now I sat staring at my calendar. After the move date, I had nothing written down. Not a single thing.

I arrived at work on Monday morning with one thought on my mind: Do not cry.

Do not become a blubbering idiot when it is time to say goodbye to Patrick at the end of the day. Hold it together, Helen. You did it at the funeral, you can do it now. *That's quite a pep talk.*

I took my time in the morning, not wanting to be early. Better if he arrived first and I made a dramatic entrance. I put on jeans and a fitted V-neck T-shirt. I thought my outfit said, "I'm here to pack you up and send you off to Moscow" without being too obvious, despite the fact that at the correct angle, anyone could see right down my shirt. I put on some perfume and lipstick. I was a basket case.

Coffee and scones were my big idea. Hoping to avoid the awkward moment when it was clear that the physical relationship between Patrick and me was over, I thought props would help. The hotel had been great, really great, especially the shower bit, which was so, *so* sudsy. But that was 24 hours ago. By my assessment, we were colleagues again. I figured having full hands when I arrived would take care of the "should we kiss" moment. Everybody knows you don't embrace someone holding a tray of coffee. Solid planning, I thought.

One look inside the office and it was clear—as usual, I had overplanned.

Patrick was already gone. His desk was cleared. Files were boxed. Post-it notes with addresses and instructions dotted the room.

He was gone.

And I thought I was bad at goodbyes.

There was a note on my desk. And a bag from the Huntington's gift shop! Well, fuck him, I didn't need a decorative paper weight. Oh my God, I was so angry I wanted to scream, but I didn't, fearful of the excellent hearing of Karen from Library. I smashed the scones into the desktop instead.

How could he just leave like that? What a coward.

Then I read the note:

Helen,

My plans changed at the last minute. I had to work in a stop-over in London to see my daughter. She is fine, but I need to be there. I didn't want to bother you at home last night, as you said you had a family obligation.

I hope you understand.

I did my best to clean up after myself, and I hope the instructions are clear about what to do with all the boxes. I will send addi-

tional instructions. E-mail if you have questions.

I never expected my time in Pasadena to yield so much for me personally or professionally. Helen, you are part of that unexpected pleasure.

Please open the bag. I kept up my end of the deal.

Patrick

I reached into the bag and pulled out the Nubby Sweater, still smelling of lemon verbena, of Patrick.

That's when I started to cry.

CHAPTER 23

Our footsteps pounded around the Rose Bowl. Was this the four hundredth time Candy, Tina and I had walked these three miles? Or the four millionth? Who knew? I only knew that it felt good to be up early, beating the blistering July-in-Pasadena heat.

"So that's the story," Candy recounted. "Candysdish is exploding, I may get a regular gig on Access Hollywood, and still my daughter refuses to go to Raleigh. Turning down a waitlist spot! I'll be over there with the exhausted Catholic moms at Sacred Sisters. At least I won't have to get dressed up for the Mother's Club meetings! I guess when it's your fifth time through high school, you don't give a shit what you look like. It's so refreshing to be in a roomful of women where nobody is a single-digit size. Who would have thought a year ago that my daughter would be going to a school with kilts and your son would be going to the *Fame* school, dancing in the lunchroom? Okay, what's next?" True to form, Candy was a fine moderator, guiding our conversation on the walk, letting each of us talk and vent before moving on to the next person or topic.

Already, Tina had updated us on her vacation plans: The La Jolla Beach Club, of course, and then a week in Minnesota with Anders's family at some "godforsaken lake house with spiders and mold. Ten thousand lakes and we go to the same miserable place every year."

Tina also filled us in on the Spanish immersion camp that Lilly would be attending soon, followed by a week at Girls Rule Leadership Camp. Then a stint of community service that included "playing chess with poor kids." The college resume-building had begun in the Chau-Swenson household.

Then Tina shocked both Candy and me by announcing her new career. After her experience pulling me up by my bootstraps emotionally, sartorially and legally, she had an epiphany. Her particular set of skills was gold to women recovering from divorce or the death of a spouse. She was marketing herself as a lawyer/life coach, specializing in "Post-traumatic Reinvention of Spirit, Closet and Contracts."

"Tina, that is brilliant niche marketing," Candy gushed, and I agreed. "I'll feature you on the site. Helen, you've got to blurb Tina. You are the poster child for post-traumatic reinvention!"

Tina looked extremely pleased with herself. "Thanks, you guys. I was worried you might think it was a really bad idea. But I think I have a gift! Sometimes that starts with a divorce settlement. And sometimes that starts with your wardrobe. And let's face it, after a decade of doing volunteer work, I want to get paid for my time!"

"Amen to a paycheck!" Candy witnessed. She was in an insanely great mood. It must be her new romance with the recently single top dermatologist in town. Forget Dr. Feelgood—Candy had found Dr. Lookgood. She'd bought a series of Botox injections at the benefit silent auction, and one shot was all it took for the relationship to blossom. Though she swore she'd never get involved with another doctor, dermatologists apparently didn't count. For the past two months, they'd been hot and heavy, but on the down low. The less she talked about a relationship, the more it mattered. And in the case of the distinguished doc, she'd barely breathed a word, except to say, "Best charity donation ever!" Could he be Husband Number Three?

"Candy, you better watch all that interaction with Hollywood. You're starting to talk like a fake person. Blurb is not a verb," I said. "But of course, I will write a ringing endorsement of your work, Tina. Do you want before and after photos, too?"

"I love it!" Candy cried. "And hey, Ms. Hollywood Producer,

glass houses. You're the one with the fancy title, not me. And I'm pretty sure I heard you say "up fronts" the other day, so you're busted."

"How is work?" Tina asked as we rounded the far northwest corner of the Rose Bowl, the conversation turning to me.

"Still a dream! It's great." My dream job had started the day after the Patrick departure nightmare. Annabeth and Olympia insisted I come to lunch in Beverly Hills, despite the fact that I was having trouble even thinking about, never mind dressing for, a Hollywood lunch. I was a victim of Paralysis of the Heartbroken. But I forced myself out of bed and into Work Outfit #5, updated khakis and V-neck cashmere sweater. Lunch at the venerable Ivy turned into a three-hour affair with wine, laughter and a Julia Roberts sighting. During lunch, Team Aphrodite offered me the position of executive producer of *The Dirty Archaeologist*. I almost fell off my chair into a potted plant.

Olympia, with her flawless diction and equally flawless complexion, insisted that they simply could not imagine doing the show without my steady, knowledgeable hand. I had proven to be the perfect candidate for the job while helping with the Patrick segment: researching topics; scheduling crew and locations; interfacing with the director; writing questions for the host; rehearsing answers with the interviewee; securing coffee for all involved. Apparently, that qualifies as producing! Olympia finished by saying that only I understood their language *and* had the practical work ethic to get the job done.

Annabeth chimed in with more ego stroking. I'd shaped the Schliemann Journals segment, gotten the best out of Patrick *and* managed to get all the production details right, down to the flower arrangements in the cottage. That's exactly the type of academic approach combined with an entertainment instinct that the show needed.

When I protested that I'd never executive-produced a television show before, they both howled. Olympia said, "Neither have we, and that hasn't stopped us! Television is full of people who only know television, not real life. You know something critical, Helen. You know how to get things done."

Though I tried to come up with any excuse not to take the job—the fifteen-minute commute, the hours, the potential for travel—there was nothing really solid stopping me. I had to take it. Right then. So, fifteen years after my last paying job, six months after my husband's death, and one day after Patrick left town, I became the executive producer of *The Dirty Archaeologist*.

For the last month, I had to pinch myself as I headed into work every day. I held down the home office in Burbank, spending my days suggesting segments, booking guests, pre-interviewing guests and making decisions about music, visuals and artwork. The kind of stuff I'd done for years as part of my volunteer work or to help Aiden with his projects. I loved every aspect of the job, especially working with Olympia and Annabeth, who were flying all over the world, shooting at archaeological sites from Peru to Stonehenge, constantly calling me for input.

"Feel free to treat the rest of the production staff like your teenage son. Repeat everything ten times, expect attitude and yell if necessary. That should work. They'll do all the nitty gritty stuff—the schedules, travel details, filming visas. We need you for the big picture," Olympia had advised, adding with a stage whisper, "And to keep Annabeth sane."

That's exactly what I did, minus the yelling at the staff. That wasn't my style. Too many years of Fairchild restraint under my belt to start screaming now. In truth, being the executive producer of a television show was not that different from chairing the Word-Write festival.

It might even have been easier.

But I didn't let on to Tina and Candy. I was enjoying the fact that people in town were impressed by my job, not my spouse's job, as had so long been the case. Plus, I needed some advice.

"So here's the deal: Annabeth and Olympia want me to go to Turkey, to the Troy site, to do a follow-up interview with Patrick. They think we need it for the pilot episode. What did Patrick learn in Moscow? Is Priam's Treasure a fake? Did he prove it? You know, basic stuff. In terms of the interview, anyway. I just don't think I can do it. I'm not sure I can face him in person. I don't know what to do."

"Go!" Tina and Candy said simultaneously.

"But what if I get there and it's all wrong? What if it's weird and awkward? I keep thinking that maybe I imagined us."

Candy had the answer. "You did not imagine the night at the Langham. First of all, more people saw you leave that hotel than you think! And second, you deserve some fun. So why not? Go to Troy and have an amazing adventure. What's wrong with that?"

"It feels like it's done, it's over." At least according to Patrick, judging from the business-like tone of his communications. He updated me on research, sent photos from the site, and requested press releases and documents about the TV show, but he made no mention of any personal relationship. He was friendly and warm but not the slightest bit suggestive. He seemed to have erased our night together.

But not me. In the eight weeks since his departure, I had not stopped thinking about him, despite my constant attempts to get him out of my head by creating enormous work and life distractions. I threw myself into planning a graduation party for Aiden and braced myself for Mitsy's reaction to Aiden's new high school plans. I packed and moved from one house to another. I watched Emilia marry Juan and go to work for the Gays with my blessing. I put Aiden on a plane to spend the summer working on the river with my brother and living with my crazy, adoring parents. I worked every free moment, trying to get up to speed. I even signed up for another round of grief recovery therapy to make sense of the last year.

And still, I couldn't get Patrick out of my head.

I thrilled at his every mundane e-mail. I blushed over the simplest instant messages. I went over the night at the Langham—hell, I went over every interaction we ever had, again and again and again. "I think I need a sign, something to tell me that flying halfway around the world and showing up on Patrick's dig site is not going to be a giant act of personal humiliation. I need an auger like the Greeks. Someone to read the birds and tell me what to do."

"You really need a flock of birds to tell you what to do? Sometimes you are more like your hippie mother than you think!" *Don't I know it.* As we rounded the northeast corner of the Rose Bowl and headed for home, Candy asked, "What does Life Coach Tina say?"

"Yeah, if you want that blurb, tell me what to do."

"Helen, take what you've learned this year and apply it." Tina said in her most obtuse Life Coach Speak.

"*What*? Is that what they taught you at Life Coach School? That's no good. Be Tina, not Life Coach Tina."

"Fine. Go. Get on that plane tomorrow. That's what I'd do," Tina said, snapping her fingers for emphasis. "But if you need some sign from the universe, then wait for a sign. Just don't wait too long! The summer will be over soon. And I don't think you want the proverbial dust to settle that long."

"Go, Helen," Candy agreed. "Be brave. And then you'll know."

That's the catch, I thought. Then I'd know.

There was no mistaking the elegant figure or the dynamic pace. Sarah White was marching toward me, signaling with her hand that she either needed a cab or wanted me to wait. Since there are no cabs roaming the streets of Old Pasadena, I assumed she wanted to talk to me. Damn. I was caught red-handed with a large pomegranate frozen yogurt with kiwi and almonds.

Eating in public, on the street, in my velour hoodie ensemble, was something the well-bred Sarah would never do.

Oh my God, did Karen from Library discover the ripped page in the journals? I was dead meat!

"Hello, my long-lost friend!" Sarah bubbled, moving in for a social hug while trying to avoid my fro-yo. "You must have the day off. Look how casual you are. What a treat. How are things? How's TV Land?"

"Great." Hallelujah, not the ripped page. What a relief! I'd barely seen Sarah since the night of the benefit. My sudden departure from the Huntington to produce a TV show coincided with her annual pilgrimage to the Smith reunion, so our goodbyes had been hasty. There had been a few e-mails back and forth, but no face-to-face meetings. As usual, she looked like a page out of the Saks catalogue in a short black pencil skirt and shiny gray top, continuing to make me feel short and underdressed. "I'm hanging in...."

"Super. Well, things are just fine at the Huntington. We miss you, of course, and we can't wait to see the Schliemann episode. And I'm sure you heard about Melanie coming on board as the new director of development. She's a powerhouse! She's going to make my job in public relations so much easier. She creates magic!" Sarah said, with complete seriousness.

"I heard. You two are some combo. Watch out!" Good for Melanie! She'd found an outlet for her ambition that did not involve firing nannies, terrorizing committee members or spending more of her husband's considerable fortune. She would be an asset to the Huntington, though the sudden early retirement of the former development director at the age of 52 was suspicious. My guess? Melanie offered him a "package" and he took it. "Melanie must be fun to have on board!"

I got the sense Sarah had something else on her mind. She did, as she explained quite dramatically. "*And* we have an exciting new Distinguished Scholar. Milton Westbrook. Of Swarthmore.

He's a Professor of Lithographic History and Ephemera. His specialty is the 19th century. He is a genius when it comes to color lithography and the impact on the social fabric of America. He's wonderful."

What the hell is ephemera? "Let me guess—he's single?"

"Well, he was until he got to Pasadena! Oh, Helen, it was love at first sight. Now I know lithography is not as sexy as archaeology. But he appreciates me. And I can learn to love vellum." By now, Sarah's well-bred veneer had given way to full-blown blushing. I thought she might ask for a taste of my yogurt, she was so far out of character.

"Sarah, I couldn't be happier for you." And I meant it. She'd come to my rescue when I needed it. I was happy she'd found what she wanted. "How long is Professor Westbrook going to be in Pasadena?"

"A year! And that's enough time, isn't it, Helen?"

"Enough time for what?"

"To figure out what to do with the rest of my life." Sarah was sincere in her concern.

"More than enough!" I laughed. That was months more than Patrick and I had, I thought. Lucky Sarah. "You look wonderful, so I would just enjoy your Distinguished Scholar and not worry too much about the future right now."

"Is that what happened with you and Patrick?"

My face drew a blank, partly because I'd never actually acknowledged any sort of relationship with Patrick to Sarah. And partly because the soupy yogurt was quickly seeping through the recyclable cup and I needed to wipe my hands on my pants, which might make Sarah faint. So, to buy time on both accounts, I stammered, "Umm...."

"Oh, Helen, everybody knew! Did you think we didn't notice the, the *thing* between you two? Even the security guard at the front gate used to talk about what a cute couple you made! He told us about the night you came back to the Huntington really late. Together." Sarah was full of surprises. And technically, it was only about nine that night, but whatever. "I thought you did, too. That's why I was surprised to hear that you broke it off."

"I'm sorry, you heard what?" I tossed the cup in a nearby garbage can and wiped my hands, propriety be damned. What was Sarah talking about? "From whom?"

"Patrick. Patrick told me. We've talked a half-dozen times since he had to fly off to London to see his daughter in the hospital. Or, 'in hospital,' as the British say. I'm sure you heard about the meningitis scare. Poor guy, he was beside himself the night he left. His daughter was out of the woods, but he wanted to see her," Sarah said.

Meningitis? I had no idea. He had never mentioned meningitis to me. There had only been the hint in his note that he needed to see his daughter. And nothing in the e-mails afterward, except that he had squeezed in a visit to London. Why? Why hadn't he explained? I didn't feel like pretending with Sarah anymore. "Sarah, what did he say about me breaking it off?'

"He told me that you didn't feel the timing was right. You seemed to want to keep it a 'one moment in time' sort of relationship." My face must have really fallen, because Sarah gasped, "Helen, are you okay?"

No, I wasn't. "I am an idiot."

"Do I have it wrong?"

"No, you have it right. I did say that. I thought … I thought I was saying what Patrick wanted to hear."

"How did that work for you the first time? With Merritt?" It was the most pointed thing Sarah had ever said to me, maybe that anyone had ever said to me. Is that what Life Coach Tina was trying to say when she suggested I take what I learned this year and apply it? Sarah looked at me with the understanding of someone who hadn't been particularly stellar in the relationship department either.

"You know, not that well." And we both laughed.

More than square footage and a prestige address, I missed my old air conditioning. In my haste to get in a bid on Sunshine Street, I'd failed to ask about central air. I discovered during the first triple-digit hot spell that my dream cottage had one tiny window unit and limited circulation.

I was still trying to sort out my financial situation with Bruno and Billy Owens in the aftermath of the house sale. "Don't do too much too soon," Bruno warned. Billy added, "Let's let the dust settle before you start making home improvements."

What Billy really meant was that investors to Fairchild Capital may still come out of the woods to sue. My strategy? Lay low and pray. By next summer, I'd know if I could afford AC. In the meantime, I took a lot of cold outdoor showers and sat around in the least amount of clothing possible. Thank God Aiden was in Oregon for the summer.

That's how Mitsy found me on a hot July night, dripping wet and barely dressed. I leapt to attention, hoping she could look beyond my tank top and batik pareo, underwear optional.

She could not. "Are you going to do the limbo later? You look positively native." Mitsy did, too, in apple-green golf skirt, pink polo shirt and Jack Rodgers sandals. Pasadena native.

Our relationship had been cool since the night of the benefit and her grand donation. Of course, we got through the mandatory family events with civility and a sense of duty, like the Mother's Day brunch at the club and Aiden's Millington graduation. We even sat together in solidarity at Mass on Father's Day, remembering that Aiden was a boy without a dad. The good thing about never having had a close relationship with Mitsy was that a sudden cold spell did not register with the general public. Mikki and Mimi would never have noticed the chill in the air, and Aiden hadn't asked any questions.

Even the dreaded task of informing Mitsy that Aiden would

be attending a public school specializing in the performing arts instead of Merritt's beloved Catholic alma mater had been cordial. Okay, I almost threw up from the stress, but Mitsy had been very gracious to Aiden. She saved her strongest condemnation for me. "I can't imagine how Merritt would have felt about this. That's a moot point. This never would have happened if Merritt were alive."

I felt refreshingly undisturbed by her outburst. I was making progress.

Mitsy's appearance at our little bungalow was unprecedented. She hadn't bothered to check out our new digs, despite the fact that we'd moved in more than a month ago. Of course, she'd been in Nantucket for three of those weeks visiting a college roommate and drinking gin and tonics, an annual rite that she referred to as her "Sojourn on the Island." Glancing around now at my new house, she held out a bag, "Isn't this charming? And so close to that chicken hut down the street! What luck! A little housewarming gift."

On a list of things I would Never Need Again in My Life, a scrimshaw of a whaling ship must rank right up at the top. Was she kidding? I had just sold every piece of decent art we'd collected over fifteen years and she was handing me Ye Olde New England souvenir? "Thanks. Please sit. Would you like some lemonade? Or a diet soda?" I deliberately left wine off the list, despite the fact that I was enjoying a spritzer with lots of lime. I didn't want her to stay.

"Yes, it is hot in here. Nothing, though, I won't be long. I just wanted to give you these," she said, pulling a large envelope out of her Nantucket basket tote.

Could it possibly be more scrimshaw? I was too hot to wait. "What's this?"

"The tickets from the benefit. The tickets to Greece. I thought you might want to go. After all, I bought them for you. And Aiden, of course."

I was stunned, but not into silence. Into a sort of rage. How dare she! "You know, Mitsy, if you wanted to send Aiden and me on vacation, you certainly didn't have to spend several hundred thousand dollars. Mexico is just fine for us. So let's not pretend that you made that donation for me or for Aiden."

"Of course not. I didn't mean to imply that I had," she said, keeping her cool like a reptile. "It was time I stepped up and did something significant for Pasadena. The tickets were an after-thought. But I did think you might appreciate them."

"You want me to be grateful? You pledged a quarter of a mil-lion dollars for other people's children to go to school and your own grandchild may not have the money for college. And I'm supposed to be grateful?" I was not holding back.

Neither was she. Mitsy straightened her spine and stared straight ahead, not making eye contact. She spoke carefully, "I know about Merritt. I know what he did to you. I know the mess he created. The one you had to clean up."

"If you knew, if you understood, then why did you tell me after Merritt's death that you wouldn't help us? Let me rephrase that. You said it 'wasn't possible' for you to help us." I didn't add that the truth was that she had the money, but she didn't have the heart.

Mitsy stood for effect. "What if I had helped? What if I had told you right then that I would pick up the tab for Aiden's col-lege? Oh, and don't worry about high school, I'd pave the way at Ignatius with a huge donation. What then?"

"Then maybe I would have gotten a lot more sleep than I have in the last six months. Maybe, maybe ..."

Maybe *what?*

"Oh, you would have slept. You would have barely been able to get out of bed. You would have curled up in a ball and waited for everything to cave in before you tried to stop the pain."

"How do you know that?"

"Because that's what I did when my husband died. I was para-

lyzed with fear. I thought someone was going to take care of me
for the rest of my life… and then he went and died! So I curled
up in a ball for a year before I could face my future. And by
then, I had almost destroyed it. The finances, my relationship
with my children, my, my … self-worth. I didn't want that to
happen to you. If I'd given you that money, the promise that I
would take care of you financially, you'd still be sitting in that
house, stunned and shocked. But you're not. You got up and you
did what you had to do. You have moved on in a way that I never
could. Look at you!" And she did. Mitsy's eyes met mine, "The
job, the new house, the environment you created for Aiden—you
did that. You will be fine because you made it so."

I was speechless. Mitsy had outdone herself. She had manipulated me in every way possible. I'd fallen right into her trap.
Mercifully. Thankfully. After winning her approval *finally*, I
found myself on the verge of tears.

"You will be fine," Mitsy repeated. "Merritt was a flawed man.
I blame myself. That period of my life when he needed me, I
wasn't there. He learned to cope, but not with honor. You were a
good wife to him." Her voice cracked a tiny bit. She pushed the
envelope forward. "Take the tickets. Go see that archaeologist of
yours."

In my fifteen years as a Fairchild, I had never seen Mitsy look
so vulnerable.

Then the Snake Goddess appeared again, calm, cool and in
charge. "It's a trip for two. You can take Aiden before he starts
school. Or simply go alone and see what happens."

I found my voice. "Thank you." *Should I hug her? Is that
what's called for?* Too late.

"I understand you've resigned from the club." Apparently,
our kumbayah moment was over. We were back to doing what we
Fairchild women do best: logistics.

"I did. Not in the budget this year."

"Yes. Even still, I hope you and Aiden will still be there for the family soiree on Labor Day. The Lobster Cookout. As my guests, of course."

"We'd love that."

"Good. Press on." With that, she was gone.

But I had my sign.

From: Helen Fairchild
<pasadenahelen@rosecity.net>
Subject: Interview/Trip

Patrick...

Quick update. First, we'd like to do a follow-up interview for the pilot episode about what you found in Moscow. We need about five to seven minutes on "Was Priam's Treasure for real or faked" from your POV. Annabeth thinks I should do the interview. Is that something I can schedule with you for mid-August?

Also, remember how my mother-in-law bought you at the auction(!) Well, in a shocking display of humanity, she has given the trip to Aiden and me. I know you may not have the time to really fulfill the whole auction thing. But, if you have any suggestions on must-see places that we should visit when we take advantage of the first-class tickets and five-star accommodations, please do advise. Thanks.

Let me know about possible interview dates.

Oh, and I heard from Sarah that your daughter had meningitis. How terrifying.

Helen

From: Dr. Patrick O'Neill
<poneill@americanschoolathens.edu>
CC: ProprietorTed@invinoveritas.com
Subject: re: Interview/Trip

Great. Yes, of course. Yes to interview. You know about Moscow and Priam's Treasure research. Am ready to say on camera that Schliemann faked find, all for the love of a questionably good woman. May be end of my career. Ah, well. Been a good run.

Yes to trip. I gave my word to that crazy friend of yours. I don't want Melanie to slit my throat with her huge diamond ring if I renege on the trip. The Gambles are coming over to tour the sites—I thought they would be excellent company if I had to spend two weeks with your mother-in-law. She scared me. Sorry. So we can all travel together.

I've cc'd Ted. You two can coordinate your trip from there. I am at your disposal in mid- to late August. Have to be back in Athens by September 1 for classes.

Helen, come a few days early for the interview. I think it would work best if the two of us do that before the rest of Pasadena arrives in Troy. I'll get you the name of a local crew who can shoot it for you.

Send confirmation of plans when you get them.

Best, Patrick

PS, Yes, Cassie was very sick. How could I not have told you that? Sorry. It was a crazy night when I tried to pack every-thing up. And get to London. By the time I could book a flight, the worst was over. Get Aiden the vaccine! You don't want to go through that, believe me.

From: Helen Fairchild
<pasadenahelen@rosecity.net>
Subject: re: re: Interview/Trip

Patrick,

We are set! What a plan. I will arrive on August 7th. The rest of the Pasadonians, as you call us, will arrive on August 12th. Aiden is flying with the Gambles. (I scheduled vaccine!) I think that should give us enough time to get in a seven-minute in-terview. It's also when the best flights worked out. Feel free to put me to work on site: digging, dusting, bringing baked goods for the crew—my new specialty.

Do you need hair and makeup, Dr. O'Neill? Or a trailer with a personal trainer? How about an accent coach or on-set mas-sage therapist? Please advise. Our budgets are modest—but for you I am sure I can arrange something special.

Yasu, Helen

From: Dr. Patrick O'Neill
<poneill@americanschoolathens.edu
CC: ProprietorTed@invinoveritas.com
Subject: Bring Cheeseburger

Dear Ms. Fairchild,

I believe I can do my own hair and makeup, but I would enjoy the Langham cheeseburger.

Hot, please.

Soon, Patrick

CHAPTER 24

It was hard not to get caught up in the romance of it all. Crossing the Dardanelles by boat to get to the Turkish city of Hissarlik, the site of ancient Troy, I felt like I was traveling in the wake of history. My ferry crossed the same body of water as the ships carrying Helen and her lover Paris, fleeing a furious Menelaus, the jilted husband. These waters had transported the Greek warriors from Sparta to avenge their leader's betrayal. Later, the dark waters of the Dardanelles would bring Heinrich Schliemann, his new bride, Sophia, and her soon-to-be lover Rudy to uncover the past and write a new chapter for the history books. I could barely take it all in, the gut-churning sensation of embarking on something momentous combined with the stunning scenery in front of me—the waves, the ridgeline, the barest outline of a city on a hill.

I felt sick.

I'd forgotten to take a Dramamine in the car from Istanbul. As if the car ride wasn't trying enough, the boat ride was worse. I'd suffered rough Aegean ferry rides before, during my student days, so I knew I needed meds. But the excitement of the moment overwhelmed my usual common sense. Maybe the subconscious reason I abandoned archaeology was the seasickness, not the feelings of inadequacy.

Breathe deeply and concentrate on the horizon, I thought. The famous shore stood a half-mile away. Unlike other ancient sites, Troy did not have any ruins. There were no temples in disrepair or crumbling walls to remind a modern tourist what had transpired here 3,000 years ago. Only rolling hillsides and tall grasses covered the opposite shoreline, to the disappointment of the uninformed, who rated Troy "not worth the effort" on travel blogs. Most visitors to this part of the world were Australians, coming to see the nearby World War I site of Gallipoli, not Patrick's trenches. But I couldn't wait to see the layers of history buried in the dirt.

The thought of Patrick made me queasy again. Please don't let him be on the dock to greet me. Green is not my color, I mused silently, cracking the barest of smiles. *What am I doing here?*

It had all happened so quickly—the tickets from Mitsy, the go-ahead from Annabeth and Olympia, the plan to meet up with the Gamble family to get our full tour of ancient sites. And the final detail: convincing Aiden. He hadn't needed much arm-twisting, nor had he asked many questions. Two weeks in Turkey and Greece with the Gambles and Dr. O'Neill? Yes. Are there beaches there? Yes. Aiden was in. He would be flying over with the Gambles in five days.

I had five days alone with Patrick, for better or worse.

The phrase "what a difference a year makes" is thrown around to describe downfalls and comebacks, but I never thought it would apply to me. Once I was pretty sure I knew what the future held for decades, not just days. But I was wrong. There's no way I would have paid a fortune teller her full fee if, a year ago, she'd intoned, "Next August, you will be sailing to ancient Troy, to connect your past with your future. You will be a widow traveling without your child. The journey will be steep and difficult, but on the journey, you will meet a very hot guy." Ridiculous! The image made me laugh.

Which in turn, made me feel even worse.

I needed to get off that boat and onto some solid ground.

"You feel better now?" Ekram, my guide and porter, asked as I emerged from what the sign indicated was a ladies room but could have easily been a broom closet, given its size, odor and lack of such amenities as light, water and a mirror. Thank God for my packet of wet wipes!

"Yes," I smiled. *Here's hoping I didn't miss my mouth with the lipstick application.*

"Dr. O'Neill said to bring your bags to his tent, then bring you to his trench right away. His apologies again, he is in the middle of something, and the ferries, well, they can be not on time, yes? My car is here or you can walk a short way and I take luggage. Sometimes, that is good to clear the head."

I must really be green, I thought. *Wait, did Ekram say he would bring the bags to Patrick's tent?* Another positive sign! Or a language barrier. "I'll walk. Thank you."

Now I was grateful Tina had talked me into the Merrell high-fashion hiking boots for the trip. "Earthy but sexy," she said. She was right about the earthy anyway; I was already covered in light dust from my knees down. I shook my head thinking about Melanie and her promise of five-star travel and accommodations. It was hard to imagine Mitsy or any of Pasadena's potential bidders making the trek to Troy. I pushed the image out of my head and immediately felt better.

I wondered instead: How did Helen of Troy make it up this hill without ruining her gown?

The Trojan dirt is a deep gray with flecks of silver limestone, but on Dr. Patrick O'Neill, who was lightly covered in the stuff, it looked like a sheen of the finest oils. He stood in the ten-foot-deep trench, glistening. His eyes were fixed on an invisible treasure in the walls, measuring and scribbling notes. A handful of students stood nearby, taking photos and notes as well. They turned to check me out, the overdressed outsider. Patrick hadn't heard me coming, so I could take in the familiar linen shirt, the long legs and the strength of his exposed forearms. I thought the guy looked good in front of a computer terminal, but here, in his natural surroundings, he was ... he was....

Ekram interrupted my festival for the eyes. "Dr. O'Neill. Your lady is here."

Patrick turned and squinted up at me, my silhouette outlined by the setting sun. The shade of dust heightened the blue in his eyes, the line of his mouth. "Helen, welcome to Troy."

As Patrick climbed up the ladder out of the trench, I had a moment to panic about the proper greeting. Hug only? Euro double-cheek kiss? Quick peck on the lips, followed by hug? I shouldn't have worried.

Patrick knew exactly what he wanted: a deep, long, full-on-the-mouth kiss. Who cared how dirty Travel Outfit #3 got? I was overwhelmed; Patrick was not. He whispered, "You're here. Finally."

Yes, finally.

I think one of the female students almost passed out.

"Okay, guys, finish up without me. Don't forget to catalogue the soil samples, Greta. Oh, Ekram, will you tell the cook I won't be eating with the crew tonight? We'll take something in my tent at 7. Leave some limeade and wine now, with fruit. Ms. Fairchild and I have some catching up to do."

Ekram nodded and disappeared like magic. The grad students stared in stunned silence. My knees wobbled a touch as Patrick firmly led me toward the small tent village in the distance.

When we were out of earshot of the others, he finally spoke. "Your trip was good?"

"I don't remember a single detail before the last two minutes."

"Did you bring my cheeseburger?"

"They confiscated it in Frankfurt. Something about the frilly toothpick."

Patrick stopped and pulled me close. "I've missed you, Helen."

"I can't believe I'm here. What am I doing here?"

"We have a few days to find out, don't we?" He stroked my hair, then bent down to kiss my neck. "Do you want a tour of the site?"

"Later." I ran my fingers over Patrick's dusty chest, then touched the moon and the stars on his forearm. "There's something I want to do first."

"What's that?"

"Take a shower."

Hours later, relaxing on the wooden deck in front of Patrick's sturdy white tent, I felt the strong pull of history from Helen to Sophia to me. Maybe there was something in the shining gray dirt that made women bolder. Or less inhibited. Or just plain stupid. Those Turkish sheets certainly lived up to their reputation. "I have a good idea: Let's spend the next couple of days re-creating some of those scenes from the Schliemann Journals. You know, Rudy and Sophia and those long summer nights. Like Journal XI, page 118. That was pretty sexy. How about that one?"

"Helen of Pasadena, I'm shocked!" Patrick mocked, pouring me another glass of wine, part of the simple feast that the cook had set out for us. "I suppose you could consider re-creating certain scenes from the journal 'research.' I only wish I'd known of this particular academic interest earlier. It certainly would have enlivened our afternoons at the Huntington."

"At the time, I wasn't quite ready for that level of … commitment to the work, Dr. O'Neill," I half joked.

"And now?"

"I think I'm ready." The sky was a deep blue, not yet black. The ancient plains stretched out before my eyes to the sea. I felt like I'd been here before. "Can I ask you a question?"

Patrick leaned forward. "Of course."

"That morning back in May. At the hotel. You were going to say something and I cut you off. I was afraid to let you finish. I thought I could make it easier for both of us if I came up with the usual 'not the right time, not the right place' speech. But I think I was wrong. Do you remember what you were going to say?"

"Yes, I do. I was going to say that I couldn't...." Patrick leaned back, avoiding my eyes. He seemed to struggle with the words. *Damn.* "... I couldn't offer you what you had: a traditional life. With the house and the stability and a man who wore a suit and tie to work. But I wanted to offer you something, part of ... me. I've been alone for years, always working. And I didn't want to be, I don't want to be, alone anymore. That morning, I wanted to ask you to be part of my life. You get me, Helen—my work, my life. I live in Athens, I work here, but still, I wanted you to be a part of that somehow."

You had me at hello.

Patrick chuckled. "Wow, that sounds pretty selfish now that I actually say it out loud."

"Does your offer still stand?"

He nodded, slightly surprised, waiting for an explanation. So I provided the best one I could. "I'm a planner, Patrick. I've been one my whole life. But after this last year, I understand that things don't always go as planned. And I'm okay with that. I don't know what the next phase of my life is going to be like, beyond getting Aiden through high school. But I'd like you to be a part of my life, too. I don't need traditional anymore, at least I don't think I do. We can make something work. Somehow."

"I'll be back in California for a fundraising dinner in December that Ted Gamble is putting together. Does that qualify as somehow?" Patrick kissed me gently on the nose.

"Yes, for now, anyway. Wait here." I was reminded of one more item on my to-do list. I slipped back into the tent, in what I hoped was a feline maneuver, re-emerging a minute later with the pink scarf in the pocket of my linen shirt. "I think I owe you this, Dr. O'Neill."

I held out the treasured accessory. Patrick stood, taking the scarf from my hands and gently tying it around my neck, kissing me softly.

"Come with me, Helen. I want to show you something."

"What?"

"*The earth, the heavens, the sea, the untiring sun, the moon at full....*"

"Deal."

ACKNOWLEDGEMENTS

Though the actual writing of a novel is a solitary pursuit, the publication of a novel is not. *Helen of Pasadena* would still be an outline in my head without the support, encouragement and cheerleading from the following:

Colleen Dunn Bates has been a friend, neighbor and work/life balance guinea pig for years; now, she is my publisher. Many thanks to Colleen and Prospect Park Books for taking a chance on a first-time novelist and doing so with such faith and fun. Thanks also to Caroline Purvis at Prospect Park, whose enthusiasm is matched only by her organizational skills.

The Hell-Raising Heroines, my online writing group, kept me on track and perfectly punctuated when grammar eluded me. Special thanks to Kate Mason and Catherine Lucey, both of whom are wonderful writers, careful readers and fabulous women. Someday we should meet in something other than a Google chat room! Thanks also to Erika Mailman, who taught the novel writing course at mediabistro.com. Her early enthusiasm for Helen was inspiring.

Linda Francis Lee shared her wisdom and wit with me, a total stranger on the phone, when I needed it. Thanks, Alana Sanko, for connecting us. Thanks also to Sally Bjornsen and Jodi Wing for their time and generosity.

My Pasadena Posse, all the women who have cheered me on and supported my far-reaching media career in all its forms—thank you for your friendship and positive energy. I really owe lunch to: Ryan Newman, my personal therapist and walking partner; Susan Pai, a true connector and friend; Sally Mann, my fashion consultant for Helen; and Candy Renick, who let me steal her name.

My family: Thanks to Brookes and Colin for your patience and understanding. And for not bothering me for hours on end so I could write. Finally, all the gratitude in the world to my husband, Berick Treidler. Enough said.

ABOUT THE AUTHOR

Lian Dolan is a writer, producer, talk show host, podcast pioneer and social media consultant. She writes the blog and produces the weekly podcast *The Chaos Chronicles,* a humorous look at modern motherhood, and she writes weekly for Oprah. com as a parenting expert.

A decade ago, Lian created Satellite Sisters, a talk show, blog and website, with her four real sisters. From 2000 to 2009, Satellite Sisters won eight Gracie Allen Awards and had a million listeners a week. Lian is also the co-author of *Satellite Sisters UnCommon Senses* (Riverhead), and her writing has appeared in many national magazines. She is a popular speaker, always using humor as hook.

Lian lives with her husband and their two sons in Pasadena, California.

Q & A
WITH AUTHOR LIAN DOLAN

Unlike your protagonist in Helen of Pasadena, *you're not the daughter of pot-smoking Oregon fiber artists—you grew up in Southport, Connecticut. Isn't that a lot like Pasadena? How did you get that outsider's perspective that allows for such a witty and smart look at the more upscale side of the city?*

I often say that Pasadena is like Southport with palm trees. There is a real sense of tradition and civic pride in Pasadena that is very familiar to a Connecticut Yankee. Many families have been here for generations, attending the same schools, belonging to the same clubs, raising money for longstanding organizations, and living in the same neighborhoods. Pasadena residents love their city and everything it represents in terms of arts, culture, education and sports. They can't imagine living anywhere else.

But even while I'm comfortable with Pasadena's societal workings, I'm not quite on the inside, having only lived here two decades! That leaves a lot of opportunity for observation.

Pomona College is what brought you to Southern California. What made you stay? And why Pasadena?

I left Southern California after graduation, but I guess it never left me. Six years later, I was back because I fell in love with a Pasadena boy. I was living in Portland, Oregon, and working in sports broadcasting when we got engaged. It wasn't much of a negotiation, because he was clearly never leaving Southern California to live in the Pacific Northwest. Plus, he already owned a house near the Rose

Bowl at age 25! Everything I owned fit in a Volkswagen. It made sense for me to move. I stayed because the beauty and energy of the city really fit my style. Plus, once again, husband never leaving, so I didn't really have a choice.

You were a Classical Studies major in college and studied in Athens your junior year. Did you want to be Indiana Jones?

I was 16 when *Raiders of the Lost Ark* came out, so mainly I wanted to marry Indiana Jones. But the movie did inspire me to love archaeology. Plus, my parents forced me to take Latin in high school, which I ended up loving. In college, I studied Greek, plus history and archaeology. After spending a semester in Athens, I really thought I would have this very rewarding, romantic career digging up stuff in the Greek Isles. But, frankly, I wasn't smart enough. Advanced ancient Greek did me in. And so did the thought of spending ten years post-college in pursuit of a doctorate. Instead of grad school, I moved to Jackson Hole to be a ski bum for two years. I think that says it all about my academic fortitude.

But I still love history and am hugely jealous of people who can make a career pursuing the tiniest historical details with passion and scholarship. That is a dream job to me.

It's said that first novels are usually autobiographical. Is the title character Helen based on you?

Absolutely not. Hahaha.

Is Patrick O'Neill based on one of your college professors?

Don't I wish! Then maybe I would have found that academic fire I needed! Actually, I did have one archaeology professor that I had a little crush on… but he owned no nubby sweaters as far as I know. To create Patrick O'Neill, I researched actual archaeologists and modeled his fictional work and resume after the real Dr. Manfred Korfmann, a famous German archaeologist who managed the excavation at Troy until his early death. For the sizzle, I turned to the Facebook group "Bringing Sexy Back To Archaeology." Yes, such a group exists, and the women of Sexy Archaeology were very helpful in describing the sexiest professors they ever had. I owe Patrick's nubby sweaters, his tattoo, his tanned forearms and his quiet, thoughtful work habits to them.

You already had a busy enough life as a mother, columnist, podcaster, blogger, volunteer, wife, sister, daughter and dog walker—how did you fit writing a novel in there?

My writing teacher said that to write a novel, you have to give up something, so I gave up yoga to write in the morning.

But before I even got to that stage, I knew I had a novel in me—but with so much going on, I couldn't focus on fiction. Then when my radio show, Satellite Sisters, ended unexpectedly, I had an opening in my schedule. I was used to creating and performing six days a week on air, so I refocused that energy on writing. Unlike Helen, I jumped right in without overthinking the situation! I took an online novel-writing class and forced myself to write for the class critique group to stay accountable. I am a big believer in deadlines as a motivator. And announcing to the world that I was writing a novel and committing my energy to the process was key.

There's never a perfect time to write. If you wait for that, you may never get anything done. Plunging in was the key for me.

You've lived in Pasadena a long time and have a lot of friends and family there. Are you worried that they might be offended when you have some fun at their town's expense? Or if they see themselves in some of the more comic characters?

Should I be worried? Dang, I hope no one eggs my house. I think most people have a sense of humor about themselves and the lives they lead. I satirize with much love. Hey, I'm the girl who gave up her career in sports for a Volvo with a keyless remote entry. Plus,

I was sensible enough not to use any one person wholesale as a character. Or one school or charity. Everyone and everything really is fictionalized—a hazy stew of the people, places and events I've experienced.

Has your teenage son read Helen of Pasadena? Does he think the character of Aiden is based on him?

No, he hasn't read it. There's one upside to having a boy who doesn't like to read! I could have made Aiden exactly like him and he never would have known. There are similarities between the two boys, but Aiden is not a carbon copy.

I made Helen's child a boy because I do know boys better, being the mother of two young men. For the plot's sake, I wanted Aiden to have that parallel with Merritt and the pressure that comes with that. Plus, contrary to popular belief, boys at that age are emotional and complicated. And they can still be very sweet to their mothers.

Is your husband anything like Merritt?

100% no! First of all, my husband is a UCLA fan, not a USC guy. Enough said.

In the novel, a lot of psychic energy is expended over education—specifically, the panic to get kids into the "right" school. Do you think American parents obsess about their kids' educations?

Of course we do! As parents, it gives meaning to our angst. I don't know why we've ratcheted up the stakes for our children, but we have. Pasadena is a town where a great number of kids attend private and parochial schools, so the jockeying for admission starts in pre-K and is out of control by college. That was new for me, having gone to public schools my whole life, only going through the admissions process as a senior in high school. But it's not just in Pasadena: Today the pressure on kids to perform academically and athletically exists in every community all over the country.

Having Aiden not attend the expected high school was my not-so-subtle way of saying that even though we may have expectations for our children, they have their own strengths and weaknesses, hopes and desires. Just a little parenting message in the fiction!

We hear you're working on two more novels in what's being called the Rose City Trilogy. Can you spill a bit about them?

Both books will combine contemporary women and their historical counterparts. Both books will continue to explore the many roles women play as wives, friends, sisters, mothers, daughters, patrons of hair salons. And, of course, both books will be set in Pasadena, using the city's rich cultural heritage as a backdrop. And you may see some familiar characters popping up again, because every book about Pasadena should include a former Rose Queen!